SPECIAL MESSAGE TO READERS

THE ULVERSCROFT FOUNDATION
(registered UK charity number 264873)
was established in 1972 to provide funds for
research, diagnosis and treatment of eye diseases.
Examples of major projects funded by
the Ulverscroft Foundation are:-

- The Children's Eye Unit at Moorfields Eye
  Hospital, London
- The Ulverscroft Children's Eye Unit at Great
  Ormond Street Hospital for Sick Children
- Funding research into eye diseases and
  treatment at the Department of Ophthalmology,
  University of Leicester
- The Ulverscroft Vision Research Group,
  Institute of Child Health
- Twin operating theatres at the Western
  Ophthalmic Hospital, London
- The Chair of Ophthalmology at the Royal
  Australian College of Ophthalmologists

You can help further the work of the Foundation
by making a donation or leaving a legacy.
Every contribution is gratefully received. If you
would like to help support the Foundation or
require further information, please contact:

THE ULVERSCROFT FOUNDATION
The Green, Bradgate Road, Anstey
Leicester LE7 7FU, England
Tel: (0116) 236 4325

website: www.foundation.ulverscroft.com

Carys Bray was was awarded the Scott Prize for her debut short story collection, *Sweet Home*. Her first novel, *A Song for Issy Bradley*, was shortlisted for the Costa, the Desmond Elliott and the Waverton Good Read, and won the Author's Club Best First Novel Award. She lives in Southport with her husband and four children.

You can discover more about the author at www.carysbray.co.uk

THE MUSEUM OF YOU

Clover Quinn was a surprise. She used to imagine she was the good kind, but now she's not so sure. She'd like to ask Dad about it, but growing up in the saddest chapter of someone else's story is difficult . . . Darren has done his best. He's studied his daughter like a seismologist on the lookout for waves, and surrounded her with everything she might want — everything he can think of, at least — to be happy . . . What Clover wants is answers. This summer, she thinks she can find them in the second bedroom, which is still full of her mother's belongings. What she's looking for is essence — an undiluted collection of things that will tell the full story of her mother, her father, and who she is going to be . . .

Books by Carys Bray
Published by Ulverscroft:

A SONG FOR ISSY BRADLEY

CARYS BRAY

THE MUSEUM OF YOU

Complete and Unabridged

CHARNWOOD
Leicester

First published in Great Britain in 2016 by
Hutchinson
London

First Charnwood Edition
published 2017
by arrangement with
Penguin Random House
London

Grateful acknowledgement is made to Rebecca Lindenberg for permission to reprint lines from 'In the Museum of Lost Objects' and 'Obsessional' taken from *Love, An Index* by Rebecca Lindenberg.

A catalogue record for this book is available from the British Library.

ISBN 978–1–4448–3136–8

Published by
F. A. Thorpe (Publishing)
Anstey, Leicestershire

Set by Words & Graphics Ltd.
Anstey, Leicestershire
Printed and bound in Great Britain by
T. J. International Ltd., Padstow, Cornwall

This book is printed on acid-free paper

N.B — as you wish.

I hope you don't mind, but I have kept
a few of your pieces

for my private collection.

Rebecca Lindenberg

Someday I hope I can become resigned
to knowing it's *not knowing* I must bear.

Rebecca Lindenberg

1

This is happiness, Clover thinks as she hefts the watering can and an old bucket. The clear arc of sky. The melty sun. The hum of insects. The smell of growing. The reds and browns of the fences dividing the Tetris pattern of plots. Every shade of green. The warm air. Her heaving effort. The way the stones crunch under her trainers and the dust rises, coating her bare legs.

She moves with deliberate, tightrope concentration, shoulder blades cresting like sails as water laps the containers' edges and she tenses to avoid spillage. No one else is here, because it's the hottest part of the day. Dad would prefer her to wait until the evenings when it's cool and the water doesn't evaporate. But mosquitoes descend as the temperature drops, and their bites weal and burn, even when she manages not to scratch. Once, she had to go to the walk-in centre because her ankle went all balloony, and Dad had kittens, literally. So she will water in the day, when the allotments are empty and the sun toasts the topsoil into a dense crust. This is work, she thinks. This is *doing*. Her face is slick and buttery in the heat. She licks her lips and tastes salt. School is finished and the summer is hers. All of it.

She uses the can first, and when it is empty she refills it with water from the bucket. She waters the onions, already big enough to fill the palm of one of Dad's hands, and then the carrots. She gives the peas, their curly stalks yellow and crispy, an extra helping, by way of apology for coming at this time of day. Although something got to the cabbages and they looked like skeletons within days of being planted out, they have, to an extent, recovered and are growing sparsely, three or four leaves to each plant. She sprinkles the last of the water over them and then scuffs back down the dusty track to the tap, empty can and bucket swinging.

She listens to the tumble of the water as it fills the can. Little spits splash her legs, damping the dust to dirt. Just before the water spills over, she twists the tap shut. Then she lifts the can aside, replaces it with the bucket and lets the water go again. When the bucket is full and the tap is tight, all is quiet. It's only as she walks back down the path that her ears rediscover the whisper and throb of the living things.

She waters the pumpkin plants. Her idea, for Halloween. Their leaves are rhubarb-ish and furry, the papery petal fingers of the remaining yellow flowers still clenched, like fists. She waters the potatoes and the different types of broccoli, and when she has finished, she hides the empty can under the corner of a large square of carpet that Dad has placed over a spare weeded bed to blind the new shoots of stinging nettles.

She unwraps one of the carrier bags tied to the handlebars of her bike and fills it with runner beans, careful to select only those that are tender and smooth, leaving the thick, stringy pods to dry in the sun for next spring's seeds. She picks six enormous onions and a few carrots, just to see. The carrots are fat at the top, near the leaves, then they taper into wispy, pencil-thin roots. 'Waste of time,' Dad will say. 'I don't know why I bother.' But he'll change his mind, and next year they'll try again.

Along the back wall, in between thickets of stinging nettles and the flowers she and Dad planted last spring for Mr Ashworth's bees — crocus and bluebell bulbs, rosemary and pussy willow cuttings — there are raspberries. Clover picks a handful and sits on the carpet, legs crossed. The berries are fat and dusty. She places them on her fingers where they sit like thimbles, and, one by one, she pops the fruits into her mouth and sucks them like sweets.

Afterwards, she lies on the carpet, eyes closed, and summer curls around her like a yellow cat. She has plans, but she will wait. Sometimes it's the wait that's the best bit; knowing something's coming, enjoying the feeling of it being about to happen — like Christmas Eve, which is always better than Christmas Day.

And there's the happiness, again. Flickering, moth-like, just under her sternum. She presses a hand up to the place. If she could leave the embered blackness behind her eyelids and travel to the spot where feelings are made, perhaps she could farm the right ones. She has recently become attuned to the way Dad takes the temperature of her mood and attempts to chart it. He'll stop once she smiles — a small smile isn't enough, it takes all her teeth to convince him, and even then he sometimes inspects her expression like a worried dentist. Every night, before bed, he says, 'Three happy things?' It's pretty easy. There's always weather of some sort: sun, snow, rain, wind. There's food — her favourite cereal or a nice pudding. And one other bit of happiness, which can be absolutely anything: clean sheets, a book, one of Dad's ideas — it doesn't matter whether the idea will actually happen, the optimism dominoes from him to her, regardless.

She would like to ask about this constant gauging of her mood, but Dad's answers are frequently lacking. She remembers, years ago, asking where babies come from. 'Between your legs,' he explained, and afterwards, as she eyed her legs from foot to thigh, she determined that the space *between* each — the soft, veiny plane of skin behind her knees — was *incredible*.

Grinning, she extends her arms and legs and spreads her fingers and toes, filling the full stretch of herself as she makes a shape on the carpet like a snow angel — an offering to the sun. Basking, that's it. Basking while the birds chatter and a slight breeze tickles the trees into motion. 'Shush,' they whisper, 'shush.' Dad doesn't realise that people aren't happy a lot of the time. But it's okay; they're daydreaming, or thinking, or planning, or waiting. That's all.

When she has enjoyed a long wait, she opens her eyes and sits up. Her skin is toasty and there are new freckles on her arms and legs. She retrieves the carrier bag of vegetables and puts it in the empty bucket, which she loops over one of the bike's handlebars. She unfastens the helmet that she had clipped around the seat post, pops it on her head and wheels the bike down the track to the big gate, which has to be closed properly, it's one of the rules. After a hard tug confirms it's fastened tight, she climbs on the bike and cycles towards the road. Past the beech hedge on one side and the neat rows of the orchard on the other, across the track that bridges the sluice, and out on to Moss Lane, bucket swinging. Her mouth still tastes of raspberries and the happiness is swelling like a gum bubble — something will burst it later, but for now it is the loveliest feeling.

When she reaches the end of Moss Lane she smells sun against tarmac and hears the sounds of real life: traffic, a pneumatic drill, and the fart of a bus as it stops at the roundabout. She slips on to the pavement and peddles past Bargain Booze, the post office and Jo Kelly's News. Up the hill that's actually a railway bridge, climbing alongside the blue railings that shield the drop to Jewson's, which remains stubbornly at ground level, refusing to rise with the slope of the bridge. Past the entrance to Meols Cop station, across the junction and then down, coasting, hands poised over the brakes as the sway of the bucket wobbles her front wheel. Past the sycamores and the tall leylandii trees that grow behind more blue railings, wheels skipping over helicopter seeds and dropped needles, reminders that autumn is already chasing summer.

At the bottom of the hill she swerves and slips into The Grove. She pedals slowly now, the grassy bank of the bridge on one side and a row

5

of semi-detached houses on the other. At the dead end of The Grove she dismounts and wheels her bike down the driveway of the very last house. It sits in the right-angled dip between the roads that cross on the railway bridge, one road climbing parallel to its front, the other along its side. The house has been waiting for her to come back, she can tell. There's something patient in the squat of it — the shuttered eyes of the sash windows, the long-suffering sag of the rusty metal gutters — a sense that there's no point in hurrying. It has sat in the same spot for more than a hundred years, rumbled by the vibrations of traffic and trains, occasionally by events, but, apart from the hairline cracks in the plaster, remaining unmoved.

Clover dodges stacks of empty plant pots and yogurt tubs and the severed milk cartons and plastic cola bottles that will hold next year's seedlings. She unhooks the bucket and unfastens her helmet before leaning her bike against the house and feeling in the pocket of her shorts. The key is newly cut and still bright, hers because in turning twelve she has crossed an unaccountable boundary. As she unlocks the door she hears a train crawl up to the station, its wheels squealing as they slip on the curve of the tracks. She glances back over her shoulder at the grassy crook where the banks meet, at the blue railings that top the banks and the tall trees that grow beside them. Cul-de-sac — it means bottom of a bag, dead end, it means no one ever passes the house on their way to somewhere else. Dad can't decide whether this is a good or a bad thing, whether she is more or less safe because of it. She steps over the mail that he will want to sort, and locks the door behind her.

The hall walls have been scraped bare and an unfastened radiator leans against the door of the understairs cupboard. There are watermarks on the carpet beside the capped-off pipe. The stairs are littered with things Dad will move or make use of one day. Several stacks of books that were twenty pence each when the library closed last year, a pile of her old clothes he's planning to give away, a couple of motorbike helmets, a pile of free newspapers for burning with the allotment rubbish in the autumn, and six tins of Dulux, Black Satin paint from the pound shop which might come in handy. Since he bought the cheap paint he has started doing the vees when they pass the new sign on the gate of the Jewson's, DULUX TRADE COLOURS MIXED HERE, as if he has got one over on them.

She dodges spare bicycle parts and a heap of folded dust sheets as she steps down the corridor, past the door to the lounge and into the dining room, where no one dines and Dad's things line a variety of shelves, some are free-standing, some are attached to the walls, and others are improvisations — slices of MDF and, in one instance, an old door, balanced on empty baby formula tins.

The kitchen leads straight off the dining room. She puts the carrier bag of vegetables on the worktop and divides the runner beans into three piles; one for the fridge and one each for Mrs Mackerel and Grandad. She adds two onions to each pile, but she keeps the carrots — they aren't worth sharing. There's a tiger loaf in the bread bin. She cuts a doorstep slice, slathers it in Biscoff spread and makes a cup of tea, one sugar — a big one since Dad's not looking, and she doesn't bother with a plate, either. She carries the tea and bread back through the dining room and into the lounge, where she settles on the leather-look PVC recliner that fell off the back of Colin's van. By the time she has finished the bread and tea, the backs of her legs are stuck to the chair, and as she attempts to unpeel herself the temperamental mechanism activates and the footrest bursts open. She clambers off and slams the footrest back until it locks.

Now it's time.

She climbs the stairs, careful not to trip on the books, clothes and newspapers. Hers is the front bedroom, the biggest of the three. Its sash windows are level with the top of the bank, and the traffic on the bridge — cars, buses and lorries — is visible between the trees and through gaps in the railings. There's plenty of space here, room for lots of stuff. A skateboard she doesn't ride, a guitar she can't play, a record player Dad is going to fix. Several shelves of children's books, mainly library rejects from the Bargain Bookcase Dad hadn't been able to resist over the years — 'You might read these, one day.' Her knitting: the five-foot Doctor Who scarf she worked on with Mrs Mackerel last summer and the beginning of the blue and white football scarf she hopes to complete this summer, for Dad. A novelty beanbag shaped like a pair of lips, Dad's music CDs from the nineties, her wardrobe and dozens of soft toys. She flips the lid of the old-fashioned school desk Colin was supposed to take to the tip, and grabs her new notebook and a black biro. The blue gloves are hiding under the bed. She kneels on the floor and feels for them, face pressed against the side of the mattress.

Somewhere between here and Liverpool, Dad is driving his bus, window open, right arm resting in the sunlight. Next door, Mrs Mackerel will be napping in her conservatory. Clover remembers other holidays, sitting in that greenhouse of a room, waiting for the sand of six weeks to pass through the hourglass of summer as Mrs Mackerel relaxed in her wicker chair and fell asleep mid-sentence, head back, possibly dead, until the breath began whistling out of her nose.

Her fingers brush polythene. There. She pulls the gloves out from under the bed. They are the kind you wear if you're putting diesel in your car. She stands and waits a little longer, extending the moment. Three happy things: the sunshine, the Biscoff on her bread and *this*, this waiting for what comes next — she can't tell Dad, she'll have to find something else to say, but, oh, *this*!

When it feels like bedtime on Christmas Eve and she is fizzing with anticipation, she slips her hands into the blue gloves and, clasping the notebook and pen, steps out on to the landing.

Museums

Museums I have visited (in alphabetical order)

Botanic Gardens Museum — with Dad, before it closed, every time we went to the park.

International Slavery Museum — with school.

Lawnmower Museum — with Grandad: 'Very informative. Let's give them a five-star review.'

Merseyside Maritime Museum — with school.

Museum of Liverpool — with Dad after doing some Christmas shopping at Liverpool One.

National Football Museum — last summer with Colin: 'Fit men in shorts, Clo, what's not to like?'

World Museum — with Dad, Kelly and the boys. There's a giant spider on the ceiling. Yikes!

My top three museums

Botanic Gardens Museum

They had a 1,500-year-old canoe, a shrimping

cart and a big collection of stuffed animals. There was an ice-cream shop next door. The council closed it to save money.

World Museum

Good, despite the giant spider. There's an aquarium and there are drawers of moths and butterflies and beautiful rocks. Upstairs, there's a planetarium.

Merseyside Maritime Museum

A museum about the sea that's right next to the docks, literally. I liked 'Titanic and Liverpool — the Untold Story'. It's where I got the idea.

2

Once, his dad talked a man off a bridge. His mum would tell the story when his dad wasn't there. Behind his back. 'Still waters run deep,' she'd say. 'There's more to him than meets the eye.'

Growing up, it seemed to Darren that his dad, like one of the rocks in the garden, was expertly masking a flurry of activity.

'What did he say to the man?'

'I don't know.'

'So he might not have said anything?'

'He *talked him off*.'

'How?'

'I don't know.'

He pictured the man balancing on the bridge in a low crouch. Ready, steady . . . and then Dad's words looped through the air, a verbal lasso, grabbing the man and setting him down on the pavement, safe and sound. Darren used to suppose that the same ability lay untapped in him, that he had inherited a reserve of words, in case of an emergency.

And where was this bridge, the scene of the talking off? Mum didn't know. It could be this one, he thinks, slowing as he reaches the top of its hump, where the railings are replaced by black bricks, laid high enough to prevent kids from climbing, yet low enough for someone his size to straddle without too much difficulty. He could sit, if he wanted. The bricks aren't topped by glass or wire, as they are on some of the other bridges. But he's content to stand for a moment and watch the tracks slither their way towards Manchester.

The tracks are flanked by brambles and grass. There are hub caps and plastic bags in the undergrowth, a partially deflated football, limp sheets of newspaper — God, people are filthy. He can hear a train in the distance. He waits. There it is, a sluggish chugger, just two carriages. After it disappears beneath him he strolls down the hill of the bridge, heading for town.

It helps to walk to work. To either the garage or Lord Street, depending on his shift. It helps to have a good breakfast. Three Weetabix and a mug of tea, no sugar. Sometimes he sits down as he eats. Sometimes he doesn't. It depends. Even after all this time, he occasionally dreams of Becky, and he wakes in the third bedroom, in his single bed, not knowing where he is. As it comes back to him, he is poleaxed by the old ache of missing her and he lies there, imagining the judgements she would levy were she to inspect the particulars of his life. When he goes downstairs he sees the house both as it is and as it was, and he eats his Weetabix on his feet, facing the worktop, his back to the jumble of the kitchen. On those mornings, when dream is clinging to him like a spider's web, and no amount of rubbing or swiping can remove the sticky feeling, the walk scours him.

He passes a yellow bin of grit salt. Winter seems a lifetime away. The sky is like glass. He hasn't brought a jacket. No point. Just his lunch and a water bottle in a carrier bag.

The thump of his feet and the in-out of his breath beat Clover's name in time with his thoughts: Clo-ver, Clo-ver. How did she get to be twelve? Twelve years old and fine, as far as he can tell — no, better than that: fine, as far as *anyone* can tell.

★ ★ ★

Once there was a bit of argy-bargy on the bus between some local lads and the buskers. 'Why don't you and your accordions go back to where you came from?' — that sort of thing. At the next stop Darren twisted in his seat and talked the lads off the bus. There's no one to tell Clover: *Once, your dad talked some racist knob-heads off a bus.* He could tell her himself, of course, but it wouldn't be the same. And there is no mystery about his words, which were: 'You! Off! Now!'

★ ★ ★

He waits halfway down Lord Street for the changeover. Switches his phone to silent and puts it in the carrier bag with his water and sandwiches.

Ed pulls in, bang on time. He lets the customers get off and on first, then he opens the cab and steps out of the bus. 'All yours,' he says. 'Okay?'

'Yeah. Another hot one today,' Darren replies.

'Hotter than a whore's drawers. I've made sure every window's open.' Ed rubs his damp forehead with the back of his hand before wiping it on his trousers. 'Look at me, sweatier than a Scouser during *Crimewatch*. It's shorts weather, this. Any reasonable company'd give you the option. One of these days I'm going to take me kecks off and drive in me skivvies. That'll learn them!'

The air on board is soupy. Darren climbs into the cab, hangs his carrier bag from the hook and shuts himself in. He checks the running board and adjusts the seat. Not a bad shift, ten till six. No need to worry about disappointing the biddies who line up early and gripe when he won't let them on board at twenty-seven minutes past nine, three minutes before their passes are valid. No late-night shenanigans, either. Liverpool and back, twice. That's it. He places his left foot on the rest, wraps his hands around the warm plastic of the steering wheel, indicates, and edges out into the traffic. A kid starts to cry and a woman begins to sing 'The Wheels on the Bus' in a wheedling, baby voice.

'The driver on the bus says, 'Any more fares? Any more fares? Any more fares?' All day long.'

Darren has never said 'Any more Fares?'. Ever. He doesn't mind crying babies, but he hates crap music. There should be a list of acceptable songs — they could stick it alongside the NO STANDING PASSENGERS ALLOWED BEYOND THIS POINT sign or the BUS TICKET TO UR MOBILE adverts. They could do a customer consultation — ha! No input from petrol heads, though, they'd get it all wrong — you couldn't stop for passengers if you were listening to 'Highway Star', you'd have to drive past them, through a foot-deep puddle. SONGS PERMITTED ON THIS BUS, that's what the sign would say, with a list below: 'Bus Stop' by The Hollies, and The Beatles' 'Magical Mystery Tour'. What else would work? The Who's 'Magic Bus' and The Divine Comedy's 'National Express,' of course — shit — he brakes and beeps at an old codger as he steps into the road, just feet away from a pedestrian crossing. Bloody hell. What *is* it with old people who do that?

'*The horn on the bus goes beep, beep, beep! Beep, beep, beep! Beep, beep, beep!*'

He waves to the weird kid who waits outside Mecca Bingo during the school holidays, bus-spotting notebook in hand, and then he slows as he approaches the last stop on Lord Street. He opens the doors. 'Wheels on the Bus' woman gets off with her still-snivelling kid. Result! And the waiting people spill on.

'It is — and no rain forecast.'

'There you are, ta.'

'Air conditioning? Ha!'

As he checks passes and issues tickets, he gradually becomes aware of Jim, standing on the pavement, ushering people ahead of him, earning smiles and thanks from a woman with a buggy and an old bloke carrying a dog. Darren tries to ignore him. In recent weeks he has noticed him, lean as a wrench, tramping around town. There is something in his walk that reminds Darren of the high-stepping Thunderbird puppets that

16

used to be on the telly. It's in the bounce of his knees, the way his feet smack the pavement and his arms swing, busy hands clenching and unclenching as he marches.

When everyone's on, Jim leans in, head first, undecided. 'All right?' he says.

Darren nods. 'You?'

'I'll just park myself here for a stop or two.' He steps aboard and positions himself in front of the yellow line on the floor that everyone must wait behind. His hands are shaking and he's got food stains on his T-shirt — ketchup or a bit of baked bean sauce. 'Giddy up,' he says.

Darren shakes his head.

'Don't worry, I'll nip straight off if any of your lot get on. Scout's honour.'

'You can *park yourself* on a seat, after you've paid.'

'Ah come on, Dazza.'

'After you've paid.' He folds his arms and nods at the wheel. No hands, no budging.

'Look at you. Working for the man when you should be sticking it to him.'

'Give over. Are you going to pay?'

'Don't see why I should.'

'Get off, then.'

'No one'd think we're family.' Jim lifts his arm for emphasis, displaying a raw elbow-ring of psoriasis.

His grubby clothes and trembling hands, his evident itching and urgent walking — these are warnings, apparent to anyone who looks closely, and, regardless of how inattentive he has been in the past, or perhaps because of it, Darren is now

17

someone who looks closely. 'Family when it suits,' he says. 'You haven't seen Clover for weeks.'

Jim seems to be about to address the issue of his absence but, after a glance at the engrossed pensioners occupying the accessible seats at the front of the bus, he reconsiders. 'Yeah. Well,' he says and steps down on to the pavement.

Darren calls, 'Have a nice day,' as the doors close, and Jim flips the bird at him. It's tempting to flip one back, but it isn't worth it.

He indicates and pulls into the traffic. Once, Darren Quinn talked Jim Brookfield off a bus — he'll have to go and see him, but not today. There isn't space in his head for new worries today. He is already preoccupied.

After Clover was born a deep seam of imagination opened and he can't help mining it once in a while. He feels a wave of pity for the daughter of his dark daydreams, the fictional creature who is, at this exact moment, pining for company. He allows himself to be afraid for a moment, to consider the possibility that this milestone, this first unsupervised school holiday, may trigger the very thing he's been seeking to avoid. Then he buries the feeling. Because, of course, this adjustment is necessary and for the good. He forces himself back to the surface, where it's possible to exist for long stretches of time, largely undaunted by her vulnerability. He remembers when she was three and had to wear the eyepatch. As he fastened the patch to her trusting, upturned face, the doctor explained that she might bump into things on her blind side and warned about watching her on the stairs. Darren suspected he'd confront the first stranger who so much as looked at her the wrong way — that, or cry, which was ridiculous, as it was nothing, just a square of sticking plaster under her glasses. But there was something so painful about watching her, suddenly runtish and teetering, that, in the weeks that followed, he taught her to say 'Arrrgh' and to answer to Dread Pirate Roberts. And when they were out and about and people spoke to her, through him — 'Would she like a drink?' 'Is she a good girl?' — he'd reply, 'I'm afraid you'll have to speak to the Dread Pirate Roberts, herself. She's the boss.' And, right on cue, she'd growl, 'Arrrgh.' People didn't know whether it was okay to laugh, which meant *they* ended up feeling awkward and embarrassed, not Clover, who was too busy returning his conspiratorial grins.

After Lord Street morphs into Lulworth Road it's like driving in a different town. Detached houses sit behind in-out driveways, and Italian-style fountains decorate manicured lawns. Darren drives up the hill and past the golf course. These houses may be posh but they're still rumbled by vibrations from buses and, a little further along the road, by the trains that pass through Hillside station. Every rut and divot in the road judders the tyres and trembles the floor. The windows shudder in their frames, and the engine belts out the high-low tune it sings around town, an undulating song of acceleration and deceleration. This noise — the rattling tremor that begins in his feet and hands before quivering into his legs and shoulders, and finally his chest — is the loudest noise in Darren's life.

He believes he's concentrating as he responds to the bell and pulls over at the last stop before the bypass to let an oldie off, but as he begins to drive away, a second pensioner staggers past the cab. She stumbles and he watches helplessly as she just about manages to right herself. He brakes, reopens the doors and calls an apology which she either can't hear or won't accept. Ninety-five per cent of accidents occur as a result of driver distraction. Concentrate, Darren.

On the bypass, air whooshes through the open windows. Although it is hot, blooming with pollen from the wheat and barley fields, it's welcome. He turns off the bypass at the first roundabout and trundles through Formby. While he waits for a minute and a half at the Formby Cross Green timing point, he resolves not to think about home and listens instead to the muted sound of the stationary engine and the turbine of an old bloke's chest. Back on the bypass he is overtaken by cars, white vans and a removal truck. He pushes for a last burst of speed on the A565, bombing down the road, before he hits the 30mph limit again, the power and weight of what's behind him — the lives of the people, fifty seats, moulded metal, plastic, foam, fabric, the hot engine — pressing on his back and shoulders. *He's got the whole bus in his hands* — ha!

The landscape and the bus get more crowded as he approaches the city. Red-brick terraces stream parallel to the roads, and motoring, smoky voices sputter into coughs. Nearly there now. He can see wind turbines, the tips of tower blocks and a glimpse of the docks; John Moores University and the Radio City Tower — buses everywhere, chugging past the World Museum, St John's Gardens and the Marriott Hotel. Finally, he turns into Queen Square bus station, the last stop of the outbound journey, and everyone gets off.

When he is alone, he edges down the hill to the number 10 stop where he opens the doors and allows the bus to fill again: a gang of lads wearing their baseball caps backwards, a bloke with a hearing dog, an old woman whose shopping is lashed into a baby's buggy with rope and a carabiner.

'Yeah, toasty, isn't it?'

'Don't forget your change.'

★　★　★

Once, he wondered whether the man on the bridge had just been sitting there. Hadn't been planning to jump at all. Was, in fact, stretching his legs. Letting them dangle. Taking a risk, the kind some people take in order to feel properly alive. A small, private gamble, before mobile phones and YouTube, before planking and skywalking. Sitting on the bridge with his legs swinging, thinking I *could*, I *could*. Maybe that was it.

★　★　★

21

He stops at the lights by The Royal and stares at the derelict building. The ground-floor windows shuttered, the second- and third-floor windows missing, along with most of the roof, except for a circular turret that grows up from one of the building's corners and is topped by an icecream cone of slate tiles. A car behind him beeps and he blinks. Concentrate, Darren.

People get off as he leaves the city. Those few who remain settle into their seats, some doze off, cheeks pressed against the glass. After he passes the shops at Crosby the streets are tree-lined again, and as he steers under the leafy canopy he feels the tug of home.

He's coming off the bypass when he realises he is chewing his cheeks. He lets the skin go and tongues the ridge on each side, stamped with the pattern of his teeth. Clover will be fine. Perhaps he'll call her when he gets back to Lord Street and it's time for his break.

It helps to get out of the cab at Formby Cross Green timing point and stretch his legs for a moment. The passengers watch and he feels obliged to exaggerate this stretching so they feel reassured, certain of his purpose. Arms up, back arched — that's it.

When he gets back in the cab he listens as the engine belts out its high-low tune, noises which verify that, in the back of the bus, under the protective layers of metal, pistons are moving, fuel is being injected into the cylinders and the exhaust valves are opening. And, as he approaches Lord Street, he finally allows himself to think about the noises Jim is making and what

22

could be happening under his protective layers of arseyness. He wonders what the catalyst might be this time and how much of the responsibility he will be expected to shoulder.

The kid with the notebook is still bus-spotting; Darren waves at him before he pulls in at the changeover stop. He lets people off and on and then he opens the cab, lifts his carrier bag off the hook and climbs out.

'All right, Terry?'

'Yeah, you?'

'Hot.'

'Don't you go wishing for rain; I'm off to Cornwall next week.'

After Terry has pulled away, Darren crosses the road and walks to a shady spot on the steps of one of the war memorial colonnades. Maybe Clover is back from the allotment now and about to eat her lunch, too. He could call her mobile. But she often leaves it in her room when it's not a school day, in case it slides out of her pocket as she cycles. He could call home, instead. But if he does and she's out, he'll worry, and that would be worse than not calling at all. He settles for a text.

Hope ur ok. Don't forget sun cream & helmet. Look after the key. Lock the door behind you. Careful crossing roads. He stops himself. Deletes everything but the first sentence. *Hope ur ok.* Adds a couple of kisses and hits send.

A hopeful pigeon lands on the step, eyeing his sandwiches. He used to sit here with Colin sometimes on Saturday afternoons, after they'd wasted all their change on the 2p machines at

23

Silcock's Funland. There was a Woolworths on the other side of the memorial back then, with two whole aisles of pick-and-mix sweets. The skater kids practised kickflips and grinding on the monument steps, but he and Colin weren't bothered about skateboarding, they were hoping the birdman would turn up and put on a bit of a show. The birdman spoke in an uncanny, avian voice. His coat was the coarse, woollen kind and there must have been bits of millet clinging to its fibres because the birds perched all over him, even before he started pulling handfuls of seed out of his pockets.

Darren shuffles down a few steps, away from the pigeon and out of the shade. The stone warms the backs of his legs through his work trousers. He closes his eyes for a moment and tilts his face skyward. As he's got older the world has shrunk. It sometimes feels as if everything is moving around him and he is stuck, feet in concrete. It's understandable when he's at home and the trains squeal past the house on their way to Manchester and beyond, but it also happens while he's driving the bus; he sits at the wheel and it's as if the houses and the trees and the fields are whipping past as he remains still, holding tight until he's allowed to get off. He thought he'd be long gone by now, and yet here he is, circling the slight perimeter of his life: his old house, his primary and secondary schools, the parks, the hospital, the hospice. If he could go back to being a boy he'd retrieve every wish for time to accelerate; his rush to reach double figures, to be thirteen, to be seventeen — he

24

made those wishes never believing there might be a day when he would wish in reverse — to be seventeen, and thirteen, and ten.

He'd like to think he's a different Darren Quinn from the one who laughed at the birdman. But he remains the boy who watched *The NeverEnding Story* six times. Who would wait in front of Dad's cuckoo clocks in the hall, a minute before the hour, trying to guess which trapdoor would spring first; who got bladdered on Diamond White and Hooch and threw up on Colin's mum's living-room carpet during a rendition of 'Boom! Shake the Room'; who, when asked by the careers teacher to list ten things he wanted to get out of life, didn't think to include happiness.

★   ★   ★

It doesn't feel like six o'clock. The sun is high and hot and his polo shirt is damp under the arms and down the middle of the back where it was sandwiched between his skin and the seat. He's finished in plenty of time to get home for the start of the new series of the baking programme Clover likes. And, given her text — *I'm fine!!! xx* — there's time to visit Dad, too.

He walks from the changeover stop on Lord Street to Dad's flat. The cafés have crept outside into the heat; the pavement is crowded by chairs and umbrellaed tables. He passes ice-cream shops, bucket-and-spade shops, rock shops and fancy-dress shops; places that almost make him feel as if he lives beside the right sort of seaside,

25

the kind with yellow sand and blue sea, rather than a stretch of salt marsh bordered by dunes.

Dad has chosen to grow old and reclusive in a modern retirement development. It's nice enough; within walking distance of a golf course, the shops, a park and the Marine Lake. At least it would be, if Dad ever went anywhere. There's a communal garden and a lift, which Dad doesn't need because there's nothing wrong with his legs. They have bingo and coffee mornings, games nights and a visiting library. But Dad doesn't join in.

Darren walks down the block brick path, presses the intercom and waits next to one of the tubs of pansies someone has placed on either side of the entrance. 'It's me,' he says, and the door jerks open.

He climbs the stairs to Dad's flat. The front door is already unfastened and Dad is waiting for him in the hall, beside the cuckoo clocks and the big photograph of Mum. It's fuzzy and over-exposed. They didn't have a digital camera at the time and it's how Darren remembers her now, soft around the edges and slightly luminous.

Dad follows his gaze. 'She never made a fuss, did she?'

Faint praise. Darren searches for the words that will agree with Dad and simultaneously expand his observation into a meaningful tribute.

'She was a good woman,' he says, and Dad nods. It'll have to do.

*   ★   ★

Once, when Darren was still a teenager, his mum was diagnosed with lung cancer. They awaited the results of the tests that would stage it. 2B was the best they could hope for. *2B or not 2B*, Mum said — a Shakespeare joke, fleetingly funny; and then the answer was 3B, median life expectancy fifteen months, and all jokes stopped.

Another picture in Dad's hall, smaller, darker, captures the three of them, together. There's Darren, twenty years old by then, wearing a black polo neck jumper and white jeans, one arm around his dying mother, smiling for the camera and for his future self, who is bound to examine and re-examine this particular photograph. There he is, assuming death is a simple thing that it happens in stages: The Preparation, The (obligatory) Fight and The (inevitable) Capitulation; followed by The Arrangements, The Mourning and The Mending.

★ ★ ★

'Beer?' Dad asks.

'Go on then.'

Dad's got all the windows open but it's still muggy. Even the glass doors that lead on to the balcony are gaping. Darren can hear applause from a game show on the telly and the low buzz of a flotilla of bluebottles as they fling themselves from one end of the flat to the other. As Dad shuffles into the kitchen Darren watches the crook of his retreating back. The kitchen smells faintly of piss. Dad says — no, *insists* that he doesn't pour it down the sink once he's measured and recorded its volume in his B&B (Bowel and Bladder) book, but he's got to be lying. That, or there's a problem with the drains. Either way, Dad can't seem to smell it and so there's a weird performance every time Darren arrives which involves him sniffing around like a cartoon hound while Dad follows in his wake, saying, 'It's you. There's something wrong with your nose. That's what it is.'

'Have you got some bleach? I'll pour a bit down the drain and see if it makes a difference.'

Dad points at the cupboard under the sink. 'You don't have to come. You're busy and I don't want to be any bother.'

'You're no bother.' Darren finds the bleach, positions the bottle over the plughole and pours.

'But Clover — '

'Clover's *fine*. She'll have been at the allotment, watering. There'll be a bag of veg for you in the kitchen. I'll bring it or she can cycle round with it. She's been dead cheerful. Humming to herself, smiling at nothing. Must be the holidays.' Darren puts the bleach back in the cupboard and pauses as he tots up Clover's round-the-clock cheerfulness to the daydreamy way she has been holding old photographs and books. 'You don't think she's . . . she's too young to be soft on a lad, isn't she?'

'Sounds about right to me.'

'Oh God.'

'No need to worry, it'll all be in her imagination.'

'What?'

'Have you ever *seen* a twelve-year-old lad?

28

Ha-ha!' Dad's laugh turns into a cough and he digs in his pocket for a hanky, which he uses to wipe his eyes. 'It'll be someone off the telly. A singer, probably. You'd better find out who it is and buy her a poster so she can practise kissing it.'

'Ugh.'

'That's what they do, isn't it, girls?'

'I don't know.'

'Me neither. Not really.' Dad lifts a few cans out of a cupboard. John Smith's and Courage Best Bitter. 'Help yourself.'

'Have you got something cold?'

'No.'

'This then. Ta.'

Dad opens one of the leaves of the fold-away table and gestures. *Sit*. They sip their beers. A bluebottle bursts in from the hall and scopes out the kitchen, hovering briefly over a neat stack of unfastened Amazon boxes on the table, ready for recycling.

'Been anywhere nice recently?' Darren asks.

'No.'

'Been anywhere at all?'

'No.'

'That's a shame.'

'No need. Everything's delivered.' Dad nods at the flattened boxes on the table and lifts his beer. 'Good shift?'

'Fine. Hot.'

'When're you next off?'

'Tomorrow. But I'm helping Colin with a job.'

'*Colin*.' Dad tuts. 'How's his *friend?*'

'Mark's okay.'

29

'Brave lad. I looked up the charity. You volunteer and then you have to go wherever they send you, did you know that?'

'Yeah.'

'Least he only went to Africa. Could have been Afghanistan or Syria.'

'I know. Colin was dead worried.'

'Colin's a scally.'

'He's all right.'

'Waste of a day off, helping him.'

'He's lonely. Missing Mark. And it's a bit of extra cash. Comes in handy. The allotment cost fifty quid this year.'

'Worth it, though.'

'Probably. Just.'

'Carrots any good?'

'Pathetic.'

'Put them in tubs. I've told you.'

'I know. I'll listen one of these days.'

Dad fills his mouth with beer, holds it between his cheeks for a moment then swallows. *Gulp.* 'You can start now, if you like.'

'Go on,' Darren says, wary of the forced jollity in Dad's voice and his not-so-subtle request for permission to speak.

'Sid's dead.'

'Sid?'

'From upstairs. Sid with the incontinent pug.'

'Ah, Sid. God, he was *old*.'

'Ninety-three.'

Darren tries to look sympathetic, but he can't muster any sadness for Sid. In fact, he feels slightly pissed off with him for having lived so long. Greedy, really, when you think about it.

'Sid got me thinking. I used to have conversations with your mum, before she got ill. *When I die, I'd like you to do such and such a thing* — that's what I'd say to her. And she'd say the same to me. We talked as if I'd see to her arrangements and she'd see to mine. I suppose you have to, really, because you don't know who'll go first. You don't think about it, do you? You don't think, One of us will get left behind and die alone, without the other. But I will — die alone, I mean. Without her.'

'God, Dad.' Darren's chair scrapes the kitchen floor as he stands. It's an abrupt, intrusive sound and he's glad of it. He can't remember the last time Dad said so many words at once. He picks his can off the table and carries it with him to the sink.

'You'll have to sort things for me. I've written it down. It's all in the envelope in the drawer next to the bed.'

'You've told me be — '

'Make sure you put me with her.'

'I've said I will, haven't I?

'I've got about four years left, in all probability.'

Darren holds his breath and silently counts to three.

'You might go first, of course.'

He snorts; he won't argue about who's going to die first. 'You're a barrel of laughs today.'

'What do you want, when you go?'

'Give over. I'm not talking about this with you.'

'Well, you haven't got anyone else to talk to,

have you? And don't pull that face. You've got to think about the future.'

'You sound like one of those adverts where you get a free pen and alarm clock if you sign up for life insurance.'

'Sit down, I'll get a stiff neck looking up at you. There's some biscuits in the tin.'

One of the clocks strikes the half hour and Darren steps into the hall to catch it. Dad kept three of the clocks when he moved here: the plainest, oldest clock, which looks like a nesting box, and two others, both shaped like alpine houses, their cuckoos hiding behind a first-floor window. The bird in the smallest alpine house sings on the half hour and, on the hour, the clock plays one of twelve different tunes. The larger house, the fanciest of the three clocks, has a garden and when the cuckoo sings a pair of goats on the lawn raise their heads while a man in lederhosen chops wood with a tiny axe. The rest of Dad's collection is in Darren's dining room, in boxes.

Darren thinks the oldest clock chimed first, but he can't be certain. He waits and then the bird bursts out of the first-floor window of the smallest house, *cuckoo*. Dad joins him and Darren points at the biggest clock — *this one, next*. Dad nods and they stand together, Mum's photograph on the wall beside them as Darren remembers clock parts arriving in the post: hands and chains and gong coils; gears, pendulums, weights, and sometimes, best of all, a new cuckoo, its extended tail giving it the appearance of a tiny, bird-nosed aeroplane. All those Saturday afternoons at the kitchen table, Mum coordinating their efforts — 'I'm sure Darren would like to help, love. Cover the table in newspaper for your dad, there's a good lad.' The quiet concentration, the cups of tea, the plate of biscuits Mum would place on the table beside them; pink wafers and digestives, in a pattern.

The first-floor window opens and the largest clock strikes the half hour, *cuckoo*. The familiar sound settles things. It's almost as if Mum's ghost is occupying the space between them, cushioning their corners.

'We had a good time doing them clocks, didn't we?' Dad says.

'We did.'

'You could always unpack some of them and have a go with Clover.'

'I could.'

He is thinking about leaving when Dad proffers the B&B book. He glances at the day's recordings.

P.U.

6.00: 270ml yellow
10.23: 185ml pale
1.14: 225ml pale
4.07: 190 ml pale

B.O.

10.23: firm, 5 inches
1.14: pellets, several — firm

'Looks fine,' he says. 'Everything seems to be in working order.'

'The bladder *should* be able to hold up to 430ml.'

'Well, there's no point in holding it in, is there? Seems all right to me. Go and see the doctor if you're worried.'

'I'm not.'

'Good. And you're keeping busy, even though you're not going out?'

'I am.'

'With . . . ?'

'YouTube,' Dad says, eyebrows raised, indicating that he was barely able to resist adding, *of course.*

'Anything in particular?'

'Documentaries.'

'About?'

'Mars.'

'Right.'

'The red planet.'

'Yeah.'

'Do you know how many documentaries there are about Mars on YouTube?'

Darren shakes his head. 'Do you?'

'No.'

'Oh. I thought you were going to tell — '

'Lots.'

'Right.'

'A hundred thousand people have applied to go there. And there isn't even any oxygen.'

'Idiots.'

'Do you know how cold it gets at night?'

'No.'

'Minus one hundred.'

'Pretty cold, then.'

'I should say so. There's a fifteen-mile-high volcano.'

'High, that.'

'You're not kidding.' Dad taps his fingers on the table. 'I'd go, you know.'

'To Mars?'

'I would.'

'Give over.'

'Nothing for me here.'

Darren won't argue. There's no point. It's a provocation — *I'd* go to Mars, and *you* won't even get yourself a girlfriend — that's what Dad's really saying.

He leaves with a bag of the outsize beefsteak tomatoes Dad grows on the balcony. He hasn't asked how Dad gets them so big or what he uses for fertiliser because he really doesn't want to know.

He strides back through town to South Garden, where he buys fish and chips for two in honour of the programme Clover likes, the one that starts tonight. It's always better to watch food programmes with something nice to eat, so you don't get hungry, and although *South Garden* isn't the nearest takeaway, the portion sizes are immense and their chips are the best in town.

He's approaching The Grove and the incline of the railway bridge, the fish and chips sweating in the plain white carrier bag, when he thinks about pudding. The thought sends him striding up the hill alongside the blue railings and the trees; past the dip in which the house sits, past Jewson's and down the hill to Jo Kelly's News, where he buys a box of Mr Kipling's French Fancies. Clover's baking programme has contestants and judges. When the judges are tasting the contestants' creations, he'll produce the French Fancies, on a plate.

'Lovely icing, Darren,' he'll say, in a high, posh voice, just like the female judge. 'Very delicate. And in three colours. Well done.'

Clover will laugh and it will be another moment he can call on, should he need it. They'll sit together, the two of them, in the dip beside the railway bridge, surrounded by their stuff; everything she might want — everything he can think of, at least — all the ingredients for a good life, so many possibilities, so many reasons to be happy.

Concept (idea): An exhibit. 'Becky Brookfield — the Untold Story'.

Purpose: Education, information, discussion, illustration (add other 'ion' words so there is lots of purpose).

Objects: The objects will come from the second bedroom and they will also be borrowed from around the house. Clover Quinn will catalogue the objects.

Story: Clover Quinn will tell the story and write any text.

Designer: Clover Quinn.

Curator: Clover Quinn.

Keeper: Darren Quinn.

Other information: This will be a temporary exhibit. Afterwards the objects will be stored somewhere safe.

3

Clover bought the notebook during the end-of-term trip to the Maritime Museum, a few weeks ago. The day began badly. As the train sloped into the station Mr Judge told people to pick partners and she was filled with a panicky, musical chairs feeling.

This school year, friendship has evolved from something easy to a complicated performance that requires a lot of pretending. It has become vitally important to like and dislike the right things; to have committed certain acts or to at least understand the acts that other people claim to have committed. Take fingering, for example, which sounds like it could be to do with playing the ukulele, but is something else entirely — something Abbie Higham claims to have had done *to* her.

Abbie Higham has the kudos that comes from having been kissed. She won't name names, but she is happy to be pressed for details and proffer advice.

'When you kiss, you have to open your mouth or you'll suffocate.'

'If you wear red lipstick it means you're a slag.'

'You shouldn't go swimming in the sea when you have your period. Sharks, duh!'

Clover glanced left and right, pulling her best not-bothered face; she wouldn't look desperate by dashing about from person to person. It wasn't a case of not being liked, just of not being liked enough, of not being anyone's first choice, of not having a *bosom friend*, something she can't ever say out loud, obviously — *bosom!* — but has been mulling over ever since she and Grandad read *Anne of Green Gables* in their book club last summer.

In the end Mr Judge took pity on her. 'You can sit with me, Clover,' he offered.

They crowded on to the train. Mr Judge secured four seats, two sets of two, facing each other, and placed his bag beside him. Clover sat opposite, in the aisle seat, and watched as further down the carriage Abbie, Jess and Emily attempted to stop Dagmar from occupying an empty seat by piling their bags on it.

'Clover!' Abbie called. 'We're saving this for *you*.'

Dagmar waited in the aisle, one eye obscured by the slope of her dark fringe.

'Clover! Get here! I'm not sitting next to Dracula.'

'She vants to bite us.'

They needed Clover's help to complete their meanness, but she didn't move. In the end Mr Judge stood, twisted and, clutching the headrest of his seat, called, 'For goodness' sake, Dagmar, just sit down.'

Dagmar looked helplessly at the piled bags.

'Clover, move up to the window. Dagmar, *come here*. There's a seat *right here*.' He sat down hard. '*Honestly*, girls.'

Dagmar sat, head bowed, hands clasped, and not for the first time Clover wondered what to say to her. It was easy to assume that she didn't care. She never blushed. Her expression remained impassive and she held herself small, as if she was used to pretending invisibility. But she must care, Clover thought, she *must*.

Dagmar felt the looking and glanced up, face cross, forehead crinkled. If she had spoken, she might have said, *I didn't ask for your help* and *Don't you dare feel sorry for me.*

The Manchester and Liverpool lines run in tandem for a few hundred feet before they split and the line to Manchester heads west, curling past back gardens and sneaking under road bridges, while the Liverpool line arrows south, right in front of people's houses. As the train barged down the middle of Railway Street and Railway Terrace, forcing buses and cars to stop at level crossings, Clover pressed her face up to the window. Once the houses and roads had been replaced by golf courses and pine woods, she turned to Mr Judge and began to tell him some of the things she'd read the previous night, in one of Dad's books, in preparation for the trip.

'Did you know some of the bodies from the *Titanic* sank to the bottom of the sea and never floated back up because of the pressure and the cold? Sea creatures ate them. All that was left was their shoes.'

He didn't know.

'Did you know the wreck was only discovered in 1985? It's covered in rusticles, which are underwater icicles.'

He didn't know that, either.

'Did you know — '

He said she could put all the details in the report she'd be writing for homework. And she could have a merit for being a good researcher. Then he pulled out his phone and played Fruit Ninja for the rest of the journey.

The museum was made of red bricks, all of it, even the arched ceiling. Standing in the foyer was a bit like standing in an enormous old tunnel. The lights hung from steel wires and the floor was made of cobbles and pavement slabs. The air stank of coffee from the museum café, and when the glass doors opened and people stepped in and out of the building, Clover could hear seagulls squawking. Outside, tall ships and tugs floated in the Albert and Canning docks, on either side of the museum.

Mr Judge said they could explore by themselves, as long as they were back in the foyer at lunchtime. Staff in blue museum T-shirts handed out trail booklets to accompany an exhibit called 'Seized! The Border & Customs Uncovered'. There would be a prize for the first person to complete the booklet, so most people headed downstairs. Clover wasn't interested in the prize. She climbed the metal staircase. It was open on one side so you could see the drop to the museum shop and a display of a wooden canoe filled with tiny human figures. On the other side of the staircase a wall had been painted to look like the side of a ship. There were glass-fronted portholes, and along the top, by the high museum ceiling, was a railing, from behind which MDF silhouettes of passengers waved.

On the first floor Clover stopped beside a

model of the *Titanic* in a glass case. It was long, perhaps as long as her bedroom, though it was difficult to tell. It had tiny lifeboats hanging from its sides and dozens of little portholes. She wished she could open the case and look through the *Titanic*'s portholes — it would be epic if it was filled with replicas of things that were on the real ship: flower arrangements, tablecloths and candlesticks; fancy curtains, paintings and cutlery; wooden beds, tools and musical instruments, all carefully placed on board to help people have a lovely time. All sliding about as the ship tilted. All crashing into the walls and ceilings as it sank. All sitting in the thick quiet at the bottom of the sea.

On the other side of the display case, Clover noticed a woman scribbling into a notebook with a stubby pencil. She was too old to be a student and she wasn't wearing a Maritime Museum T-shirt like the people who guarded the exhibits that visitors weren't supposed to touch. Her navy jeans were smart and her painted toenails poked out of red wedge sandals. Clover edged around the case, pretending to examine the *Titanic*. When she got close to the woman, she glanced at the open notebook. The woman wasn't drawing and her writing was too small to read.

'Do you like the model?'

Clover nodded, embarrassed to have been caught staring. But the woman seemed friendly, so she asked, 'What are you doing?'

'A gallery check.'

'What's that?'

The woman tucked the pencil behind her ear,

like a builder. 'Once a week, we check to make sure everything's working: the lighting, the touch screens on the computerised parts of the displays, and the objects themselves — some of them have environmental controls so we check to make sure everything's okay.'

'And that's your job? Checking things?'

'Part of it.'

'What are the other parts?'

'Coming up with ideas — *concepts*, that's what we call them. Thinking about which exhibitions will be permanent and which will be temporary. Selecting the objects and deciding how we'll interpret them. Making sure we get the text right — '

'Did you always want to work in a museum?'

'For as long as I can remember. When I was a little girl, my mum was a keeper at Liverpool Museum. That's what the job used to be called.'

'A keeper?'

'Lovely name, isn't it?'

'Like a zookeeper or a park keeper, but for museums? Someone who's in charge of *keeping* stuff?'

'Yes! But we're called curators now; it's a good word, too. An old word — it's Latin. We take care of the displays and objects. And we make lots of lists.' She waved her notebook to demonstrate.

'So you're *in charge* of *all this?*' Clover glanced at the displays, the models and the wall-mounted screens showing black and white footage of passengers waving from skyscraper-high decks.

'There's lots of people involved: designers,

conservation people — '

'What do they do?'

'The designers work on the displays. They decide how to mount things and they think about the best way to show the objects. The conservation people clean things, they have to — '

'Do you have stuff that isn't on display at the moment?'

'Oh yes.'

'Where do you keep it?'

'There's some onsite storage. But we keep a lot of it in a big object store for Liverpool Museums.'

'Where's that?'

'I can't say, sorry. For security.'

Clover imagined a library, but with *things* sitting on miles of shelves, and curators pacing down the endless aisles, their footsteps echoing in the vast space as they agonised over which objects to display. 'But how do you get all the stuff in the first place?'

'Sometimes we borrow objects from other museums and sometimes we buy things. Often, people give us objects, things that have been in their families for ages.'

'And they don't mind having their stuff on display?'

'No, I think people like sharing their lives.'

'How do you decide what to display and what to leave in the store?'

'Well, it's all about which objects fit the narratives we're telling. We do some research — there's a database; every object has a unique catalogue number that stays with it. We have photographs and text about the history of each piece. And a section about its provenance — that's the story of the object: where it came from, why it's important and so on.' She pulled the pencil out from behind her ear and tested its end with her front teeth. A moment later she lowered it, leaned forward and whispered, 'Do you know what the best bit about this job is?'

Clover shook her head.

'Touching things — with gloves on, you have to be careful — touching things that are part of the past, especially personal items. You get a feeling about them as you hold them. You're doing something special . . . looking after culture and history, looking after people's stories. That's what it's all about.'

That was how the idea started.

Light streamed through the big windows of the industrial building and the idea sat in the warmth all afternoon as Clover explored the main exhibit, 'Titanic and Liverpool — the Untold Story'. She had to pick a card about a passenger to carry with her until the end, when she would find out whether the person lived or died. She picked two, just in case. Violet Jessop, a pretty, soft-faced nurse, and Mildred Brown, whose features were completely obscured by the shadow of an enormous hat. 'My name is Violet Jessop,' the first card read, and it was as if Violet's voice was calling across the years. At the bottom of both cards it said, 'Discover my fate at the end of this exhibition.' She held the women's cards against her chest and hoped for happy endings.

Clover learned that there were five grand pianos on the *Titanic* and twelve dogs, three of which survived. She saw a display of items salvaged from the debris field: a ceramic sink, a chamber pot, a ventilation grille, tiepins, glasses, a watch and a letter opener. Perhaps Violet and Mildred had touched some of the things. The curator had almost certainly touched them before they were placed in the glass display cases. Did she really get feelings about objects just by touching them? Did the stories seep out of the metal and glass and leather, through the protective gloves and into her fingertips? Clover thought of Violet and Mildred; she wished them lifeboats, life jackets and childhood swimming lessons.

The idea fed on details. By the time Clover reached the end of the exhibit it was ready — full of energy and wrapped in a protective coat of patience, like a seed. She paused to read about the women whose cards she'd carried. Violet Jessop survived and went on to work as a nurse in the British Red Cross during World War One. Mildred Brown also survived. It was a good sign, further evidence of the idea's rightfulness.

She sat beside Dagmar on the train home and was daunted to silence by her stillness and the way she kept eyes trained on some distant spot, lips locked like cockle halves. Dad says the danger in spending your kindness on other people is that you might not have any left for yourself — it doesn't stop him from being kind, though. Shielded by the dark as they passed through a tunnel, she whispered, 'Are you okay?'

'I am fine, thank you,' came the reply.

Clover couldn't think of anything else to say, so she opened the notebook she'd bought in the museum shop and slipped the passenger cards between the pages. There were plans to make, words she might forget if she didn't write them down: *concept, object, text, curator, keeper, exhibit, display*. She pulled a pen out of her blazer pocket and, for the rest of the journey, toyed with the notebook and tended the idea.

When she got home from school, Dad was kneeling in the hall. He'd unscrewed the radiator and his thumb was pressed over an unfastened pipe as water gushed around it. The books and clothes and newspapers that used to line the hall had been arranged in small piles on the stairs. Beside him, on the damp carpet, was a metal scraper he'd been using to scuff the paper off the wall.

'Just in time!' he said. 'Fetch a bowl. A small one, so it'll fit.'

She fetched two and spent the next fifteen minutes running back and forth to the kitchen emptying one bowl as the other filled, Dad calling, 'Faster! Faster! Keep it up, Speedy Gonzalez!' His trousers were soaked and his knuckles grazed, but he wasn't bothered. 'Occupational hazard,' he said, as if it wasn't his day off and plumbing and stripping walls was his actual job.

Once the pipe had emptied he stood up and hopped about for a bit while the feeling came back into his feet. 'I helped Colin out with something this morning,' he said. 'The people whose house we were at had this dado rail thing — it sounds posh, but it's just a bit of wood, really — right about here.' He brushed his hand against the wall beside his hip. 'Underneath it they had stripy wallpaper, but above it they had a different, plain kind. It was dead nice and I thought we could do that.'

Dad found a scraper for her. The paint came off in flakes, followed by tufts of the thick, textured wallpaper. Underneath was a layer of soft, brown backing paper which Dad sprayed with water from a squirty bottle. When the water had soaked in, they made long scrapes down the wall, top to bottom, leaving the backing paper flopped over the skirting boards like ribbons of skin. It felt like they were undressing the house.

The bare walls weren't smooth. They were gritty, crumbly in places. As they worked, a dusty smell wafted out of them. It took more than an hour to get from the front door to the wall beside the bottom stair. That's where Dad uncovered the heart. It was about as big as Clover's hand,

Darren + Becky

4ever

etched on the wall in black permanent marker, in Dad's handwriting.

'I'd forgotten,' he murmured. And then he pulled his *everything* face. The face he pulls when Uncle Jim is drunk. The face he pulls when they go shopping in March and the person at the till tries to be helpful by reminding them about Mother's Day. The face which reminds her that a lot of the time his expression is like a plate of leftovers.

She didn't say anything, and although she wanted to, she didn't trace the heart with her fingertips. Instead, she went up to the bathroom and sat on the boxed, pre-lit Christmas tree Dad bought in the January sales. When you grow up in the saddest chapter of someone else's story, you're forever skating on the thin ice of their memories. That's not to say it's always sad — there are happy things, too. When she was a baby, Dad had a tattoo of her name drawn on his arm in curly blue writing, and underneath he had a green four-leaf clover. She has *such* a brilliant name, chosen by her mother because it has the word *love* in the middle. That's not the sort of thing you go around telling people, but it *is* something you can remember if you need a little boost; an instant access, happiness top-up card — it even works when Luke Barton calls her Margey-rine. Clover thought of her name and counted to three hundred. As she counted she drew her finger through the dust on the Christmas-tree box. Once she'd finished counting she wondered about the factory where the tree was made — who assembled it, who

49

touched it and packed it? 'Made in China', it said. There were probably workers' fingerprints all over the box; there might even be specks of skin and hair inside it. She thought of all the things her mother might have touched in each room of the house. Had she a favourite mug? Was some of the dust in the second bedroom made up of her skin? If the police came, might they find her fingerprints?

When she went downstairs Dad had recovered his empty face and she couldn't help asking a question, just a small one.

'Is there any more writing under the paper?'

'I don't think so.'

'She didn't do a heart as well?'

'Help me with this, will you?'

They pulled the soggy ribbons of paper away from the skirting and put them in a bin bag. The house smelled different afterwards. As if some old sadness had leaked out of the walls.

★ ★ ★

Clover kneels on the small square of floor she has cleared. Dad used to sleep in this room. Before. It isn't quite as big as hers — it's almost square shaped, whereas hers is rectangular. The sun stabs a sharp slice of light through the window — there's only one here; it's larger than either of hers and it looks out over the back garden. On the first day, she squeezed past the boxes and tried to push up the sash, hands already sweaty in the blue plastic gloves she'd taken from the dispenser at the petrol station.

50

But the window wouldn't budge.

Underneath the jumble of boxes and other stuff there's a double bed. No duvet and no sheets, just the base and the bare mattress, topped by sheaves of papers, envelopes, shoes, books, a pile of folded-up material — bed sheets? curtains? towels? — a few cushions and several carrier bags that are beginning to dissolve, snowing plastic on to the floorboards below. From in among the piles of stuff she can see the sharp poke of picture frames. Wait there, she thinks, I'm coming for you.

The bed sits in front of the chimney breast. In the alcove on either side of it are matching wardrobes. They are old, with corrugated fronts like window shutters; they were probably white before the sun sleeked through the window and toasted them yellow. Access to the wardrobes is blocked by bigger boxes, the kind Colin keeps in his van for when people are moving house. Some of these are fastened with brown tape, others are open. She'll reach the wardrobes, eventually.

The walls are wrapped in old paper. Swirls of orange, yellow and lime-green flowers on a milky blue background. Some of the flowers are definitely roses. There are daisies too, but she isn't sure whether the others have names or are just flower shapes, like the kind you draw when you are small. The paper is interrupted by a picture rail. Above the rail, the wall is painted lime green. The floor-length curtains are green, too. After she failed to push up the sash, she held one of the curtains and fanned it open. It was striped where the sun had bleached the material;

the stripes were light, dark, light, dark, like bamboo stalks.

The room is half and half, which is to say, if a stranger stepped into it, they might think it half packed or they might think it half unpacked; it seems it could be either. She imagines Dad beginning the packing, initially determined, sustained by the idea of how it would look once it was done; folding, lifting, arranging, and then standing with one hand on his hip, rubbing the fuzz of his hair with the other, thinking about the best way to proceed. At some point he must have got disheartened. Perhaps it made him sad. Perhaps he was too busy; looking after a baby is hard work. Or it could be that he had another idea in the meantime and the enthusiasm trickled down his arms and out of his fingers until, shoulders slumped, he closed the bedroom door.

But now she's here. And she will sort it out.

The floor is wooden, not polished and shiny, just exposed, bare. It is already making divots in her knees. She lifts a pile of paper off the end of the bed and places it beside the boxes and the carrier-bag flakes. Specks of dust take flight and she blows a following wind after them. Then she unfastens her red mock-Converse trainers and settles, legs crossed.

A quick rifle reveals that the pile consists entirely of unopened mail addressed to her mother. She slides her hands out of the blue gloves and unwraps letters offering double glazing and conservatories, and credit card applications, along with shopping surveys and requests from charities. Catalogues:

clothes, kitchens and seeds. And holiday brochures: cruises, skiing, beaches and canal boats.
All sorts. Nothing important. When she has finished, she has a new pile that's bigger and messier
than the one with which she started. But that's
okay. If she's going to get all this cleared up,
she'll have to make a mess first.

She doesn't need to record any of these things
in her notebook. Instead, she pops downstairs
— mind the motorbike helmets, and the
newspapers, and the Dulux Black Satin paint
— for a bin bag. As she heads down the hall the
letterbox snaps. Yikes! But it's not Dad,
inexplicably back from work early. It's just the
postman. Her breath escapes in a relieved puff.

Dad has never said she isn't allowed in the
room, he just says:

'Oh, it's such a mess.'

'Don't go in there, you'll break your neck.'

'I'll sort it out one day.'

On the few occasions when they've stepped
inside together he has allowed her to have a brief
look; opened a few of the boxes, lifted the odd
thing off the bed and stroked it while she
watched, mouth closed tight, because to speak
would break the spell and return them to the
other side of the door.

Back in the room, she chucks the junk mail in
the bin bag and, having slid her hands into the
blue plastic gloves again, lifts another pile of
papers off the bed. Just as she begins to flick
through the pile, the telephone rings and she
dashes down the stairs — *careful* — to answer, in
case it's Dad.

'IS THAT YOU, CLOVER?'

Mrs Mackerel is a bit deaf. When she talks she cups her mouth and, if you didn't know better, you'd think she was about to whisper. Then her voice explodes out of her, literally. She has two settings: loud, for normal words; and extra loud, for the words she wants to be certain have been heard.

'I've got some SWEETS. Will you COME AND GET THEM?'

'You mean now?'

'No, I mean next week — OF COURSE I MEAN NOW.'

Clover trudges up the stairs. She places the gloves on the bed and picks up her red trainers before stepping out on to the landing and closing the door. Mrs Mackerel doesn't usually buy her sweets, she's just checking up on her. Still, there's plenty of time. Weeks and weeks of it.

⋆ ⋆ ⋆

Mrs Mackerel's bell plays a selection of tunes on a loop. Today it does 'Jingle Bells'.

Mrs Mackerel opens the door. 'NOT TODAY, THANK YOU,' she says, and then she closes it in Clover's face.

Clover waits. The door opens.

'It was a JOKE! Now, COME IN.'

She follows Mrs Mackerel down the hall, past poor bleeding Jesus on a cross as long as her arm, and into the lounge, which is a mirror image of hers and Dad's and almost as crowded.

'You'd better SIT DOWN, then.'

54

Clover sits on the edge of the two-seater sofa.
'NOT THERE.'
She flits to the three-seater instead.
'THAT'LL DO.'
Mrs Mackerel's lounge is full of chairs. It's as if she went to the furniture shop, found a fabric she liked — turquoise with a spattering of fat pink roses — and ordered everything they had in it: a three-seater, a two-seater, an armchair and a matching footstool. She picked the same material for her curtains, the swoopy kind that look like they should be in front of a stage. Everything is so big, it's a wonder it was able to fit through the door. Clover wouldn't be surprised if the furnishings started out tiny like those dehydrated flannels she used to like when she was a little girl, and Mrs Mackerel watered them until they swelled into three flowery sofas and a fancy pair of curtains.

There's not much room for any furniture besides the chairs. Instead, Mrs Mackerel has filled the remaining space with cottage ornaments. Every surface — windowsill, television stand, a small display cabinet and the mantel-piece — is decorated with them, all slightly different but essentially the same: whitewashed walls and thatched roofs with tiny flower-filled gardens wrapped by hedges. The houses have names like Rose Cottage, Thistle Cottage and Midnight Cottage. Clover used to line them up on the carpet when she was younger, deciding which she liked best, which she would live in if she were a centimetre tall. Although she knows several collectors — Grandad (clocks), Uncle

Jim (jigsaws), Dad (well, everything) — and could, if pushed, suggest reasons why Grandad and Uncle Jim and Dad keep the things they gather, this particular collection mystifies Clover. Mrs Mackerel has lived in The Grove since she got married, nearly fifty years ago. Her house, like Clover's, is made of red brick; the windows are encased in white plastic and its roof is protected by thin slices of slate. She doesn't have an allotment, and many years ago she paid workmen to bury her back garden and driveway under paving slabs. She would *hate* living in the countryside — if anything from outdoors ever sneaks inside she takes off her slipper and fights it to the death.

'And what have YOU got to SAY FOR YOURSELF today?'

The question makes the visit seem like her idea, and she doesn't have *anything* to say for herself. She only came for the sweets.

'CAT GOT YOUR TONGUE? Well, I'll tell you what I've been up to then, shall I? Now, I'm telling you this IN CONFIDENCE . . .'

Mrs Mackerel says a lot of things *in confidence*, but because she says them so loudly, she pretty much ends up saying them *with confidence*, instead. Dad's always telling her to go and see the doctor. 'Hearing aids don't cost anything, they're *free*, Edna,' he says. But Mrs Mackerel won't put any old rubbish in her ears. What she wants is some of them proper digital hearing aids from the telly, not a pair of NHS whistlers. She goes on and on, until Dad gets all huffy and says, 'You haven't listened to a word

I've said.' Then she looks pleased, as if the whole point of the conversation was to get a rise out of Dad.

' . . . and so I told Mrs Knight, *God forgive me*, IF YOU THINK I'M GOING TO BRING YOUR BIN IN AGAIN, YOU'VE GOT ANOTHER THINK COMING . . . '

Mrs Knight is a nice old lady from round the back. Mrs Mackerel keeps an eye on her and they seem like best friends — they shop together every Wednesday and Saturday, they have lunch in the café at BHS, and they do little favours for each other, like lending Catherine Cookson books and telling each other which supermarkets have gin on special offer — but Mrs Mackerel keeps a mental count of every good deed and Mrs Knight is in arrears. Sometimes it seems Mrs Mackerel is Mrs Knight's best friend *and* her greatest enemy, all at once. On Tuesday afternoons Mrs Knight comes round to Mrs Mackerel's and they drink gin and orange squash. Just one or two, they say. And then it's three, and four, and five. Last summer, Clover endured trips to the café at BHS and stagnant afternoons in Mrs Mackerel's conservatory, but she looked forward to Tuesdays. Once, Mrs Mackerel even said a rude word. Mrs Knight started it, by trying to rest her glass on her tummy, which rolled out like a little hill when she sat down. Some of the gin splashed on to her trousers.

'GET YOUR AUNTY PEARL A CLOTH,' Mrs Mackerel said.

Clover did as she was told, even though she

doesn't have any aunties.

Mrs Knight dabbed at the mound of her waist. 'Oh dear, it's my belly, it's — '

'Your chest's ON YOUR BELLY and your belly'll be ON YOUR KNEES before you're finished, Pearl.'

'Oh!'

'You need a PANTY GIRDLE.'

'Really? I — '

'SEVEN POUNDS AT BONMARCHÉ.'

'Well, I don't know what I'd . . . I've never — would you wear knickers with one, Edna?'

'OF COURSE. I always wear knickers with mine. In fact, in the WINTER, when I've got my KNICKERS, my GIRDLE and my TIGHTS on, I'm always LOVELY AND WARM! I can't be doing with a cold B.T.M.'

'A cold what?'

'BEE — TEE — EM.'

Mrs Knight rubbed at her damp patch and shrugged.

'A cold ARSE, Pearl.'

And then — funniest of all — Mrs Mackerel did a burp. Not a loud one, just a little pop that she tried, and failed, to swallow.

Clover smiles as she remembers.

' . . . I won't have her HOLDING ME HOSTILE with her power washer. And I don't know what's SO FUNNY about that,' Mrs Mackerel is saying. 'I SUPPOSE YOU'LL BE WANTING YOUR SWEETS.'

Her nylon trousers crackle when she gets up from the armchair. She is wearing a sort of jacket like the ones the school dinner ladies wear. She calls it a housecoat; she has several in different pastels — there must be a catalogue or a special shop — and she wears them over her clothes, only taking them off when she goes out or has important visitors. Mrs Mackerel likes to keep things for best: blouses, trousers, glasses, biscuits — even the turquoise, rose-spattered sofas have white napkin-ish flaps dangling over their arms and tops, just where your arms and head rest. While she is gone, Clover peers at the silver-framed wedding photograph that sits among the cottage ornaments on the mantel-piece. You can tell it's Mrs Mackerel, it's exactly how she would look if you excavated her face: remove the wrinkly topsoil, dig under the eye-bag mounds, flatten the badlands of her neck, and there she is, young and skin-tight, looking wonderfully glamorous in a sparkly crown and a white lace dress with sleeves like bells, her hands covered by little white gloves that stop at the wrist, fingers clasping a small bouquet — lilies, gardenia, iris? It's hard to tell because the photograph is black and white. Mr Mackerel is smart in a dark suit and a striped tie. He is tall and slim, his hair so short and shiny-slick that it could pass for plastic, like Barbie's Ken.

'CUP OF TEA?' Mrs Mackerel calls from the kitchen.

'No, thank you.'

'DON'T ANSWER, THEN. Why do I bother?' She bursts back into the lounge, holding a bag of Jelly Babies. She usually buys mints: soft mints, humbugs, mint imperials, Murray mints,

Tic Tacs, Polo mints and Werther's butter mints. She must have stood in the sweet aisle of the shop, imagining what Clover might like; the thought makes Clover happy.

'HERE.'

'Thank you.'

'ROT YOUR TEETH.'

Clover nods.

'FULL OF SUGAR.'

She nods again, clasping the yellow packet in case Mrs Mackerel changes her mind and takes it back.

'DON'T EAT THEM ALL AT ONCE.'

'No.'

'AND I FOUND THESE.' She delves in her knitting bag for something that is clearly not knitting, because it rustles when she touches it. 'THERE. We were cleaning out the cupboard at CHURCH and LO and BEHOLD.'

Clover opens her hand to receive a small stack of colouring books — *Our Lady of Fatima, Our Lady of the Miraculous Medal, The Story of Mary* — and a booklet, browned and curling at the corners, called *Latin Words and Phrases for Beginners*.

'Oh. Thank you.'

'YOU'RE WELCOME. What are you UP to? Aren't you BORED on your OWN all day?'

'It's not *all* day, and I've got jobs. I'm doing the watering — '

'And you'll be KNITTING THE SCARF FOR YOUR DAD, won't you? Bring it with you NEXT TIME and I'll HAVE A LOOK. What does HE THINK about you being at home ON

YOUR OWN ALL DAY?

'Well, I'm not, it's not *all* day, but he's — '

'HE'S A GOOD MAN — *God help him*. He wears his HEART on his SHOULDER.'

Clover makes an agreeing noise.

'Well, you've got JOBS to do. You'd better BE OFF.'

As Clover leaves, Mrs Mackerel presses a £2 coin into her hand. 'THERE,' she says. 'You could BUY YOURSELF some of those LOON BANDS.'

'Loom bands?'

'That's right. Someone made a DRESS out of them and got a MILLION POUNDS for it. YOU COULD DO THAT — *God love you*.'

Clover hurries to the door, conscious of Mrs Mackerel's partiality for what Dad calls the tablecloth trick.

'And Clover?'

Here she goes, everything's lovely, now she'll whip the cloth out from under it.

'Tell your dad he'd better SORT YOUR BACK GARDEN OUT. He's been PROMIS-ING to do it for TIME AND MEMORIAL.'

★   ★   ★

Clover sits on a stack of empty milk crates in the back garden, the Latin booklet and Jelly Babies resting on her lap. The colouring books top a pile of papers in the kitchen destined for the recycling bin. She rearranges the press of her bottom on the criss-cross of the crates — Colin borrowed them from somewhere when he was having a go at being a milkman; one day Dad will line them with plastic and use them as planters.

Mrs Mackerel is right, the garden could do with a tidy. The shed is bursting with tools, buckets and spades, canes for the allotment, collapsed lilos, a stack of six plastic garden chairs and a matching table, jars of screws and nails, half-emptied seed envelopes, two sleds, and a dressmaker's dummy Dad thought she might like in her room — she didn't like it; it terrified her, that's why it's out here. Other stuff rests against the shed's outer walls or lounges on the lawn, waiting to be put somewhere. All the bikes she has ever owned lean up against it like a sculpture of her growth to date, in metal and rubber. A boat engine Dad bought on eBay is beached on the grass beside her. At least Dad keeps the grass quite short; Mrs Mackerel can't complain about *that*. When it's time to cut it he gets Clover to lift everything — the plastic slide she played on as a toddler, the slimy-bottomed paddling pool, the balls and water pistols — while he trails behind her, not mowing neatly, in stripes, but backwards and forwards, in a vacuuming sort of pattern.

A car alarm whistles and every dog in the neighbourhood answers. She flicks the Latin booklet open and scans the words: *collector, curator, idea, museum* — she recognises lots of them. The sayings are trickier. *Acta non verba* — deeds, not words. She likes that, it makes her think of her notebook, upstairs, waiting.

Knock, knock.

Shielding her eyes, she stares up, past the cusp of the garden fence, at the square window of Mrs Mackerel's second bedroom, where she is standing, draped in the net curtain, jabbing the pane with her index finger, pointing, pointing, pointing . . . at the bag of Jelly Babies. Her lips are moving. NOT ALL AT ONCE, she'll be saying. And possibly, YOU DON'T WANT TO END UP LIKE YOUR MOTHER. Clover puts the bag down on the crate and waves.

Mrs Mackerel knew her mother. That's what everyone calls her — *your mother*. It's not friendly like mum, ma or mam, but she quite likes it because it sounds special and a bit posh, and she is used to it now; she couldn't call her anything else if she tried. It's the same with Mrs Mackerel: by the time she said, 'Call me Edna,' when Clover was about eight, it was far too late. She would like to put Mrs Mackerel in a juicer and squeeze the story of her mother out all at once, but Mrs Mackerel trickles her comments and sometimes says mean stuff on purpose.

'She could have done with losing a few pounds, *God love her.*'

'She wasn't much of a mother, *God forgive me.*'

Mrs Mackerel always mentions God after she has been mean. Sometimes she is not a very nice person — *God help her!* Dad says she's had a hard life, so allowances must be made. When she is especially mean he calls her 'Evil Edna', who was a witch of extreme wickedness, from a cartoon he used to watch when he was a little boy, and sometimes, when she's going off on

63

one, he says rude things under his breath, very quietly. Dad has had a hard life, too. But he isn't mean.

Clover was a surprise. Dad has always been clear about it. When she was small he delivered the story while pantomiming a surprised face. 'One day your mother had tummy ache and then, suddenly, you arrived! She had to go to the hospital in an ambulance. When it was time for my break, someone met me on Lord Street and told me to go to the hospital. I jumped on the 44, and when I got there I couldn't believe it. What a surprise!'

She had always imagined that she was the good kind of surprise, like when it's a party and everyone jumps out and shouts, 'Happy birthday!' But the way Mrs Mackerel told the story of her birth made her wonder whether she had in fact been the kind of surprise someone might get if, after the party, they got home and discovered their house had been burgled.

'I suppose you know the FACTS OF LIFE, now?' she began, one afternoon last summer.

Clover did — does, in fact, know a lot of *disgusting* facts, even more than she knew last summer. She shifts slightly on the milk crate; her knickers are climbing into her bum, they're a bit too small, and since Dad told her his version of the facts there has been a growing carefulness between them when it comes to things like snogging on the telly and romantic songs, and she has been putting off saying *I need some new ones*. The carefulness intensified last autumn when Dad announced that he thought it would

64

be a good idea if they went to Marks and Spencer to buy some new underwear. She knew he had to be talking about bras, because they usually grabbed knickers and vests in packs of fives or sevens from the supermarket, chucking them in the trolley with the fish fingers and ice lollies. She wondered how he knew about Marks and Spencer and who had told him about the measuring service. Girls at school joked about it, said the ladies who worked there volunteered specially so they could cop a feel. It was probably Kelly, she thought. Which also meant that Kelly might have said, 'Clover's getting boobs,' or words to that effect. Clover couldn't decide if it was worse for your dad or a family friend to notice your boobs first. 'Would you like Kelly to come with us?' Dad asked. Clover absolutely DID NOT want Kelly to go on a boob-measuring trip with them. Kelly would want to make it into a special occasion. There would be a cosy chat afterwards: *How does it feel to have your first bra?* So she went with Dad. He accompanied her through the forest of under-wear, right up to the fitting room, where he mumbled something about measurements to one of the women. The woman was friendly and brisk. 'You'll want at least three,' she said, and she helped Clover choose. Dad retreated to the border of Lingerie, occupying the no man's land between it and Menswear. He kept a lookout and joined them at the till once the measuring and choosing was over. Afterwards, they went to the café for the first time. It was full of old people. Dad bought hot chocolate and shortbread squares. She held the bag of bras tight on her lap, half scared that, given the opportunity, they would slide out and expose themselves. Dad said she was growing up fast and cleared his throat. Then they talked about burning the rubbish at the allotment before winter, and Mrs Mackerel, who had recently described herself as a DEAD-IN-THE-WOOL TORY. 'We live in hope,' Dad said, and they sniggered. It was a sort of celebration, but without any fuss. Later, he did a clearly rehearsed speech and presented her with a precautionary packet of sanitary towels. 'Nothing to be embarrassed about,' he said, as his face and neck turned red. 'I bought these at Lidl. In broad daylight. And I wasn't bothered at all.'

Clover was born at lunchtime. In the kitchen. There was a racket. Mrs Mackerel banged on the wall, and when the noise didn't stop she came round to see what was happening. No one answered the door, so she rushed round the back, let herself in and found Clover's mother kneeling on the floor like an animal. Mrs Mackerel knew what was happening, she has had four children, all boys, which means she might as well not have bothered, because boys are no use whatsoever.

Clover has seen people having babies. Not in real life, obviously, but on the Scientific Eye video everyone watched at the start of Year 7 and on *One Born Every Minute*. It's quite frightening. The worst bit is right at the end when the mothers make these mooing noises. Sometimes it looks like things are about to go wrong, but they don't — or maybe they don't show those bits — and people cry (with happiness) and say things like, 'It's a miracle' and 'What tiny fingers.' The dads talk about how amazing it was to be part of it all, and when they phone family and friends their voices wobble. A lot of babies seem to be born in the night, which might be the best time because everything is quiet and it's not long until morning when you can wake up with your brand-new baby beside you. What a lovely beginning.

Every time Clover asked her to repeat the story last summer, Mrs Mackerel added something. If Clover asked about any of the new bits, Mrs Mackerel made out she'd always told the story that way, so Clover zipped her lips and listened.

'There's absolutely NO NEED to MAKE A RACKET,' Mrs Mackerel said. 'I told your mother — *God help her* — to SHUT HER GOB and OPEN HER LEGS.'

Her mother was what Dad calls *cuddly*. Mrs Mackerel says she was *big-boned*; a woman who *liked her food*. Clover has seen photographs. There is one on the mantelpiece in the lounge which Dad took on the beach. Her mother is facing away from the camera and the wind has lifted her hair and spread it skyward, which means you can hardly see her face. There is another in her bedroom, a high-school picture, taken when her mother was all teeth and nose, before she had grown into her face. And there are also two photographs of Clover and her mother together, in a small plastic album in a kitchen drawer. What she would really like is a photograph of her mother with Dad, like the one of Mr and Mrs Mackerel on Mrs Mackerel's mantelpiece. Of course, it wouldn't be of a wedding because Dad and her mother never got married, but to have a picture of the two of them dressed up smart would be epic. In the pictures she has, her mother looks like the kind of person who would be really good at hugs; soft and pillowy, not massive — not like people on the telly who can't get out of bed. But big enough, perhaps, not to notice Clover attaching herself, cells dividing and multiplying, settling in, certain of a welcome.

Her mother had probably realised that she was having a baby by the time Mrs Mackerel burst into the kitchen, but Clover sometimes worries that she hadn't and the exact moment it dawned on her was when she heard, 'SHUT YOUR GOB and OPEN YOUR LEGS.'

That is not a lovely beginning.

'The air may have been BLUE, but you CAME OUT PINK,' Mrs Mackerel said. 'And that's the MAIN THING.'

Mrs Mackerel meant that her mother was swearing. Clover wishes she had asked about that. It would be nice to know her mother's swearwords of choice; whether she stuck to the usual or got creative, like Uncle Jim, who calls people 'lard-fondlers' and 'twunt-biscuits'.

'I *CAUGHT* you, Clover Quinn. A catch IAN BOTHAM would have been PROUD of! I cut the cord with THE KITCHEN SCISSORS, and I wrapped you in a TEA TOWEL. Looking back,

I probably should have PASSED YOU STRAIGHT TO YOUR MOTHER, it might have been GOOD FOR BONDAGE, but I didn't think of it AT THE TIME.'

Instead, Mrs Mackerel carried her into the hall and telephoned for an ambulance, leaving her mother on all fours, skirt rucked round her waist. The ambulance drove right to the end of The Grove, blue lights flashing. Everyone came out to look.

'I was going to CARRY YOU OUT,' Mrs Mackerel said, making it sound like she'd hoped to hold her up to the neighbours, like in *The Lion King*. 'But one of the PARAMEDICS took you while the other PUSHED your mother IN A WHEELCHAIR. Nothing wrong with her. NOTHING BUT STUBBORNNESS. She could have walked if she'd wanted to.'

One of the neighbours had parked awkwardly, which meant the ambulance had to reverse out of The Grove. 'Backwards and downhill,' Mrs Mackerel muttered when she got to that part of the story. 'Like everything that happened next.'

Since listening to Mrs Mackerel's account, Clover wants to hear a longer version of Dad's story. The version he tells is short, learned and always the same. It has a careful feel about it. She suspects she will feel better about Mrs Mackerel's story when she hears the whole thing in Dad's words. So far she hasn't managed to ask. Sometimes the question is there, in her mouth, all the words lined up in the right order: 'You know the story of when I was born?' Once or twice the beginning of the 'Y' has slipped out

69

like a string of spaghetti and Dad has said,
'What?' But each time, she has retreated: 'Oh,
nothing.' She doesn't want to upset him or,
perhaps worse, lead him to shrug and say,
'What's done is done, Clover. Don't waste time
thinking about it.' But she does, she thinks about
it a lot.

Exhibit: 'Becky Brookfield — the Untold Story'

Told through her belongings, this compelling exhibit will give a unique insight into Becky Brookfield. (Add some unique insights below)

EXPLORE a room where she slept.

TOUCH some of her personal items.

Other highlights include:
(Think of some other highlights)

Location: First floor. This exhibit will be in the second bedroom, which is next to her daughter Clover Quinn's room and across the landing from the bathroom. See floor plan. (Draw floorplan)

Entry: FREE.

Opening times: 10am — 5pm daily from the beginning of September.

Facilities:
Café located on the ground floor, offering cups of tea and a selection of biscuits.
　Free Wi-Fi
　Toilet
　Parking

4

When Jim gets like this, it helps to go and see him. He should have gone last week, should have checked on him the same day he talked him off the bus, instead of visiting Dad. But although it helps to see Jim, it's also hard work and he has to brace himself for it. He'll stay for a bit; long enough to have a chat and make sure there's food, that's all. It's only a five-minute walk from the bus stop on Lord Street. He strolls past the war memorial and the station, glad to be outside and on his feet after another sticky day at the wheel.

Jim lives by Asda in a room in a big old house; a bedsit, or *studio flat*, as he prefers to call it. The house was probably nice once, before its front gardens were paved and jammed with unroadworthy cars and communal wheelie bins. Its bay windows add character, but the inconsistency of their coverings indicates decline: some are shrouded by grubby net curtains, others by roller or venetian blinds and, in one case, the glass has been shattered and replaced with a square of MDF and a few strips of cardboard secured by brown tape. A group of lads straddle the crumbly, red-brick front wall, sitting between the beheaded posts of redundant TO LET signs, lean and tired, shirts off, smoking as they soak up the last of the day's sunshine. Polish, Darren thinks. Jim says they live upstairs, squeezed in like sardines. They're picked up in minibuses, early, and taken to work in the meat- and fruit-packing units outside town. He nods to them as he turns into the drive.

The front door is open: someone has left it on the latch. Darren steps inside and heads down the tiled corridor to Jim's door, which is also open. He leans in and announces himself by knocking on its thick layer of once-white paint. Jim is lying on the sofa, one that houses a pull-out bed which can be hidden away during the day, though he never bothers with the bed, preferring instead to curl up on the cushions. He is barefoot, dressed in striped boxers and a stained T-shirt, perhaps the same one he was wearing the other day. He waves and Darren enters, making a point of closing the door behind him.

The place is a shithole. It smells like an ashtray and the floor is littered with empties and jigsaw pieces. At first Darren tries not to stand on the jigsaw pieces, but it's useless. The bundle of Jim's duvet takes up the spare half of the sofa and Jim makes no attempt to rearrange it, so Darren sits on it, noting the cigarette burns on its cover as he nudges the lids of two jigsaw boxes with the toe of his shoe: a 1,000-piece Where's Wally? and a 2,000-piece Mona Lisa. There was a time when he would have tried to retrieve and regroup Jim's scattered jigsaws, momentarily comforted by the thought that he was at least putting something back together.

The telly's on a rolling news channel. A couple of suited blokes are discussing Ebola while a ribbon of text runs along the bottom of the screen: air strikes targeting Islamic State fighters, possible negotiations between Israel and the Palestinian Authority, residents in Hawaii preparing for a hurricane — anyone'd be miserable listening to this all day.

Jim jabs the remote with a swollen finger. 'I'd turn it off but it won't bloody work,' he says, as if it's doing it on purpose, to piss him off.

'Probably just the batteries. I've got loads at home. I'll bring some, next time.'

'It. Just. Won't. Argh.'

Darren watches as, head bent, Jim continues to assault the buttons. Jim's hair is like Becky's, but yellower. Perhaps the cigarette smoke has stained it, along with his teeth and fingers. The skin on his elbows is scaly and white, scabbed so thickly in places that it looks like it could be lifted with the tip of a spoon, like the crust of a pie. Darren reaches across and rescues the remote.

He talks about the allotment and his latest job with Colin, a house clearance on Lancaster Road. In an effort to cheer Jim up, he makes self-deprecating jokes and exaggerates his and Colin's ineptitude.

Jim picks an almost empty can off the floor and tips his head back to catch the dregs.

'Your psoriasis tablets and those — you're not supposed to, are you?'

Jim folds his arms and gazes past the TV, at the bare wall behind.

'I've seen you, out and about. Wearing down the pavement. What's up?'

74

He's wasting his breath, Jim never listens — he just waits for his turn to talk. But it helps to calmly point out the bleeding obvious; it's what Becky used to do.

'Are you feeling stressed? It looks like you've been scratching — your elbows are a right mess. Shall we get a bin bag and get rid of some of this crap?'

Darren asks these questions in a lilting, cheerful voice he probably should have used when Clover was a baby. The one time he went to the Mother and Baby Group — 'and Father', someone added hastily, on his arrival — he was struck by the way everyone spoke to their babies, almost as if they were singing. He'd thought it might help to go to a group, but it didn't, it just made him feel as if he was doing it all wrong. Although he never went back, he did a bit of actual singing afterwards, at bedtimes, in case it was important. Just him, by himself, before Colin gave him the ukulele. Mostly hits from the 1990s; he found a few cheerful staples: 'Rhythm Is a Dancer', 'Roll with It' and 'Three Lions'. Clover seemed to like it.

'You don't want Clover to see you like this, do you?' he asks, shaking his head, effectively answering his own question.

Jim finally stops staring at the wall. 'Have you finished boring the shit out of my arse?'

'Yeah, I suppose.'

'Question for you.'

'Go on.'

'When was the last time you picked Clover up and carried her?'

Darren is surprised to realise he can't remember, and he braces himself — sometimes Jim says stuff that makes him feel sick; Jim doesn't just get under his skin, he digs a tunnel and drives a bus down it.

'So, one day you were carrying Clover around, right? And you put her down, yeah? And then you *never* picked her up again. Never. Ever. And you didn't tell her it was the last time you'd ever pick her up, did you? You didn't explain. You just stopped doing it.'

'What?'

'I'm saying there was a time, a *very last time* that you *ever* carried her, and you don't even remember it.'

'You're serious?'

'It's true, isn't it?'

'No, not the way you're saying it, you're making it sound — '

'True is true.'

This is *not* helpful. There is a new separateness in the way he and Clover belong to each other. At home he has started to step around her, hands hesitating on either side of her bony shoulders, hanging in the air like a pair of brackets. When they are outdoors there is room to resurrect the old physicality; to loop an arm through one of hers or swing his hand around her waist. Outdoors, she has the space to lean in or spin away, to clasp him back or evade him with a playful push — it's up to her. So much of the intimacy has ended: the carrying and the tickling, the piggy-backing and the fireman's lifts. Colin has stopped, too. They haven't conferred, it just seems to be time. Jim's relationship with Clover is different. It is punctuated by winks and nudges and the pulling of daft faces. There's no point in trying to explain, no point in talking to him at all when he gets like this. It's a matter of resisting the impulse to shout, and coming back later in the week for round two.

'It doesn't matter *how* you say something, as long as it's the truth,' Jim continues. 'Not that you'd know the truth. Not if it grew legs and chased you.'

'Stop being such an arse crack.' Darren stands and rubs his hands together in a busy, I-was-just-about-to-leave way. 'Right, is there anything you need?' He steps over the cans and into the kitchenette, where he checks the fridge. It's brimming with cheap lager, but there's also a packet of ham, a carton of milk, a six-pack of cola and a box of eggs. The cupboard beside the fridge houses a half-empty multipack of crisps and a couple of tins of baked beans. 'No? I'll be off, then,' he says. 'Next time I'll bring some batteries.'

As Darren opens the door to let himself out, Jim mutters, 'I've got toothache.'

'Well, take some painkillers and phone the dentist.'

★   ★   ★

There's a bus stop right outside Jim's, but the walk home will give him twenty minutes to decide whether things have reached the stage where he has to do something. It's difficult — sometimes Jim has a social worker and sometimes he doesn't; sometimes he takes medication and sometimes he doesn't; sometimes there are meetings and care plans and sometimes there aren't; sometimes Darren goes to the meetings — just so they realise someone is watching — and sometimes he doesn't. His kindness comes in bursts and he tires quickly. It was easier in the early days, when it seemed as if it was going to be more of a sprint than a marathon. He is tired. And he has discovered that tiredness is not the bottom of it; there are moments when his resignation subsides and he tumbles into a shaft of anger. He is not as good as Becky. Not as patient or kind, not as understanding.

He increases his pace as he approaches the hill of the railway bridge. He has been enjoying the newness of returning to an occupied house. Years ago, after work, before he collected Clover from Edna's or Dad's, he occasionally sneaked home in search of echoes of his old life. He eased the front door open, as if by not startling the house, he might catch it reminiscing. But he never heard Dune FM playing; never smelled food cooking or saw the post stacked on the side in tidy piles of catalogues, holiday brochures and the surveys Becky used to complete in exchange for the chance to win £100.

He stops at the top of the bridge. Leans up against the warm of the wall for a moment and glances at the ripening blackberries growing in tandem with the tracks, not entirely reconciled to the way the present shunts and rearranges memories so all that came before, even the good things, leads to this sunny evening in August, to him, heading home to Clover, on her own.

★ ★ ★

Clover is already watching *Bake Off* when he gets back. She glances up at him from the recliner, skin golden brown and freckled. People used to say she looked like Becky when she was small, but the resemblance has lessened as she has grown — a matter of both sadness and relief. Although it's not quite as fair as her mother's, her wild hair has been bleached by the sun and is getting there. Such impossible hair, spiralling and bright, like the shiny ribbon people wrap around presents and curl with scissors; the kind of hair people want to stroke. He remembers buying Super Noodles when she was little because they were shaped like her hair. He'd mix them with a jar of passata and whatever was cheapest on the deli counter — salami, pepperoni or ham, back when they had the cutting machines in the supermarket and you could ask for just two or three slices. Then he'd top the curly mountain with grated cheese; pizza-pasta, that's what he used to call it. It's been a while, he'll have to make it again, she'd like that.

'Did you remember your suncream today?'

'Course.'

He glances at the scar on her knee. The skin has zipped neatly shut and is darkening in the sunshine. Girls her age shouldn't be shaving their almost invisible body hair — it's far too dangerous. The horror of hearing her yelp and subsequently discovering her in the bathroom, bleeding, razor in hand, is not something he can easily forget.

'Have you watered?'

She nods.

'Had some tea?'

'Yeah. I did beans on toast.'

'Good girl. I'll make myself some toast in a minute — oh, I found some colouring books in the recycling pile. You should probably keep them. You might want them one day.'

'They're *really old*. From Mrs Mackerel. They've been in a cupboard at her church for *centuries*.'

'I've left them on the side for you, just in case.'

'All right. How's Uncle Jim?'

'Oh, you know.'

'He's not himself?'

'That's right.'

'Kelly called.'

'Did she?'

'She said to tell you that she booked a lane at Premier Bowl for her and the boys and some of their friends tomorrow evening. But the friends can't come. And she wants to know if we'll go instead.'

'Hmm,' he says, pretending uncertainty. 'What do you think? Fancy a bit of bowling?' He mimes a shot. 'Str-ike! Could be fun . . . '

'All right.'

'But?'

80

'She can be a bit . . . '

'Much?'

'I don't mind her messing with my hair while she's cutting it.'

'She's just trying to be nice.'

'But I don't want to go for a manicure.'

'All right.'

'Or a facial.'

'Okay.'

'And I don't want a Katniss braid.'

'I'll tell her.'

'No you won't.'

Kelly is usually good at talking to people, she does it all day — *Going anywhere nice on your holidays? Shall we try a different colour?* And she's got kids of her own. But her boys are younger than Clover and there's something easy and animal about them. They've always liked Darren; perhaps they like anyone, everyone.

'She isn't used to girls. That's all. What do you want me to do? Reckon I should shout, 'GET YOUR HANDS OFF MY DAUGHTER'?' he asks, mimicking the Australian in their favourite YouTube video, the man who yells, 'GET YOUR HANDS OFF MY PENIS!' at the police while they're trying to arrest him.

The unspoken *penis* dangles for a moment. Maybe he shouldn't joke about things like that any more. Perhaps it's inappropriate.

'Yeah, I reckon you should,' she says. 'Do it just like that, Dad. I *dare* you.' And then she laughs. Which helps.

★ ★ ★

After he's wolfed a couple of slices of toast and downed a cup of tea, Darren sits on the couch and watches the rest of the programme. The best part is the showstopper, the fancy thing the bakers have to make at the end. This week, it's a 3D biscuit scene. He is gobsmacked by their creations: a train, a sea monster, even a bloody *carousel*! When it's finished, he goes into the kitchen and roots about. He heads back into the lounge holding a baking tray upon which he has placed two knives, a packet of Biscoff biscuits and the jar of Biscoff spread.

'Here,' he says, 'look at this.'

Clover watches as he unfastens the jar and smears two blobs of Biscoff spread on the tray.

'I'll just . . . hang on . . . yeah, like this.' He stands two biscuits upright, facing each other. Then he pastes spread on to the underside of a third biscuit, which he places on top of the other two, like a roof. 'Come on,' he says. 'You, too. Get building.'

When the tray is smeared in spread and populated by a series of triumphal biscuit arches, Darren purses his lips, dog's arse tight, like the lady on the programme, and does his best posh voice.

'*Now, Darren, what have you made for us today?*'

Clover grins.

'I've made Stonehenge. Out of a packet of biscuits and a bit of Biscoff spread.' He lifts the biscuit roof off one of the Stonehenge arches and breaks it in half. '*That's a lovely snap,*' he trills, crumbs spraying out of his mouth as he pronounces, '*Well done, Darren! It's a good bake.*'

Clover laughs and he gets his phone out of his pocket and takes a photo of her holding Stonehenge, evidence that she was happy, to show her later, should he need it.

★　★　★

Once Clover is in bed he gets a beer out of the fridge and calls Kelly. She's had a drink — drinks, in fact. A couple of glasses of wine, she tells him. It's been one of those days. The boys are in bed, though, she adds.

He puts his phone on speaker and rests it on the arm of the recliner. Kelly talks like she drives: quickly, changing gear at the last minute. Her voice zips out of his phone sharper, thinner, but otherwise it's almost as if she's there in the room with him, chatting as the sun steers past tips of the trees at the top of the bank and slips beneath the railings.

' . . . and the thing with you, Darren, if you don't mind me saying — which I'm sure you don't, you're a good listener, aren't you? — you don't get all fidgety when someone's talking to you, and I like that about you, I do — but the thing with you is . . . remember the time when I'd just started school and there was a boy in my class — I can't even remember his name now — who kept following me around and calling me Smelly Kelly? God, I was only four — and I was used to Colin teasing me, that's what brothers

83

do — but this was different, meaner somehow. So I didn't know what to do, and I remember one lunchtime *you* followed the boy for a bit and gave him a taste of his own medicine, and he stopped after that. Anyway, the thing with you is, you're not a walkover, but you don't say much, do you?'

'Well . . . ' he says.

'Do you remember that?'

'Not — '

'So,' she begins again, and he senses a gear change. 'Today Tyler asked if he could make his own toast and I said yes — they've got to learn to be independent some time, haven't they? And do you know what he said? He said, 'Do I put it in portrait or landscape?' Portrait or landscape! Can you believe that? God, I felt old.'

He smiles. One of the surprising things about adulthood is how few people accompany you there and what a relief it is to occasionally talk to someone who knew the child-you and the teenaged-you; someone who has seen all your versions, every update, and stuck with you through all of it. That's really something.

' . . . knackered by the time I fetched the boys from Mum's.'

'Did you carry them at all, today — Tyler and Dylan?' he asks.

'You mean actually pick them up?'

'Yeah.'

'Probably. Hang on . . . yeah, I did, but Tyler's getting big for it now, he's like a little tank — why?'

'Just wondering.'

84

'You all right for tomorrow? Did Clover tell you?'

'Yeah.'

This is where he should mention Clover's hair; say that Kelly is not to offer to braid it like the girl from *The Hunger Games*. Or stroke it. Or try to pass on free samples of Frizz Ease treatments. But he can't.

The hair thing started when, years ago, before she married and had her boys, Kelly came round to babysit so he could go out for a drink with Colin. She'd looked after Clover before, but hadn't ever put her to bed.

When he got back later, slightly soused, Darren popped upstairs to check on Clover. Her face was clenched and blotchy, as if she had fallen asleep crying.

'Was everything okay?' he asked, downstairs.

'I gave her a bath,' Kelly said. 'I just wanted — she's got such lovely hair, and I thought it would be . . . You haven't got a hairdryer. Unless you've . . . unless there's one somewhere in the middle bedroom? I'm sorry. I wasn't snooping. I popped my head around the door, but then I saw . . . and I . . . I just assumed you'd sorted it all . . . Would you like some help with it?'

He shook his head, once. No, underscored.

'Okay. I just . . . you're my friend . . . and I . . . ' She lifted her hands, surrendering easily. 'So I called my mum and got her to bring a hairdryer round. I've got a diffuser — they're good for curly hair. But when I turned it on, Clover went mental. She shouted, 'Hot, hot, hot!' and ran away. I thought she was messing at

85

first. I made her sit on my knee. And she howled. Then I tried to coax her into it. I offered her a treat, but she got dead angry with me. How do you dry her hair? You don't take her out with it wet, do you? Her little head will get cold.'

'She doesn't go out with it wet. I'm not stupid.'

She was upset. And he'd had a few. That was how it happened, he thinks. She sat down and they talked about the salon where she'd been working since she finished her NVQ, about her plan to open Kelly's Cuts one day, and Colin's joke that it sounded more like a butcher's than a hairdresser's. He remembers all that, but he doesn't remember how she came to unbutton her shirt. She wasn't wearing a bra. Her nipples sat on the bony stave of her ribs like a pair of crotchets. His hands hung limply by his sides until she lifted them and placed them on firm skin, marbled like wet plaster. He tried not to think of Becky, whose naked body had been creamy and soft, so soft.

He was careful; they were mates and he didn't want to spoil things. 'Shall I . . . Is it okay if I . . . There?'

'Hmm.'

'And — '

'Hmm.'

'Do you — '

'Yes.'

'This okay?'

'Hmm.'

'Is it all right if I — '

'Darren?'

'Yeah?'

'Shut up.'

'Thank you,' he said afterwards. And he knew it was wrong, even before she scrunched her face and curtsied.

'No, thank *you*, Darren.'

'I'm sorry,' he added, immediately aware he'd got that wrong, too.

He called her in the morning to make sure things were all right between them and was relieved when she was herself: chatty, casual.

The next time she babysat, she kissed him on his return. Or maybe he kissed her. Either way, it started in the hall and she finished it — finished him — on the dining-room floor.

He went out with Colin more frequently. Sometimes he'd say he was tired and pick up a couple of beers on the way home. One night, as she sat on the kitchen worktop, legs around his waist, head resting on his shoulder, she said, 'We could go out for a drink some time.'

'I'll get Edna to have Clover.'

'Colin'll do it.'

'Edna won't mind — that way Colin can come, too.'

She unwrapped her legs and arms. Slid off the worktop. Closed her zip and fastened her buttons. 'I don't want to go for a drink with Colin. I want . . . '

He willed her to stop before she spoiled everything, and she did stop, for a moment.

'Maybe you *should* ask Edna in future,' she said. 'That might be better for everyone.' She didn't offer to babysit again. And he didn't ask.

Kelly carries on talking. He listens to the sound of her voice rather than the individual words: the up and down of it, the light and bright of it, until, eventually, she says goodnight and, alone in the dark and quiet, he dozes off in the recliner.

★ ★ ★

He wakes in the early hours, tiptoes up the stairs, pees, strips down to his pants and slips into bed. Too hot, he kicks off the covers and lies there, thinking about the way Edna stopped him a while ago as he passed her house on his way home and congratulated him for telling Clover about the Facts of Life. It was also his responsibility, she announced, to teach Clover HOW to be a WOMAN. In fact, she'd been in the bookshop, the lovely, old-fashioned one in town, and had seen a book called exactly that: *How to Be a Woman*.

He rolls on to his side and stuffs his arm under the pillow. It might help, that book. Might fill him in on a few things. Let him know what to expect and what he needs to cover. Even when you think you're doing well, you miss stuff. He remembers years ago when Clover started doing swimming lessons at school.

'Can you teach me how to do a towel-hat on my head?' she asked.

'A what?'

'A towel-hat. In a pile.'

'You mean a turban?'

'Yes, one of those. All the girls do them after

swimming, in the changing rooms.'

It was something he hadn't thought of, and there's bound to be a shedload of other stuff. He should be prepared. It helps, that feeling of having stuff at his fingertips, should he need it. It really helps.

Exhibit: 'Becky Brookfield —
the Untold Story'

Catalogue

Object: Book.

Description: 'Winnie the Pooh and the Honey Tree' (Little Golden Book). In good condition.

Item Number: 1.

Provenance: This book must have been bought by Becky Brookfield (my mother) for Clover Quinn (me). On the inside cover it says 'Love from Mummy xxxx' in blue biro.

Display: Display this book open, so 'Love from Mummy' is visible.

Curator: Clover Quinn.

Keeper: Darren Quinn.

5

Uncle Jim is not himself. Last time he was not himself it was Christmas and there weren't any beds at the special hospital by the park, so he had to go to Liverpool. He hates being sent to Liverpool. It's like being deported, he reckons. Like being forced into exile or extradited. Dad says it's not like being extradited at all; you'd have to commit a crime in Liverpool first, in order to be extradited there. Uncle Jim says that could be arranged.

When he is himself, Uncle Jim does armpit farts, impressions, Mexican waves with his eyebrows, volunteering in the charity shop and dead hard jigsaws. He sleeps at night-time, remembers to eat, and sometimes pops round for a cup of tea or a beer with Dad while they watch old films like *Top Gun* and *Indiana Jones*.

When he is not himself, Uncle Jim stops taking his medicine and believes everything he thinks. He responds to volunteer opportunities in the paper, like massage therapist for the Liverpool Marathon or van driver for the British Heart Foundation, even though he's got no massage qualifications and he can't drive; he starts up conversations with people he doesn't know and tells them all the stuff he wishes was true, like he owns a pet shop and he could have been a professional footballer if he hadn't busted his knee when he was younger. Once, he decided there was no reason why he couldn't get a proper job, so he filled out a form to say his circumstances had changed and he didn't need his benefits any more. Dad spent a whole afternoon on the phone trying to sort it out. When he is not himself, Uncle Jim gets fizzy on the inside — literally — and the fizz makes him walk really fast for hours at a time, even in bad weather.

It rained a lot last December and Uncle Jim walked so much that he wore holes into his shoes. He came round on the evening of the 23rd, all muddled up, thinking it was Christmas Eve when there's always a special tea with him, Grandad and Mrs Mackerel, and all the best bits from the frozen Christmas buffet section of Lidl: sausage rolls, bite-size pizzas, prawn vol-au-vents and mini chocolate éclairs. He was wet from the rain and limping, scared because he thought someone had been following him. Dad made him come in and sit down. He cooked cheese on toast and brought it in on a tray. As soon as the tray was balanced on Uncle Jim's knees and he wasn't going anywhere, Dad knelt on the floor, unfastened Uncle Jim's trainers and peeled off his socks. The bottoms of his feet looked like strawberry crumble. Dad said he would take him to the walk-in centre as soon as he finished his toast, but Uncle Jim didn't want to go and they had a big argument. She doesn't like it when they shout at each other. There's no sparks — they're firing blanks, but still. Uncle Jim called Dad a nutsack-wiper and Dad called him a royal pain in the arse. She had to go next door and sit with Mrs Mackerel because she wasn't allowed in the house by herself back then. Mrs Mackerel held her rosary, said a Hail Mary for Uncle Jim — *God help him*. Then she did some prayers to St Dymphna, light of those in mental darkness. Dad got back from the hospital late, by himself. The doctor at the walk-in centre had sent them over to Accident and Emergency, where Uncle Jim had been sectioned.

When Uncle Jim is not himself she isn't allowed to visit on her own. Dad says it's in everyone's best interests; that way, no one will get upset. But Dad and Uncle Jim are more likely to upset each other than she and Uncle Jim are. This afternoon, when she has finished at the allotment, she'll cycle to Grandad's with a load of vegetables, and then she might pop to Uncle Jim's, just to say hello — he won't want any vegetables, he only likes brown or yellow ones, like potatoes and baked beans.

Outside, the sun is drumming on the path. She locks the front door behind her, slips the key into her pocket and wipes greasy hands on her shorts. The suncream smells of coconut. When she was small, Uncle Jim told her that coconuts were bear eggs. He bought one from the supermarket and told her to keep it somewhere warm and light. Such an exciting wait, tipping the bristly ball from hand to hand, holding it up to her ear, listening for the bear. Dad told her in the end, said Uncle Jim was being unfair. But she didn't mind, it had been like listening to an especially exciting story, it didn't matter that it hadn't been real.

She fastens her helmet and ties a couple of carrier bags and the bike lock around the handlebars. All ready. She pedals to the end of The Grove and then back on herself, passing the house as she plugs up the hill of the bridge, bucket swinging with the effort. Once she has crossed the road at the top she takes her feet off the pedals and coasts down the other side, past Jewson's, past Jo Kelly's News and the post office. She's pedalling again, just approaching the roundabout where she'll turn off on to Moss Lane, when she notices Dagmar sitting outside the corner shop at the foot of the wheelchair ramp, a red and black tartan trolley beside her, the kind old ladies drag around. There's an instant during which she could pedal on, pretending she hasn't seen her, but she misses it — her timing is all wrong, her feet don't move fast enough. Dagmar looks up and Clover freezes, like a statue when the music has stopped. She squeezes the brakes and her tyres skid on the scatter of stones that dust the pavement.

'Hi.' She glances at the shop door, checking for the owner of the shopping trolley, Dagmar's nan, perhaps. 'Who are you waiting for?'

'I am waiting for no one.'

'So that's *your* trolley?'

'Yes.'

Clover can see how the trolley might come in handy if you had a lot of things to carry. It is also a bit strange — if Abbie Higham saw it she would declare it ridiculous and die laughing, literally. That is enough to make Clover decide to like it. 'It looks very useful,' she says. 'What're you doing here, then?

'I am watching the men with the dog.'

On the other side of the roundabout, in the empty parking spaces beside the hairdresser's and the bakery, two men are talking. One of them is holding a small dog.

'I am deciding what they are saying.'

'Oh.'

'Would you like to buy this dog?' Dagmar asks, her voice gruff and mannish. 'It is your turn,' she explains, using her own voice again. 'You must say what is next.'

'Oh. Okay. Er . . . no, thank you. A dog is a big commitment.' Clover doesn't even attempt to adopt the second man's voice.

'It is your turn, still. Your man is talking.'

'Right . . . I don't have time to walk it. And dog food is very expensive.'

'If you do not buy her, my wife is leaving me.'

'Why?'

'Shush, it is not your turn. My wife is leaving me because the noise is making her crazy.'

'But I don't want a noisy dog, either.'

'Then I am being alone.'

'You'll have your dog,' Clover says, and the men separate and walk off in different directions.

Dagmar smiles. It's quick; a twitch of her lips, before her face returns to impassivity. She looks different outside of school. If Clover didn't have very important plans, this could be interesting. They might find something to say to each other, something that doesn't involve One Direction or who hasn't been tagged in

Twenty-Five Beautiful Girls on Facebook.

'Where are you going?' Dagmar asks.

'The allotment. It's this place where you grow stuff. Down there. Just to water things.'

'I can come?'

Clover likes her time at the allotment: the work and the thinking, the quiet hum of the living things and the feeling of being responsible for it all. If she lets Dagmar come she might end up with less time to visit Grandad and Uncle Jim, and less time to sort through her mother's things before Dad gets back. But she is curious.

'All right then.'

*   *   *

Clover walks beside her bike, not minding the quiet. She gets the feeling that Dagmar is comfortable with it and would speak if she wanted to. They turn off Moss Lane and head down the track. Past the beech hedge on one side and the neat rows of the orchard on the other, until they reach the gate.

'And all this is yours?'

'Oh, no.'

Clover unlocks the gate and Dagmar follows, the hard wheels of her trolley scratching the ground. They pass a couple of neglected plots that are chock-a-block with thigh-high weeds, brambles and old vegetables gone to seed.

'Here,' she says, stopping beside a low wire fence. '*This* is ours. We've had it for *ages*. It used to be my grandad's, like fifty years ago, or something.' She leans her bike up against one of the canes that support the fence and then steps over the wire. 'Come on,' she says.

Dagmar explores the perimeter, leaning over dividing bits of fence and shrubbery to see into the neighbouring allotments. Clover glances at the enormous apple tree in the overgrown allotment to the left, its limbs piled with ripening fruit; at the tidy rows of Mrs Grindle's allotment on the right, all topped by wooden frames that have been stapled with chicken wire. She listens to the drone of Mr Ashworth's bees. Dad says, 'Bees are the canaries in the mine of climate change' — he didn't make it up on his own, he read it somewhere, but it's a good comparison. Last autumn Mr Ashworth gave them a jar of his honey. It tasted different from the honey from shops; it tasted like flowers. Clover hopes he will do it again this year.

'You are not having a shed?' Dagmar calls.

'No, not here.'

Clover looks at Mr Ashworth's shed. He used to sit in it with the door open when he needed a rest, making it look like a guardhouse. He wore a Puma baseball cap and drank home-made elderflower cordial. Dad says the old men used to wear flat caps. But since flat caps got fashionable and you can buy them in all the clothes shops, even at the supermarket, the old men have started wearing baseball caps. This is true — even Grandad has got a baseball cap. Mr Ashworth's wife had a stroke at Christmas, so he can't come as often as he used to.

When Dagmar has made her way back, Clover walks her down the strip of turf that dissects the

97

plot, naming everything: onions, carrots, cabbages, potatoes, pumpkins, lettuce, broccoli, strawberries, raspberries, runner beans, beetroot and peas. Dagmar nods seriously, like she's memorising it for a test.

'Want to try some?' Clover opens a pea pod and pops the peas into Dagmar's open hand.

'They are different. Crunchy.'

'Good, aren't they?' She collects a strawberry and a few of the raspberries that run along the back fence. 'Try these, too.'

'You come here every day?'

What to say? She doesn't mind Dagmar being here today, but she can't afford to have regular distractions burning up her summer.

'Me or my dad.'

She lifts the carpet that covers the empty bed to reveal the watering can, and retrieves the bucket from her bike. They walk to the tap and back, side by side, feet kicking up dust. Dagmar's black trainers turn grey. She's a mouth-breather; Clover can hear the air wafting in and out of her, blowing her lips dry. Dagmar lifts a hand to scratch her bare neck and Clover notices her bitten nails and the purply transparency of the skin under her eyes.

'You are doing this all holiday? The gardening?'

'Yeah,' Clover says, thinking that gardening is the wrong verb, but not sure what to suggest as a replacement.

'You are not going anywhere?'

'No.'

'I am not going anywhere, also.'

'Well, we might go to Blackpool for the day.'

Once they've finished the watering, Clover hides the can and they sit side by side on the dusty carpet.

'This is very nice. I am having a yard. No garden.'

'Did you have a garden where you came from?'

'A flat, with balcony. But there is a river. And mountains. And not far away, a castle. In the town it is . . . the colours are different. The buildings are in white and yellow, with red and orange roofs.'

'It sounds very different.'

'There is a Tesco.'

Clover catches the small smile again. 'Are you okay, at school?' she blurts. A silence follows and she worries she might have overstepped.

'In stories, people are being horrible because they are sad. My dad says this is not true. People are being horrible because they can. And that is it. The end.'

'Oh. That's sad.'

'It is true.'

'How was it in your primary school?'

'I come very late. In Year 6. People are already having friends. And my English is very bad then.'

Clover lies down and shields her eyes from the disc of the sun with the flat of her hand. 'What's your favourite time of year?'

'What is yours?'

'The summer holidays. Right now.'

'Why?'

'Because all the time's mine. There's no

school, no nothing. Dad doesn't care if I go to bed a bit late, and I don't *have* to do anything, except come here. But I like this, so it doesn't really count.' She pauses for a moment, searching for the right words. 'It's so warm — I love it when you don't need a coat or anything. You get that inside-outside feeling. You know? The feeling you get when you can go anywhere without even thinking about it. You don't have to think, Will my feet get wet? Are my hands going to be cold? Might I need an umbrella? You step out of the front door, and it's so warm; and the days are longer and time gets all stretchy: that's the inside-outside feeling.'

Clover can't see Dagmar's face, because she is still sitting, arms propping her from behind like tent strings. But she hears the thinky sound she makes as she deliberates.

'I think . . . I like October. The field is not so muddy, so the boys are not bothering me, they are playing football. I am going to the after-school clubs and when I go home it is dark. And soon it is bedtime.'

'I like October, too,' she says, hoping Dagmar is happier at home than she is at school, though her answer suggests otherwise. 'What's in your trolley?'

'My things.'

'What things?' Clover waits but Dagmar will not be goaded by silence and in the end it's up to her to fill it. 'I've got this,' she says, sitting up as she pulls *Latin Words and Phrases for Beginners* out of the back pocket of her shorts.

'What is it?'

'Latin. I'm learning the words.'

'Why are you doing this?'

'Because they sound good.'

'This is what you think?'

'Yeah. They're old words. And they remind me of Hogwarts — that's the school from *Harry Potter*.'

'I know this.'

'Plants have Latin names — they're called botanical names. They put them on seed packets to tell you stuff like the colour or smell and what kind of shape the leaves will be. Long names — they're a bit tricky. I like these words better.'

'What words?'

'*Ad astra*.'

'What is *ad astra*?'

'It means 'to the stars'. And *ad astra per aspera* means 'to the stars, through difficulties', which is even better.'

'I have this.' Dagmar pulls a sketchbook out of her shopping trolley.

Clover takes it from her hand and leafs through the pages. There are pencil drawings of trees and flowers and arrangements of objects like fruit and ornaments. Some of them are crossed out, scribbled over, the perspective is wrong or the shading too dark; others are really good.

A pheasant screeches, the noise accompanied by a drubbing of wings so loud that it almost sounds like the coughing start of a motorbike. Dagmar jumps and Clover laughs and stands up.

They do a bit of picking before heading back

up Moss Lane, carrier bags of fruit and vegetables sitting in the bucket.

'What are you doing now?' Dagmar asks as they arrive back where they started, outside the corner shop.

'I'm going to see my grandad.'

'And you will see your grandmother, too?'

'No, she died before I was born.'

'You have another grandmother?'

'Yes, but I don't see her very often. She lives in Portsmouth.'

'And that is very far?'

'Yeah.'

'And she has no car?'

'She doesn't drive.'

'And there are no trains?'

Of course there are trains. Every so often Dad talks himself into inviting Nanna Maureen. She won't stay overnight. Up and down in a day, that's how she does it. The idea of Nanna Maureen is always better than the reality. She is like those lemon sherbet sweets: when you haven't had one for a while, it's easy to forget that they are hard and sour, and burn the skin off the roof of your mouth.

'I need to go now,' Clover says, rather than explain herself.

'I can come?'

'Oh. My grandad's old. And you can't just — '

'I wait, outside.'

'He hasn't got a garden.'

'I wait on the pavement.'

'It's a while away. By the Marine Lake.'

'It is not far,' she says.

102

Despite Dagmar's protestations, Clover locks her bike to the railings outside Grandad's flat.

'You might get tired of waiting,' she says.

She presses the intercom, announces herself and the main door jerks open. Once upstairs she walks straight into the flat; Grandad must have unlatched the door and shuffled back to his armchair.

'I've brought some stuff from the allotment,' she calls as she steps down the hall, past the cuckoo clocks and the photograph of Dad with Grandad and the nanna who died before she was born.

'Put it in the sink, love.'

The smell in the kitchen reminds her of Year 3, when they had a class pet, Harvey the hamster. She dumps the carrier bags in the sink and joins Grandad in the lounge. He is wearing shorts with a proper buttoned-up shirt. It's as if his bottom half is complaining about the heat, but his top half is saying, 'Don't be silly.'

'How are you, Grandad?'

'Old and disappointed. Now park yourself. And shush. I want to see what happens.' He's watching *Jeremy Kyle*. A woman has taken a lie detector test and Jeremy is kneeling beside her, hissing nasty things in her face so she'll shout at him and he can tell her off for being rude. 'We're about to find out if her boyfriend is the baby's father,' Grandad says. 'I reckon she's at it.'

The results are handed to Jeremy. He holds the card up, starts reading, and the woman's protestations begin.

'I knew it.' Grandad lifts the remote and fires it at the telly. 'What a load of rubbish. Who watches it?'

Clover grins.

'I'm not *watching* it,' he says. 'It's just on, for company. What've you brought me?'

'Beans and peas, a lettuce, some strawberries and raspberries and an onion.'

'Good girl. You all right?'

'Yes.'

'Good. Well, that's good.'

Grandad runs out of things to say if you don't help him. Last summer's book club was epic because every time he got stuck he read a discussion question: 'Why was it so important for Anne to have a dress with puffed sleeves?' 'Would you prefer to be called Anne with an 'e' or Ann without an 'e'?' 'Why did Anne want a kindred spirit or a, um, a . . . *bosom* friend?'

Clover glances at the laptop resting on the floor beside his chair. 'What are you doing on your computer at the moment?'

'Shakespeare.' He reaches for the laptop, lifts the lid and logs in. 'I've finished Mars — if you want to know anything about it, I'm your man. I've got *Hamlet* this afternoon. See, all ready, on the right page. The BBC one with Derek Jacobi. I'm going in alphabetical order. *All's Well That Ends Well, Antony and Cleopatra, As You Like It* — right through to *The Winter's Tale*. Sometimes I can only find a radio version. It's hard to stay awake without pictures.'

'And what's next?'

'Haven't decided yet. It'll take another month to get through this lot.'

'Seen any good cat videos this week?'

'Too busy. Want a biscuit?'

'Yes, please.'

'Get me one while you're at it, love. And a cup of hot water. Use the beaker by the sink. Two hundred and fifty mil.'

Grandad has written measurements on the plastic beaker in black permanent marker. She fills it up to 250ml with warm water from the kettle. Today he's got ginger nuts in his tin. She takes two and slips a third into the front pocket of her shorts. Ginger nuts are really hard, it shouldn't break.

'Thank you muchly,' he says when she gives him the cup. He sips like it's tea or something nice.

One of the clocks in the hall calls the half hour. A few seconds later, the others announce it.

'You know, you should get your dad to unpack the clocks. You could help him. It'd be fun. Tell him I said so. Are you having a good summer?'

'Yes.'

'Well, why wouldn't you be, at your age? So . . . ' He closes the laptop and nods at the telly. 'Want to watch the rest of that bun fight?'

'All right,' she says, and he switches it back on.

★　★　★

Dagmar is waiting by the doors. 'You are a long time,' she says.

'You didn't have to wait.'

'I am doing nothing else.'

'Won't your mum be worried?'

'She is working.'

'What does she do?'

'She is deputy hotel manager.'

Clover hands Dagmar the warm ginger nut before unfastening her bike from the railings.

'Thank you. Where are you going?'

'To see my Uncle Jim.'

'Where is he living?'

'By Asda.'

Dagmar clasps the handle of her trolley. 'I can come?'

Clover wonders whether there's a polite way to deter her and, on a scale of one to ten, how upset she'd be if she said she didn't want her to come.

'Come on,' Dagmar says, and it's too late to do anything else.

★　★　★

There's nowhere to fasten her bike at Uncle Jim's. Dagmar offers to watch it.

'I might be a while,' Clover says, opting to wheel it past the parked cars and hide it behind an enormous wheelie bin.

The main door is open, so she steps into the building and heads down the tiled corridor. Uncle Jim's door is open, too. When he is not himself he finds closed doors more frightening than burglars. He is sitting on the floor in front of the sofa, legs crossed, elbows on his knees, head resting in his hands. She knocks on the

106

edge of the door to let him know she's there, but he doesn't look up. The TV is muted and the room is a mess.

'It's me. I've come to say hello. Are you all right?'

'Got-toothache,' he mumbles.

Clover hears the trundle of wheels in the corridor behind her and makes a shooing motion with one hand.

'Can I do something?' she asks scanning the empties and the dirty clothes, the jigsaw pieces and the cigarette butts. Where would he keep painkillers — the kitchenette, or the bathroom, perhaps? 'Have you got any medicine? Shall I come in and have a look?'

'S'all-right,' he says, still cradling his head. 'Had-something. You-get-off-home. Come-and-see-me-when-I'm-better.' The words waddle fatly into each other on their way out of his mouth.

'Are you sure?' she asks, nudging Dagmar away from the open door with the point of her elbow.

'Hmmm.'

'Can I get you anything?'

'Uh-uh.'

'Shall I . . . would you like a cup of tea?'

'Uh-uh.'

Sitting there, he almost looks like a little boy in a school assembly, about to recite the Lord's Prayer, and she is struck by the thought that one or more of the children who sat, legs crossed, in her own school assemblies might one day find themselves sitting on the floor of a dirty bedsit in that same, cross-legged position.

'Well . . . I'll just go then,' she says. 'But I'll definitely come back another day.'

'Hmm.'

As she turns she bumps, half on purpose, into a goggle-eyed Dagmar and forces her back down the corridor, hard, so the trolley bumps the skirting and they almost trip over it.

'What is wrong?'

Clover steps out on to the drive and disappears around the back of the enormous bin to fetch her bike. 'He's not himself,' she says, wheeling the bike past Dagmar and the parked cars and on to the pavement.

'But *what* is wrong?'

'He's . . . '

'Yes?'

'He's just . . . not himself.'

Dagmar seems about to press her further, but then she shrugs. 'Where are you going now?'

'Home,' she says. And, fed up of being shadowed, she adds, 'I'm not allowed anyone in the house while my dad's not there.'

'Your dad is scaring you?'

'He's a bus driver.'

'And he is scaring you?'

If she says Dad isn't scary, Dagmar might insist on coming back to the house with her. 'Well, maybe a bit,' she fudges.

No one from school ever comes to the house. When she was small enough to have birthday parties, Dad booked them at KidzKlimbz in town. For as long as she can remember she has been aware that other people don't have as much stuff as she and Dad do. When she was at nursery school she was invited to have tea with a couple of girls. Their houses seemed empty, cavernous.

'My dad is scaring me,' Dagmar says.

Clover listens, not wanting to interrupt the interesting words that will surely follow. Their feet smack the hot pavement. The bike's wheels *tick, tick, tick* and the bucket sways gently from its handlebars. Dagmar's trolley drags and the dry puff of her breath makes her very existence seem a matter of great effort.

'My dad,' Dagmar says eventually, pausing before continuing, as if she is already thinking better of it, 'is not himself, also.'

★ ★ ★

Clover has an hour in the second bedroom, tops. Last time she was here she spotted a wire sticking out of a pile of stuff near the headboard and, breaking her self-imposed rule about working methodically, tugged it gently until a portable CD player and headphones on a thin metal band emerged. She found some batteries and listened to the old songs on the CD it contained: 'Born to Make You Happy', 'Spinning Around', 'Beautiful Day' — cheerful, summery songs, from ages ago; she already knows some of them from Dad's nineties CDs. They are the perfect accompaniment to her work, and she clips the CD player to the waistband of her shorts, arranges the headphones and presses play before lifting another pile of paper off the bed. Rubbish, rubbish, rubbish. When she realises there are even more holiday brochures, she goes back through the bin bag and retrieves the others. Then she sorts them into piles: winter sports, canal boats and sailing, beaches, cruises, and adventure. The beach pile is the biggest, closely followed by winter sports. She keeps those two piles on the floor and slips the other brochures back into the bin bag.

Downstairs, in the dining room, she roots through a pile of MDF offcuts. You can make all sorts of things with MDF: photo frames, magazine racks, Christmas decorations — she and Dad haven't made any of these things yet, but they might, one day. Grandad's cuckoo clocks are here, in among the other stuff: plugs, owner's manuals for various electronic devices, an old-fashioned overhead projector and a sizeable collection of empty sweet tins that Dad likes to save, just in case. She flicks the lids of a couple of clock boxes and sees roofs topped by ridge tiles, some flat, others corrugated, each carved out of a different coloured wood. But there's no time to look properly now. She selects a slice of MDF that's poster-sized, grabs a pair of scissors and a glue stick, and negotiates the stairs — careful!

She cuts out the best beach pictures, the ones with palm trees, white sand and turquoise water, so different from their beach with its dark sand and churning grey-brown sea. Then she cuts out the best of the winter pictures: tiny skiers gliding down jagged mountains against sapphire skies; grinning families drinking hot chocolate in log cabins. She glues the beach scenes to one side of the board and the snowy scenes to the other. Of course, she has no idea which of these places her mother has visited. They interested her, though, that much is clear. She must have requested the brochures and she must have spent time thinking about what it would be like to lie under a palm tree or speed down a mountain. In a sense, these are *personal items* — they came in envelopes, addressed to Becky Brookfield. The lady at the museum said you get a feeling about things as you hold them. Clover closes her eyes and skims the tips of her fingers over the collage; first one side of the board, and then the other. The feeling she gets is this: a day at Blackpool is a bit rubbish. The pictures are like a message from her mother, who seems to be saying: there's more to life than candyfloss, donkey rides and Pleasure Beach. Clover wonders about going on a proper holiday. Perhaps to one of the places in the pictures. It might even be that while visiting one of her mother's favourite places — because that's surely what these places are — Dad would be unable to prevent himself from talking about her. That'd be epic! She opens her eyes and leans the board against the foot of the bed. Not long until Dad gets home. She'll update her notebook and then she'll plant herself in the recliner with a cup of tea and a biscuit.

★ ★ ★

When it's time for bowling, Kelly comes to the door by herself. The boys wait in the car, licking the windows like monkeys. They are called Tyler and Dylan but they are mostly known as the boys: 'Come on, boys,' 'Don't do that, boys' and 'Sit down, boys.'

'Oh God, don't look at them. My mum let them overdose on e-numbers this afternoon. They're high as kites.'

Dad laughs.

'You encourage them, Darren, and I'll kill you.' She kisses Clover on the cheek and leaves a sticky print behind. 'You're looking lovely, so grown up. Oh, sorry.' She licks her index finger and rubs. 'There. Let's go.' Her heels click-clack as she hurries down the path back to her car, and her hair, which is silvery blonde today, swishes.

Although Kelly is Colin's younger sister, she doesn't look anything like him. Colin's got a shaved head and massive muscles. When Clover was small he used to lift her above his head with one arm and, if she was wearing trousers, he'd turn her upside down and boost her so high that her feet could actually walk on the ceiling. He doesn't do that any more. She's too grown up. Instead, he says things like, 'Anyone messes with you, Clo, and I'll sort them,' which sounds scary, but he's a big softy, really — last time she was at his house, she saw a little home-made chart, counting down the number of days until Mark gets back, every X like a kiss.

Kelly is long and straight, like her hair. She talks fast, walks fast, smokes fast and always seems a little bit nervous. She wears heels all the time, even with jeans, and she always has dead nice nails because her friend is a beautician and they give each other freebies. Clover could have freebies too, if she wanted. And she might, one day, when she has grown into the new bits of herself. In the meantime, she'd just as soon not.

The boys mash their faces against the glass, tongues out, noses flattened. Kelly knocks on the window. 'Stop it, you monsters.'

Clover sits between the monsters. They go to her old primary school and like to tell her about things that have happened since she left. She is planning to ask about school when Dylan shouts, 'Let's have some music!'

Kelly slides a CD into the player. 'Sing quietly,' she warns as she drives out of The Grove. But they don't.

It doesn't matter that there's a queue at Premier Bowl, because your hour only starts when you bowl the first ball. They take off their shoes as they wait. Kelly holds Dad's shoulder for balance, and the boys climb him like a piece of playground equipment.

'Can you lift us both at the same time, Darren?'

'Maybe.'

'Not like that — get me in one arm and Tyler in the other. Like two rolls of carpet! Uncle Colin can do it.'

Dad pats and chucks them like puppies. They stand on his feet and tug his arms, rubbing at the tattoo of Clover's name. She is too big for all that. The top of her head is level with his shoulder. Too tall to scale him, too big to be turned upside down — she is the wrong size for those dad things; she'll get used to it before long. As she watches him playing with the boys, she thinks up a new question to add to the growing list in her notebook: did Dad and her mother plan to have other children?

The wait stretches. The boys get fed up with grappling with Dad. They go a bit bananas in their socks, running between the arcade machines, flinging themselves on the motorbikes and the racing cars: *brum-brum, brum-brum*! The queue inches forward and Clover feels Kelly's hand on her hair.

'I could do a lovely wrap-around braid.'

She tries to catch Dad's eye — *look, she's playing with my hair again* — but he is watching the boys. And it's not so bad, really. Clover has been doing her own hair for a while now, but she remembers the feel of Dad's big, painstaking hands as they made a plait. Kelly's fingers are gentle and quick as they section and smooth, and weave and tuck, and Clover discovers that she is exactly the right size for this; this . . . tending, by a mother.

Eventually, they reach the counter and a girl hands out the bowling shoes. Clover's are still hot. She dips her feet into them and tries not to mind. In and out again. In, out. In, out.

'Come on,' Dad says, and she just has to get on with it, even though the shoes are steaming.

Up to six people can share a lane, and when their five names flash up on the screen Clover can't help thinking of Uncle Jim, who is literally all over the place at the moment and might have liked some company. They should have invited him to come with them. If not him, then Colin, who has been a bit lonely since Mark went to

Chad. She's about to mention it to Dad when Kelly gets up.

'Tyler, take my go for me. I'm just popping outside for a cheeky ciggie.'

'Aw, come on, I thought you were giving up. Would you like some cheeky heart disease or a cheeky stroke?'

'Are you going to give Mum a cheeky stroke, Darren?'

'I *am* giving up,' Kelly says, the SMOKING KILLS warning peeping out of her clasped fist. 'I'm only on two a day. I'm mostly vaping. And there's not going to be *any* cheeky stroking, boys. All right?'

Dylan climbs on Clover's knee while Tyler takes Kelly's go.

'Do you know what happened at school before the holidays, Clover? There was this writer who wrote a joke book. And guess what? He came to do an assembly. He talked about bogies and he made up some funny things to say to people you don't like.'

'This isn't going to be rude, is it?' Dad asks.

Dylan shakes his head. 'The funny things to say to people were: 'Whatever, McDonald's toilet cleaner' and 'Whatever, Tesco shelf-stacker.''

Tyler, back from scoring a seven, tuts at his younger brother. 'You missed out the actions. Watch me.' He makes a big W shape with his thumbs and index fingers: 'Whatever, McDonald's toilet cleaner.' *That's* how you have to do it.'

'Mum said it wasn't funny,' Dylan continues as he climbs off Clover's knee and slithers along the bench seat, eventually draping himself over

115

Dad's legs like a blanket. 'Because Alfie Ashcroft's dad works in Tesco on the night shift — this is my upside-down voice, can you hear it? — and teaching kids to laugh at their parents for working hard is a — '

'*Fucking disgrace,*' Tyler finishes for him.

Dad coughs. 'I'm sure your mum didn't say that.'

Dylan slides on to the floor and he lies on his back with his eyes closed. 'She did!'

'Well, not to the teacher.'

'She went in to school,' he says, climbing back on to Dad's lap, 'and gave Mrs Carpenter a piece of her mind.'

'A great big slice of it,' Tyler adds, 'with cream and cherries on top.'

Dad grins, as if it's the best thing he's ever heard. They sit there, like a trio of hyenas, and Kelly hurries back, her walk strangely muted in the flat bowling shoes; past the arcade games and the pool tables, past the rollercoaster simulator and the bar, while Dad and the boys watch her as if she is the bees' knees. Literally.

★   ★   ★

Three happy things today are, firstly, bowling. Dad won, he always does because his throws are the hardest, but she came second, with 102, her highest score yet. Secondly, the thought of going on holiday. Dad nods when she says this; he's looking forward to their day in Blackpool, too.

'Could we go on a proper holiday, though?' she asks.

'What do you mean?'

'Away, somewhere.'

'Where?'

'I don't know. Somewhere else. Somewhere hot or cold. A different country.'

He frowns and she feels she has done something wrong, but she isn't sure what.

'You don't have to go somewhere foreign to be happy; you can just as easily be happy at home.'

'I know, but — '

'And who'd look after the allotment?'

'Kelly and the boys? Or Colin and Mark?'

Dad snorts.

'But we wouldn't have to go in the summer, we could . . . ' she tails off because the last happy thing is tricky enough without making a big deal about imaginary holidays. 'And thirdly,' she says, 'I'm happy about Uncle Jim coming for tea tomorrow.'

'Very funny.'

'*Please.*'

'It's not a good idea at the moment.'

She could mention going to Uncle Jim's earlier; describe the open door and his school assembly sitting — it might help her cause, but it would also annoy Dad. Instead, she gives him a long, hard stare.

'Oh, all right,' he says, and then he hugs her tight, like he used to when she was little, filling her ear with the human noise of his heart. And it's actually her top happy moment of the day.

Exhibit: 'Becky Brookfield — the Untold Story'

Catalogue

Object: Letter.

Description: A note from Jim Brookfield (my uncle) to Becky Brookfield (my mother). **It says:** 'I tried to be sorry but I'm not. And I'm not sorry for not being sorry. Shall we run away? Tomorrow? I've got a bag of white mice and my torch. Write back.'

Item Number: 4.

Provenance: There are lots of notes from Uncle Jim. I'm not sure about the order because he hasn't written the date on any of them. I think he must have read a lot of adventure stories.

Display: Put the funniest, most imaginative notes in an order and display them together.

Curator: Clover Quinn.

Keeper: Darren Quinn.

6

Darren waits at the foot of the bridge for Colin's transit van. It's easy to spot, bright yellow with 'The Handyman Can' in curly letters down each side. Colin originally wanted to go with 'Mr Handi-Job, big or small, I'll do it!' And while it was a somewhat accurate description of his role as handyman and jobbing labourer, it was, of course, utterly tasteless and completely unsuitable, which is probably why he liked it so much in the first place. Years ago, the two of them spent a boozy evening racking their brains, Clover fast asleep, upstairs. It'd been a right laugh. They'd even come up with a handyman version of 'The Candy Man' song, which was subsequently fixed to each of the van's back doors in vinyl letters.

*Who can take
a house move*

*Handle it with
care*

*Cover it in bubble-
wrap*

*And float it down
your stairs?*

*The Handyman
Can!*

*Who can take
a bare wall*

*Skim it smooth
as glass*

*Paper it or paint
it, leave*

*your whole house
looking class?*

*The Handyman
Can!*

There he is. Darren waves as Colin indicates

and pulls over. The passenger door is sticky; Darren gives it a tug and jumps aboard. That song is playing on the radio, 'Happy' — he really needs to sit down with his ukulele and work out the chords, Clover will love it.

Colin holds a hand up to his mouth and sneezes, once, twice, three times; his eyes are red and the skin around his nostrils is cracked and peeling. He pulls into the traffic and immediately slows as the lights at the top of the bridge switch to amber. Driving one-handed, he rummages in the glove compartment and the side-door pocket for a tissue. The lights turn green again and someone behind them beeps. Colin sighs, wipes his nose on the back of his hand and rubs it on his shorts.

'What's up? You look like shit.'

'I feel like shit. I didn't even go to the gym this morning,' Colin says, voice scuffing the back of his throat.

'God, you *must* be ill.'

'It's crap having a cold in this weather. Didn't want to get out of bed. Then I remembered the cure.'

'For colds? What's that?'

'Self-employment.'

'Ha!'

Today's is a simple job: a house move, no packing, the boxes should be ready, they just have to pick them up, move a few bits of furniture and drive it all to the other side of town. Three or four trips should do it. Colin doesn't do many of these nowadays, just the odd favour for someone who is moving at short notice and can't find anyone else or, like today, a friend of a friend who wants it done on the cheap. It's an interesting job. Once, they arrived to find that the bloke they were moving hadn't even started packing. He'd not been able to make himself get on with it and was half hiding behind his open front door, face stiff with shame. Colin lied and said it happened all the time. Then they rolled up their sleeves and got on with it. Today's family, a mother, father and two little girls, is prepared. The girls race around the almost empty lounge. They lie on the floor, perform consecutive roly-polys and attempt handstands. Darren has seen it before; there's something about kids and empty houses, they turn into little dogs, try to mark every last bit of territory before they leave. The father is bearded and bespectacled, built like a garden cane. He's wearing fashion-ably faded jeans and a T-shirt that reads: 'Greed is the knife and the cuts run deep'. He addresses his wife and children, interchangeably, as darling — 'Darling, could you just . . . ' 'Don't do that, darling' — and he's got one of those bracelets, the ones that tell you if you had a good night's sleep and how many times you've farted. He's probably in IT. The mother looks horsey, it's in the thighs: sturdy and firm.

'A hot drink?' she asks in a soft, posh voice. 'There's an open box in the kitchen, for the kettle and so on. Tea? No? Are you sure? Fruit tea? Chai tea? Peppermint, ginger . . . ?'

Colin smirks. 'Nah, ta,' he says.

'I've got some biscuits; would you like a Viennese whirl?'

'You're all right. We'll just get on with it.'

They jog upstairs to gauge the weight of the empty wardrobes and check out the bed frames that they'll disassemble in a moment.

'Viennese whirl!' Colin mutters. 'Sounds more like a dance than a biscuit. *Would you like some chai tea?* Bloody hell. What's that when it's at home?'

'I dunno. I thought it was those slow exercises old people do. I think Edna does it at the leisure centre.'

'That's tai chi, you knob.'

'Well, maybe it's for colds or something. You should have tried it.'

'Sounds like something they drink in *Landan*.'

They hear footsteps on the stairs and stop talking.

'Everything all right?' Mr IT asks.

'Yeah,' Colin says.

'I've packed the office equipment. It's all ready for you to carry downstairs. Keep the printer upright.'

Colin salutes.

'We'll leave you to it, then.'

'Great, we'll see you at your *new abode*.' Colin likes to say that at least once — he thinks it adds something to the occasion.

They lift the packed boxes down the stairs and place them in the lounge. Back upstairs, they take the doors off the double wardrobes and bag up the screws. They wrap the mirrors and fit foam corners, disassemble the beds and carry the frames and mattresses out to the van. While Colin does a last inspection of the upstairs, Darren cases the kitchen. The box containing the kettle is open on the worktop. He peers in; there's a couple of mugs and several different types of tea. He finds the box of chai and reads the description: cardamom, ginger, cinnamon — sounds like curry. He discovers a small package, wrapped in greaseproof paper — the Viennese whirls. Home-made, that's a first. And they're good. Crumbly, round biscuits, sandwiched together with jam and buttercream. He helps himself to another while he rummages in the bottom of the box, which is littered with fridge magnets: letters of the alphabet, numbers from zero to nine, and some cutesy sayings. He digs out the sayings and lines them up.

Someone else is happy with less than what you have.

Life isn't easy for those who dream.

A daughter is a little girl who grows up to be your best friend.

He can hear Colin's feet through the ceiling as he checks, making sure there's nothing, not so much as a micro screw left upstairs. He fingers the magnet about daughters. This has been a happy house. The bloke with the anti-austerity T-shirt, the dark-haired, soft-voiced woman and their little girls have been contented here. He catches echoes of their life in the room . . .

Chai tea!

Viennese whirls!

Darling!

★　★　★

123

The first time he took something it was a book. He was back at work on the buses, but once in a while, on days off, he helped Colin. Edna took Clover, as she did when he was working, and the cash in hand was welcome — nappies cost a bloody fortune, so did formula. He'd played plasterer's lackey, lugging buckets of water back and forth and wiping skirting boards clean; he'd done a bit of gardening and a house clearance, and then he found himself accompanying Colin on a removal job: a couple and their baby, graduating from a three-bedroom semi in Churchtown to a detached fixer-upper in Birkdale.

The man was grey and rumpled. He rubbed his head habitually, hard, right where his hair was thinning. The baby had been wrapped in a big scarf and somehow tied to the woman. It dangled, outward-facing, like a joey.

'He only sleeps like this,' she said, 'skin to skin. Every time I try to put him down in his cot, he wakes up *immediately* and *screams* the place down.'

Darren opened his mouth to commiserate and closed it as he realised she was proud of the baby's dependence.

'Say hello to the nice men, *sweetie*,' she said. The baby couldn't speak, he was only a few months old, barely able to manage the weight of his own head. 'Shall we watch the nice men pack our things? *Shall we?* Mummy needs to feed you first, though, *doesn't she?*'

He and Colin traipsed in and out of the house, carrying the empty boxes they'd brought with them. Upstairs, there wasn't much to pack. The master bedroom was minimally furnished and the second bedroom contained a desk, a few shelves and a swivel chair. The third bedroom was the baby's. Blue and yellow, everything matched: the cot, the bedding, the wallpaper border, the wall stickers, the lampshade, the tiny bookcase — all of it. And the baby didn't even sleep there, did he? He slept *skin to skin*, so the whole room was a monument to an imaginary baby, one that enjoyed his own company.

Darren untied the cot bumpers and stripped the bedding; he unhooked the curtains and unscrewed the lampshade. The miniature bookcase was full. It was like a library: Thomas the Tank, Winnie the Pooh, Elmer the Elephant and a whole set of Little Golden Books. As he packed the Little Golden Books, he opened one. Just a quick look to see how small the writing was. Tiny — it'd be ages before the boy would understand the stories, and years before he'd be able to read them himself. While he was flicking through its pages he noticed that the woman had written in the book's front: 'Love from Mummy xxxx'. He opened another and it said the same. And another. She'd written in *every* book; dedicated them all. There was something desperate about it: *this is from me, and so is this, and this, and this, and this — see what I've given you?* It made his skin prickle. He could hear her voice coming from the second bedroom, where she was feeding the baby. The way she talked to him, as if the word *I* didn't exist: 'Mummy thinks you might have had enough to eat for now!'

'Mummy's just going to change your nappy.' What was that saying? *There's no 'I' in team.* She was the kind of person who'd say things like that, wasn't she? He couldn't get over the way all the stuff in the room matched. It was so *staged*. He felt shown up by it. None of it was necessary. Babies needed to be fed and clothed. Kept warm and dry. All the other stuff was bollocks. Wasn't it?

She appeared in the doorway, announcing her arrival in another one-sided interaction with the baby. *The man is putting your things away — yes, he is!* And then he'll take them to the new house — *yes, he will!*

Darren knelt on the floor and took the drawers out of a small chest, placing them in a neat stack.

'Are you married?' she asked. 'Is there a lucky lady in your life? Someone *special*?'

He shook his head.

'Just you wait.' She smiled at him, beatific and wise. 'One day you'll know what it's like to survive on three hours' sleep, and you won't mind at all. *He won't mind, will he?*' she asked the baby. '*No, he won't!*'

Darren smoothed a sheet of paper over the contents of each drawer: neatly folded baby clothes and various accessories — a pair of tiny Nike trainers, a replica England rugby kit, a bow tie on a Velcro fastener, a crocheted monkey hat, with ears.

'Do you want children?'

Her baby was ugly, he thought. Flat-faced and pasty, skinny. Nothing to recommend it.

'You will, one day. Your biological clock will

start ticking and you'll suddenly get all broody. *Won't he? Yes, he will!'*

He tipped the mattress out of the cot, slipped the fitted sheet off and folded it, placing it with the curtains and cot bumper.

'A little boy to — I bet you're a football man, aren't you? — a little boy to play football with. That'd be lovely, wouldn't it? Who d'you support?'

'Wigan,' he muttered.

'A little Wigan kit. Tiny football socks. That'd be lovely, wouldn't it? *Yes it would!'*

Clover wasn't quite one at the time. She was teething; waking in the night, *every* night. He frequently felt drunk with tiredness. Everything was fuzzy. It was as if waking throughout the night allowed the dark to seep into you. There were black bits of it floating in his eyes. It had stolen into his ears, which felt blocked and woolly. The shadows had slipped between his fingers, making his hands blunt and clumsy. Clover's crying would start and he'd force himself into a sitting position, drag his feet out from under the covers, stand on wobbly legs and shuffle down the hall to the front bedroom, where she lay in her cot: half-swaddled, a wriggling, angry, wet-chinned grub of a girl. He'd check her nappy and rearrange her blankets. Fumble for the tube of Bonjela. Rub his finger along bone-hard gums and wipe it dry on his boxers. Then he'd kneel beside the cot, inhaling liquorice and dark as he murmured her back to sleep with whispery word-fragments. He absolutely *did* mind waking in the night. There was no question about it. He minded a lot. This woman said she didn't, but she had to be lying, engaging in some sort of elaborate performance — she was like Jesus, nailing herself to a cross of tiredness; look at me hanging here, aren't I great?

'Excuse me,' he said, and he crossed the hall to Colin, who was lifting the clothes out of the wardrobes in the master bedroom and hanging them in special boxes. 'I'll be back in five, okay?'

Colin nodded. He looked as if he'd like to say something, but he didn't; he never did back then. He didn't dare.

Darren was glad to get out of the house. He sat on the front wall and breathed for a bit. He'd thought he might suffocate in that room: it was so full of expectation — dense with hope and anxiety, each matching item begging *love me, love me, love me*.

When he went back in the house, the husband was standing at the bottom of the stairs, rubbing his head and calling, 'Mummy! Mummy! Come here, please.'

Darren glanced up, looking for the bloke's mother, wondering where she had been hiding when he and Colin cased the rooms. But *she* appeared at the top of the stairs: *Mummy* — one boob out, her skin milky white and veined like Stilton.

'Yes, *Daddy?*'

The baby's suction broke and her nipple popped out of his mouth, distended and wet. Darren looked away, allowing her time to cover herself.

'It's okay,' she called, in no hurry. 'It's natural. It's what breasts are for.'

He let them have their conversation, and when they'd finished he returned to the baby's room and finished the packing.

It was after Mummy, Daddy and Sweetie had left for their new house, and he and Colin were loading the van, that Darren did it. He didn't think about it, he just grabbed one of the Little Golden Books from the box, shrugged off his hoodie and wrapped the book in it. The enveloped book sat on his knee all the way to the fixer-upper in Birkdale. When they got out he left it in the footwell of the van, and afterwards, once everyone was settled and Sweetie's things had been arranged in a less pristine bedroom, Darren climbed back in the van, lifted the hoodie on to his lap and held it during the drive home.

Colin dropped him off at the bottom of the bridge and instead of going straight to Edna's to collect Clover, he hurried to the bottom of The Grove, past the FOR SALE sign fastened to his front wall, and down the path. He took the stairs two at a time and burst into the second bedroom; he always did it fast, like ripping off a plaster. It was a mess. People kept asking whether he'd *dealt with* Becky's things. They offered helpful suggestions: find new homes for them, throw them away, give them to a charity — *you have to accept that she's not coming back.* He would sort everything out when the house sold. It would be both a conclusion and a new beginning. In the meantime, he'd bought a single bed and moved himself into the tiny third bedroom, the room he'd imagined would be occupied by the baby they would surely want, one day. He'd moved Clover into the front bedroom and replaced her Moses basket with a cot.

Becky's things entered the second bedroom via a weathering process; there were occasional downpours, when he swept up the stairs, arms full of her belongings, and there were times when he was surprised by a single object — an odd sock, a hair bobble, a book, a scarf, a letter — and he cradled it all the way to the bed, laying it down where she had slept, where he could no longer sleep. It was a monument, and a dump.

He chucked the book on the bed. Mummy would miss it one day. She'd think it had inexplicably got lost in the move, like a sock in the wash. It wouldn't occur to her that it had been nicked. But it would bother her, he thought. She'd wonder where it had gone. She might occasionally look for it; might try to find a second-hand copy on eBay to complete the set, although it wouldn't be the same, would it? It pleased him to think he had brushed against her perfect world and smudged it.

*   *   *

A daughter is a little girl who grows up to be your best friend. It's the sort of magnet he should have on his own fridge, an affirmation of cosiness and familial love. In the past, he might have slid it, or something like it, into the back pocket of his jeans. But not today. When he hears

130

Colin coming down the stairs, he chucks the magnets back into the box and carries the small package of greaseproof paper into the hall.

'Viennese whirl?'

'Don't mind if I do.'

★　★　★

He's doing a proper tea tonight, even though he's tired and he's got work in the morning. Jim's favourite is macaroni cheese with bacon, so that's what he's made. He's done runner beans, too. Strung and sliced them, nice and thin. To make a point. Jim won't eat them, of course.

The house seems especially crowded this evening; it usually does when he gets back from helping Colin. One day he'll sort it out. It was easy to put it off in the beginning, when he imagined it would sell. He kept it on the market for months but no one ever made an offer. Sometimes the people who came to look around asked about the baby's mum or realised there was something familiar about his face. And as time passed the thought of leaving was harder than staying. He could just about keep up with the mortgage, and he started to think about schools and how he'd manage without Edna next door. It had been easier to stay, mostly. Every so often he and Colin do a house clearance and he is reminded that all his belongings are only his while he is alive, afterwards they'll just be a job for someone else to sort out, and he comes home feeling panicked at the thought of Clover inheriting the

131

mess and having to sort and dispose of it.

Jim turns up early and plonks himself on the sofa. He smells of arse and cigarettes. Darren considers telling him to go upstairs and get in the bath. He reckons he could get away with it, but there'd probably be a bit of a fuss, which might upset Clover.

'When are we eating?'

'It's not ready yet.'

Jim tuts and gets off the sofa. He paces to the window, paces back, sits down and stands again.

'Going somewhere? Got a date?'

'No.'

'You're okay to wait, then.'

'How long?'

Jim's pained expression pisses him off. 'It'll be ready when it's ready,' he says. 'What do you want me to do? Climb in the oven and blow on it?'

'Dad!'

He returns to the kitchen. Clover was right to pester him. Jim looks dreadful: haggard and fidgety, puffy-faced too, as if he's just got out of bed. Later he'll google the side effects of the medications Jim's supposed to be taking, although chances are he's stopped them and that's why he's not himself.

The kitchen smells of melted cheese and bacon fat. Proper food. He should do this more often. They eat too much toast and too many fish fingers, too many tins of soup and frozen pies — with fresh vegetables, of course, but he could do better. He checks the pasta. The cheese on top has browned. He takes the dish out of the

132

oven using a tea towel and divides the food into three. He adds a big helping of runner beans to each and carries the plates into the lounge, Clover's and Jim's first.

When he returns with his own plate he stands in the hall for a moment, beside the unfastened radiator which he needs to reattach before winter, and listens.

' . . . he was all, 'Who watches this rubbish?' And then he switched the telly back on. And there was this woman who had no teeth, and her son was smoking weed all day and robbing her blind, that's what she said.'

'Huh.'

'But in the end, her son went off with Graham, who's the counsellor, which means he isn't allowed to shout at people. And he promised not to smoke weed any more. So that was good.'

'Hmm.'

'Did you have a nice walk here?'

'Hmm.'

'It's hot, isn't it?'

'Hmm.'

'Are your feet okay at the moment?'

'Hmm.'

Darren steps into the room. 'Tuck in,' he says.

Their forks chink the plates. The pasta is cheesy and the bacon pieces have just the right amount of crunch. But Jim puts his fork down. One mouthful and he's already pulling faces.

'What's wrong?'

'Have you got any painkillers?'

'What's up?'

133

'My tooth.'

'Still?' Darren sighs and puts his plate on the floor.

He jogs up the stairs, dodging the stuff he'll get around to sorting at some point. The key to the medicine cabinet is hidden in his room. He kneels on the floor beside his bed and lifts the mattress. There. In the bathroom he unlocks the cabinet, grabs a new box of paracetamol, locks the cabinet, checks it and checks once more, before returning the key to its hiding place.

'You can keep these,' he says to Jim. 'Been to the dentist yet?'

'Uh-uh.'

'Will you just go, please? It might be something they can fix without an injection.'

'Is that why you haven't been yet?' Clover asks. 'That's really silly. It doesn't hurt. I had a filling and the injection's just a scratch — that's what they say as they do it: 'just a scratch'. And there's a sign on the ceiling: 'Life is short, smile while you still have teeth.' You can see it while you're lying on the up-and-down chair.'

She flashes Jim a huge smile and Darren loves her for it, for everything.

★   ★   ★

Jim hardly touches his tea and he won't stay and watch telly or play on the Wii afterwards, even though he doesn't have to be anywhere. Darren gives him a pack of batteries for his remote and stands at the door, waving him off, watching as he strides out of The Grove and heads down the main road towards town.

Most of Jim's tea ends up in the food recycling bin. What a waste. What a git. Still, he came, didn't he? He's not well, but he walked over and tried to eat with them.

'When Uncle Jim's not himself, it's not really *him*, it's just something that happens *to* him,' he reminds Clover as she waits, tea towel at the ready. 'Things'll carry on like this for a bit and then, well . . . ' He raises his arms and makes a you-know-what-comes-next gesture. 'And after he comes out of hospital he'll be better for a while. Snakes and ladders, eh?'

'We should be nicer to him,' she says.

'We are nice to him.'

'Nice-*er*. Friendlier.'

'Your Uncle Jim and me aren't really *friends*. Don't pull faces! I bet there's loads of people at school who aren't your friends — it doesn't mean you don't like them, it's just that they're . . . they're not like you.'

'Colin's not like you.'

She's got him there. He slides the plates into the sink and tries again. 'Your Uncle Jim and me put up with each other because of your mother.'

Clover goes very still, as she does whenever he mentions Becky. It's like watching the hackles rise on an animal and he immediately regrets bringing her up.

'You know that. 'Happy' song? I heard it on the radio again this morning. When we've finished the dishes I'll get online and see if anyone's done the chords. That'll be fun, won't it?' he says.

She agrees, and he hums the tune as he scrubs melted cheese off the plates. The kitchen is hot. But it smells of cheese and bacon. And it sounds like happiness.

Exhibit: 'Becky Brookfield — the Untold Story'

Catalogue

Object: Baby teeth.

Description: A resealable envelope containing several baby teeth.

Item Number: 6.

Provenance: I think these belong to Becky Brookfield (my mother). It's possible they belong to Darren Quinn (my dad), but that's not the feeling I get when I hold them. I think they contain DNA, but I don't know how to get them tested (Jeremy Kyle could do it, but we'd have to go on the telly and have a big fight). Becky Brookfield's mother (Nanna Maureen) must have kept the teeth when she was being the tooth fairy.

Display: Either in the original resealable envelope (which might stop being sticky if opened too many times) or in a tiny Tupperware container (plenty in the kitchen).

Curator: Clover Quinn.

Keeper: Darren Quinn.

7

'THERE YOU ARE.'

Clover jumps.

'You were JUST ABOUT TO GO, weren't you? Did I give you a FRIGHT?'

'Yes!' She leans her bike back up against the house and turns to face Mrs Mackerel.

'I've been WATCHING. I was SLOTHING from the WINDOW.'

'Oh.'

'Off to the ALLOTMENT?'

'Yes.'

'THIS AFTERNOOON you can bring that SCARF you're SUPPOSED TO BE KNITTING. Your AUNTY PEARL'S coming.'

'But, I — '

'I got some RIBENA in, SPECIALLY.'

'Oh. But I . . . '

'NO, I won't be FLOGGED OFF.' Mrs Mackerel steps back inside her porch and calls, 'SEE YOU LATER,' which makes Clover think of Uncle Jim, who, when he is himself, likes to say, 'See you later, terminator' and 'See you later, percolator.' He uses every kind of 'ator' he can come up with: elevator, calculator, navigator, and, if he is feeling particularly cheerful, mashed pota-tor.

★   ★   ★

138

She returns from the allotment with one bag of new potatoes and another of runner beans. She dumps the bags in the sink and leaves the kettle to boil while she fetches the beginnings of Dad's scarf from her room. So far there are two stripes of blue and two of white. That's all. Yikes! There's going to be trouble. She sips her tea and dunks her biscuit before starting the next section of the scarf. Knit one, purl one, knit one, purl one.

★　★　★

Mrs Mackerel won't open the windows in case an insect breaks in. It's so hot that the carpet is practically cooking and it smells like slippers and dust. The party hasn't moved to the conservatory yet. The orange squash rests on the floor beside the armchair, and the gin bottle sits on the mantelpiece among the cottage ornaments, like an alcoholic lighthouse. Mrs Mackerel follows Clover's gaze.

'NOT FOR YOU, MISSY. We'll keep you on the RIGHT AND NARROW until you're older.'

Clover has no interest in it: it smells disgusting, like disinfectant. She fetches the carton of Ribena from the fridge, and when she comes back Mrs Mackerel examines the scarf, squeezing its thickness between finger and thumb.

'You've been WEAVING IN when you CHANGE COLOURS?'

She nods. Of course she has! You can't knit an entire Doctor Who scarf if you don't know how to change colours properly. But there's no point in saying anything: this exchange is for Mrs Knight's benefit — she can't knit.

'Not got VERY FAR, have you?'

'Not yet.'

'Better HURRY UP.'

Clover sucks Ribena through the tiny straw, careful not to show Mrs Mackerel up by slurping. Although she has more important things to do, it's actually quite nice to be invited to attend the event that used to be the best bit of her week in holidays past. There is a new fun in being here in a different way, as a guest, who can, she hopes, get up and leave at any time. Sitting on the turquoise, rose-spattered two-seater, she feels magnanimous and benevolent.

Mrs Knight complains that it's very hot. She usually sits outside in the afternoons. For the fresh air.

'Yes, and THAT'S why you look like a RAISIN, Pearl.'

'I haven't been well. I've had a funny tummy.'

'ARE YOU EATING?' Mrs Mackerel eyes Mrs Knight's glass, which is already half empty.

Mrs Knight notices and tightens her grip. 'Oh yes.'

'WHAT?'

'Soup.'

'That'll go STRAIGHT THROUGH YOU. What you want is a SLICE of DRY TOAST to CLEAN your DIGESTIVE TRACK.'

'How does that work, Edna?'

'THE CRUSTS.'

'Ah.'

Mrs Knight sips her drink and melts into the middle of the three-seater while Mrs Mackerel rehashes a well-worn moan about the charity shops on Lord Street.

'The place is going to HELL in a HAND-BAG,' she says.

Mrs Knight explains that the state of Lord Street doesn't matter if, like her, you've got a nice daughter round the corner who can buy you things from the internet and arrange for them to be delivered straight to your door. A nice daughter can source peach toilet paper to match your bathroom suite, instead of the boring white stuff that's everywhere nowadays.

Of course, Mrs Mackerel hasn't got a nice daughter round the corner. Her sons live in Australia, Hong Kong, California and Glasgow. They are ungrateful toads, and they don't send her things from the internet.

'YOU'RE A MEMBER OF THE INTERNET, AREN'T YOU, CLOVER? You've got ALL THE MODS AND CONS, haven't you?'

Clover nods.

'SEE?' she says, as if she has proved something.

'You should try Liverpool,' Mrs Knight says. 'The shops are *lovely*.'

'Oh, we've DONE THAT, haven't we?'

It's true, they have, despite the fact that Mrs Mackerel doesn't hold with Liverpool — she doesn't hold with Birkdale or Ainsdale or Formby or Crosby or any of the places on the way to Liverpool either, but especially not Liverpool, which is where cars have their tyres nicked and people get stabbed. One day last summer, the two of them went together. They used their passes, Mrs Mackerel's older person's pass and Clover's family pass, to catch the bus to Lord Street, and from there they caught the 47. Dad's 47. Mrs Mackerel was adamant. She had never been on one of Dad's buses. It was a ONCE IN A LIFETIME experience, she said. They stayed on the 47 all the way to Liverpool and back. Mrs Mackerel picked the closest seat to Dad, the special high one for disabled passengers. People got on with sticks and walking frames, but no one asked her to move, because she's old. She sat there, like a queen on a throne, pop-socked legs dangling, and cupped her hand around her mouth as she said things like, 'YOU WEREN'T EXPECTING THIS, WERE YOU, DARREN?' and 'It's SO NICE to see you being the CAPTAIN OF THE BUS.' Dad didn't reply. He's not supposed to talk to people while he's driving. But the back of his neck went all pink and sticky, like a slice of bacon.

'Don't let her do that again,' he said afterwards.

'I can't stop her!'

He made a noise like the whoosh of the bus doors and pointed at an imaginary Mrs Mackerel. 'You. Shall. Not. Pass,' he said, and they both laughed.

'Try Liverpool again, Edna,' Mrs Knight suggests.

'It *is* quite nice, you know,' Clover says. 'It's better if you get off the bus and have a look around. There's loads of shops — big versions of

142

the ones we've got, and posh ones like John Lewis where ties cost fifty quid.'

'They NEVER DO!'

'Honest. We bought one for Grandad for Christmas. He put it in the wash and it fell to pieces.'

'NO!'

'It was silk.'

'Well, that's Liverpool for you.' she says. 'You can't make a SILK EAR out of a SOW'S PURSE.'

'And how are your boys, Edna?' Mrs Knight asks, half hoping, it seems, for another opportunity to talk about her daughter.

But it turns out that Mrs Mackerel has some news about her oldest son, Thomas, the one who is BIG DOWN UNDER.

'Very big down under?' Mrs Knight asks, emptying her glass and smothering a giggle.

Mrs Mackerel explains that Thomas has, once again, *God love him*, invited her to visit him in Australia. This means she will spend the next month or two asking everyone's advice, before deciding not to go.

'He can't HONESTLY expect me to travel ALL THAT WAY. What do YOU think, Pearl?'

'Well, I've always liked *Neighbours*.'

'It's such a LONG JOURNEY.'

'*Australia*,' Mrs Knight says, in a strange, high voice.

'TWENTY-TWO HOURS.'

'*Hel-lo, possums.*'

'You have to wear those SPECIAL STOCK-INGS.'

143

'*G'day, darling.*'

'ARE YOU LISTENING, PEARL?'

'Of course,' Mrs Knight says, and then she toasts Mrs Mackerel with her empty glass and sings, '*Waltzing Matilda, waltzing Matilda, you'll come a-waltzing Matilda with me —* '

'You're CERTAINLY not going to WIN ANY PRIZES for your IMPERSONATIONS. Or YOUR SINGING.'

'*Fair dinkum.*'

'If I get there in ONE PIECE, it'll be like that programme with ANTON DECK. I'll be up against the GIANT SPIDERS. And the SNAKES. And the SHARKS.'

Mrs Knight pours another gin and adds a shot of squash. 'But would you be going swimming, Edna? Would you really?'

'I MIGHT.'

'Do you think so?' Clover asks, not at all convinced. 'In the sea?'

'WHY NOT? I've got ALL MY FACILI-TIES.'

'But what if you died, Edna? What if a snake bit you? Or a shark ate your leg? It costs a fortune to fly bodies around. They might have to bury you there. In *Australia*,' she does the funny voice again. 'In *Australian* ground; your bones forever covered in *Australian* soil — '

'I GET THE MESSAGE.'

'It all sounds far too dangerous to me. You're right, I really think you should stay at home, with us. Where it's safe.'

Mrs Mackerel beams. 'I EXPECT I'LL GO.'

When the two women get up to go into the

conservatory, Clover excuses herself. 'I'll go home and do some more of my scarf,' she says, before pausing in the doorway to add, 'I think you should go to Australia. If I was your son, I'd want to see — '

'LOOK AT YOU,' Mrs Mackerel interrupts. 'So GROWN UP all of a sudden. All that HAIR. You're the SPLITTING IMAGE OF YOUR MOTHER, *God forgive her.*'

Clover nods. Hoping for more.

'And your POOR FATHER — the way he put her on a PEDAL STOOL.'

She waits, breath piling in her throat.

'Go on, then. OFF YOU GO.'

Outside, Clover notices that Mrs Mackerel has put her wheelie bin out early, for tomorrow — she always leads the charge. She peeps under its lid as she passes. There's only one bag inside; loads of space for another. She hurries down the path and unlocks the front door before scrambling up the stairs to fetch the black bag of opened post and envelopes. If she leaves all the rubbish in the second bedroom, it will never look nice. She manoeuvres the bag past the stuff on the stairs and rushes down the driveway to the pavement. Thud goes the bag. Flip goes the bin lid. All gone.

She heads back to the room feeling lighter, almost feathery. She could float to the ceiling like Jane and Michael in *Mary Poppins*, inflated by happiness; buoyed by the belief that, in removing extraneous objects, she will more easily find her mother. What's that saying? *You can't see the wood for the trees.* She can't see her mother for the mess! Volume is not important, what she is looking for is essence, the undiluted bits: a collection of things that will provide her mother's flavour.

★ ★ ★

There are cards. To do with love. Love with a capital 'L'. Epic love. Like in *Romeo and Juliet*, which she hasn't done yet in English, but she's heard of it — who hasn't? *Romeo, Romeo, where are you, Romeo?* The love cards are covered in hearts and teddy bears and flowers, with really soppy words written in them. Imagine getting that soppy about someone, so soppy that you'd write all those unguarded things, leave yourself completely defenceless, like a snail without a shell. She pops downstairs for another piece of MDF, aware that she must be very careful — these cards are a part of history in ways that the holiday brochures were not.

Three of the cards are birthday cards from Dad to her mother — that's all they had together, just three birthdays.

When you stepped on to my bus and into my life it was the BEST day ever xxxxxxxx.

I love you babe, you're amazing xxxxxxxx.

Love you loads and loads xxxxxxxx.

She won't cut them. Instead, she uses Blu-Tack to stick them to the board. She will make a big heart and colour it with her special-occasion Sharpies. Then she will place it in the middle of the display.

There are several piles of books. Romance ones. She sits cross-legged and flicks through the pages, looking for rude bits and dying, literally, when she discovers them.

Jed's mouth captured hers in a tender kiss. He drew a ragged breath, before claiming her lips again. 'Are you taking your contraceptive pill?' he husked.

'Yes, baby,' she said, clinging to his solid arms.

'Good,' he replied, melting her bones with his crooked grin.

'I love you, Ruby,' Clint murmured, his voice gravelled, desperate.

Ruby's belly clenched. 'I love you too, Clint.'

'Ruby!' A growl escaped his lips.

'Clint!' She gazed at the most male part of him, longing to feel it inside her.

'We're different people from ten years ago. If I'd only told you I loved you,' Belinda cried.

They were both free of other responsibilities. It was time for the loneliness to end. Silence settled, like snow.

'Say you love me now,' Cole said finally, lowering his lips to hers.

She peels off the gloves, cheeks flaming, hands sweaty. Love is *very* embarrassing. She stuffs the books into a bin bag, one after another, after another; every pink and purple and red cover; all the glistening men with bulging muscles and the pretty, wide-eyed ladies with big boobs — bosoms, even. There. That's the lot. It's a good job Dad isn't a crooked-grin, gravelled-voiced sort of man. Even if he was, there's no one who'd like him to melt their bones.

Except Kelly — the thought pops up like a little jack-in-a-box. Ta-dah! *Kelly* — oh.

Clover leans against the bed and replays the other evening. Kelly holding Dad's shoulder as she slid her feet out of her shoes. Kelly sitting beside him after she'd been outside for her cheeky ciggie, thigh pressed right up against his, even though they weren't short of space. Kelly turning to smile at him in the car on the way home when she should have been watching the road, et cetera, et cetera. Yikes. But Kelly is not a crying, clinging, belly-clenching woman with enormous boobs. She's a let's-do-something-fun, the-boys-think-you're-great, would-you-like-a-free-haircut sort of woman. Which is different. Isn't it? And not so bad, maybe.

★   ★   ★

She finds the article under a pile of towels while 'Seasons in the Sun' leaks through the portable CD player's funny headphones. The towels are ordinary, pink and blue and green, different sizes. She opens each towel and refolds it neatly, and that's when she finds the sheet of newspaper, folded into four. It has been out of

148

the light, so it's not faded or anything, just very creased along the folds, like a napkin or a new shirt.

SPECIAL DELIVERY FOR EDNA!

When a local pensioner set out to investigate a strange noise she got more than she bargained for. Intrepid Edna Mackerel discovered her next-door neighbour giving birth in the kitchen.

Mother-of-four, Edna is no novice when it comes to childbirth, but she admitted that this was the first time she'd been on the receiving end. Brave Edna delivered her neighbour's baby and called an ambulance. 'I just did what anyone would have done,' she confessed modestly.

It wasn't just the venue of the baby's arrival that was surprising. 'I didn't know she was having a baby, and neither did she,' Edna revealed. 'You don't believe someone could be pregnant and not realise. But now I've seen it with my very own eyes.'

Edna's neighbourliness didn't stop there. The generous retiree gave the new parents' kitchen a thorough going over with a mop and bucket. Well done, Edna! We'll be sending Edna our Resident of the Week bouquet, courtesy of Sweeneys Florist.

Mother and baby are thought to be doing
well in hospital. If you know the family,
call our news hotline.

The article is accompanied by a photograph of
Mrs Mackerel holding a mixing bowl and spoon,
as if she is just rustling up a baby. It is captioned
'Edna Mackerel, pictured in her own kitchen'
and it's the most promising object she has found
to date. It was printed just days after she arrived
in the world. At the exact moment when paper
boys and paper girls were slipping the newspaper
through people's letter boxes, she, Clover Quinn,
was in hospital, with her mother. Dad was
probably too busy to do an interview. And too
surprised! But it would have been nice if he had
agreed and the newspaper had sent a photogra-
pher to the hospital to take a picture of the three
of them, together.

There are only two photographs of her with
her mother. Dad took them with an old-
fashioned camera. She slips off her gloves and
hurries downstairs to retrieve the album from the
kitchen drawer.

The first photograph was taken at the hospital.
Her mother is sitting up in bed, legs hidden by a
white blanket. She is wearing a black baggy
T-shirt, with something written across the chest
that's difficult to read because she is cradling a
tiny baby in a rock-a-bye pose. The baby's face is
scrunched and she is wearing a yellow woollen
hat.

Her mother looks tired. But that's to be
expected. And a bit startled. No wonder! Her

hair is loose and it reaches her waist. The camera has missed her smile. Dad says this happened all the time with old cameras because you couldn't check the photograph until you picked up your order from the shop; you didn't know what you'd got until it was too late.

The second photograph was taken at home, in the kitchen. Her mother is wearing another big T-shirt and a pair of baggy trackie bottoms. Her hair is still loose and her mouth is open, as if she is saying something or — Clover thinks — about to smile. You can't see the baby's face because she is holding it against her, one hand resting on the bump of its nappy-covered bottom, the other supporting its back. The baby is wearing a pink baby-grow. It looks bald. It's not possible to say whether the baby is asleep or awake, but Clover feels that she was definitely awake and that the hold was more of a hug than a carry.

That's it. One and two. There's nothing else of them together. Unless there's something here, in among all the stuff. An overlooked photograph or another newspaper cutting; both, even. Perhaps she'll get really lucky and discover something amazing — a long-forgotten interview accompanied by a family picture: SPECIAL DELIVERY FOR DARREN AND BECKY! That would be epic.

The other pictures in the album are of Clover by herself and, occasionally, with Dad. She flicks through, amazed at her smallness. Dad says the doctors decided that she was about five weeks early; that's probably why she had to wear an eyepatch when she was a toddler. She was lucky, he says, some early babies have respiratory problems and developmental delays. And, he teases, she was clearly determined, in arriving early — in arriving *at all* — to surprise as many people as possible.

She slips the gloves back on. The two photographs of her with her mother don't seem to belong in the little album any more. They belong with the newspaper article. She slides them out of the plastic pockets and places them on the floor. She will make a display. Draw a special heading — 'SURPRISE' in bubble writing. But not yet. She'll need to arrange things properly. And she might find more stuff to add, things from her own room, like the tiny clothes Dad bought on the day she was born — there he was, buying baby-grows, and he'd never even held a baby until that afternoon.

She examines the photographs side by side, scanning the just-missed-smile and about-to-smile face of her mother for a reflection of herself — an echo or an impression, an answer to the question *what will I be?* She is incomplete, a part-written recipe. How can she imagine what she will be if she only knows half of her ingredients?

Exhibit: 'Becky Brookfield — the Untold Story'

Catalogue

Object: School report — one of several.

Description: Becky Brookfield's school report, summer 1989.

Item Number: 9.

Provenance: Becky Brookfield (my mother) is described by her teacher, Mrs Sylvester, as a solitary child who sometimes needs encouragement. Mrs Sylvester's pen pressed hard into the paper and her writing is very spiky. Becky Brookfield was often absent. I expect I would be absent a lot too, if Mrs Sylvester was my teacher.

Display: In its brown envelope which doesn't have a stamp (Becky Brookfield must have carried it home from school with her).

Curator: Clover Quinn.

Keeper: Darren Quinn.

8

It's been a while since he visited Broadhursts. He used to come here with Mum when he was a boy, and he came a few times with Clover to collect the free World Book Day books and to spend the tokens Edna used to give at Christmas and birthdays. He'd forgotten how nice it is. The walls are wrapped in bookcases and glass-fronted cabinets, and the air is warm with the grassy smell of paper and leather. A book-packing station with a string dispenser and sheets of brown paper sits below an antique sign: *Pleasant Books for the Children*. The place feels old and trusty and a little bit magical.

He glances around, hoping he won't have to ask, but he doesn't know the author's name. Perhaps he should have ordered the book online, but he practically passes the shop on his way home from Lord Street; he'd be daft not to do it while it's on his mind. He tilts his head and inspects the spines of the books in the nearest case. It's such a small shop; he won't get away with browsing for long before someone —

'Can I help you?'

'There's this book I'm looking for. It's about women.'

'Hmm,' the girl says. And as she purses her lips thoughtfully, he notices a book just behind her, front-facing: *Vagina*. Oh God. What if she thinks he wants that book? — it's practically bellowing, *I'm a book about women!*

'Something about *how* to do it. How to be a woman, I mean,' he adds, quickly.

'Ah, I know.' The girl lifts a green paperback from a shelf just behind him. 'This'll be the one,' she says, holding it up for his inspection.

There's a picture of a woman on the cover. She has long black hair with a white streak, like Morticia. Her expression is one of mild amusement, but her raised eyebrow says, *Mess with me at your peril.*

'Is it a present?'

'No.'

'Oh, that's *great*.'

'I mean — '

'Good for *you!*'

' — well, I'm a man — '

'You'll love it.'

I'm a man? Good one, Captain Obvious.

'Especially the bit where she tells you to find a chair to stand on.'

'Right.'

'I am a feminist!' the girl cries, toasting him with an imaginary glass. 'Would you like it wrapped?'

'Oh, I — '

'There's no charge.'

And before he can respond she is folding brown paper around Morticia's face and the quote on the book's cover — 'The book EVERY woman should read' — disappears under creases and a criss-cross of string.

He hurries home in the early evening sunshine, clasping the wrapped book. In it's

155

pages lies the promise of certainty. He feels better already, comforted by the anchoring assurance of another solid object.

★ ★ ★

The runner beans have grown dark and wild, overwhelming the bamboo frame he built. Several of the thickened knotty pods have dried in the sun. He tears them away from the plants and opens them up. The seeds inside are speckled purple and black, smooth and shiny like pebbles. He empties them into the palm of one hand and slips them into a ziplock bag. He will plant them next spring and they will begin their lives in the kitchen, on the windowsill and the worktop, where it's warm and light. One day he'll get a greenhouse. One day.

The mozzies are out. He can hear them whining past his ears. Bastards. He windmills his arms and jumps on the spot, sending the seeds spinning around the bag. There weren't mosquitoes like this when he came here as a boy. Of course, it was a different world — God, he sounds ancient, like Dad, but it *was* — when you missed something on the telly or forgot to set the video recorder, that was that; if you finished your book you had to wait until the shops or the library opened, you couldn't download another one or pop to a twenty-four-hour supermarket. On light evenings, when he was small, and he'd finished watching *Inspector Gadget* or *Banana-man*, he happily helped Dad with the growing; it wasn't as if there was much else to do. And he

156

enjoyed it. Just the two of them, Bob Quinn & Son, growing things in the back garden, tending them until they were big enough to be lifted into the boot of the car and transported to the allotment.

When Dad stepped into the back garden, he turned into someone different: Grandmaster of the Greenhouse, conjurer of life in yogurt pots, seed trays and margarine tubs. Years before Darren was born, when Dad lived in the house alone, he had laid a stepping-stone path down the middle of the lawn. It pointed like a suggestion to the bottom of the garden where the greenhouse lived. The greenhouse had an aluminium frame. It was shaped like the kind of house you draw when you're a kid, with a pitched roof, a little door bang in the middle of its front, and fruit trees on either side. When the door opened, warm air steamed out, thick with the peppery smell of generations of tomato plants. In addition to the growing things, the shelves that lined its perimeter were filled with treasures: balls of string, wooden clothes pegs, a tub of slug pellets, twine, leather gloves, pot brushes, insect catchers, a folding pruning saw and a pocket knife. Bags of compost and fertiliser slouched on the floor alongside watering cans and bubble-wrap rolls. There were cobwebs and all manner of pupa — some fat and occupied, others derelict, dried-up husks. And spiders: hairy beasts with legs like pipe-cleaners that waited out the winter under the shelves and inside the empty pots.

In the early spring he and Dad lined up the

pots and trays. They filled them with compost and labelled them with plant sticks, a task Darren was allowed to perform as soon as he was able to shrink his bloated, quivering letters small enough. Dad kept the seeds in a long box, separated by alphabetised index cards: bean (broad), bean (green), beetroot, broccoli, cabbage, carrot, celery, chives, cucumber, and so on. He'd written notes on the cards, in capitals:

START INDOORS
SOW AFTER DANGER OF FROST HAS PASSED.
PLANT 2 INCHES APART.
SOAK SEEDS 24 HOURS BEFORE SOWING.

One year, when he can't have been more than five, Darren sneaked into the greenhouse before Dad got home from his job at the Philips factory, with the intention of doing him a great kindness. He filled the biggest watering can using the outside tap — once, twice, three times — and he watered *everything*. There was nothing much to see at that stage: they had only recently buried the seeds under the compost. Perhaps he had hoped to hurry them up; he can't remember his precise thoughts, but he remembers heaving the can with both hands, swamping the yogurt pots of peas (garden), submerging the trays of lettuce (round) and sopping the tubs of beans (green). Not content with soaking all the growing things that were concealed under compost, he refilled the can and saturated the onion sets. Then he sluffed the seed potatoes. And finally, he opened the long, indexed seed box and filled that with water, too.

When Dad got home they had tea and then they went outside together as usual, Darren carrying the battery-operated radio, tuned to John Dunn's Radio 2 drivetime show. Dad opened the greenhouse door and froze. He didn't shout. He waited for a few moments before turning and heading back down the stepping-stone path and into the kitchen.

Darren followed.

'Carol, come and look at this.'

'What is it, love?' Mum asked.

Dad inclined his head and she stepped into the garden in her slippers. Again, Darren followed, radio at the ready.

They stopped at the greenhouse door. It looked like there'd been a storm. Water dripped from the shelves: plop, plop, plop.

Mum put her hand on Dad's shoulder. 'Oh, love. I *am* sorry,' she said. 'I really *am*.'

Dad nodded, accepting her condolences.

'He'll have done it to be helpful. You were trying to help, weren't you, Darren? He didn't understand what he was doing, did you?'

Darren realised they weren't going to thank him. And that he might be in trouble. So he hurried back into the house, put the radio on the side where it belonged and crept up to bed.

'It wasn't the best idea you've ever had,' Dad observed, the following morning.

Over the subsequent evenings they restored order. Dad tied lines of string to the greenhouse ceiling and pegged the index cards out to dry. It looked like bunting and while it was up, whenever they walked down the garden, it felt they were on their way to a party. Some of the seeds from the box were salvageable because the envelopes were waxy, pretty much waterproof. Where the soil and seeds had been washed out of pots and trays, they replanted. They put the onions in the earth earlier than planned in case of mould. The potatoes were fine. It was all right in the end. Dad never shouted at him. Not when he doused the greenhouse. Not ever. Perhaps his patience was a product of his age.

His mum and dad were older than other parents, something that dawned on Darren during his first sports day, when he experienced an unexpected flare of panic at the announcement of a dads' race. He looked at Dad, who had taken the afternoon off work specially, and realised that, compared to the other men, he was slow, deliberate. Darren didn't mind this. In fact, he felt a great wave of tenderness for him, an overwhelming feeling that it would be the worst possible thing in the world for him to feel obliged to enter the race and come last or, worse still, fall and hurt himself in front of everyone. So while his mates dragged their half-laughing, half-posturing dads to the starting line, Darren studied the band of elastic on the front of his plimsolls.

There was a tremendous thudding on the grass as the dads ran. They were like animals, a herd of strapping chaps. Darren felt the stomp of their feet in his chest and he cheered and laughed with everyone else, but afterwards, during the walk home, he held Dad's hand extra tight. *I might have cheered for them*, his hand was saying, *but don't worry, I like you the best.*

★ ★ ★

Darren grabs the watering can from under the carpet and jogs down the path to the tap. The peas are struggling. Clover's daytime watering isn't doing the trick. Still, it's better than nothing and at least *she's* not being eaten alive. He drops the can and whacks a mozzie on his forearm. Splat — ha!

Once the watering is done, he banks a line of emerging potatoes and weeds between the older plants. It'd be good if he could drag Dad down here. He saw a little wooden sign not long ago, when he was in Lidl, doing the shopping. What was it? — TO PLANT A GARDEN IS TO BELIEVE IN TOMORROW. Dad won't get involved in any material plans for tomorrow. All he wants is to stay at home and shop from his armchair. He orders everything: groceries, clothes, the latest technology — he's got wireless headphones, chargers that don't need to be plugged in, all sorts of shit. He'd rather watch telly and look stuff up on YouTube than go outside and do something. He's on to Shakespeare now, Clover says. There are thirty-seven plays — Darren checked, to see how long it will last: clear through until September. And what's the point? What'll Dad have to show for it in the end? He should do one of those adult courses at the college if he wants to learn stuff. Otherwise, what's the difference between him and other people who never leave their houses, the ones who sit in bed all day eating, only to shit it out the next morning?

Some people are all right by themselves — Darren is absolutely fine. Dad says he is fine too, but Darren can't help wondering whether his mother would have managed better on her own. She had friends. A whole group of them. They worked at Kwik Save together, before he was born. When he was small they came round for coffee and chats and card games. He liked their paraphernalia: scarves and bags, hats and coats, gloves and cardigans. He liked the way they filled the room with their soft things, and soft noises, the sympathetic *hmms* they made, the similar sounds that meant a variety of things: *no, yes, really? Never!* They fussed and petted him. Sometimes he'd get to climb on a comfy knee and listen to his favourite Ladybird books: *The Enormous Turnip* and *The Little Red Hen*. When he'd had enough of their attentions he would sit on the rug with his colouring book while they smoked and laughed and called, 'Last card!' In between rubbers they talked about men he didn't know: Alan, Steve, Ian, Paul. Later, after he started school, it troubled him to know that Mum's friends were meeting without him. He knew when they'd been, because the house smelled of their bodies: of talc, extra cigarette smoke and instant coffee.

One day after they'd been — he was a little older, definitely school-aged, so perhaps it was during the holidays — Mum got a picture out of the dresser drawer.

'I expect you've been wondering who Paul is.'

He hadn't. But she seemed about to say something interesting, so he listened.

'Before I met your dad, I was married to Paul. He died. And I was very sad. But then I met your dad and had you. And now I'm very happy.'

She showed him a picture of a wedding. It was her, *his mum*, in a floaty white dress, head wrapped in a piece of material that looked like a net curtain, getting married to someone who wasn't his dad.

'Why did he die?'

'Something went wrong in his brain. It bled, inside.'

He looked at the photo of the man who wasn't Dad, the man with the brown suit, the thick moustache and the bleeding brain, and he was glad that the man was dead.

'And did you have another boy?'

Mum laughed. 'Oh, *no*,' she said. 'Why would you think — no! There's only you. You're my only boy.'

Dad never had friends round. He spoke warmly of people at work and occasionally went to the pub on a Friday, but more often than not he stayed in, content with Mum's company. On a Friday or a Saturday, she would have a glass of wine after tea. And sometimes she would rehearse the story of how they met at Kwik Save. It was like a performance. She said her lines while Dad played supporting actor and Darren took the part of the audience.

'I noticed your dad. He always came in on a Saturday morning. Early.'

'I did,' Dad would say.

'I thought he was nice. Very smart.'

'I was,' he'd agree.

'He used to come to my till, even if there was a queue. And we always had a little chat.'

'We did.'

'He noticed I wasn't wearing a wedding ring.'

'That's right.'

'He kept coming back.'

'I did.'

'The shopping wasn't all he was checking out!'

'It certainly wasn't.'

'So one day, after he'd bagged all his shopping and it was time to pay, he said, '*I*'ve got a special offer.' And I said, 'Oh, what's that, then?' 'Tickets to the cinema,' he said. 'Buy one, get one free: I've bought one and you can have this one for free.''

'It's true.'

'It was meant to be. It was fate.'

Dad would smile and shake his head, a mild, unspoken mode of disagreement, undertaken with a courtesy he'd struggle to muster nowadays.

Darren attended to these performances, but he felt very little curiosity about his parents' beginnings. Later, when he learned in biology that a woman is born with all the ova she'll ever produce, it may have briefly occurred to him that this story, and all Mum's stories, were in some ways his — that the egg of him was present at that supermarket checkout, and at the wedding

164

to the man who wasn't Dad — but he didn't give it very much thought. There were odd occasions, as he grew older, when he slipped the picture of his mum and Paul out of the drawer and wondered about fate. Although Mum was a great believer in it (she was also a great believer in the royal family and a five-thread overlock hem), Darren remained unconvinced. The photograph did not make him feel as if his existence was fixed and fated. It made it seem as if he'd arrived on the planet by a hair's breadth, by a whisker. And he felt lucky.

★　★　★

He tucks the watering can back under the carpet. Next year he'll put the peas here. There's a notebook in the garden shed containing diagram after diagram of the plot, one for every year since Dad signed up. Crop rotation reduces the chances of soil deficiencies and keeps things balanced, healthy. If only you could do the same with people. Determine their requirements, identify their problems and pests, group them in the right families and keep moving them away from trouble.

He pulls an empty carrier bag out of his pocket and begins to fill it with raspberries. They're fat and juicy, the kind you pay extra for in the supermarket. He should probably save them up, stick them on trays and freeze and bag them, like Mum did. He could make jam or something. He remembers the things Mum used to make with the raspberries: cheesecakes, trifles,

165

tarts, fools and mousses. They could have a go, him and Clover, she'd like that. He has had these ideas before but it's a struggle to make them materialise; by the time he gets home there will be something else to occupy his thoughts — the detached radiator, the hall walls, the worry that there may be something else she needs. But time is passing and he knows it won't be long before she'll have better things to do.

He pauses to eat some of the fruit, and pictures Mum, apron strings wrapped twice around her waist, sleeves rolled past her elbows, writing RASPBERRY JAM and the date on a roll of sticky labels. He remembers the hot smell of boiling sugar and raspberry juice in the kitchen. 'I wonder what'll have happened by the time we eat this,' she'd say. She used to say something similar each time they put the Christmas decorations back in the loft: 'I wonder what fate has in store for us in the next twelve months.'

He can't decide whether Mum's belief in fate was stupid or stoical, a means of conciliation or consolation. Fate's all right if everything's going well. Makes you feel all important. Deserving. Like your happiness is *meant*. But when things are shit, you're trapped by it, helpless, like those myths where the gods muck about with humans, for a laugh.

He much preferred the idea of luck. It seemed different from fate. Better. A skin-of-the-teeth, relieved feeling; the way you feel when you're playing dodgeball in PE and the air beside you whooshes, but you don't get hit. Luck's not so set as fate. Even when things are shit, you might get better luck, it could be just around the corner. Course, he grew up eventually and realised life's a crapshoot and most things, good or bad, happen by chance and accident.

★　★　★

His and Colin's was an accidental friendship. They didn't live on the same street and they didn't sit next to each other at school; they didn't even share the same table. Although Miss Richardson never said which of the tables was top, everyone knew it was the Lions. Darren was on the Tigers, which was second, but Colin had to sit with the Hippos. Darren assumed this was a mistake or a temporary measure. Some kind of punishment perhaps, because Colin was funny and clever and quick — sometimes he shouted out the answer before Miss Richardson had finished a question.

When it was their class's turn to do a school assembly, Colin had a really small part. During rehearsals he mucked about. After he took his shoes off, smelled his feet and pretended to die of asphyxiation, Miss Richardson moved him.

'Go and sit next to Darren,' she said. 'He's sensible, let's see if it's contagious.'

Colin passed his words to Darren. 'Bet you can't read that.'

Darren glanced at the sentence. 'Can,' he said.

'Bet you can't read it out loud.'

' "Seven local fishermen got lost on the marsh during the fog." '

Colin folded the paper and put it in his

pocket. When it was his turn to speak he stood up and said his line without it, which proved Darren right: Colin *was* clever and definitely didn't belong with the Hippos.

'Do you want to play *Dukes of Hazzard?*' Colin asked at break time. 'I'll be Luke. You can be Bo.'

Darren was up for that. The next day it was British Bulldog, the day after it was *World of Sport* wrestling.

'You can be the announcer,' Colin said.

It was easy to be the announcer — Darren watched the wrestling on Saturday afternoons with Mum and Dad. 'On my left, in the red corner, at six foot eleven, is *the Masked Emperor,*' he said in a special announcing voice. 'And his opponent, on my right, at twenty-four and a half stone, is *Bi-i-g Daddy*! Two submissions or a knockout decides the winner. *Ding-ding!*'

Colin balled his jumper and stuffed it up his shirt. The other lads ran into him and he fended them off with belly blocks, just like Big Daddy.

That was how they became friends. And they remained so, their roots forever connected by that early meshing. Colin was cheeky and often in trouble. He remained with the Hippos that year and graced the bottom sets in every subject except maths throughout his time at school. Eventually, Darren noticed his difficulty reading. Sometimes he helped him with his homework. And he chose to work with him when they had to read in pairs. But he never felt sorry for him. Colin was funny and he had a largesse that other kids lacked; he shared everything — sweets, toys, football stickers — with a casual optimism, confident that life would bestow more sweets, more toys and more football stickers. When it was bring-a-toy day he let Darren have a go on his Major Morgan. The hand-held electric organ was the first instrument Darren had ever touched. He matched the symbols and colours on the push-in cards and played the whatsit out of it. In return he lent his Rubik's Cube to Colin, who got fed up when he couldn't solve it and peeled off some of the stickers to complete the red face. This pretty much wrecked it, but Darren didn't mind. Not a lot, anyway. They were friends, after all.

Colin's dad had a Kawasaki bike and, according to Dad, a bad attitude. Darren had seen him shove Colin into a corner and attack him with his index finger: 'You.' *Jab.* 'Little.' *Jab.* 'Git.' *Jab.* Colin said it hadn't hurt at all, but Darren wasn't convinced. Colin's mum was small and skinny with peroxide hair and a smile which she propped up with tense, bony shoulders. Colin's parents were young. They'd been born on the cusp of the sixties. Dad was born just as Europe geared up for the Second World War, and Mum was born right at the end of it. The years between Mum and Dad and Colin's parents, between war babies and the start of Generation X, made a world of difference. Dad remembered rationing. He didn't talk about it often, but when he did it connected him to the war and gave him a past that seemed, to Darren, to have been shot in black and white, and slow-motion frames.

Colin didn't come round very often. It was always a bit awkward when he did. Mum fussed in the kitchen, cigarette lolling between her lips as she checked the microwave seal with her radiation counter, before pureeing the zapped vegetables in the Magimix. She called Colin 'love' and repeatedly asked whether he was enjoying himself. Every time she said 'love', Colin flinched.

The soundtrack to tea was the scrape of knives and forks against china. In Colin's house it was the telly. Dad didn't make small talk at the table. Darren was used to this, but when witnessed by another person his silence seemed rude, as if he was cross with everyone or too ancient to have anything interesting to say. Of course, he wasn't *that* old but, once noted, the differences between him and Colin's parents stacked up: the way Dad's skin bagged slightly, the rooty veins on the backs of his hands, the puff of his knuckles, his stiff-collared shirts, his paisley ties and his utter lack of strut.

Once, Colin came round for tea in the early spring. In Darren's imagination, the two of them were going to have a great time afterwards, helping Dad in the greenhouse. They helped, but it didn't go well. Darren found himself stuck between Colin and Dad, uncertain how to accommodate them both. They trooped down the stepping stones and stood in that hot little space together while Darren bestowed kindness and condescension on Dad, speaking on his behalf and providing Colin with a running commentary of greenhouse-related information. When his helpfulness went unacknowledged and unremarked upon, he felt resentful. There he was, being kind to Dad because he wasn't quite the same as the other dads, and Dad didn't even have the good grace to notice either the kindness or the difference. Eventually, he ran out of things to say and Colin, who approached silences like swimming pools, dive-bombed the conversation with jokes. Darren had to laugh extra loud to make up for Dad's silence.

'Where do the Irish keep their armies? Up their sleevies!'

'Ha-ha!'

'What's black and white and red all over? A sunburnt penguin!'

'Ha-ha-ha-ha!'

'Why did the one-handed man cross the road? To get to the second-hand shop!'

'HA-HA-HA-HA!'

Afterwards, he and Colin sat on the pink and grey sofa in the lounge, drinking ginger beer and listening to Mum's time-worn Beatles singles on the record player, a novelty for Colin, who only had a portable ghetto blaster at home. While Darren changed the records, Colin made up silly songs.

'Old Bob Qu-inn had a greenhouse, e-i-e-i-o.
And in that greenhouse were some seeds, e-i-e-i-o.
With a yawn, yawn here and a snore, snore there,

Here a flower, there a plant, everywhere a
  frigging branch.
Old Bob Qu-inn had a greenhouse, e-i-e-i-
  o.'

'HA-HA-HA-HA! The greenhouse is so
boring,' Darren said.

And, of course, Dad was standing in the
doorway, wasn't he? He didn't even look cross.
He just cleared his throat and disappeared down
the hall.

'Oops,' Colin whispered.

The following evening, when it was time to go
outside, Dad said, 'It's all right, you sit down. I
expect you've got better things to do.'

'No — no, it's fine.'

'No, you're all right,' Dad said, and he stepped
outside by himself.

★   ★   ★

Darren ties the handles of the raspberry-stuffed
carrier bag in a knot and places it on the carpet.
He picks up the shears and crouches to trim the
grass pathways that dissect the beds. It's not long
before his biceps and pecs are burning. It's
almost as good as going to the gym; perhaps he'll
wake up in the morning with guns like Colin
— ha! Once he's finished trimming the pathways
he straddles the back fence; he'll do Mr
Ashworth's too, it'll be a nice surprise for him
when he next manages to come.

Colin was wrong — it wasn't boring helping
Dad and it's not boring here. The sun and the

172

soil are reliable, they do their jobs and he does his: if things look dry he gives them more water, if the potatoes get blight he cuts off the tops to stop it getting into the tuber. He knows where he is, here. Knows why Dad enjoyed it.

After the incident with Colin's song he still helped Dad sometimes. But he felt like he was imposing. He'd lost his share in the greenhouse. It couldn't have been more obvious if there'd been an actual sign saying 'Bob Quinn & Son' and Dad had crossed through the '& Son'. It didn't matter too much, because not long after Dad got his first cuckoo clock and they shared that, instead. Mum bought it for his birthday. It came all the way from Austria, where a friend of hers had been on holiday. Dad *had* to discover how it worked, and then he wanted another, and another, until there was a line of them in the hall: *tick-tock, tick-tock, cuckoo, cuckoo*; measuring out the seconds and the minutes, segmenting the hours into halves and quarters.

Time passed. Unlike Colin, who couldn't get out of bed in the mornings once he started puberty, so weighed down was he by his new carpet of body hair and the voice that had dived into his boots where it sat like concrete, Darren remained an early riser. As soon as he was thirteen he started doing a paper round. He loved his daybreak circumnavigation of the neighbourhood, *Now 20* playing on his Walkman as he cycled on the empty pavements. Initially, his mind was occupied by memorising the route, then he graduated to imagining how he was going to spend his wages, but after a while he

173

started to notice things: the waxing and waning of the moon; the different types of clouds; the wind direction and the warning of red skies, heralding wet and windy weather.

Mum waited by the front door at 7.30 each morning to receive his coat as he returned. 'Ta,' he'd say and hurry upstairs. Each weekday when he got back, his bed was made and his school uniform was laid out on it in the shape of him. Like Flat Stanley — ha! He'd dash to the bathroom, shuck off his Air Jordans, his trackies and his baggy T-shirt and step into the shower. Two minutes was all he needed. He flung his uniform on and hurried downstairs where breakfast awaited him: milky tea with white-bread toast that Mum cut into triangles and slotted into a rack. The toast was served with Marmite, marmalade or home-made raspberry jam, while *TV-am* played on the portable telly in the kitchen and he admired Ulrika Jonsson.

That was life. It consisted of the daily orbit of his paper round, six hours of school, a quick trip to Colin's for a turn on his Sega Megadrive, tea with Mum and Dad — something home-made or Findus Crispy Pancakes for a treat — fol-lowed by *Coronation Street*, while Mum did her knitting and Dad read from one of the encyclopaedias or replaced the bellow top flaps on a clock. Afterwards, there might be a documentary that Dad had spotted and circled in the *Radio Times*, something about extreme weather or space, and then it was time for bed. Darren got glimpses of other lives and was aware that some people's existences weren't quite like his; some people were lonely, others were unhappy at home. But as far as he could see, things generally turned out for the best — it was less about fate and more about goodness, he decided. Good people, on balance, experienced good luck. One day, Colin's dad climbed on his motorbike and never came back. See? Things turned out.

Back then everything was predictable, linear. He would follow a predetermined path: school, college and university. It was the way to *get on*, Dad reckoned — it's what he would have done, had he been given the chance. And after college and university, Darren would be rewarded with a life not entirely dissimilar from that of his parents, only better: a bigger house, a nicer car and a more exciting place of work than the Philips factory.

Like the potted seeds in the greenhouse, he grew into his surroundings, warm and fed and watered. And all the time he was growing up he anticipated the day when he would be too big, too important for his container, when a transfer would be necessary and he would be uprooted and transplanted to somewhere better, a place where he could grow without restraint. In the meantime, life was ordinary, unremarkable and occasionally boring. It was, looking back, wonderful.

Exhibit: 'Becky Brookfield — the Untold Story'

Catalogue

Object: Holiday brochures (numerous).

Description: Brochures about beach holidays and winter sports holidays (in original sealed envelopes which were opened and then discarded).

Item Number: 13.

Provenance: Becky Brookfield (my mother) must have ordered lots of brochures because she and Darren Quinn (my dad) were planning to go on holiday together. It is quite likely that she enjoyed some epic holidays as a little girl and wanted to show Darren Quinn all the wonderful things she had seen.

Display: Reversible collage of the two most popular types of holiday brochure: beach and winter sports.

Curator: Clover Quinn.

Keeper: Darren Quinn.

9

There's an art book, *Rubens' Drawings*. It's turquoise, with a sketch of the head and shoulders of a thoughtful toddler on the front. Clover flicks through the pages. The drawings are of people. Black and white, mostly done in chalk, it says. The people are fleshy, soft. They have round shoulders and feathery hair.

As far as she knows, her mother didn't draw. Perhaps she just liked the pictures. But what, in particular, did she admire? Clover can't decide whether her mother preferred the muscly, bare-bottomed men or the group sketches, like *The Holy Family and St John*, which has a mother holding a very fat baby boy while a man, presumably St John, leans in close and a chubby toddler grabs at the mother's skirts. The group is completed by a fluffy dog, though it *could* be a sheep — Clover isn't sure. The best thing about the picture is the way the mother's hand cradles the whole sweep of her baby's calf and it is as clear as day, literally, that she adores him.

Clover looks through the book again, more carefully this time. She likes *The Annunciation*. Like the other pictures, it is black and white — 'a pen and ink wash over black chalk', it says in the description underneath. A sturdy angel and two chubby, cherub-ish creatures are floating just above the ground, reaching out to Mary, who seems surprised, one hand held against her chest, as if she's asking, *Who, me? Are you sure?* Mrs Mackerel has a full colour picture of the Annunciation on the wall in her lounge; it's gaudy, not as nice as the one in the Rubens book. Mrs Mackerel's angel is holding a bunch of flowers — the small, £2.99 kind, not what you'd expect from a heavenly messenger. And the ring of yellow around Mary's hair looks very much like the foam shampoo shield Clover used to wear in the bath when she was small. But at least Mary looks surprised, that's the main thing.

Rubens' picture of the Annunciation was probably her mother's favourite, too. After all, Becky Brookfield, like Mary, was taken by surprise. Clover has a vision, then, of a series of heavenly encounters cut out, mounted and lined along the bedroom wall. A mural of angels and surprised women. It would be epic! She can use the colouring books Dad rescued from the recycling. They are full of heavenly figures, hovering just above the ground, with straight lines shooting out of them to indicate radiation. No, *radiance*.

The next pile is a mix of sheets and towels. She places it on the floor. She doesn't want to miss anything and so, as before, she unfolds and shakes each item before making a new pile. Some of the towels feel new. They're still soft; they don't have that coarse, crispy texture that towels get when they come out of the washing machine. It's the other way round with the sheets: the crispy ones feel new and the soft ones have a smoothed, slept-on feel. She smells them, rubs any softness with the flat of her hand in case it was made by the press of her mother's side or back. When she has worked her way through all the towels and sheets she fetches a whole roll of bin bags from the kitchen. Dad won't notice, there are others in the cupboard. She rips off a bag and packs the towels and sheets into it, keeping a navy bath sheet to go with the holiday display and one set of very soft bedding that *might* bear her mother's stamp. There's a danger the bag will split, so she carries it downstairs carefully. She moves the unfastened radiator and opens the understairs cupboard, where Dad keeps the charity bags people are always stuffing through the letter box, and searches for one with WEDNESDAY written on it. It's tricky to fit the charity bag over the bin bag. It's like putting a sleeping bag back in its cover, something she did once or twice with the sleeping bag Dad bought in case she preferred it to a duvet. Eventually, she manages it. Where to put the bag? Dad started work at eight o'clock this morning, so he'll be back just after four. The charity van should have driven past by then. But will it definitely spot a bag at the dead end of a cul-de-sac? She isn't sure, and she doesn't want to keep watch all afternoon, so she struggles along The Grove with the bag, careful not to scuff it on the pavement. She takes the first left, and then turns left again, down Mrs Knight's road. No one is about, so she leaves the bag outside her house.

* * *

179

Folded up on the bed, previously crushed by the sheets and towels, she finds a T-shirt. It is black with 'I'm flying without wings' written on it. It looks like it could be the one her mother is wearing in the first of the pictures of the two of them together, the one that was taken in the hospital. She examines the T-shirt in the photograph, which is waiting to be incorporated into the 'SURPRISE' display. It is black and baggy with some partially obscured white writing across its chest. It might be the same one, and if it is, it's an actual piece of history and she should display it properly. She is considering attaching a hanger to the picture rail when she has an amazing idea. She peels off the blue gloves, dashes down the stairs — careful! — through the kitchen and into the garden.

It's not a small job: it isn't just a matter of getting it out of the shed, there's other stuff to move first. She steps into the tropical, timbered space and lifts buckets and spades and canes and tools. One by one she puts things on the grass, glancing up at Mrs Mackerel's window, just in case. The dressmaker's dummy has no head and no arms or legs; it's just a wooden stand that supports a dark velvety torso. It has a pair of bumps for boobs, a pinched waist, and a sort of hook-ish handle growing out of its neck in place of a head. There are cobwebs on the velvet and she nearly dies, literally. There's no way she can lift it into the house like that. She finds one of those sticky roller things under the kitchen sink and runs it up and down and over the bumps. Once she is certain that the possibility of spiders has been eliminated, she places her hands around the nip of its waist and lifts the dummy indoors. Then she stuffs the other things back in the shed in any old order and dances the dummy up the stairs.

She places the T-shirt over its head. It looks horribly creased and far too baggy, so she fetches a hair bobble from her room and pulls the T-shirt tight at the back before wrapping the bobble round the clumped material. There. It's not quite right, it looks like a minidress on a one-legged woman, but it'll do for now.

The last of the things on the bed are pillows (without cases), cushions (with covers — plain, cream), a book — *Faster Pasta: Good Value Family Meals*, two pairs of shoes (flip-flops with pink sparkly flowers on the toe-divider and a pair of plain, black patent heels), three framed pictures (one of a sunset, one of a puppy that looks like it's been cut out of a calendar — the grid of the days is ghosting through the dog's golden coat — and, best of all, an old school photograph of Uncle Jim and her mother), a key ring (YOU ARE THE KEY TO MY HEART), a selection of fridge magnets and a couple of other kitchen-ish things with nice sayings on them, a box containing a half-used bottle of perfume (J'adore by Christian Dior) and a blizzard of carrier-bag flakes. She sprays the perfume and follows the mist with her nose, inhaling deep and long. It's a bit like oranges . . . and also flowers. It's as close as she will *ever* get to smelling her mother. She lifts her arm up to her nose to sniff the bare crease of her elbow — funny how you can't smell yourself. Dad smells of soap and deodorant and sometimes of outdoors, especially when he has been at the allotment and the soil has snuck under his nails and into the whorly creases of his fingers. She sprays again, this time directly on to the inside of her arm, and as the perfume smells like her mother, she decides to like it.

Now the bed is cleared she can climb on it. She tries to brush the carrier-bag flakes off the bare mattress but they cling to her fingers and arms like feathers. The more she brushes, the clingier they become. In the end she has to fetch the hoover.

The room looks much better afterwards, despite the fact that it is still quite crowded. She opens the first of the boxes by the window. It strikes her that the air in the box might be old, from the time when she was a baby; air that passed in and out of her mother's tissues. She leans into the box and breathes it in.

The box contains underwear. Bras and knickers, all different colours; some are matching sets, others are plain. Several are slightly grey from the wash. She fastens a red and white polka-dot bra around her torso and slips her arms through the straps, just to see. It is massive. If she ever needed to be winched off a mountain, she could probably lie in it.

There are tights and socks and some of those longer, fancy bra things with hard bits in, like ribs, but going down instead of across. There is a moment when she feels like she might be poking her nose into something that is not her business.

But the feeling doesn't last long — these are her mother's belongings, after all.

She keeps the polka-dot bra and the matching pants. She also keeps two pairs of socks one for the display and another — black, patterned by small pink rabbits — for herself, to wear in the winter, under jeans. She unfastens and flattens the now empty box and stuffs the remaining underwear into a bin bag. She'll dispose of it later.

Her stomach is rumbling. Time for lunch and then her jobs at the allotment. This has been her best day yet. She has got so much done. Before she goes downstairs, she slips her feet into her mother's high-heeled shoes. They are slightly big: both a little too wide and a little too long. She steps along the floor at the foot of the bed, her toes and heels pressing in the exact same places that her mother's toes and heels pressed. She wobbles over to the window, feet knocking against the floorboards. She squeezes around the boxes and looks out at the gardens: hers and Dad's (untidy), Mrs Mackerel's (paved), and beyond. This was her mother's room. This was her mother's view. These are her mother's shoes. She teeters over to the cleared space at the end of the bed. Back and forth she treads, back and forth, and back and forth, as if, eventually, she might step into her mother's life.

* * *

Dagmar is sitting outside the corner shop with her trolley. Clover brakes and stops. This is the third time she's happened upon her waiting here. She hopes she doesn't wait every afternoon on the off-chance, but she suspects she might.

'We are going to the allotment?' Dagmar asks, as if *she* is inviting *her*.

'Okay,' Clover says. But she stays on her bike, skating it along the pavement with the tips of her toes. Dagmar will have to keep up.

'You have gone to Blackpool?'

'Nope. At the weekend.'

'You are lucky.'

'I suppose. It might be fun to go on a proper holiday, though,' Clover says. 'Somewhere abroad. I'm trying to get my dad to think about it.'

'And is he saying?'

'*You don't have to go somewhere foreign to be happy; you can just as easily be happy at home.*' She speaks in a mean voice that doesn't sound at all like Dad. '*Who'd look after the allotment?*' she says in the same silly voice.

'And your mum is saying?'

'It's just me and my dad.'

Dagmar makes the usual surprised face and Clover braces herself for questions, but Dagmar continues, 'I am looking after it for you.'

'Oh, it's okay — it won't, he won't . . . ' she tries to explain, suddenly ashamed of herself for making so much of Dad's refusal.

'He is not letting me?'

'We aren't going.'

'But *if* you go, he is not letting me?'

'It doesn't matter.'

She is going too fast. She slows a little and lets

her red trainers drag. Dagmar's trolley wheels scrape against stones and her breath hisses in and out. She sounds like a bicycle pump.

'What does your dad do?'

'He is watching television.'

'Is it his day off?'

'No.'

'Mine gets two days off every week. One week out of five, he gets a long weekend. He sometimes helps Colin, his mate, with jobs if he's got a day off in the week.' She pauses to allow Dagmar to reply. When she doesn't, Clover carries on. 'He'd get more money if he did some overtime on the park and ride, but he likes to do stuff with Colin. They've known each other since they were tiny. They're like b — ' she nearly said it, the *bosom* word, ' . . . like best friends,' she says.

'My dad is not working.'

She feels as if she is forcing Dagmar into a corner. But Dagmar could change the subject and talk about something else if she wanted, couldn't she?

'Maybe he'll find a job soon,' she says firmly, ending the awkwardness for them both.

They turn off the road. Clover dismounts and they walk down the track. She takes the key out of her pocket, but when she tries to place it in the lock, the gentlest of nudges sends the heavy gate swinging open by itself.

'Oh, it's dropped again.'

'Dropped?'

'The gate. It's heavy. Sometimes it drops and then you don't need a key to get in. You can just give it a little push and it opens on its own. Someone will tighten it up, eventually.' She holds one of the bars so the gate doesn't pivot all the way back. They step through and she closes it carefully, making sure the latch has caught.

It's hot. The air is thick with dust and pollen and the thrum of growing. Someone has trimmed the long grass at either side of the path. It's so hot that the sun has bleached the offcuts to hay. It lies there, white and soft, like fur. They kick it as they walk.

Dagmar grabs the bucket from the bike and Clover lifts the carpet to uncover the watering can. It takes a few journeys back and forth before they've watered everything.

'Want to do some weeding?'

'How are you knowing what is a weed?'

'Basically, it's anything you didn't plant. If something's not growing in the right place at the right time, it's a weed. So you could say the raspberries are weeds. We didn't plant them, they just keep growing every year. But we let them, because we like them. The nettles keep growing, too. But we don't like them, *obviously*, and you mustn't weed them without gloves, not even if you get them right at the bottom — they'll wreck your fingers.

'I don't know all the names of everything, Dad does, he's epic at it, but it doesn't really matter, you don't need to know what everything's called. See these ones? And these? They're weeds. Just rip them up and chuck them on the grass.'

They crouch on the pathways that dissect the plot and pick the weeds. The soil is so dusty in

186

the places they haven't watered that it only takes a gentle tug to make the roots slide right out.

'My dad, he was in Afghanistan,' Dagmar says.

'I thought it was just America and us.'

'No.'

She would like to ask if Dagmar's dad killed anyone. But it might be rude.

'He was working in the field hospital in Kabul.'

Clover looks down: it will be easier for Dagmar to keep talking, she thinks, if she carries on with the job, uprooting the weeds and dropping them on the grass beside her.

'He was seeing things.'

Clover stands for a moment and stretches the crouch out of her knees before squatting again. Dagmar's face is pinched. There is a stripe of colour along each cheek.

'Very bad things. And now . . . he is like you say about your uncle. He is not himself.'

Dagmar's dad is big. Clover saw him at parents' evening: a pale-skinned, mournful-looking man, the tallest person there by miles. Luke Barton called him Frankenstein, afterwards. 'Dracula's dad looks like Frankenstein — course he does!' he said.

'This is a weed?' Dagmar asks.

'Yeah.'

'What is the name?'

'I don't know.'

'And this one here is a weed?'

'Yeah.'

'What is the name?'

'Clover.'

'Your name is the same as a weed?'

'It's only a weed if it's in the wrong place at the wrong time, remember. Some farmers grow clover. On purpose.'

The clover roots mat the ground. Dagmar pulls, and a whole network lifts.

'Maybe your dad will get better.'

'The field hospital was closing when I am seven.'

Clover slides from the crouch on to her bottom and sits cross-legged on the grass, all pretence of weeding abandoned.

'It is not so bad when I am going to school. In the holidays I feel the shouting coming. And I go out.'

'All day, by yourself?'

'If he is having a bad night it has to be very quiet.'

'*Recalculating*' — a harsh, computerised voice blasts out of Dagmar's trolley.

'What's that?'

'Oh, it is . . . ' Dagmar reaches into the trolley. She stirs its insides, her hand eventually emerging with a chunky rectangular device. 'It is a satnav,' she says, passing it to Clover so she can see it properly. 'From eBay.'

'Like Google Maps, but old? Where are you going?'

'Nowhere.'

'Why is it recalculating?' There's a sliding button on the top of the device. Clover flicks it with her finger and a map appears on the matte, old-fashioned screen. Despite what Dagmar said, there's a route and, in the bottom left-hand corner, an estimated time of arrival: early tomorrow morning. 'So where are you going, really?'

'I am going nowhere.'

'All right. Where is it *set* to go?'

'Home.'

Clover puzzles over this. She doesn't know where Dagmar lives, but it can't be all that far away. At the moment the map fills the screen, but it only shows as far as the roundabout at the end of Moss Lane. There must be a way to zoom out.

'Last holiday we drive home and use the satnav. I press here: Recently Found. See? And I am finding all the places. Now I know how far I am from Uherské Hradiště.'

'From where?'

'Uherské Hradiště.'

'Oo-her-ske Rhad-deesh-de-yeh,' Clover tries. 'Where's that?'

'Home.'

'I thought you meant *here* when you said home. So how far is it?'

Dagmar takes the satnav and presses the screen. 'One thousand, nine hundred and twenty-five miles.'

'You miss it.'

'Yes.'

Clover thinks. Sometimes when people miss things they'd rather not talk about them. Like Dad, for example. Perhaps Dagmar is different. 'What do you miss?' she asks.

'The Christmas market.'

'We have one, you know. In December, at the weekends.'

'I miss name days.'

'What are they?'

'All the names are having their own day. Mine is the twentieth of December. I get a present. The window of every flower shop says DAGMAR, to remind people.'

'What's the day for Clover?'

'Clover is not on the list.'

'Oh.'

'There is a list of the names and a calendar. One name for every day. People are choosing names from the list in the old times. Now they don't have to.'

'What else?'

'Going to Vlčnov to see *Jízda králů.*'

'What's that?'

'In English, it is . . . the Ride of the Kings. There is a boy riding a horse. He is being the king, but he is dressing as a lady because he is in a . . . he is pretending . . . in a . . . '

'Disguise?'

'Yes. And the horses — lots of them — are covered in flowers. And there are costumes. The ladies have folded sleeves . . . ' She demonstrates, bending the edge of her T-shirt over and over itself.

'Pleats?'

'Yes, pleats. And big skirts and long boots.'

'Do you have one of those costumes?'

'Yes. And I learn the dancing. I think it is a bit silly at home. But here, I am missing it.'

'And friends?'

Dagmar tugs another web of clover roots. 'Yes. At home I am having friends.' She clears her

190

throat. It's an impatient, *that's enough*, sort of sound. As if she is cross with herself for talking like this. 'You will tell people about my dad?'

'No.' Clover considers telling her a secret too, by way of reassurance. A sort of information exchange. Then she remembers Uncle Jim and supposes that Dagmar witnessing his bedsit counts for something.

'And you are promising?'

'Yeah.'

'Thank you.'

When someone tells you something, you like them more, not less, she thinks. It's nice to hear stuff from Dagmar that she would never have guessed. If only Dad would tell her stuff, too.

They finish the weeding in silence then walk back up the path to the gate, accompanied by the tick of her bike, the knock of the bucket against its frame and the scrape as the hard wheels of Dagmar's trolley graze the ground.

At the end of Moss Lane, outside the corner shop, Dagmar extends her hand. Her palm and fingers and the translucent skin of her wrist are bobbled by a series of nettle stings.

'It is the weeds. The last one I pick is wrong.' She rubs the stings against her shirt and the leg of her trousers and laughs in a pained, funny-bone way.

'Come with me.'

'But your dad is not — '

'Oh, he's fine,' Clover says. It seems that they may be turning into friends, which means Dagmar will have to meet Dad at some point, and she'll realise he's not scary at all, won't she? 'Come on. We've got some cream.'

★ ★ ★

When Dagmar steps down the hall and into the dining room and sees Dad's makeshift shelves and all the *stuff*: cuckoo-clock boxes, shoe boxes, unstrung ukuleles, empty sweet tins, reference books, candles — *everything*, she whispers, 'Wow,' and it is fine.

The cream is in a box in one of the kitchen cupboards with other medicine that isn't dangerous if it's taken by accident. Clover hands the tube to Dagmar and watches as she smears it over her hand and wrist.

Next, she loads two spoons with crunchy Biscoff spread and passes one over. 'You have to try this. I think it might be the yummiest thing in the world.'

Dagmar sniffs the lump and licks its edge before sliding the whole spoon into her mouth. She nods her head and makes a noise of agreement. It seems she thinks it might be the yummiest thing in the world too, and Clover enjoys the dual pleasures of biscuity spread and sharing.

★ ★ ★

She and Dad watch *Bake Off* together. Tonight it's bread. When the bakers are doing the signature challenge, which is rye bread, Dad starts talking.

'Edna says she saw you this afternoon as she passed the shops on Bispham Road.'

'I didn't see her,' she says, hoping he'll shush.

'She was on the bus. You were with a friend?'

'Yes,' she says.

'A boy?'

'No.'

'Edna says it was a boy.'

'It wasn't.'

'Is he your boyfriend?'

She turns away from the rye bread. 'No! It was Dagmar. She's a girl. With short hair.'

'Are you sure?'

'Am I sure she's a girl?'

'I just want you to tell me the truth.'

'I am!'

'Does she come here while I'm at work?'

'No! Well, only — '

'I don't want people round while I'm not here.'

'I *know*.' She feels in the wrong, like she's in trouble, but she hasn't done *anything*.

'And if — *if* — you had a boyfriend you could tell me, you know.'

'I haven't!'

'All right. I'm just saying. Because you're growing up. And one day you will — have a boyfriend, I mean.'

She turns back to the telly. Stares straight ahead at it, trying to focus on the rye bread.

'Or a *friend* who's not a boy — if that's what you . . . you can tell me anything.'

Rye bread, rye bread, rye bread . . . Is he asking whether she fancies boys or girls? Why does he think it's okay to do this on a Wednesday evening, completely out of the blue, when she is trying to watch her programme?

'You might not want to tell Colin, though. He'd probably have a heart attack. Say you're far too young.'

She wishes he'd stop trying to smooth things over and just shush.

'He loves you.'

'Uh-huh.'

'He's thought the world of you since you were a baby.'

'I know.'

'Remember that time when you were little and he said, 'I really don't want to go to work today,' and you said, 'I bet you don't want to be bald, either'? He thought it was hilarious.'

'Dad.'

'Yes?'

'Can we watch the baking?'

'Sorry.'

For the showstopper the bakers make pesto pinwheels, cheesecake brioche, a Spanish crown topped with gold-foiled olives, and all sorts of amazing, bready delights.

Dad gets up while the judges are deliberating and returns a few minutes later with a couple of rounds of buttered toast cut into triangles.

'I reckon it's a nice structure and a good consistency,' he says.

'Me, too.'

'A soft white bread with hidden wholegrain and no bits,' he adds.

'I didn't *knead* to know that, Dad.'

194

'Do you want me to *prove* it to you?'

'No, it's okay, I'll use my *loaf*.'

'I give up. In fact, I *seed* . . . no? Really? All right, you win,' he says.

★   ★   ★

It's too hot. She lies in bed, duvet kicked into a bundle on the floor, listening to Dad, who is downstairs trying to work out the chords for 'Happy'. '*I'll be just fine, I'll be just fine*': he sings the same line again and again, testing different strumming patterns.

The house feels different. It's as if her mother is seeping through the walls. She presses her arm to her nose; she can still smell the perfume on her skin. She has a new sense of the fact that she is made of her mother. Bone of my bones, flesh of my flesh — she has heard that somewhere, it's probably religious, in which case Mrs Mackerel will have said it. Her mother runs through her bones and flesh.

Her feet, if she stretches, can almost touch the end of the bed. She is growing into herself. She wonders what her mother looked like age twelve. Had she started her period? Is everything you will ever be already there, inside you, like a seed, or are you only partly put together, like those cake mixes Dad sometimes buys — just add oil and water? Once, her mother was inside Nanna Maureen, and once, she, Clover, was inside her mother, like those nesting dolls: inside, inside, inside.

Since she bought the notebook, she has

written down the things she remembers people saying about her mother. Colin: 'Becky thought I was a bit of a twat, which I probably was.' Grandad: 'She knew how to be quiet and didn't talk all the time, unlike some.' Uncle Jim: 'She was good at looking after people.' Mrs Mackerel: 'A big girl, *God bless her*. I've seen bigger, mind.' They're scraps. Fragments. A jumble. But jumbles are sometimes nice, she thinks. Like the back wall of the allotment with the raspberries and nettles and rosemary, the crocuses, bluebells and pussy willows, all higgledy-piggledy. Anyway, once she has arranged the displays and written the text, her mother's life will be less of a jumble, and when she finally shows Dad the room it'll be like one of those renovation programmes where they do a big reveal. It will be a nervous moment — it always is because no one knows how people will feel about the newness, and it sometimes takes them a moment to get used to it, but they are mostly pleased. There are times when they aren't, of course. She rolls on to her stomach and buries her face in the puff of her pillow, allowing herself a moment of worry. Rolling back, she decides it will be okay. She'll have thought of a proper speech by then, an explanation of what she's done and why. And once she's explained, she'll open the door slowly, and Dad will be shocked but pleased, and he'll tell her about the items, and why he kept them; he'll make sure she's got all the pieces in the right places. There'll be details and descriptions. No fobbing off, no cul-de-sac conversations.

And then, and then . . .

And then, maybe after a little while, once the exhibit's purpose has been achieved, it will be okay to move it, like they do at real museums; to box it up and put it in the object store — otherwise known as the loft — and use the second bedroom for something else.

Dad's singing floats up the stairs: '*Clap along if you feel like happiness is the truth.*' Happiness is so many things. They made a list in English last term, a mixture of other people's ideas and their own. Happiness is a warm gun (The Beatles) and a warm blanket (Schulz). Happiness is Mini-shaped (Mini). You can't buy happiness but you can buy tea and that's kind of the same thing (Lipton). Happiness is amazing first impressions and having breakfast outside every morning (Jet2). Happiness is a super-comfy sofa bed, a few side tables and a strong Wi-Fi connection (IKEA). Those things *may* be true, but she suspects they're not. She has her own list. Happiness is Grandad saving links to cat videos in a Word document so he can share them when she visits. Happiness is when Uncle Jim and Dad accidentally get on with each other. It's eating Biscoff out of the jar with a spoon. It's Mrs Mackerel getting her words mixed up and Dad making crappy things to eat during *Bake Off*. And it will be learning all about her mother.

The sheet is warm. She moves her legs around, searching for a cool spot. Her room is crowded with shadows; it is almost as full of stuff as the second bedroom was. It occurs to her that she could also empty and arrange her own things.

There is so much she doesn't want, despite Dad's concern that she might one day need it. But it will have to wait. The summer is melting away and she hasn't finished her mother's exhibit.

Exhibit: 'Becky Brookfield — the Untold Story'

Catalogue

Object: Art book. 'Rubens' Drawings'.

Description: A book of drawings by the artist Rubens. It says in the book that he did not sign his drawings because he did not think they were as important as his paintings. They are still very good, though.

Item Number: 15.

Provenance: Becky Brookfield (my mother) chose this book because she especially liked Rubens' drawings of families.

Display: On page 40, 'The Annunciation', a drawing of Mary, a big angel and two small fat angels that is done in pen and ink wash over black chalk.

Curator: Clover Quinn.

Keeper: Darren Quinn.

10

She's gone up to bed early. He's meant to think she's tired, but she'll be knitting the scarf he isn't supposed to know about. He missed *University Challenge* when he was doing a late on Tuesday and he couldn't watch it last night because it was the baking programme, so he's found it on the iPlayer instead. There's something razor-ish and wit-sharpening about the violin music at the beginning of the programme. Ready, steady — *think*, it seems to say.

In this episode the University of Sussex is up against St Peter's College, Oxford. They're all dead posh and there isn't a woman on either team. It wouldn't have even registered before he had Clover; having a daughter does that to you — makes you wonder where all the women are.

He always aims to get at least one question right. If he gets two or, God forbid, three, he allows himself a beer before bed. The first question is about The Beatles. It's a gift. 'What short adjective links a tea, lighter in body than green tea, and The Beatles' ninth official album?' Any old fool'd get it. Now he can relax. Questions about poetry, Shakespeare, Charles Dickens and politics follow. He doesn't know any of it. But a cloud formation question saves him and he gets up from the sofa to fetch a beer from the fridge.

He was supposed to go to university.

Birmingham — far enough to leave home and near enough to come back regularly. He still has the letter offering him a place. The prospectus will be somewhere, too. And the letter agreeing to a one-year deferral. In the dining room, perhaps. Or here in the kitchen, in one of the drawers or a cupboard. He used to get them out and look at them sometimes when Clover was small — idiot. He read that bloody prospectus a thousand times when he was still at college. He used a luminous highlighter to score through the words he was looking forward to appropriating: *meteorology, deforestation, globalisation, geomorphological processes* — pretty soon the page headed 'Geography BSc Hons' was a resplendent yellow.

'Darren's not going anywhere, are you?' Dad said that summer, after the exams, when Mum was first diagnosed. 'He wouldn't dream of it, would you, son?'

It was a warning, disguised as reassurance. *Don't you dare leave me to cope with this by myself* — that's what Dad was really saying. It was hard to take in: university had always been part of the map of his life. And Mum didn't offer any encouragement. There was no 'you go on, love, I'll be fine', no sense that it would be okay for him to continue with his life as planned. So he didn't.

He slumps back on the sofa and slurps the beer. If he'd gone away he'd be someone else entirely now. If wishes were horses.

★   ★   ★

201

When Mum was first ill he got a part-time job working in the newsagent where he'd been a paper boy. Something to do while he waited for her to get better, he thought. Somewhere to go when he wasn't taking it in turns with Dad to ferry her back and forth to radiotherapy and chemotherapy and laser treatment and photodynamic therapy. Somewhere to go in between hospital visits. Somewhere to go in between hospice visits. Something to do while he waited for her to die, he later realised.

On the mornings when he wasn't at the newsagent from daybreak, folding papers for the boys and girls who would deliver them, he looked after Mum, just as she'd looked after him. He helped her down the stairs and made her milky tea and white-bread toast. He cut the toast into triangles and slotted it into a rack, serving it with Marmite, marmalade or the last of the previous year's home-made raspberry jam, while GMTV played on the portable telly in the kitchen.

The prospectus remained on his desk. Bedtime reading. It was easy to believe that the world it contained was as flat and two dimensional as its pages, just waiting to be animated by his arrival. Easy, until mid-December, when people who'd gone away started coming home for the holiday, and the sight of them in town or at the social club on a Friday night nudged his equilibrium.

Weekends back then began with *TFI Friday*, which he and Colin watched through a cloud of Lynx and hairspray. Darren arranged his curtained locks à la David Beckham. Colin's hairline was already creeping away from his forehead, it wouldn't be long before he'd adopt the Jason Statham, but back then he still brushed what hair he had forward and sprayed it into a brittle, Shredded Wheat-like fringe. Sometimes they'd walk to Bliss and pick one of the building's three sticky-carpeted floors: pop, indie or dance. They'd wonder whether they were dancing or drinking in the exact spot where Tom Jones and The Beatles once stood. And when they'd had a few drinks they'd engage in a game of spot-the-Everton-player. Other times, they'd go down the social club for an evening of passive smoking, karaoke and snooker. They'd drink. Talk to girls — it'd be another couple of years before Colin came out. Provide a bit of hands-on snooker tutelage — *let me help you with that, love.* Follow up with a snog in the car park — cop a feel, if they were lucky. Go back to Colin's for a few more beers and watch *Eurotrash* with Kelly until Colin teased her away.

'She's stayed up specially, just to be in the same room as you, haven't you, Kel?' he'd say. 'She gets the fanny gallops whenever she thinks about you, don't you, Kel?'

Kelly'd take so much, and then she'd rise from the armchair like a queen and disappear upstairs.

★   ★   ★

Mum died in the November, just over two years after she'd been diagnosed. It was too late for him to start university — he was going to have to reapply anyway, he'd lost his deferred place when he hadn't taken it up the previous October. There were the new tuition fees to consider; he'd done a bit of reading, it seemed he'd be all right, but maintenance grants were in the process of being scrapped and replaced by loans. Dad watched the news, muttering, 'Neither a borrower not a lender be.' Christmas happened. Darren wondered how to stay with Dad and how to leave.

They settled into a routine. Between them they mastered an adequate, if somewhat boring, menu: beans on toast, cheese on toast, omelettes, ham and salad, frozen fish with oven chips, and, for an occasional treat, Fray Bentos pies with mushy peas. It would be better in the summer, when the vegetables came in. After they'd eaten, someone did the washing-up, and the other someone dried the dishes and put them away, and then there was the rest of each evening to get through. They put the telly on, but *Coronation Street* wasn't the same without Mum's exclamations and commentary. They still had dial-up back then, so Dad would boot up the second-hand Intel Pentium PC he'd bought and allow himself thirty minutes of clock browsing on eBay. He set an alarm and repeatedly glanced from it to the clocks on the screen, racing against time. Before he logged off he'd reread the 'Know Your Prostate' section of the 'Chronic Prostatitis' web page. 'There's no link between prostatitis and prostate cancer,' he'd say, as if voicing the facts was its own kind of preventative medicine. Afterwards he'd flip open an encyclopaedia. And sigh. Flick through a couple of pages. And sigh again. It was difficult to figure out how to be a good son without Mum acting as mediator: 'What your dad means is . . . ' And perhaps Dad was experiencing a similar lack: 'Darren would really like it if you'd just . . . ' They'd always been spokes on the wheels of her conversations.

Darren turned twenty-one in the March, decided he was fed up of sorting and folding papers and selling Mars Bars, and, having seen a recruitment advert on the back of a number 43, got a proper job driving a bus. He was accompanied for two weeks, initially travelling as a passenger, memorising the route until he was allowed to drive in service, colleague at the ready, just in case. Then he was on his own. He circled the town, like a plane in a holding pattern, the knowledge that he'd soon be taking off making him view the place with a new fondness.

It wasn't a bad job. Something to do while he waited for Dad to get better, he thought. Something to do when he wasn't tiptoeing around the house, when he wasn't answering the phone which Dad left ringing, when he wasn't assuring concerned callers that they were fine because they had each other. Something to do when he wasn't wondering how two people who had lived together for so long could have so little of each other, could come ungrafted so quickly.

While Mum was dying he felt sorry for himself and Dad: sorry that she was going away and leaving them. He felt sorry for her in a different way: sorry that she was ill and suffering. It didn't occur to him that as much as they were losing her, she was losing them; that it may have felt to her like he and Dad were the ones who were going somewhere and leaving her behind. It was only after Clover was born that he considered how he would feel if he discovered he was dying. *Considered* — ha! It was only after Clover was born that he lay awake at night *agonising* over what would become of her if anything happened to him. It was only while looking at her that he finally began to get some small understanding of how his mum must have felt about him; how difficult it must have been for her to leave him, just out of his teens; how hard-fought her outward bravery had been. The mere thought of leaving Clover, even in many years' time, once she is happily settled, is appalling because surely no one will ever love her in the unconditional, no-holds-barred way he does, and he knows how it feels to be left alone in the world without anyone who loves you like that.

Not that he was completely alone after Mum died. He had Colin, which was something. Colin, who had been working his way through a series of diplomas since he left school: bricklaying, electrical installation, painting and decorating. Colin, whose insubordinate attitude and low boredom threshold repeatedly led to trouble. He'd had a few jobs, but he never lasted long. A week or two of any kind of repetitive work — stripping and glossing doors, sanding and varnishing floorboards, slapping emulsion on ceilings — and he was ready to explode.

'I can't help it,' he said. 'Remember how we had to sit quietly in assembly? Especially during the Lord's Prayer? It was so boring that you'd start wondering what would happen if you shouted. No? Really? You never sat there wondering what would happen if you yelled 'fart' or 'bugger'? Thing is, once you've had the thought and you're awake to the possibility of doing it, it's a battle between your brain and your mouth. I know, it's your brain that tells your mouth what to do, so it's not actually a battle, but it feels like one. And when you've spent two weeks mixing plaster and wiping down skirting boards, or getting the drop right on a fancy wallpaper — the stuff with big patterns — you start to get that school assembly feeling, and the thought that you've got to do the same thing *again* and *again* for *days* makes you wonder what would happen if you said, 'Fetch your own water' or 'I'm *not* wasting paper, it's your own fault for choosing such an arse-backwards pattern.''

Colin had a go at being a postman and a milkman. But the daily sameness invited the possibility of all kinds of imagined *coulds*. He *could* peep inside an interesting parcel and pretend it had been damaged in transit, he *could* ring the bell when he delivered the milk — *wakey, wakey!* So he started working for himself. Doing a little bit of everything. Less chance of getting bored. He joined a gym, which also helped. It tired him out a bit. If his workouts were essentially the same, at least the music channel varied from week to week.

After Darren started work on the buses, Colin prodded him about university at regular intervals.

'You *are* going, aren't you? You can't just stay here.'

Of course he was going. Of course he was. But the longer he stayed, the more he felt that there was an underlying vanity in the whole scheme, and the idea that he could make himself different — better, somehow — by filling his head with stuff his friends and family had never needed to know began to unsettle him.

'You'll go away, like you always planned, and afterwards you'll come back here and do something different.'

'Like what?'

'I don't know, do I? Some sort of geographical thing.'

Darren found he didn't know, either. It was becoming harder to imagine another version of himself. Harder to believe that he *could* go away and come back. Colin might be egging him on, but his legs felt as heavy as if someone was crouched beside him, arms clasped around his knees.

★ ★ ★

They call people by their surnames on *University Challenge*. If he was one of the contestants, the voiceover bloke would call out 'Quinn!' when he buzzed with the right answers.

Buzz — 'Quinn!' — 'White!'

Buzz — 'Quinn!' — 'Mother-of-pearl clouds!'

'Hello, my name's Darren Quinn, from Merseyside, and I'm reading Geography.' That's the way he'd say it if he was sitting behind one of the *University Challenge* desks. *Reading*, not studying.

The gong sounds. Paxman tells Sussex that they could have taken it. But, of course, they didn't. 'It's goodbye from me,' he says. As the violin music spikes back to life, Darren's phone also sounds. He glances at the screen. It's late and it's not a number he knows.

'I'd like to speak to Darren Quinn, please.'

'Speaking.'

'We've got you down as next of kin for Jim Brookfield?'

'That's right.'

'Mr Brookfield was admitted to the Emergency Assessment Unit earlier this evening . . . '

He stands and slides his feet into his shoes without undoing the laces. As he twists to allow the shoes' crushed heels to unfurl, the woman's words register: she *isn't* calling from the psychiatric hospital. Why not? His ears are lagging behind; he hears the words *poorly* and *overdose*. His knees slacken. He sits back down and checks the bump of his pocket for his keys. It was just the one beer. He'll be fine to drive, won't he?

' . . . bring some things?'

'I'll come now, shall I?'

There's a pause and then she speaks again, slowly, and it's clear that she is repeating herself. 'He's not in any immediate danger, so you *don't* need to come now. If there's any change during the night, we'll call you. If you could bring a few things in the morning?'

'All right.'

After he hangs up, it's the usual: he didn't ask the right questions, didn't find out exactly what has happened. He thinks about calling back, about making a list before he dials, so he doesn't forget anything:

1. Who brought him in?
2. What's wrong?
3. What do you mean by *poorly?*
4. What do you mean by *stable?*

And the question that will bother him all night:

5. Was it on purpose?

He'll wait, though. He doesn't like to make a fuss.

The beer is fizzing around his stomach. He should go to bed. Get some sleep. He's going to have to tell Clover in the morning and he doesn't have anything nice to give her. There's a balance to strike in these situations. Bad news needs to be offset, neutralised: 'Uncle Jim's in hospital again — I thought you might like these roller skates'; 'Uncle Jim's not coming for your birthday — here's a book about drawing animals.' It's always better when he can plant something in her hands, replace what he has stolen with something real.

It's perfectly possible to have a happy

childhood. He should know. If he thinks very hard he can retrieve a wisp of annoyance about the times when Mum made banana Angel Delight instead of butterscotch; he can mine some residual embarrassment at the way Dad insisted on wearing a shirt and tie whenever they went anywhere, even to the supermarket, as if without the reinforcement of the tie his neck might fall off; and he can access an ounce of indignation (tempered by a measure of relief) at not being allowed to go to a rave in Sheffield with Colin when he was sixteen. No one died; no one lost themselves. If only he could arrange equally inconsequential sadnesses for Clover.

Of course, Becky had a shitty childhood. Whenever she spoke about it she began with the words 'This really happened', as though she thought he wouldn't believe her. 'This really happened', and then she'd say something terrible: we went to school hungry; she hit us in the stomach because it didn't leave a mark; we were locked in our room after tea; Jim would wet himself when she shouted. He knew there was more, stuff she couldn't think about, let alone repeat. At least the sadness in Clover's life isn't her mother's kind. Still, it's more than he ever wanted. And Jim is a regular contributor. He picks his moments: Christmas, birthdays, week-ends off — all right, he doesn't exactly pick them, but still.

Darren remembers the drive to Liverpool on Christmas Day, the roads empty because everyone else, all the normal families, were relaxing after dinner, playing charades or whatever it is they do. As he drove he remembered Christmas in his own home. The long afternoon, Mum perched on the sofa with a small glass of sherry ready to toast Her Majesty at the end of her speech. Dad rolling his eyes, pretending irritation as a means of gaining brownie points for indulgence. And Darren, sitting on the pink and grey armchair, full of roast potatoes and Fry's Turkish delight, surrounded by his booty. It was cosy, predictable. Nothing like the ghostly drive to Liverpool, *The Best Christmas Album in the World, Ever!* playing in the car. '*Simply having a wonderful Christmas time*' — ha!

Clover had grabbed the ukulele as they left the house. When they got there Darren did 'Jingle Bells' in the day room. Everyone joined in, even Jim, who skipped his usual jokes about George Formby and pervy window cleaners. He had a bash at 'Chestnuts Roasting on an Open Fire' too, which he'd been practising in the evenings. Made a few mistakes. No one minded. Clover was cheerful on the way home, apparently contented to have spent the afternoon with a festival of makeshift relatives. Maybe it wasn't so bad.

★　★　★

His room is so stuffy he can almost feel the air brushing against him like cotton wool. He opens the window, hoping the cooler, outside air will push its way through the fuzz and into the room. The bed creaks as he sits on it. He pulls off his

212

shoes and unpeels his socks. Stands. Unzips his trousers and sheds his polo shirt. All the while his thoughts are penduluming between *selfish git* and *poor sod*; his stomach tilts with the sway of it.

The book he bought the other night sits on the chipboard bedside unit, still wrapped in string and brown paper. He unfastens and unwraps the book — it doesn't matter if he has a bad night, it's his long weekend off. No work tomorrow, Saturday, Sunday or Monday. No jobs with Colin, either. Just him and Clover. And Jim, too, now.

He reads the prologue. The book isn't what Edna imagined. It can't possibly be. She's got the wrong end of the stick again. It's funny, but not in ways she'd appreciate or understand. It's also horrifying. In the opening scene a chubby girl, who turns out to be the Morticia woman on the front cover, is bullied by a gang of boys. There's a bit about feminism, which explains some of what the woman in the shop was going on about — nothing about standing on chairs, though; not yet, anyway. And then the poor chubby girl has her first period and there's no one for her to talk to; no one will explain what's going on. She's clueless and it's awful. He shuts the book and sticks it on the floor.

It's so bloody hot. He lies on his back, staring at the ceiling. The last train squeals as it rounds the corner and comes into the station. He thinks of those final passengers, stealing back from Manchester, Bolton and Wigan. They'll be stepping on to the lonely, unmanned platform, climbing the metal steps to the brow of the bridge and hurrying along familiar streets made strange by the dark. The tug of home — he feels it as he drives the bus back to the garage when he's on lates; the way, at the end of a long day, it reels you in. The train cries as it snakes out of the station. It's too hot to settle. He rolls the duvet over and over until it sits at the end of the bed like a hay bale. There. He lies down again. Slides a hand inside his boxers and closes his eyes.

★   ★   ★

'ARE YOU UP?'

Of course he's up. He ran for the phone in case it was the hospital, but it's the first day of his weekend off — he should have known who'd be calling.

'I DIDN'T GET YOU OUT OF BED, DID I?'

'No.' He always says no, even when the phone stabs deep into his sleep, puncturing his dreams and sending him stumbling down the stairs, half-blind, heart thudding, morning erection tenting his boxers.

'HAVE YOU GOT ANY PLANS?'

'Not much — '

'You could GO ON A DATE.'

Oh God, not again.

'I'm happy to LOOK AFTER Clover. She could STAY OVERNIGHT.'

'I'm not going on a date.'

Clover appears at the top of the stairs,

bleary-eyed, hair wild. He waves her back to bed.

'NO MAN IS AN ICEBERG.'

'I'm fine. Clover and me are — '

'It's NOT GOOD for a man to be ALONE.'

'I'm not alone, I've — '

'There's a LID for EVERY POT.'

'Well . . . I'm not sure I — '

'You'll be off to the ALLOTMENT soon?'

'Later. I'm going to visit Jim. In hospital.'

'OH NO!'

'I'm not a hundred per cent sure what's happened, I — '

'You always get THE BLUNT OF IT.'

'It's all right,' he says, feeling, as ever, obliged to stick up for Jim in the face of external criticism. 'I don't mind.'

'YOU'RE A GOOD MAN — the way you CARRY ON in the FACE OF ABSURDITY. If you'd just TIDY UP YOUR GARDEN, I'd have NO COMPLAINTS.'

'Okay,' he says. 'I'll do it.'

'I DON'T BELIEVE YOU.'

'I will. Promise.'

★　★　★

Jim is hollowed out. His bones are pushing into his face, wheeling his eyes and whittling his cheeks. An oxygen tube rests on his upper lip and loops behind his ears like a fancy moustache. There are scabs all over his bare arms, and his fingers are swollen and knotty. A nurse checks a machine beside the bed. Darren can't make himself smile. An old anger is

215

climbing around inside him. His cheeks feel stiff, the skin stretched tight over the bones, hot and stingy.

'What happened? They said you took an — '

'It was an accident. I wouldn't . . . '

'Are you sure?'

'I wouldn't, you know I wouldn't.'

'You'd better not.'

'I said, didn't I?'

'I thought you might — '

'I wouldn't. All right?'

'What happened?'

'It was a mistake.'

'How?'

'My bloody teeth. I just — they really hurt.'

'Oh, for fuck's sake.'

'Too much Nurofen. Had some Disprin, too. I thought you could. And some of them Night Pain tablets as well.'

'You can't do that. It's the same stuff, in different boxes.'

'I got confused.'

'You mean drunk?'

'Where's Clover?'

'Do you think I'd bring her before I knew?'

'Suppose not.'

'Well.'

'Well.'

Ding, ding, ding. Round one over, Darren sits beside the bed in the pink vinyl-coated armchair. At least it's a side room, which means Jim won't regale the rest of the ward with stories about his job as an RSPCA inspector (he wasn't) and the time he saved twelve Bengal cats from

216

extermination (he didn't).

'Could you wheel me outside? I'm dying for a ciggie.'

Darren looks at the machine beside the bed. Jim is attached to it in two places. Blood appears to be flowing out of him and into the machine before streaming back into him again.

'I don't think you can go anywhere.'

'Now, Jim, what have I said?' the nurse asks, folding her arms beneath a bust that is mountainous and unyielding. 'You can't go out, and even if you could, you're not allowed to smoke. Oxygen accelerates combustion. It's a fire hazard. People have died because they fancied a quick smoke while they were on oxygen. You've got your patches.' She turns to Darren. 'We're also giving him something called chlordiazepoxide hydrochloride, which should help with the alcohol withdrawal. That's his lot, I'm afraid.'

'It's not enough,' he whines.

'Well, it'll have to be,' she says, and Darren feels a stab of pleasure at his discomfort.

'How did you get here?'

'One of the Polish lads saw me, on the floor. He called an ambulance.'

'So your door was open? God, how many times have I told you about that?'

'He wouldn't have seen me if it had been closed.'

'That's not the point.'

'I might have *died* if the door had been shut.'

'That'd have been nice for Clover, wouldn't it? 'Jim Brookfield Found Dead in Bedsit.''

'Studio flat.'

'Whatever.'

'He'd been sick, hadn't you, Jim?' the nurse prompts. 'He'd been bleeding from his tummy and he was very poorly when he came in. I don't think he realises how lucky he is. We're giving his kidneys a rest. He's going to have to make some *lifestyle changes*, aren't you, Jim?'

Jim is so far past pretending, he doesn't even nod.

'I brought you some stuff.' Darren puts a carrier bag on the bed. 'Just from Primarni and the pound shop.'

He went straight to town, as soon as the shops opened. Didn't bother going to the bedsit to look for Jim's things. At the very least they'd have needed washing, if not binning. He dashed around for the usual: pyjamas, pants, socks, shampoo, deodorant, a toothbrush, toothpaste and a couple of jigsaws. They only do 100-piece puzzles at the pound shop; he chose a Labrador puppy with a red ribbon around its neck and a Dora the Explorer. Wait till Jim sees them, he'll do his nut.

'Ta.' He doesn't even look in the bag.

'You're lucky to have such a nice brother,' the nurse says.

'He's not my brother.'

Jim works his way through various iterations of 'we're not related' and 'he's got nothing to do with me' every time he's in hospital. He thinks he's making some big point by saying it.

'We'll get him seen by the hospital dentist while he's in. His mouth's a mess. And he really shouldn't be drinking while he's taking methotrexate. That's the name of his psoriasis medication.'

'I know.'

'We've done some liver function tests. Livers are surprisingly resilient. Yours needs some time off, doesn't it, Jim? We've had a chat about this, haven't we?'

Jim pulls faces as she talks. Like a teenager.

'You're going to listen to the nurse, aren't you?'

They stare at each other and all the years and all the things between them crowd the room. Darren breaks off first. 'You *are* listening, aren't you?' But Jim looks right through him and Darren knows that none of it matters. Jim won't stop drinking. He won't promise to take his medication. He won't stop smoking. And he won't eat properly — he can't even remember to clean his teeth. He wouldn't do it for Becky. He won't do it for anyone.

'What about his mental health?'

'Someone's coming to talk to him this afternoon.'

'I *am* in the room, you know.'

'Sorry. Do you want to watch the telly while you're in?'

'Yeah. Ta.'

Darren manoeuvres the bedside screen with one hand and fishes in his jeans pocket for his debit card with the other.

'It must have been hard for you . . . ' Jim begins.

Darren stands there, debit card pinched

between his fingers. It *has* been hard. He's had *years* of it. Jim's words are a concession of sorts. An acknowledgement of all the shit that's happened. That's all it takes, just a *smidgen* of recognition settles the roving of the old anger, and he is glad to help, happy to pay for the telly, even though it costs a bloody fortune.

' . . . really hard, knowing Becky preferred me.'

He stuffs the card back in his pocket. One of his shoes squeaks as he turns. The door to the room swings shut behind him and he strides past the nurses at the desk and down the long corridor, past the hand sanitisers and the signs for the X-ray department, past the café and the hospital shop, and through the double doors. Outside, he pays £3 to retrieve his car. He reverses out of his space carefully and drives home, windows down, radio off, hands wrapped tight around the wheel.

★　★　★

Kelly is hurrying down the path and back to her car as he pulls up. She has parked in his way, blocking the drive. He leaves his engine running and climbs out.

'Clover says you're going to Blackpool tomorrow. It's my weekend off, too. Why don't me and the boys come with you?' Her hair is brown today, shiny, like a conker; and she's done something to her eyebrows, they look like she's drawn them on with a black felt tip. She looks nice; she always looks nice.

A day with Kelly and the boys will be full, bursting at the seams with chat and laughter. And Clover will enjoy herself, he knows she will. So he says yes, even as he wonders whether he is becoming a project; if Kelly is so kind because she feels sorry for him. He doesn't want anyone to feel sorry for him, *least of all Kelly* — but that's not something he wants to examine right now.

Exhibit: 'Becky Brookfield —
the Untold Story'

Catalogue

Object: Framed school photograph.

Description: A school photograph of Becky Brookfield (my mother) and Jim Brookfield (my uncle) in a black frame, with plasticky sort of glass. They are wearing a uniform, white shirts with navy and yellow striped ties. They both have blonde curly hair. Becky Brookfield's hair is tied back in a ponytail. Jim Brookfield's hair is tight and woolly like a sheep's. The skin under Jim's eyes is purple. There are red and white crusty patches on his cheeks and forehead. Cracks in the skin around his lips have been bleeding, they are running into his face like tiny streams. He is smiling. Becky Brookfield is not smiling. She has got her arm around Jim Brookfield. Their heads are touching. If you look carefully you can see that her fingers are curled around his shoulder, tight.

Item Number: 19.

Provenance: This photograph was taken in primary school. Jim Brookfield has one of his bottom middle teeth missing, so he is probably in reception or Year 1, which means that Becky Brookfield is in Year 1 or

2 — the oldest she can be is seven.

Display: On the wall (find some nails and hammer one into the wall. Hang the picture with the other chosen pictures in an arrangement).

Curator: Clover Quinn.

Keeper: Darren Quinn.

11

For the first time this summer there's cloud, the thick, pillowy kind that buries the whole sky. The inside-outside feeling has vanished and it's a day to dress for the weather. A blustery wind races along the promenade, teasing hair, wafting jackets and whipping the sea into stiff-peaked waves. They wear jeans, T-shirts and coats, except for Kelly, who is sporting tiny shorts and a pair of grey tweed platform shoes. Clover remembers the wobble of her own walk when she experimented with her mother's black patent heels. She studies the way Kelly trots, feet clopping like hooves, and admires her legs, which are the same shade of bronze as the rest of her. There is a walk-in spray-tanning booth at her salon; she must hop inside it when she hasn't got any customers.

It's only a five-minute walk from the car park. Blackpool is nowhere near as pretty as the locations on her holiday board. Everything is grey: seal and smoke, slate and shadow, iron and pebble — beautiful in its own way, she decides in a burst of happiness. Wires and cables from the trams and the illuminations criss-cross above the road. Light-up models of SpongeBob, Squidward, Mr Krabs and Patrick hang from lamp posts ready for the switch-on at the end of the month. Pleasure Beach looms, the scaffold-like structure of The Big One rising up from behind brightly coloured shopfronts: a chippy, an ice cream and souvenir shop, Pizza Hut and the Beach Amusements arcade.

'Whoa, The Big One is massive!' Tyler says.

They all stop briefly to admire the twist of red and blue metal.

'You're going to tell me *exactly* what it's like, aren't you?' Dylan asks.

'*Exactly*,' Tyler promises.

There's a queue to buy tickets. Clover watches Kelly while they wait. Kelly touches Dad's arm as she talks, her hand doubles as a full stop, comma and exclamation mark. And sometimes she gives him a look like butter, a look that melts all over him. She thinks he is the dog's bollocks, literally, and he doesn't seem to notice.

Clover finds she doesn't mind Kelly coming as much as she did yesterday. Dad had a bad afternoon, pulling his *everything* face when he thought she wasn't looking, and not listening when she spoke.

'Are you all right?'

'Yes.'

'Were there any jigsaws in the pound shop?'

'Yes.'

'Did you get some?'

'Yes.'

'How was Uncle Jim?'

'Yes.'

'Are you pretending to listen to me?'

He said he had some sorting out to do and went into the garden, but he couldn't decide what to keep and what to throw away and ended up rearranging things. Mrs Mackerel watched from an upstairs window, initially nodding encouragement and then shaking her head in annoyance. Afterwards, it looked like the bikes, the milk crates, the boat engine, the paddling pool, the slide and the water pistols and balls had been enjoying a game of musical chairs.

He is better today. Maybe because of Kelly. It's a shame Colin couldn't come too; they've known each other for so long, they can fill Dad's gaps and smooth his edges. Dad probably thinks Kelly coming is a happy coincidence, and perhaps it is. But Clover can't help wondering whether he mentioned having this weekend off at some point and that's why Kelly also arranged to be free. The boys are all over him like a rash — 'Watch me, Darren!' 'Will you race me on the Steeplechase, Darren?' 'Mum says we can have lunch at Pizza Hut. Are you coming too, Darren?' Whatever was bothering him yesterday is fading. At this rate he'll be fine by teatime.

★ ★ ★

While Dad was shopping for Uncle Jim's things and visiting him in hospital yesterday, she was opening boxes in her mother's room. Clothes mostly. And shoes. She emptied and collapsed the boxes and piled the clothes she didn't want into bin bags. Her mother mostly wore casual things: jeans and T-shirts, tracksuit bottoms and leggings, trainers and flip-flops. She discovered a couple of blouses and a few pairs of smart-ish trousers. It was all big. Nothing she *could* wear and nothing she *would* wear, even if it was smaller. She piled up the collapsed boxes ready to sneak into Mrs Mackerel's bin next week.

Once the boxes on the window side of the bed were all emptied, she could finally open the wardrobe. It was an exciting, Christmassy sort of moment. What did she expect to find? A succession of accessorised outfits, lined up like shed skins? Two rows of fur coats and a lamp post in the distance? Nothing so grand. She just expected something. *Anything*. But when she pulled back the door, the rail was deserted and the wardrobe, which had felt like a destination, was more of a dead end. She was silly to be surprised — where did she think all the boxed clothes had come from? Dad must have started the packing and not quite finished. It was just like him, wasn't it, to start something and then give up. She immediately felt mean for thinking it. Starting things is a sort of talent in itself. Some people never try anything new; some people never even talk about it.

All that was left in the wardrobe was a jumble of stuff covering its bottom. On the top of the mound was a red handbag. It was old. You could tell because there were places where the leather was really scuffed and the stitching was unravelling on one side. The bag had a handle and a long strap. Inside, she discovered some tissues and a rectangular, red leather purse. The purse contained some change, a National Insurance card, a book of first-class stamps, some receipts and a library card.

In a zipped compartment at the back of the purse she discovered a strip of four photographs, folded in half between photos two and three. They were like the one she has on her bus pass, but each photograph was different. In the first photo Dad and her mother were facing the camera, which had caught them, mouths wide, laughing. In the second photograph Dad's head was turned slightly; he was at the tail end of the earlier laugh, smiling at her mother, his face all gooey. In the third photograph they were looking at each other, and what Clover saw there was love. Both faces were soft, and not just from being young; their expressions were the kind people do when they are mad about each other. In fact, there was so much love that looking at the picture felt a bit like spying. In the last photograph they were kissing, of course. It was as if the kissing *had* to follow because it was the next bit of the story. The photos were amazing. Firstly, because her mother was smiling, and secondly, because Dad didn't look worried or preoccupied or as if he was trying very hard to have a good time. He just looked happy.

She hung the bag's long strap around the dummy's chest and shoulder, and put the photo strip with the love-related objects. It was proof. Evidence that, once upon a time, her mother and her dad had lived happily, even though they didn't manage an ever after.

In the bottom of the wardrobe, underneath a navy duffle coat and on top of a folded duvet, she found the strangest thing. A plaited piece of hair as long as her arm, one bobble at the top and another at the bottom, where the hair tapered. She held it with the tips of her fingers. It dangled like something dead, reminding her of the wild animal collection she and Dad used to visit at the Botanic Gardens Museum, before it closed. One day, when they were visiting, the fire alarm sounded and Dad wasn't sure if it was a drill or for real; he didn't know whether to evacuate or stay put. While he was deciding, the fire door closed by itself, shutting them in the big, high-ceilinged room with all the stuffed animals doing unconvincing impressions of their former selves. It felt as if the room had captured them and it seemed possible that by the time the door reopened, she and Dad might find themselves imprisoned behind a sheet of glass, with fixed grins and buttoned eyes. It was a delicious fright, one they remembered and reconstructed on numerous occasions, tiptoeing into the animal room, half hoping the alarm would sound again and trap them for a second time.

She held the plait up to her own hair; it was a shade or two lighter. She wrapped it around the hook of the dummy's head and placed the black patent shoes beside the stand. There. It looked as if she was building something.

* * *

The tables in Pizza Hut are sticky with tomato sauce and spilled pop. A biting wind licks around the restaurant every time someone opens the heavy door. Clover sits beside Kelly, whose legs are dimpled by goosebumps. They watch Dad standing at the buffet counter with Tyler and

Dylan, laying slices of pizza on their waiting plates.

'I married someone like my dad,' Kelly says. 'People do that sometimes. It probably won't turn out as badly if you do it.'

No one likes Pete. Except the woman he replaced Kelly with — she must like him.

'So do men marry women who are like their mothers?'

'Hmm, maybe. I'm not sure.' Kelly tries to spear a crouton with her fork. 'I used to babysit you, when you were little.' She gives up and uses her fingers.

'I know.'

'Do you remember?' Kelly's face has gone all mushy — the croutons must be really nice.

'Not really. You know . . . you know my mother?' she asks, not wondering whether it's okay until after the words are out and it's too late to take them back.

'Ye-ess.' Kelly's lips worry the word.

'What was she like?'

Kelly licks her fingers and thinks. 'Your dad really loved her.' She pulls a face, a sort of apology for not answering the question. 'When a friend who's a boy falls in love, you don't see them as much. Things change and you only bump into them sometimes. You see each other at parties, but you don't . . . ' Her face twists again. 'Becky was . . . she seemed nice.'

Nice — it's not much, but she'll add it to her notebook. 'Did you cut her hair?'

'I wasn't her hairdresser.'

Clover steals straight into the gap between her

question and Kelly's answer. 'But did you ever cut her hair?'

'Once.'

She doesn't know what to say next. She'd like to try, 'Did you love my dad back then, before you married Pete?' But she daren't, and moments later Dad and the boys are back, their plates stacked with pizza, arguing about whether the wind will drop enough for The Big One to open. Dad reckons it's unlikely, but the boys are desperate.

'The Big One goes at eighty-seven miles per hour,' Tyler says. 'It's more than two hundred feet tall and there are warning beacons for aeroplanes on the two highest bits.'

'Is that right?'

'Yes, Darren.' Dylan tuts and waves a slice of pizza for emphasis. It's hard for him to believe that anyone doesn't know these important facts. 'The Big One is *an experience of a lifetime,*' he claims in a stilted, word-for-word voice, clearly repeating something that's been either read or said to him.

'You're not big enough for it, mate. And growing takes a while. I hate to break it to you, but you're not going to reach a hundred and thirty centimetres this afternoon.'

'*Darren!* I *know* that! I want it to be open so *Tyler* can go on it.'

'Aww, you're a good lad.'

Dad noogies Dylan, and Kelly looks like she might dissolve all over the sticky table. Once you've spotted love with a capital 'L' you can't stop seeing it. It's plain as a pikestaff, literally.

231

★ ★ ★

The Big One doesn't open, but they go on everything else: Avalanche, Infusion, Revolution and The Big Dipper. They leave Valhalla to last because it's an absolute *soaker*. Afterwards, they stick pound coins in the human-sized dryers and stand in front of the blasting warm air until their clothes have gone from sodden to slightly steaming.

Dad buys two large bags of chips, which they eat in the car on the way home. Clover shares with the boys, who dig in, all fists. Dad uses his fingers to feed himself, but he spears chips with a tiny wooden fork for Kelly and slips them between her lips as she drives.

By the time they reach Preston, the boys are fast asleep, heads flung back, mouths open, hands glistening with chip fat, and Kelly is talking about people she and Dad used to know at school. Clover wipes her hands on her jeans and digs in her coat pocket for the Latin booklet. There are so many Latin phrases that she already knows, like *ex libris*, which you sometimes see in books, and *hosanna in excelsis*, which is a line from 'Ding Dong Merrily on High' and means 'hosanna in the highest'. And then there are words and phrases she has never heard of but wants to learn because they sound epic when she whispers them to herself. Like this one: *nil admirari*, which means 'to be surprised by nothing'.

'What did you say, Clover?'

'Nothing.'

232

'You did, I heard you.'

'*Nil admirari.*'

'What?'

'She got this Latin book from Edna, but no one speaks Latin, do they? Shall I get you a French book?'

'Mark's fluent, you know. He can help with her French, when he gets back. That'll be better than a book.'

'It's fine, I don't need a book and I — '

'So what does *nil-mirary* mean?'

'To be surprised by nothing.'

'Oh. Good plan,' Kelly says, and carries on chatting to Dad.

Clover whispers the words to herself, committing them to memory. She will write them on a piece of paper and colour them in; they'll provide a nice contrast to her mural of surprised women.

When Kelly pulls up outside the house Clover climbs through the gap between the front seats and out of the passenger door so as not to wake the boys.

'I had a really good time,' she tells Dad as Kelly turns her car around.

'Me too,' he says, and they wave Kelly down the road.

While they watch the first episode of the new series of *Doctor Who* she colours some of the pictures from Mrs Mackerel's books: *Our Lady of Fatima, Our Lady of the Miraculous Medal* and *The Story of Mary*. And, sneakily, when she is sure Dad isn't looking, she colours the tiny hearts she has drawn on the sheet of paper that

233

will head the LOVE board.

'I *knew* you'd use those colouring books one day,' Dad says, and she smiles and lets him enjoy being right.

★ ★ ★

Early on Sunday morning they pop to the allotment to water. It's cool and still windy, but at least it's dry. They pick a big bag of raspberries, a selection of vegetables for Grandad, and some new potatoes for Mrs Mackerel, which Dad delivers on the way home.

Mrs Mackerel comes to the door in her dressing gown, the crown of her hair sticking up like a label.

'Oh *dear*, I didn't get you up, did I?' Dad asks.

'OF COURSE NOT,' she says, lips baggy without the scaffold of her teeth.

★ ★ ★

Dad has this big idea for the raspberries. He gets baking trays out of a cupboard and arranges the berries on them. The trays go in the freezer. Once the fruit is frozen they will put it in bags and keep it for cooking. Next time her programme is on he wants her to watch it with a pen and paper at the ready in case there are any good recipes. Easy ones, mind. He acts like he's asking a big favour, but she is dead happy to do it; just think of all the things they might make.

★ ★ ★

They visit Uncle Jim in the afternoon. Dad is cross with him. She doesn't know why, but she can tell because he explains how to get to the room and, instead of accompanying her, he stops in the corridor and coats his hands in antibacterial gel. He does it so thoroughly that you'd think he was a vet getting ready to shove his arm up a cow's bum.

'Go on,' he says. 'Don't wait for me.'

Uncle Jim is sitting up in bed. He is attached to a machine and he looks very tired.

'Am I glad to see you!'

He extends his arms for a hug. She is careful. He looks like he might break.

'Are you feeling better?'

'I'm fine, it was just a stupid mix-up. Look at the jigsaws your dad bought.'

She laughs when she sees the boxes sitting on the overbed tray.

'He was trying to annoy me.'

'Oh no, I'm sure it was just a mix-up, too.'

He waves a hand, dismissing her protest. 'Thing is, they're not as bad as you'd think. Push them over to me. That's right. You can do this with them,' he says, and he gets both puzzles out of their boxes and creates two mixed-up pictures, using alternating pieces. 'You can go with every other piece, every other line, half and half diagonally, half and half horizontally — the possibilities are endless.'

'Really?'

'No. Endless is the wrong word, but I thought it sounded impressive.'

'It did.'

'Oh, good.'

He must be very bored to have tried so many different combinations of jigsaw pieces. 'Is the telly broken?'

'It's different here. You have to pay. And it's expensive.'

'Is the food okay?'

'My mouth hurts. I have to choose the soft things.'

'You know what's soft?'

'What?'

'Vegetables.'

'They make you choose some every day. I don't eat them, though. They can't force me. I'm seeing the dentist on Monday.'

'That's tomorrow.'

'Oh. Yeah.'

'Don't worry. I expect they only let the best dentists work in hospitals.'

'They're all rubbish,' he says. 'That's why they let them practise on people who can't run away.'

'How do you know that?'

'I just do.'

'No you don't.'

'Yes I do.'

'Don't.'

'Oh, all right,' he says. 'Where's your dad?'

She walks to the door and pokes her head around it. Dad is standing at the nurses' desk, chatting.

'At the desk,' she reports.

'Ahh. The silent treatment.'

'No, he's talking to the nurses.'

After twenty minutes Uncle Jim starts to flag.

He asks about school, forgetting it's the holidays, and he starts to tell her a story about a time when he had a pet rat, which is probably not true because he's not very good at looking after himself, never mind an animal.

Dad appears in the doorway. 'Jim.'

'Dazza.'

That's all they say to each other. They *are* cross. She glances at Dad, wondering whether he's too cross to sort out the telly.

'It's very boring here,' she says.

'Not guilty. I haven't complained, honest. Wouldn't dream of being such a turd nugget.'

Dad gets his debit card out of his jeans pocket. 'Would you like him to watch telly?'

'Yes, please.'

'I'll sort it for you, then,' he says, tugging the telly's movable arm.

Uncle Jim snorts. Clover catches his eye and gives a small shake of her head. If he's not careful, he'll end up with nothing. She puts a finger to her lips as Dad messes about with the screen.

When it's done, Dad says, 'Let's go,' and heads straight for the door, without saying goodbye, which means that she has to be extra nice to Uncle Jim on the way out in order to make up for it. She hugs him and says she hopes it all goes really well with the dentist. As she heads out of the room, she looks back and waves.

'See you later, detonator,' he calls.

★　★　★

Dad always goes out for a drink with Colin on one of the nights of his long weekend off. He doesn't want her waiting up for him by herself, so he sends her over to Mrs Mackerel's with a DVD. Mrs Mackerel calls the cinema 'THE PICTURES'. She hasn't been to THE PICTURES since the Odeon on Lord Street closed in 1979. Her favourite films are usually about the past because it is WHOLESOME and GOOD CLEAN FUN, even when terrible things happen. Films she has especially enjoyed on Dad's weekends off include *Les Misérables*, which she pronounces like it's named after an unhappy man called Les — SUCH LOVELY SINGING — and *The Great Gatsby* — SUCH LOVELY COSTUMES. The fact that neither film has a happy ending doesn't bother her at all.

There is a rhythm to these evenings. Dad escorts Clover to the door and says exactly where he's going, in case of an emergency. Mrs Mackerel makes him promise not to get drunk with THAT COLIN and then she says HE'S A QUEER ONE. Dad tells her that it's called being gay now and she pretends to be shocked because she didn't MEAN ANYTHING BY QUEER. When she has shut the door in Dad's face she says, 'Make yourself at home,' and goes into the kitchen. She always comes back with Ribena or Lidl cola and a whole packet of Tunnock's tea cakes arranged on a fancy silver tray. In the summer when it's hot and it's still light at night, you can sometimes see her fingerprints on the chocolate.

Tonight she asks about Jim before she presses Play.

'He's very tired.'

'*God help him.*'

'And bored.'

'*God love him.*'

'And there's a machine next to his bed. For his blood.'

'He'll be having a BLOOD TRANSMISSION.'

'I think it's cleaning his — '

Mrs Mackerel presses Play. The conversation is over.

Tonight's film is *Gravity*. Clover picks the outer layer of chocolate off a tea cake while Mrs Mackerel shouts at the telly. She seems to think that if she shouts loud enough, the actors — whom she insists on addressing by their real names — might hear her and save themselves a lot of trouble.

'WATCH OUT!' she warns Sandra Bullock.

Clover nibbles at the froth of the marshmallow. Underneath, there's a blob of jam. She licks it off the biscuit base, which is always disappointingly soggy.

'I wouldn't do THAT if I were YOU,' Mrs Mackerel advises George Clooney.

It's strange to think that Mrs Mackerel would have been around Dad's age when the moon landings happened. It must have been very exciting.

'Space is VERY BIG, isn't it?'

Clover agrees and slips off her shoes. Now she is allowed to put her feet on the sofa. Before she does, she helps herself to another tea cake.

'MAKE AN EFFORT, GEORGE! If he'd just do a BIT OF FRONT CRAWL in the air I'm SURE he could SWIM BACK TO EARTH.'

Mrs Mackerel pauses the film so she can SPEND A PENNY. This happens at least once during every film because she has a BLADDER LIKE A CHEESECLOTH. Clover has no idea what a cheesecloth is. She imagines it must be very small, with lots of holes in, like Swiss cheese in cartoons — a sort of miniature cheesy colander.

'You'd better HAVE A GO, too,' Mrs Mackerel says on her return. 'I don't want you INTERRUPTING THE SECOND HALF.' She talks about the second half as if there's a natural break in the film, a spot where the first half ends so old ladies can have a wee.

Clover takes herself off upstairs. It's easier than arguing about the capacity of her bladder. Mrs Mackerel's bathroom suite is powder blue. So is the carpet. Dad says only optimists and ladies who live by themselves have carpet in their bathrooms. The bath is the corner kind, with special taps that look like shells, and the bowl of the sink is scalloped like a cockle. It was ALL THE RANGE when Mrs Mackerel had it done. Beside the toilet there's a powder-blue bidet, which Mrs Mackerel calls a BJ. You can wash your feet in it, or your bottom, apparently. When Clover was small they'd go upstairs and wash their feet in it, for a treat. Afterwards they dried their feet and plastered them in peppermint foot cream. Then they'd sit on the sofa sucking humbugs, a clean, minty smell emanating from between their toes and teeth. 'CLEAN AS A BRISTLE,' Mrs Mackerel would say.

Once she has squeezed out the smallest of wees, Clover takes her usual snoop around the bathroom. Mrs Mackerel's things are different and therefore somewhat interesting. A pair of nail clippers that look like shears sit on the edge of the bath beside a bottle of Silver Shampoo and an Avon Timeless Cologne Spray. On the floor beside the toilet are some Tena Lady pads — 'New Body-Shaped DryZone' — and a packet of Lady Pants, which aren't for periods, but cheesecloth bladders. Clover has seen the adverts: women laughing hysterically with not even the tiniest bit of wee running down their legs. On a shelf above the sink she finds a tub of peppermint foot cream, a white plastic container for dentures that looks like a teeny cool box, and a tube of Poligrip, which is the sticky stuff that's advertised on telly by people who bite into apples and manage not to leave their teeth behind. Above the shelf there's a mirror-fronted medicine cabinet. It's locked. After she's finished having a good snoop, Clover heads back downstairs to *Gravity*.

Mrs Mackerel becomes increasingly animated in the SECOND HALF of the film. Despite the fact that she has lived by herself for a long time without a man and seems to have got along just fine, she doesn't think SANDRA should be ALLOWED up there without a RELIABLE SPACEMAN to fix things.

'HAVE ANOTHER TUNNOCK'S.'

'I'm a bit full.'

'They'll only GO TO WASTE.'

'All right.' Clover takes a third tea cake. The waxy chocolate is beginning to edge away from the marshmallow all on its own.

'SANDRA!' Mrs Mackerel shouts as the film reaches its climax. 'FIND THE EJACULATE BUTTON!'

★ ★ ★

When Dad and Colin pick her up they are bleary round the edges and especially polite.

'Good evening, *ladies*.'

'Was the film *to your liking?*'

'Oh YES. I was HANGING ON by the FINGERS OF MY NAILS.'

Colin puts his arm around Mrs Mackerel and says she's priceless. She pretends to be insulted, before asking him how much he'd charge to come and clean up her untidy neighbour's garden.

Colin laughs. He says he can't imagine that any of her neighbours would *dare* to have an untidy garden, but if they did — and he looks meaningfully at Dad as he says this — he'd sort it out for free. Then he asks whether she'd like any other favours while he's at it.

She swats him on the arm and asks about THE LOVELY BOY who's gone to NURSE THE SICK and FEED THE HUNGRY. Colin says Mark is doing a great job of saving the world and the Pope will probably make him a saint before long. He's only joking, he's dead proud of him really.

Colin comes back to the house with them for a bit before Dad calls a taxi. Because it's the holidays, she doesn't have to go straight to bed. Colin says he'll give her a game of Wii tennis and she thrashes him. He demands a rematch, this time with Just Dance. Of course, he wins hands down — hands down, legs up, and bum in the air, to be precise.

Exhibit: 'Becky Brookfield — the Untold Story'

Catalogue

Object: Comb.

Description: A yellow plastic wide-tooth comb. There are some hairs in it, which means there is also DNA.

Item Number: 21.

Provenance: This comb belonged to Becky Brookfield (my mother). It's the kind of comb people like us (with curly hair) use. We probably have lots more in common, too. Like looking after Uncle Jim, loving Dad, and other things, et cetera.

Display: In a clear plastic bag with various hair bobbles and scrunchies that were in the second bedroom.

Curator: Clover Quinn.

Keeper: Darren Quinn.

12

After Colin leaves, Darren sends Clover to bed. She goes up without any fuss; she's a good girl, and it's late. He's nicely pissed; his head feels ever-so-slightly too heavy for his neck, and his resting expression has slid to sloppy smile. He's drowsy. Full of optimism. He'll think of something fun for them to do tomorrow . . . sledding at the sand dunes, that's what. And he'll do a bit of tidying too, if he gets the chance. He reaches for the arm of the sofa and picks up the colouring Clover left behind last night. *Our Lady of Fatima* — Fatima Whitbread, remember her? Muscles like Colin. *Our Lady of the Miraculous Medal*, *The Story of Mary*, and, under the three colouring books, a sheet of A4 paper, the word LOVE written across its middle. Behind LOVE there are hundreds of tiny hand-drawn hearts which have been coloured with red, pink and purple felt tips.

So there *is* a boy. Shit.

The picture is bursting with joy. He should be worried — he *is* worried, well, he will be, tomorrow, when he can be more certain of the appropriate volume of parental concern. In the meantime he sits on the sofa, loose-limbed, lazy, and hums the opening bars of 'All You Need Is Love.' *Love, love, love.*

★ ★ ★

245

It all began on the bus. He'd been driving for three weeks when someone presented him with a red handbag at the start of his shift.

'Found this on the seat beside me.'

He thanked them and hung it in the cab, behind him. That might have been all. He sometimes thinks about it when he's on a late, and he checks his bus before the cleaners climb aboard, looking on and under the seats for abandoned bags, forsaken coats, disregarded umbrellas; he makes sure no one is left behind, dozing on the back seat — it's happened to other drivers — and when he finds something, he wonders about the person to whom the item belongs and thinks about the way a lost hat or a forgotten coat can change an entire life. That might have been all, but while he was waiting at a timing stop, the red bag rang. He unzipped it and rummaged for the phone.

'Hello?'

'You've got my phone?'

'Yes.'

'And my bag?'

'Yeah.'

'Can I have them back, please?'

'Course! You left them on the bus. I'm the driver.'

'Oh, thank God! How shall I — '

'Where are you now?'

She was in a phone box at the end of Lord Street. He wasn't far away: he was driving the 43 back then — he was never far away. He told her where to wait.

It was April. Freezing. No sign of spring. It felt

like winter — had been winter, in fact, ever since Mum died in the November. There was a weather warning for northerly gales, and the temperature was dropping as low as zero overnight in some parts of the country. It was driving Dad potty. He was desperate for things to do in the evenings, but there was no point getting started in the greenhouse with the weather as it was.

When Becky stepped on to the bus to claim her bag, the first thing Darren noticed was her hair, the way it whirled over her shoulders, right down past her elbows. There was snow that day. Not much. Just a few icy flakes, sailing about in the wind. They'd collected in her hair and made it sparkle.

'You have my bag?'

Her voice was low and soft, her hands clasped. He noticed her fancy nails, the ones with the transparent, shiny polish and the white tips. Dead pretty. No rings. She had a high, wide forehead, and almost invisible eyebrows, which levelled her expression, making her seem serene and unflappable.

'I'm Darren.'

She nodded and reached for the bag.

He passed it to her as slowly as he dared. If only he'd thought to open her purse, he might have discovered her name.

'Thank you,' she said, and she stepped down on to the pavement.

'I'll be stopping here at 10.20 tomorrow,' he called.

She glanced back at him and didn't smile.

The girl with the bag. That was how he thought of her. She reminded him of something: a familiar place or a feeling — he couldn't quite think what. He spent the rest of the shift wondering. Finally, it came to him. When he was at high school there were these pictures in the art room. Soft, partially naked women with waterfalls of hair and skin like white marzipan. He'd liked the art room. It was different from the rest of the school. The art teacher wore stonewashed jeans and black T-shirts, and during lessons he played classical music on a portable CD player. 'Just have a go,' he'd say, and once you had, he'd lean over your shoulder and find something to compliment before setting to with a soft-tipped pencil: an addition here, a deletion there and he'd discover the shape of your intentions. Although Darren lacked an aptitude for the subject, he enjoyed it. When they visited the school library during an English lesson, he looked in the art section and found a book about Rubens. He took it out with the ticket still inside the cover. The library worked on an honour system of sorts. You were trained in how to take out a book and then it was up to you to find the little ticket holder with your name, remove the ticket from the inside jacket of the book and place it inside the holder. If you didn't do this and someone found out, you'd get into trouble. But if no one noticed, you could keep the book as long as you liked — for ever, in fact, which is what he did with the Rubens book, it's in the house somewhere.

The women he ogled on the covers of the top

shelf lads' mags at the newsagent's — nipples screened by stars that really said *ta-dah!* — were carefully posed in hip-tilted, head-angled, arm-raised stances that couldn't possibly be maintained for more than a few moments; positions that were, if you thought about it (and he often didn't) pretty ridiculous. But the women in the coloured prints on the art-room wall and the black and white sketches in the library book were casual, unguarded, and seemed, to Darren at least, timeless. Rubens' pictures were drawn hundreds of years ago. The women looked patient and unruffleable. They reclined and slouched, stomachs creased, dimpled thighs splayed, with barely a glance at the viewer; no half-parted lips, no winks or self-conscious smirks. And, of course, they were beautiful: fulsome and robust. Like the girl with the bag.

The 43 route started in High Park then headed over the railway bridge at Meols Cop, past the house he'd buy one day, through the town centre and out to Birkdale, before looping back. He started to look for her when he was driving through town. How strange to think of the many times he may have passed her without knowing it.

A few days later she boarded his bus accompanied by an old chap with enormous ears and a woolly, Sherlock Holmes-like cape. Her red bag had a long strap. She wore it sideways, streaming between her breasts. Days after that, he saw her waiting at a stop on Lord Street, standing behind a different elderly fellow in a wheelchair. And later still, supporting the elbow of a tiny, desiccated woman as the wind buffeted her on the corner of Eastbank Street.

She worked in an old people's home, Peacefields, on the promenade. They had a mix of residents: some who needed nursing care; others who were just a little frail, recovering from surgery or staying for a few weeks while family members had a break. When she got on his bus he talked to her. He tried to ask questions that couldn't be answered with yes or no; he even planned some in advance so she'd have to respond with more than a word at a time. Eventually, having taken courage from the oft-repeated story of his mum and dad's courtship, he asked her out and she said yes.

He'd bought a second-hand Fiesta Mark IV. It had a 1.0 litre engine and all the oomph of a chicken korma. Still, he was pleased with it, it was a car and it was *his*. That was their first date, going for a drive in his new car. He drove them up Rivington Pike, a summit on Winter Hill, a destination he suggested casually, pretending he'd only just thought of it. In truth, he'd found the walk beforehand in a leaflet from the Tourist Information booth at the bottom of Eastbank Street. When they couldn't drive any further they got out of the car. It was May, still cool, breezy. Her hair went everywhere, as if it was alive. The walk to the summit was steep, muddy in places. The leaflet came in handy. He commented on the blanket bog, like it was something that had just occurred to him, and he told her about the legend of the spectral horseman, hoping she'd think him interesting and informed.

On a soggy section of high moorland he held her hand for the first time. His heart was thumping, and he had to wipe his palm on his jeans first because it was sticky with anxiety. There were opportunities for her to pull her hand back. She didn't. And he knew, with the kind of certainty some people evoke when they talk about Jesus or politics, absolutely *knew* he would love her, if she'd let him.

When they got back in the car she was pink-cheeked and windswept, but she didn't rearrange her hair or pull down the visor to check her reflection in the little mirror; it was as if those small vanities were beneath her. He liked that. She had more important things to worry about, but he didn't know it then.

She'd bought him a present, for the car. It had been sitting in her pocket the whole time. She passed it to him, shyly. It was a wooden clown on a pull-string, about as big as the palm of his hand. When you pulled the string its arms and legs shot up. She hung it from the mirror, and in the years that followed she'd pull the string and make the clown perform star-jumps each time she got in the car. '*Hooray*,' the clown seemed to say — 'off we go, together, *hooray!*' Once the clown was in position he took her hand again. She liked his hands, she told him. She'd noticed them resting on the steering wheel of the bus and thought how strong and capable they seemed. Afterwards, when she was his girlfriend, he would take his hands out of his pockets or off his lap and rest them on the table in front of him when she was around, just in case she fancied a look. On that day he held her hand all the way home, adjusting his grip when he needed to change gear, knocking the stick with the heel of his hand so he wouldn't have to let her go.

* * *

Colin called her Mizz Frizz to begin with. She refused to smile and take it in good part. 'Tell him to piss off and polish his rapidly balding bonce,' Darren suggested. But she wouldn't. In the end Colin used her name, though he never quite forgave her for refusing to take the part of tease-ee. He found her stand-offish and humourless, said he couldn't understand why *some people* never laughed. She agreed, said she couldn't understand it either — she *always* laughed, *if* something was funny. It sometimes felt as if they were playing tennis and Darren was the net.

Colin had only recently come out and was sensitive to any perceived coolness. Darren had been both surprised and not surprised by the revelation, in the same way that Colin managed to be both sorry and not sorry whenever he was a twat. Darren carried the news around with him for a day or two, taking it out every so often to examine it, eventually concluding that Colin's predilections were none of his business; no one wants to think about their mates having sex with *anyone*, male or female, do they?

He wanted Becky and Colin to get on. He tried to explain her to him: yes, she didn't laugh at his jokes, and yes, she had a way of being quiet that sometimes made her the loudest person in the room, but she was optimistic and kind and genuine — she never fake-smiled out of politeness. She was touched by the smallest of gestures: a card in the post, a chocolate bar, the cheap gold-plated necklace he bought for her nineteenth birthday, weeks after they met. He wanted to make her laugh. He had the feeling that making her completely happy would be a worthwhile occupation, more worthwhile than Geography BSc Hons or any of the other things he'd imagined for himself.

Colin was unimpressed, said it was his dick talking. 'Knob her for a bit, then get away while you still can.'

Darren cringed. 'It's not a matter of *knobbing.*'

'You're serious, then?'

'I am,' he said.

'Why *her*, what's so — '

'I love her.'

And Colin groaned, unaware that he was the first to know, that he had heard the words before Becky.

★   ★   ★

On the day when she'd lost her bag, Becky had been visiting Jim in the hospital by the park. It was the first time he'd been sent there. She was worried but hopeful; he was in the best place and he was going to get better. She talked a lot about Jim. Enough for Darren to create a likeness of him in his head: benign and stoical, bearing his illness with bravery.

He still occasionally relives that first visit to her mother's, finds himself twenty-one years old again, trapped in a nightmare of horrified politeness. The door to the flat opens and he is assaulted by a matchlessly vile stink. He'll learn later that it comes from Jim's rat Derek, who lives in a cage on the kitchen worktop. On that day, he wonders how Becky can live there and not smell of it. He hasn't seen her room yet, the plug-in air fresheners, the perpetually open window, the tidy piles of clothes and books. The door opens straight into the lounge. Maureen is parked in the middle of a pink leather sofa. She doesn't get up. The telly stays on. He had pictured an ample, soft woman; someone who had caused significant harm, yet meant none of it. The real Maureen is hard, tiny. Bones knuckle her neck and her complexion is grey. She looks hungover and not pleased to see him. He forces the hinge of his smile wider, embarrassed at the way the word *mother* has infused his expectations. Uninvited, he sits on one side of Maureen, and Becky takes the other.

'Not your *usual*,' Maureen says to Becky, her voice like stone.

'Don't,' Becky warns. And, leaning forward, to him, 'There isn't a *usual*.'

'I hope you're earning good money.'

He is nudged by the poke of a twiggy elbow, and a potent blend of booze and sweat seeps from Maureen's sealish skin.

'She'll eat you out of house and home, this one.'

Becky's cheeks and neck flush pink.

'You never know, he might marry you, if you lose some weight. *Ta da, da-da — all fat and wide.*'

It is done in a *playful* way, only a joke.

'I might marry her if she stays exactly the same as she is,' he says. 'Or if she puts weight on,' he adds, in case that is the next line of attack.

Maureen laughs, but he can tell he has pissed her off. Jim appears, eyes bloodshot, also the worse for wear, though he's barely old enough to be drinking. There are white crusts on his elbows and around his hairline. His hands are pink and scaly. It looks so sore. Darren's heart goes out to him. It's an actual feeling, like a leak in his chest. He's so full of love for Becky, he still feels it should be easy to love the people she loves. He explains how pleased he is to finally meet Jim, who replies 'Likewise' in a silly voice, making it clear that he is not pleased at all.

They don't like him. He is disappointed and discomfited, uncertain about what he has done wrong.

'What did you think?' she asked afterwards.

'They're not what I'd expected.'

'What were you expecting?'

'I thought they'd be more like you,' he said carefully.

'They're my family.'

'I know.'

'But?'

'She was horrible to you.'

'She doesn't mean it.'

255

'Hmm.'

'You don't know her.'

He agreed that he didn't and he learned to be quiet, listening as she told him about living with her grandparents on and off, before they died. About the six different schools. The difficulty of making friends when she knew she'd likely move again. The barely remembered time before her dad's suicide, when her mum was better — kinder, nicer. Jim didn't remember it, but she'd told him all about it, probably made it sound better than it actually was, in fact, but never mind. She didn't want Darren to feel sorry for her, though; didn't want him to think she was complaining.

Of course he didn't think she was bloody complaining! As he listened to her, he realised how lucky he was that the people he loved had never been cruel. And each time he was tempted to interject, he reminded himself that the people she loved were hers to criticise. He could loathe them silently. Which he did.

★   ★   ★

They walked a lot that first summer, especially in the evenings, after work. When the weather was fine, walking was preferable to spending time at either of their homes. They strolled down Lord Street, walked around the Marine Lake or ambled along the south end of the beach, which was usually empty by dusk — tourists tended to leave at the same time as the ice-cream vans and donkeys, and the locals went to Formby, which was prettier, sandier.

On a particularly quiet evening they skated up and down the sandy slopes of the dunes, hands clasped, stumbling, giggling. They sat down in a sheltered dip. Eventually lay down, on her jacket. He rearranged the sweep of her hair as he kissed her mouth, shoulder and neck. Her stray curls tucked away from the sand, he kissed the square and slope of her jaw. Unbuttoned her shirt and tongued the gorge between her breasts. Kissed the hard pearls of her nipples while she unfastened his trousers and shucked hers past her hips.

'Go on,' she whispered.

'What if someone comes?'

'You. And me. *We'll come.*'

The beat of her breath was syncopated by laughter as he dug his fingers into the round curve of her arse and lost himself in the coast of each repetition.

Afterwards, they lay side by side as the temperature dropped and gaps in the cloud revealed the stars. They would come back to this exact spot, every summer, he thought. Even when they needed walking poles, and blister plasters, and a rest on the way up the hill, when they were old and their skin was wrinkled, when there were lines around their eyes and mouths and they'd had kids and grandkids and knew the up and down and inside-out of each other by heart.

'You,' she murmured, 'are the best thing that's ever happened to me.'

And he let himself believe it.

* ⭐ * ⭐ *

In the beginning there are no favoured courses. Those first feelings run where they will. But it isn't long before they form a stream and subsequent feelings have no option but to wash that same way. As they do, the stream deepens into a creek, a river. And then you can't help it: the someone you have chosen to love abrades your banks; they run right through you, and it is easy for their plans and dreams to become yours, for your hopes and wants to be subsumed by theirs.

Becky wanted to move out of her mum's flat. She dreamed of progressing at work and going on holiday. And she planned to look after Jim. How tempting it was to assume that he could grant her all wishes. His own wants were increasingly malleable.

'Would you still like to go to university?' she wondered.

'What would you like?'

'I asked you first.'

'I'd like whatever you'd like.'

'I asked you.'

That's how it went. They played hot potato with his plans.

⭐ ⭐ ⭐

They'd almost been together for a year when he surprised her with the holiday. Although he'd never gone on a proper holiday before, he didn't feel as if he'd missed out. He'd enjoyed day trips with Mum and Dad: Blackpool, Morecambe or the Lake District, topped off with a bag of chips on the way home. Becky, though, hadn't been anywhere. Facing the unavoidable 'What I did in the holidays' assignment every September had been worse, she said, than 'What I got for Christmas', which could be fudged with the inclusion of seasonal television programmes and the excitement of Christmas Eve.

He built it up — that was a mistake. He tore a sheet out of a calendar, circled the days — the final of which was Valentine's Day — and sent it to her in the post: *surprise!* He told her to pack her swimming things. When she asked about changing money, he said not to worry, he'd be taking care of that.

Becky had a very particular definition of what constituted a holiday, something he learned later, when she demoted his surprise holiday to 'weekend break'. According to her, a holiday occurred in a destination that had to be reached by plane or boat. It meant a visit to a different country (not Wales). Friday to Monday in an apartment at Pontins was *not* a holiday.

It poured. Fat, maximum-wiper, Welsh rain. But there was a swimming pool with a wave machine and a slide, and the cabaret wasn't bad — better than the Bon Jovi tribute act, that's for sure. She *said* she was having a good time. She managed to juggle a smile. But he wasn't stupid. On the way home, the wooden clown dangled from the car mirror and it occurred to him for the first time that there was something circus-like about her optimism; it was precarious, balanced on stilts.

When they got back from their not-holiday, Maureen had gone to Portsmouth to meet someone she'd met on the internet, leaving Jim by himself. Derek the rat was dead. Jim was pretty sure he'd remembered to feed him, but he couldn't be certain. After Maureen returned it was determined, via a process Darren never quite understood, to be Becky's fault.

★　★　★

Dad didn't mind Becky. When she came round in the evenings she commented on the telly, a bit like Mum, and as winter thawed and the weather improved she followed Dad out to the greenhouse and helped quietly, passing the test Colin tanked all those years ago. Still, when Dad spoke about her, an unspoken *but* hovered at the end of his sentences.

'She's a nice girl . . . She's got a kind heart . . .'

He'd be sure to follow up with: 'So you're staying here, then, son? Just driving a bus for the rest of your life?'

Prospectuses he hadn't ordered started arriving. From all over the country, the further away the better, it seemed.

★　★　★

At the end of the summer Darren came home from work and encountered a FOR SALE sign. He tried to make a joke out of it. Asked whether Dad was planning to emigrate. But it wasn't funny. It

260

felt like a punishment for being a rubbish son, for falling in love while he was supposed to be grieving. Of course he was gutted about Mum, but you can't keep things separate; feelings don't line up neatly like Neapolitan ice cream.

'I don't want to be looked after, when the time comes,' Dad said.

It was the bother with his prostate — that was all. He wasn't *properly* ill, though you wouldn't know it from the attention he was paying to his bodily functions: examining, measuring, listening, smelling, making a note of every small change and plotting his decline. He bought slippers — he *never* wore slippers, before — and he started to shuffle. Maybe it was the slippers: he'd chosen the open-backed, flip-flop kind. Even so, he was only in his early sixties back then. There was no excuse for any of it, especially the shuffling. It got on Darren's nerves; he'd lost Mum and he hadn't been expecting Dad to disappear, too. He offered repeated assurances. When and if the time came he would be happy to do any looking-after; they could live together indefinitely; no one's style was being cramped, and that was the truth. The moment he realised that perhaps *Dad* didn't want to live with *him*, Darren shut up and Dad started looking at retirement flats, even though he hadn't yet retired.

'There'll be a bit of money in it for you, son,' he said. 'Enough to go to university. I've read up on going through clearing — it's a doddle. You won't need to borrow a penny, long as you're careful.'

261

The semi-detached house in The Grove had been empty for more than eighteen months. The previous owner, an elderly man, had died there. It was beside the railway line and hadn't been decorated since the 1970s. Becky picked up the details during her lunch hour. Just a thought, she said.

The estate agent who showed them round was resigned. He sloped through the empty rooms, muttering, 'Lounge . . . hall . . . dining room . . . kitchen' — not even attempting a 'conveniently located', 'hidden potential' or 'in need of some updating'.

Dad said the money was Darren's to invest in The Future. They made a silly offer. It was rejected, but their follow-up, only somewhat silly offer was accepted. With the money from Dad and their combined wages they could afford it. It wasn't exactly difficult to get a mortgage, they were handing them out like hot dinners back then. They wanted the house to seem like theirs when they stepped through the door, so they decorated the hall first. It was a hard place to begin, with the long drop of the paper and so many door frames to cut around. Colin offered to help, but they wanted to do it themselves. The walls were cracked, uneven. Before they hung the lining paper, Darren drew a heart with their names in.

'We'll redecorate one day and *ta-dah*,' he said.

Once they'd papered and the paint had dried, he knocked nails into the wall for the five clocks

Dad hadn't taken to his new flat. He wound the weights each morning and the cuckoos sang on the hour and the half hour, making it feel like home.

They took up all the carpets and cut them into pieces for the allotment. Without his greenhouse, Dad's interest in it waned and it gradually became more theirs than his. Then came Christmas and the cold weather and they wished the carpets back as draughts breathed between the floorboards.

★   ★   ★

He wishes he could remember more of the year that followed. But contentment lacks specifics, it's easily swallowed and effortlessly stomached. He looked forward, welcoming each new morning as a means to an end, losing the detail of the days as he anticipated the moment when the house would be completed.

They started work on the kitchen. Its pine units and tongue-and-groove ceiling had oranged over the years — it looked like a sauna. They sanded the wood and caked it in white gloss. It took longer than planned. But these things did, didn't they? Becky worked towards her NVQ 3, they managed the allotment, listened to Colin as he fell in and out of love, drove Maureen back and forth to the station each time she went to Portsmouth, checked on Jim, who was in and out of the hospital by the park, and when the hospital by the park was full, they rattled along the M57 to Liverpool in the Fiesta, singing along to Nelly Furtado and Robbie Williams on the radio, Becky absolutely certain that *this* time Jim would have returned to himself.

They didn't take a holiday that summer; not so much as a long weekend away. They were saving up. When they had enough money they'd get cheap flights to somewhere exciting and a deal on a hotel. They picked vegetables and uprooted weeds. They decorated the dining room and the lounge, and finally the downstairs was finished.

★   ★   ★

Autumn drew in and Becky watched cookery programmes during the darkening evenings. She tried things out, determined to make them like they did on the telly. She grew herbs on the kitchen windowsill. He couldn't see that they made any difference to the food, but if putting green bits in everything made her happy, he was all for it.

At night she curled into him, breasts and thighs pillowing his back and bum. She wrapped her arm around his waist and he grabbed her hand. Sometimes he held it, other times he stuffed it down the front of his boxers; sometimes she laughed quietly, other times her soft fingers wrapped and wrung him. They were sleeping in a second-hand bed in the second bedroom. There were old-fashioned fitted wardrobes on either side of the bed; Colin had given them some boxes for the rest of their things. Becky's shoes and books were arranged

264

in neat piles on the floor alongside the things she was collecting, in anticipation of the conclusion of the work: cushions, towels, bedding. It felt like camping, a sort of adventure while they painted and cleaned and arranged the backdrop to the rest of their lives.

Christmas crept up on them, the house still unfinished. Maureen moved to Portsmouth and Jim's CPN found him a room in a B&B in town when he came out of hospital. One night Darren walked back from the garage after a late. As he reached the brow of the bridge he saw Becky through one of the first-floor windows, roller in hand. She was painting the biggest of the three bedrooms. It ran along the front of the house and would be theirs. He'd seen a king-sized bed with a brass-look headboard which he reckoned Becky would love because it looked old-fashioned and romantic, even though the 'brass' was made of some sort of coated plastic. It would be months before they could afford it, but he knew exactly where it would go and he'd imagined the way the light would stream through the two windows during the lazy mornings of weekends off. The way he'd sneak down the stairs in his boxers and wake her up with a cup of tea, after which they'd entertain themselves until lunchtime. Perfect.

He opened the front door carefully and tiptoed up the stairs to surprise her, only realising she wasn't alone when he heard her gentle, cajoling voice.

' . . . promise not to say anything until I've had a chance to talk to him.'

He waited.

'I want one of them beds with drawers in. And a telly. There, by the window. And a new Derek.'

'Derek stank.'

'He couldn't help it.'

'I'm not having a rat in the kitchen.'

'I'd keep him up here, with me.'

'You'd have to keep the windows open during the day.'

'All right.'

'We'd get some of that spray for smelly pets.'

'And I'd like one of them chinchillas.'

'One thing at a time. And no smoking — of *anything* — in the house. Darren doesn't like it. His mum died of lung cancer. You have to behave. Promise?'

He heard the wet wipe of the roller against the wall and the creak of the floorboards as she adjusted her stance. And he heard Jim's silence.

★ ★ ★

Becky *was* happy, he thinks. He doesn't *know*, though. The rehearsing of old memories can only uncover so much. He lacked imagination, he knows that much. If he had understood then what happens when someone you love steps out of the front door one day and never comes back, the way it marks a person, he likes to think he'd have been more careful. More observant. More . . . just *more*. If he'd understood the weight of caring for Jim. If, despite the easy supplanting of his own plans, he'd found room to imagine the way frustrated hopes might catch like hangnails.

266

If he had known, if he had thought, he might have done better.

Love. It fills you up. It's not that you can't eat or sleep, just that you don't need to because you're running on feelings — buzzing, elated; surging with it. Where does it go after its object is gone? His mum had an illustrated edition of *Pilgrim's Progress* when he was a little boy. She'd won it at school, a prize for something or other. Christian, the man in the story, had a bundle tied to his back. It looked uncomfortable, heavy, but he got on with it, did all his climbing and running and fighting with it fastened to him. It's the same with love, he thinks. It doesn't go anywhere. You can decrease its volume and increase its density, you can bundle it up, tight, but you still have to lug it around with you.

★   ★   ★

He rises from the sofa and the room tilts ever so slightly. Not a spin, thankfully, just a momentary slip in the axis of things. He stands, hands in pockets, and waits for stillness. He is sorry for himself — twat. He'll be on YouTube listening to The Smiths, if he's not careful. There. The room is righted and, slightly pissed and trawling for better thoughts, it is suddenly easy to consider the entirety of a notion that has been half formed for some time. And it is this: rivers must follow a particular course, and it may seem that feelings, like water, have no option but to wash a certain way. But, downstream from obstructions, an eddy can form, flowing in the opposite direction from the rest of the water: a place where you might go to experience a rest from currents and waves.

He trudges up the stairs, chucks his duvet on the floor and lies on the bare bed, head full of the river diagrams in his old textbooks. He thinks of mouths and plunge pools and V-shaped valleys, and it is only a small step to tiny shorts, burnished legs and a pair of platform shoes.

Exhibit: 'Becky Brookfield — the Untold Story'

Catalogue

Object: Gold necklace with a heart pendant.

Description: It looks like a pendant you might be able to open, but it isn't. It is probably very valuable. There is a green bit on the underneath side — it probably needs to be cleaned specially by someone who cleans gold for a job.

Item Number: 24.

Provenance: Darren Quinn (my dad) probably gave this to Becky Brookfield (my mother) as a present.

Display: Perhaps I can wear it. (Now? After the exhibit has closed?)

Curator: Clover Quinn.

Keeper: Darren Quinn.

13

Dad says he'd better visit Uncle Jim by himself because he may have seen the dentist, and if he has, there's a chance he'll be upset, and Uncle Jim wouldn't want her to see him upset. She agrees, not because she's worried about seeing Uncle Jim upset — that's happened before and he is always himself again, eventually — but so she can spend some time in the bedroom, which is shaping up nicely, even though it still needs more work.

She removes the folded duvet that lines the bottom of the wardrobe. There's something else underneath, one last thing that she'll get to in a moment. First, she unfolds the duvet and shakes it. Then she unfurls the soft sheet and duvet cover that she kept back and makes the bed. It does something to the room; she can see its shape now, the form it will take once she has removed the bin bags and the flattened boxes and arranged all the things exactly as she wants them.

The last thing in the wardrobe, if you don't count stray hairs and chunks of dust, is a skirt. It was rolled up in a ball. Initially, she thought it was a scarf. It's beautiful. There are two layers. The outer one is filmy, black with dark red flowers. The underskirt is also black, but it's made of a thicker, opaque material. She removes her gloves and strokes the fabric. She holds it up against herself. It's floor length; you could swirl in it. She lays the dummy on the bed and slips the skirt over the wooden stand and up to the nip of its waist. The drawstring can be tied tight. There.

When she tilts the dummy back to standing, its one legged-look has vanished and it seems as if there might be a pair of real legs hiding under the twirl of fabric.

She pops to the toilet. On re-entering the room, the dummy catches her unawares and tricks her into conjuring a person.

'Hello,' she says, her voice filling the new contours of the room. 'Do you like it here? It's my museum.' She pauses to smooth a crease in the duvet cover. 'There are so many kinds of museums, I've looked online: bus museums, tea museums, puppet museums, magic museums and quilt museums. There are even sex museums,' she says the S.E.X. word quietly — she doesn't think her mother will mind. 'This is a special museum. It's the only one. It's the museum of you.'

The dummy holds its position, indifferent and immobile, and she starts to feel like a wally. She doesn't have time for pretending — she still hasn't made a card like the ones she carried through the *Titanic* exhibition.

The cards are tucked into the back of her notebook. She reads them. They were written as if the passengers were talking to you: 'My name is Violet Jessop' and 'My name is Mildred Brown'.

'My name is Becky Brookfield,' she writes. 'I

271

was born on 21st June 1980.' She isn't sure what to put next.

'My name is Becky Brookfield. I was born on 21st June 1980. I had a brother called Jim and a boyfriend called Darren.'

No, that's not right, those things don't really say anything about her mother.

'My name is Becky Brookfield. I was born on 21st June 1980. I worked in an old people's home. I liked . . . '

What to write here? She could put travel, because of the brochures. Or she could put books, because of the romance novels and the library card. Or Westlife, because of the T-shirt. When Dad talks about her mother he says what she was *like*, rather than what she *liked*. He says she was kind. And very patient with Uncle Jim.

'I liked travelling and Westlife,' she writes. 'I was kind. I looked after my brother.'

How to finish? She checks the fronts of the cards from the *Titanic* exhibition and copies the same last line on to her mother's card: 'Discover my fate at the end of this exhibition.'

* * *

In the afternoon they pack the sleds into the boot and go to see Grandad. They take a carrier bag of vegetables: potatoes, onions, peas, runner beans and a lettuce. Dad messes about in the kitchen for a bit, opening cupboards and muttering about the drains before trying to tempt Grandad out of the flat with a walk to

Rich's Ice Cream for a single scoop of whatever they fancy. But Grandad thinks it's too windy, and he fancies a quiet afternoon, with Shakespeare — he says it as if they're friends.

They can't compete with Shakespeare, so they just stay for a bit. After they've watched a video of a cat dressed as a shark riding an automatic hoover they go out to the balcony. Grandad hands out enormous tomatoes and they eat them like apples. He keeps a container of salt on the balcony, in case of slugs. They sprinkle it on the tomatoes and the juice dribbles down their chins, warm and sweet. Dad invites Grandad to the dunes, but he snorts and points at his slippers.

'You could put shoes on, Dad. You know, those things people wear outside?'

'I go out every day.'

'Since when?'

'Since I read that sitting is the new smoking. I got myself some trainers. On the internet.' He shuffles back into the flat, slippers slapping at his heels, and returns holding a pair of white high-tops. 'I put these on in the mornings and then I walk round the block. Twice.'

'That's great, Dad. Good for you.'

'They're dead posh, Grandad.'

'I know, love. I read the reviews.'

'Good for you,' she says, just like Dad, and they all stand on the balcony feeling pleased with themselves.

★　★　★

273

Dad bought the sleds after the Christmas when she was seven and there was ten inches of snow. There hasn't been another winter like it, but the sand dunes are here all year long, bumping along the coast like a sleeping beast.

They climb the biggest dune. It's crescentic, Dad says, which means it's shaped like a C with a windward side and a slip-face side. There isn't a proper path and the marram grass spikes her legs. At the top, Dad holds the back of her sled so she can climb in. She sits, and for a moment it feels like she is waiting at the top of the world. She can see the bare beach and the distant line of the sea. She can see Blackpool on the other side of the estuary, tiny, like a model of itself — the tower, the swoop of The Big One and rows of houses as small as pencil dots. Then Dad lets go and she is flying down the windward side of the dune, her stomach trampolining to the back of her throat as she cuts through the sand.

When the sled comes to a stop she gets out and draws a line along its front with the tip of her shoe, marking the distance travelled. Once she is out of the way, Dad descends, hollering and laughing as he thunders down the drop. He passes her line and whoops.

'It's because you're heavier,' she says.

'But you don't press as hard into the sand as I do,' he replies, 'so you'd think that you'd go further.'

'You weigh more, so you slide faster.'

'I don't think that's how it works.' He clambers out and brushes sand from his jeans. 'But I'm not sure. It's physics. You can do it

274

when you get older, for GCSE, and then you can tell me. Race you!'

He grabs his sled and begins the slip-sliding run back to the top. She chases after and gives him a small shove as she passes. He trips and she can hardly run as she overtakes him, gasping with laughter, literally choking with the fun of it.

★ ★ ★

Afterwards, they play Monopoly. Dad buys everything he lands on, just in case, which means he rarely gets a whole set and almost never builds houses or hotels. She waits for the good stuff. The wind whipped salt into her hair; she smells like the sea and when she licks the skin around her lips she can taste the beach.

'Has it been a good few days?'

'Yes.'

'Three happy things?'

'Too hard to choose,' she says, and from his expression she can see that it is exactly the right answer.

★ ★ ★

Dad is on an early. It's warm today. Summer hasn't quite finished with them; this last burst of heat and light will crisp up the leaves as a parting kindness to autumn.

Now that the boxes aren't blocking the way, she can have another try at opening the window. She pushes hard. Nothing. Never mind. She sprays some of the perfume instead — it's almost as good as fresh air. She attaches the CD player to the waistband of her shorts and puts the headphones on, arranging them so they serve a dual purpose, music conduit and hairband. 'Beautiful Day' plays as she sticks the completed colouring pages to the wall with Blu-Tack. In each illustration a surprised woman is being visited by a heavenly figure. She has coloured and cut out the word SURPRISE and now she sticks it to the wall next to the window, beside the colouring pages and the two photographs of her with her mother. She adds the cautionary, bubble-written NIL ADMIRARI. Remembering the baby clothes Dad bought on the day she was born, she pops to her own room. There are two baby-grows, one white, the other pink, and there is a tiny red dress. In the bottom of her own wardrobe are several carrier bags stuffed with hangers, which Dad is keeping, just in case. Whenever people say, 'Would you like the hanger with that?' in a shop, he says yes. She returns to the second bedroom and hangs the tiny clothes from the picture rail. When she has finished this arrangement she props the MDF holiday collage and LOVE boards against the skirting board. She dashes downstairs to fetch her LOVE heading and sticks it in the middle of the board. The filled bin bags make the room look untidy, so she piles them into the space behind the door before arranging the dummy at the foot of the bed and repositioning the plait so it hangs from one shoulder. The black patent heels sit beside the dummy's base, like feet.

A pile of small things, many of them her

favourites, awaits her attention: the Little Golden Book, the notes from Uncle Jim, the teeth, the school report and school photograph. But she decides to finish the exhibit card first.

On the back of the *Titanic* cards it tells you *the fate* of the characters that accompanied you on your journey around the exhibition. She turns her mother's partially completed card over and writes:

The Fate of Becky Brookfield
Becky Brookfield died when her baby, Clover Quinn, was six weeks old.

When she has done this she places the completed card on the bed. The wardrobe on the right-hand side of the bed is still blocked by boxes. She has had a glimpse in one or two of these and they appear to be full of Dad's belongings from years ago: old clothes, school books, bits of paper, letters — possibly from her mother, but these things feel forbidden because Dad is alive and could sort them himself, if he chose. Still . . . she flicks the flaps on a small box into which she hasn't yet peeped. It's just old textbooks: *Study Advice for Geography A Level, Advanced Geography through Diagrams, Changing Environments* — boring. But, in between *Geography Direct* and *Britain's Changing Environment*, she discovers a sheet of newspaper, folded in half. She opens it and sees a picture of Dad wearing a suit, head turned slightly as he tries to avoid being photographed.

MISADVENTURE RULING
FOR YOUNG MOTHER

The death of a 21-year-old mother who was hit by a car involved no wrongdoing by the driver.

Rebecca Brookfield suffered serious chest injuries when she was struck by a Land Rover Defender driven by Michael Norberry and died at the scene, an inquest heard. Mr Norberry was not exceeding the speed limit for the road. He told the hearing that he didn't see Miss Brookfield until it was too late.

Coroner Julia Davy ruled that Miss Brookfield died as a result of misadventure.

Rebecca's partner Darren, pictured, wept as he said, 'We will miss her so much.'

Clover knows all these facts. But she has never seen them laid out like this. So bare. Lacking Dad's gentle explanations and elaborations. *Misadventure* — it sounds like an unlucky holiday. She retrieves the other newspaper sheet, the one about Mrs Mackerel — she needs to put it on the wall with the 'SURPRISE' display. And she grabs the passport photos. She lines the objects up on the floor in order, one, two, three: Dad and her mother, laughing and kissing; her surprise arrival; the misadventure.

Everything was fine and then she was born. It has occurred to her before, of course. Not everyone likes surprises. It might be a coincidence, like the way Uncle Jim finds he isn't feeling himself when something important is coming up — Christmas or Dad's birthday, for instance. But the one, two, three of it suggests otherwise. She places the latest newspaper sheet on the freshly made bed, beside the card, uncertain where to display it.

Once, last summer, she asked Dad *where* her mother had been going.

'To the other side of the road,' he said, which sounded like the punchline to a joke.

'But *where*, exactly?'

He pulled a face: made a sort of shrug with his mouth.

'And where was I?' she asked.

'Next door.'

'Why?

'I took you round, before work.'

'Why?'

'To give your mother a rest.'

'From me?'

'From everything.'

'And she went out, instead?'

There it was again, the mouth-shrug, a gesture that was part 'I don't know' and part 'I don't want to talk about this.'

'Why?'

'A change is as good as a rest. That's what they say.' He sounded like Mrs Mackerel.

⋆ ⋆ ⋆

She is sorting through the pile of small objects, lining them on the floor, when the air moves beside her, and she jumps. A gust of breath escapes her with an *umph*, and she scrambles to her feet, one hand held over her chest.

'Dad! You scared me! What are you doing?'

She pushes the headphones back so she can hear his reply. When he says nothing, she tries to explain.

'This is my — I've been making this — but, I'm not finished — it's nearly — you can't . . . '

She stops because of his face. It is *more* than everything. Piled with expressions, a combination that is completely wrong, like pudding and cereal and gravy all on the same plate. His mouth moves, but no words climb out. He looks at the coloured-in pictures on the wall; nudges her mother's black patent shoes with the tip of his toe; makes a small noise in his throat when he sees the hair; reaches out a finger to touch it and changes his mind.

She hears the winding in his chest and throat. It begins with one knot of breath and is followed by another and another. He's going to cry, properly. And because she doesn't know what to do, she leaves him there and hurries down the stairs.

★   ★   ★

She waits in the kitchen, supposing he'll join her once he's soaked up the surprise of it. But he doesn't come. She boils the kettle and works on the as-yet-unfinished speech that should have accompanied the *big reveal*. What had she hoped to say? Something about looking after culture and history. Something about taking care of people's stories. Her lips practise the words while her hands lift the mugs out of the cupboard and her head marks the time it's taking him to come and find her. She shouldn't have left the newspaper sheet on the bed. *Rebecca's partner Darren, pictured, wept.*

She steps back into the hall and treads carefully up the first stairs. He just needs a few moments, she decides. And then it will be fine. She will explain it all. They'll go through each element of the display together and he'll realise that it's a much better way to remember her mother than keeping her stuff in a great big jumble.

But when she rounds the corner, the bedroom door is closed.

★   ★   ★

Colin will be at work. So will Kelly. Mrs Mackerel will be dusting her cottage ornaments in preparation for Mrs Knight's visit — she's not the right person to ask anyway; she'd probably march upstairs and say, 'PULL YOURSELF TOGETHER!' That leaves Uncle Jim and Grandad. Uncle Jim is still in hospital — they say he'll be home by the weekend, if he behaves. He's probably the last person in the world Dad would want to see, literally.

She fetches the phone and dials Grandad's number.

'It's me,' she says. 'Can you come?'

★ ★ ★

Grandad arrives in a taxi wearing a pair of shorts, his new high-tops, a shirt and tie and a baseball cap. He pays the driver and shuffles down the path, squinting in the sunshine.

'I'm here,' he says. 'Is everyone all right?'

She doesn't know what to tell him. How to explain what she has done. She points up the stairs. 'I did it.'

'Did what, love?'

'And I don't think he likes it.'

Grandad looks at all the things in his way and tuts. 'Break my neck,' he says as he steps over and around the newspapers, the tins of paint, the books, clothes and motorbike helmets.

She follows.

When he reaches the landing he points at the closed door, eyebrows raised. She nods.

'A cup of warm water, please,' he says, as he fishes in his pocket and pulls out his notebook. 'You can leave it just here, on the floor, love.' Then he steps into the second bedroom and closes the door behind him.

Exhibit: 'Becky Brookfield — the Untold Story'

Catalogue

Object: Small wooden clown with pull-string.

Description: A wooden clown. He has a white face with a red nose and blue hair. He is wearing yellow dungarees and purple shoes. There is a loop of cotton behind his head so he can be hung up. He has a pull-string between his legs and his arms and legs shoot up when you pull the string, making him do star-jumps. He is a very happy toy.

Item Number: 27.

Provenance: It would be a bit fiddly for a baby to operate this toy. I expect Becky Brookfield (my mother) bought it for later, when I could use my fingers properly. She probably thought it would make me laugh.

Display: Hanging from a nail on the wall so its string can be pulled.

Curator: Clover Quinn.

Keeper: Darren Quinn.

14

He was coming off the Formby bypass in the 47 when a Fiesta slid over the intersection like shit off a shovel. The driver was only young; she must have thought she had time to nip out in front of him. He braked, but he couldn't avoid her. Smacked straight into the driver's side of her car. Wrecked every panel. And then, *bang!* — a white van went up the back of him. Jolted everyone. People yelped. It sounded like he was carrying a bus full of animals.

It wasn't his fault, a fact he supposes he will eventually find consoling. He pulled out of the way of the traffic, got out of the cab and moved down the aisle. 'Everyone okay? Everyone all right?' he asked. Back at the cab, he retrieved his phone from his sandwich bag and stepped off the bus. Someone was already leaning into the passenger window of the Fiesta, talking to the girl. He walked over. Didn't get too close. Didn't say anything. Just looked at her. She was bleeding from a long cut on the side of her head where she'd hit the window. But she was conscious, talking.

The van driver approached, uninjured and pissed off. 'I called an ambulance. They're sending the police, too.'

'Sorry you couldn't stop in time.'

'Yeah. Well. *You'll* be all right, won't you? Just say 'My neck hurts' and it's an instant thousand pounds if you're in the union. That's what I've heard. You in the union?'

'My neck's fine,' Darren said.

He needed to take photos of the damage. Needed to call his supervisor to arrange a replacement bus. Needed to take the names and addresses of the people who'd seen what had happened. But it felt like his feet were stuck to the road.

The ambulance arrived. Someone put a hand on his arm and said, 'Maybe you should sit down for a moment.' So he did. He sat on the grass verge and watched as an elderly passenger holding his wrist joined the girl in the ambulance.

★   ★   ★

By the time he'd spoken to Brian, his supervisor, and the police had finished with him it felt as if his head was bolted to his shoulders. If he wanted to look to one side or the other he had to pivot on his feet.

They sent an engineer and a relief driver with the replacement bus. The engineer drove Darren and the damaged vehicle back to the garage and then Darren caught a bus to town so he could go to the office and fill out the incident report. He had to go through everything again: his direction of travel, the speed he'd been doing, the weather, the details of the damage to the vehicles. When he reached the part where he had to draw a picture of the accident, he took a break; his head felt like it was trapped in a mangle.

Brian sent him home. The important thing was to keep moving, he said. In the old days people wore collars and kept still. Now the advice was to move as normally as possible. So Darren walked, trying to move in his usual way, even though his hands were trembling and he felt like Eagle Eyes Action Man.

He called out as he unlocked the front door and stepped into the house. He wasn't surprised at Clover's absence — she'd be at the allotment. He fancied a cup of tea and some anti-inflammatories and was about to boil the kettle when he heard something above. Went to check. Reached the halfway point on the stairs and noticed the door to the second bedroom was open. Carried on climbing. Arrived. Stepped into the room. Felt something in his stomach stretch and tauten like a skin on a drum. Stood there for a moment while every breath beat against it.

He couldn't make sense of what he saw. The bed made with their bedding, his and Becky's. Exactly as it used to be. The boxes on her side of it, gone. The dressmaker's dummy retrieved from the shed, wearing Becky's clothes, the bag across its chest, exactly as she used to wear it. Becky's *hair*. Oh God. Each breath smacked the drum of his stomach: harder, faster, harder, faster. Photographs, baby clothes, pictures of *beaches?* And there was Clover, bending over a small pile of things, Becky's portable CD player clipped to the back of her shorts.

When she noticed him, he was already past adjustment. The old helpless rage was back and it was bigger than him. He could feel it filling his

286

chest, blocking his legs, cementing his shoulders, making it seem as if he'd been pretending for years — how dare he forget the details of this particular pain? How *dare* he?

He had no words. And even if he'd been able to locate some, they wouldn't have made it past the latch of his jaw. Clover said something and waited for him to speak.

He couldn't.

And then he was alone in the room. He closed the door to protect her, and himself. To keep it all from escaping on to the landing and down the stairs.

★   ★   ★

The room smells of Becky. He glances at the little pile of things on the floor — the perfume, that's why. He likes to think he has been a good dad. But he isn't actually sure. He has tried. That much is certain. A for effort — ha! If Becky was here, and if she was herself, he knows she would adore Clover. She'd love her in the same unequivocal way she loved Jim; she'd speak to her in the way she spoke to the old people, her voice laced with patience and kindness; she'd read to her, bake with her, and there'd be a pet, something Jim could pretend to own when he came to visit.

He glances at the wall beside the window. At the word SURPRISE and the silly Latin writing beside it. At the photographs of Becky with Clover, and the religious colouring pages. Baby clothes hang from the picture rail — the tiny red dress he picked that first evening as he hurried round the supermarket, feeling not entirely dissimilar from the way he feels now.

* * *

It was terrifying. He skidded through the A&E entrance, knowing nothing, only that Becky was there and she needed him. They directed him to the postnatal ward and he dashed down the corridor, no idea what it meant. She was sleeping in a side room, and okay — *she was okay*. He was barely able to believe the woman's — the *midwife's* — next words. Minutes later he met the baby and her words became flesh.

The love. That was surprising. The instantaneousness of it. Standing beside the incubator while inexplicably crying. Laughing at himself for crying. Explaining that he was fine, and no, it wasn't the incubator that'd set him off, he was just surprised, really, *really* surprised.

There was nothing to her. She was wizened and skinny like a little bird, her tiny bones wrapped in papery skin. He could hardly stand to hold her. She felt so breakable. What if he dropped her? What if he pressed the dip in her head where the bones hadn't yet joined? He watched the way it moved up and down with her pulse. She wasn't even *finished*, and yet there she was, his and Becky's. A person made entirely of them. There were other ingredients, of course: bottles of Chardonnay and Pinot Grigio, fish and chips from South Garden, Toffee Crisps, Boost bars and experimental pasta dishes speckled by chopped-up herbs. The baby had been grown in a house-decorating, furniture-lifting, sand-dune-walking, old-people-caring, Westlife-listening, romance-reading body. And despite the less than optimal growing conditions, and his and Becky's lack of preparation, everyone said she was going to be fine.

* * *

Dad arrived with his cheque book and pen and a list he'd copied from the internet, detailing the safest car seats.

'Your mother would have loved this,' he said, and 'Everyone's all right then?', a question Darren answered with a 'yes' that almost sounded as unequivocal as he'd hoped.

Jim scuffed down the corridor, trainers squeaking. Grabby as ever, he lifted and turned things, touching stuff that didn't concern him. Becky let him hold the baby and Darren watched, hoping her arrival would annul any plans for him to move in.

'Look at you! *Uncle* Jim,' Becky teased.

'You can't put your finger in her mouth, *Uncle* Jim — it's not clean.'

'All right, *Daddy*.'

He left a series of messages on Maureen's mobile. She responded eventually, but gave no indication that she was planning to visit.

* * *

He used the holiday money. What else could he

do? If he's honest, he quite enjoyed spending it. He asked one of the female shop assistants to help, chose her specially because he was thinking about how much his mum would have enjoyed this task, and the woman looked motherly, as if she'd make exactly the right kind of fuss, which she did. She escorted him around the supermarket, advising him on essentials: the Moses basket, the rocking stand, the special, Tiny Baby-sized dresses and baby-grows, the nappies and wipes. She instructed him on the things Becky would need, laying them in the trolley herself: breast pads, disposable knickers and sanitary towels in packs so thick they could conceivably double as pillows. And a card, from him to Becky, thanking her for the baby; that was essential, she said. She gave him a big kiss at the checkout and told him he'd make a brilliant dad. He liked her. He saw her again, after everything happened. She asked how he was getting on. When he told her she had a little cry and kissed him again.

He drove home and made a list of the things he was leaving there, before returning to the hospital with the other stuff. Becky worked her way through the carrier bags. It should have been like Christmas. That's how he'd imagined it. But the more things she unpacked, the more worried she looked, and when he showed her the list — the Moses basket, the rocking stand and the various clothes he'd left behind — the extent of the expense dawned on her, along with an understanding of where the money had come from.

Colin told him to fuck off on the phone the following morning. 'April Fool's was last week,' he said. He called back in the evening. 'Meet me at the bus stop outside,' he said.

They sat beside each other on the yellow bench seat. Colin opened the carrier bag on his lap to reveal a six-pack of Stella, and Darren accepted a drink.

'You know what condoms are for, right? Here's a clue, they're not for making balloon animals.'

'Ha-ha.'

'Is Becky okay?'

'Yeah. Tired. A bit shocked.'

'And the baby?'

'Yeah. Tiny. You wouldn't believe it.'

'Everything's all right with you two?'

'Yeah. Course.'

'That's good.'

They drank and Darren waited.

'There's no reason why she'd keep it a secret? She's not scared of hospitals or anything?'

'No.'

'So the baby was doing somersaults and Becky was getting bigger and she just thought . . . '

'Neither of us thought anything.'

'You're still having sex though, right? I mean, surely you must have noticed — '

'I didn't.'

'If I ask something, do you promise not to lamp me?'

'I wouldn't fancy my chances.'

'Are you sure it's yours?'

'Course I am.'

'And Becky didn't know.'

'Yeah.'

'All right then,' he said.

The meeting ended awkwardly, Colin managing to simultaneously appear sorry *and* largely unrepentant about everything he'd said.

The next day, he turned up at the hospital with a jumbo teddy and a bouquet that was so ridiculous it wasn't allowed on the ward and had to be belted into the passenger seat of Darren's car.

★ ★ ★

How *could* someone not know they were pregnant? He found it hard to believe. It was bloody ridiculous. But he should have noticed, too. And he hadn't. People were sometimes surprised by babies, weren't they? Years of watching *Coronation Street* with Mum had certainly left him with that impression. Not many people seemed to make the discovery at such short notice, but even that wasn't entirely unheard of. The midwife told him that Becky's wasn't the first denied pregnancy she'd seen. And by 'denied', she didn't mean that Becky had necessarily known, it was just the name they used when the mother was unaware of, or unable to accept, a pregnancy. She sounded so reasonable and assured. Becky could have misinterpreted the physical changes, she explained, and that made it a bit easier to believe. Despite what he'd said to Colin, he *had* wondered — a horrible feeling, doubting her. He'd got no idea why she'd need to lie; he loved her and there was no way he'd have pissed off at the news of a baby.

He went over it again and again, looking for signs. They'd been decorating the third bedroom in the evenings and on his days off. Becky had been walking carefully, head stiff, like something might slosh out of her if she moved too much. She'd had back pain, but they'd been standing on ladders, painting ceilings and crouching over skirting boards. She'd put on a bit of weight, but it wasn't surprising, because they'd eaten a lot of takeaways while sorting out the house. She'd had indigestion. He remembered her crunching her way through rolls of those chalky tablets and glugging that pink stuff that settles your stomach. It never occurred to him to wonder if she might be pregnant.

★　★　★

There was a meeting before they were allowed home, to make sure they were ready. There were questions about Becky's childhood and how she felt about pregnancy in general. They asked what he thought of the baby and whether he smoked. It felt like an exam. The people asking the questions were apologetic. It was important, they said, in such circumstances, to monitor the attachment between parents and baby. Darren didn't mind the questions. The protocol helped — it couldn't be that unusual, he thought, if there were rules to follow and lists of questions to ask.

Later, one of the midwives escorted them to the car, insisting, despite his protestations, on carrying the car seat Dad had recommended and paid for. He didn't understand why he couldn't carry the baby himself. It felt like the midwife was making sure she didn't come to any harm while on hospital property. He drove home like a learner, hands at ten to two, ducking the speed limit, hardly able to believe they were allowed to transport such a teeny human.

Mrs Mackerel pounced as soon as they unfastened the car seat. 'Welcome HOME!'

'Where would we have been without you?' he said and thanked her again, which had her beaming.

'Isn't she GORGEOUS? What a SURPRISE! Have you THOUGHT of a NAME?'

'Not yet.' He answered for Becky, whose skin looked grey in the daylight.

'She's so SMALL. Are you WORRIED? Well, DON'T be. You'll be FINE. You're GREEN behind the EARS, but it's the same for EVERYONE in the BEGINNING.'

'We should go in now,' he said. 'Don't want her to get cold.'

As they stepped into the hall the clocks went off, a welcome-home fanfare. He closed the front door and they were a family.

* * *

Becky was in pain. Although the baby was small, she'd arrived quickly, ripping skin and tissue as she burst into the world. He'd seen the stitches.

294

Becky had shown him in a fit of despair. *Look.* They weren't at all as he'd imagined: more like a series of knots than the neat lines his mum had made with her sewing machine.

'It will be fine,' he said. 'It happens to women all the time, doesn't it?'

There was another tear, one they hadn't stitched, higher up. It would heal by itself, the midwife explained. In the meantime, Becky moved slowly and cried when she had to pee. They'd told her to pour a jug of warm water over herself as she did it, but she couldn't coordinate the urge with the pouring. He tried to help.

'I'll pour,' he said, pretending to be posh as he knelt beside the toilet.

She said she was ready and held the slack, empty nest of her belly out of the way, but when he poured she couldn't do it. 'Hurry up,' he called, which didn't help. She ran a bath instead, then stripped from the waist down, climbed in, peed and got out.

He knew it was hard. He also knew women all over the world had babies every day. And they fed them and changed them and loved them. So it was hard, yes, but it was also doable. People did it all the time, didn't they?

★   ★   ★

'We should take the baby to Peacefields,' he said. 'Everyone will want to see her. And they'll be missing you.'

'Maybe next week,' she said.

He returned to work, leaving the house reluctantly, hurrying home the instant he could. When he got back after his second shift, the baby was listless. Her skin seemed loose. He picked her up and she sagged, little legs dangling like skinny drumsticks.

'Don't disturb her,' Becky said. 'She'll wake when she's hungry.'

'When did you last feed her?'

'This afternoon.'

'When, though? I think we should wake her.'

They'd given them a book at the hospital. A sort of instruction manual for pregnancy. Most of it was irrelevant, but the last chapter was about newborns.

'Small babies mustn't go more than three hours without feeding, otherwise there's a danger of dehydration. Told you,' he said, cross with Becky for not knowing something he hadn't really known himself.

He set an alarm. Every three hours he lifted the baby out of her basket, changed her and passed her to Becky to be fed. Before he left for work he made sure the alarm was set for the next feed. Within twenty-four hours the baby looked better, but he kept setting the alarm, just to make sure.

★ ★ ★

There was such an enormous amount of shit for Becky to put up with: the stitches and the soreness, the constipation and the peeing arrangements. He hadn't expected the bleeding. She showed him the blood collecting in the nappy-like sanitary towels; it was coming out in chunks, like liver. And he hadn't counted on the state of her nipples. Everyone said breastfeeding was beautiful, natural. He'd never imagined that it might hurt. The midwife said Becky wouldn't bleed if she latched the baby on properly, but she couldn't get the hang of it.

'You've got no idea how much this hurts. It's like needles in your balls — imagine that.'

'It shouldn't hurt,' he coached as she struggled. 'Is she latched on properly? Is her head tipped back enough? I should be able to see her nose. You have to relax.'

She endured one humiliation after another; she leaked milk, and blood and tears. She was so brave and good. God, he loved her.

★ ★ ★

Mrs Mackerel came round with a bunch of daisies.

'Becky doesn't LOOK RIGHT,' she said as she left. 'Has she got some of that POST-MORTUM depression?'

'It's just baby blues,' he replied, parroting the words on the website he'd found. 'She'll be better in a few days.'

★ ★ ★

'You know when someone dies and you wake up in the morning and there's a moment when everything is okay?'

'Yeah.'

'And then it dawns on you.'

'Yeah.'

'And everything is ruined.'

'Yeah.'

'When I wake up and remember her, that's how I feel.'

'No you don't,' he said. 'Don't be silly.'

★　★　★

He bought flowers. Nice ones from a proper shop. Chose them himself. Pinks and whites with some of that fluffy stuff — 'baby's breath', the florist called it. That'd cheer her up, he thought.

★　★　★

When the midwife came, he covered for her.

'How are you getting on, Becky?'

'She's doing really well, aren't you, babe?'

How could he say otherwise? Becky covered for Jim and Maureen, always casting their actions in the best possible light. That's what she would expect of him, so he did it, newly aware that loving someone for herself involved also loving her when she was not herself.

★　★　★

'We should take the baby to Peacefields,' he said. 'Everyone will want to see her. And they'll be missing you.'

'Maybe next week,' she said.

* * *

Becky leaned against the worktop, vague and preoccupied. His words seemed to float past her. He asked again, determined to be patient.

'What do you think? We've got to choose.'

He'd lifted the Moses basket off the stand in the lounge and carried it through to the kitchen, where it lay on the floor beside him while he made tea. The baby was entering the restless stage before waking: her limbs were twitching and she made an occasional mewl. Becky eyed the basket with a wariness that made him uncomfortable.

'Daisy,' she said.

'Hmm, I don't know.'

'Rosemary.'

'Not bad. I think — '

'Clover.'

He glanced at the yellow tub on the worktop, at the bunch of white flowers from Mrs Mackerel, at the herb tray on the windowsill.

'Are you just saying random stuff? Working your way round the room? You are, aren't you? God, Becky. I've got an idea, how about Toaster? Eh? Daisy, Rosemary, *Clover!* You want to name her after margarine?'

'It's butter.'

'Butter? Oh, *that's* all right then!' He strode to the fridge, tugged it open and glanced at the contents. 'Tell you what, let's call her Stella. That'll make a good story when she's older.'

He slammed the fridge shut and carried on, racking his brain for edible names. He knew he was being a dick but he couldn't stop.

'Olive — too posh. Sherry? Come on, what do you think?'

When she replied, her words came out slowly, as if uttering them was the most enormous effort. 'I. Really. Don't. Care.'

'All right, all right.'

She looked like she was about to cry. He knew she cared, underneath.

'So let's have one of yours.' He considered her suggestions: Daisy and Rosemary were girly, names he'd never have chosen, not in a million years. 'How about Clover? It's not bad, actually — sounds nice, soft. She'll be the only one in her class, won't she? I think it suits her. What do you think?'

'If you like,' she said.

The baby — *Clover* — started to cry. He lifted her out of the basket and passed her to Becky. It was years later, when Clover was learning to write, that he noticed the word *love* hiding in the middle of her name.

★ ★ ★

He was adaptable, a veteran of abandoned plans. But Becky seemed to be grieving the loss of hers. There was something steely in her that resisted a change of course. Something broken, too, he noticed, a crack in her characteristic optimism. And he began to see how, despite her persistence and patience, Jim broke her heart, as did her mother and the dad she so carefully remembered — her whole fucking family broke her heart and, if he didn't act, he could see how he might join them.

★ ★ ★

A four-pack of Boost bars. Her favourite treat. Wrapped in shiny paper and ribbon.

'This should give you a boost,' he said.

She would have laughed, before. At the very least, groaned.

★ ★ ★

He drove round to Dad's and asked if he would mind writing a cheque for a steriliser. Although he was on board with *breast is best*, something had to give.

Becky leaked through the breast pads as she bottle-fed Clover, soaking her T-shirts with circles of milk. She still cried during feeds. Now it was guilt.

★ ★ ★

'We should take Clover to Peacefields,' he said. 'Everyone will want to see her. And they'll be missing you.'

'Not yet,' she said.

★ ★ ★

Clover was sick on Becky after every feed. It was

301

funny, a coincidence that had the potential to turn into a running joke, like Colin getting sprayed when he opened bottles of fizz, or the way half-drunk autumn wasps always dive-bombed Dad. It was one of those things, that's all. But Becky took it personally — she was taking everything personally. He began to wish Clover would be sick on him, just to level it out. Once or twice he winded her especially vigorously, goading her gag reflex.

The sick got in Becky's hair and she didn't have time to wash it every day, so she started tying it back in a plait. It made her look different, older. Like a mum. He was used to it down; even for work she only ever tied up a piece from the front, always leaving the back part loose.

'I must be feeding her wrong,' she said.

He tried to help, watched as she did it, making suggestions: perhaps if she held Clover differently, sat straighter, was more relaxed.

'You do it,' she'd say. 'You're better at it.'

★   ★   ★

He went to the library on his way home from work. Once he'd registered and received his ticket, he grabbed a small stack of novels from the Romance section. He was about to present them for stamping when it occurred to him that it might be good if there were some babies in the books. The covers were child-free, but that didn't necessarily mean the stories were. He found a chair and made himself at home, flicking through the last pages of each book. A couple ended in weddings, one in a very steamy sex scene — he rearranged the pile on his lap — another with news of a pregnancy. The characters fell in love and then what? What came next? Perhaps the next part of the story was not appealing to the writers; he hoped it was appealing to women in general, and to Becky in particular.

He gave up searching and took the stack of books to the desk. 'These aren't for me,' he explained. 'They're for my girlfriend.'

The woman nodded. She didn't care and her expression indicated that she only half believed him. He could feel heat creeping into his cheeks and around the back of his neck.

And after all that, Becky didn't read them.

*   *   *

The midwife's visits ended and the health visitor made an appointment.

'Tell her how you feel. She'll know what to do.'

'She won't take Clover away, will she?'

'Why on earth would she do that?'

'If I say I'm not looking after her properly.'

'You *are* looking after her properly. You're just worried. You're very worried. And tired. That's what you'll tell her.'

'What will she do?'

'She'll talk to you. And then you'll feel better.'

'Is that all?'

'Yes, that's all she'll do. Promise.'

'But if that's all, how will it help?'

He didn't know. He didn't know anything.

The health visitor said she needed to wash her hands, but he was on to her: she was checking up on them, seeing whether the bottles were sterilised and the dishes washed. They were: he'd got wise to the midwife's hand-washing and had made sure everything was tidy.

He was on a late that day and wanted to give them some privacy, time to have a proper chat, so he waited in the kitchen with Clover, enjoying the chance to hold her while she slept. But after a while curiosity got the better of him and he tiptoed through the dining room and into the hall, where he could hear them talking.

' — questions we ask. Is that okay?'

'Yes.'

'And are you having any difficulty sleeping?'

'Not really.'

'Feeling anxious or worried?'

'Sometimes.'

'Have you been crying more than usual?'

'I don't — I don't think so.'

'Are you enjoying the things that you used to enjoy before the baby was born?'

'I *think* I would, if I had time.'

The health visitor laughed sympathetically as he loitered in the hall, twitching. If he interrupted, what would the health visitor think? Bursting into the room to contradict Becky would be a betrayal. As were her denials. If he interrupted there'd be an argument and Becky would cry. Could they really take Clover away if they knew she was struggling? He waited and pretended a timely arrival when the health visitor commented on the baby's unusual name.

★ ★ ★

A cookery book from Oxfam: *Faster Pasta: Good Value Family Meals*. No wrapping paper or jokes this time. No words, either: his actions would express things better than he could — *I love you, I've been thinking of you.*

'I know I haven't been doing much cooking, but — '

'That's not what I meant.'

' — every time I try to do something she starts crying. I can't get anything finished — '

'I didn't mean for you to — '

' — I know I'm not doing enough, and I'm sorry.'

'No, it's my fault,' he said, retrieving the book. 'I'm sorry.'

★ ★ ★

There were purple-brown smudges under Becky's eyes. If she could get some proper rest he knew she'd feel much better.

'You need to make sure you sleep when the baby sleeps,' he said.

She flinched, and although he hadn't done anything wrong, her response made him feel as if he had slapped her. She was like a cactus, there was no handling her.

They needed help during the day, he decided.

She wouldn't go out, so he'd provide her with company, someone to keep an eye on things and see that she got some rest. He asked Dad, who was still working at the Philips factory during the week, but potentially free during the weekends Darren had to work. Dad recommended caution: child-rearing was up to women, and if there was one thing women didn't like, it was interference. Anyway, he'd never fed a baby or changed a nappy. He wouldn't be averse to giving the garden a bit of a once-over, though, if that was of any use? Darren said he'd get back to him and instead asked Mrs Mackerel if she'd mind popping round for a couple of hours on the odd afternoon. But she was supervising the tiling of her roof, and once that was completed she was having her back garden paved, which meant she needed to be in the house to make cups of tea and oversee everything. Ha! — needed to let them know who was boss, needed to interfere and tell them off at every opportunity, more like. Colin laughed when Darren asked if he'd like to come round and have a go with the baby. In the end he called Maureen.

'I think Becky would really like to see you,' he said. 'And you've not met Clover yet.'

Maureen came up from Portsmouth on the train, just for the day. Becky was terribly anxious. Unfinished projects loomed large: the uprooted upstairs carpets, the bare walls and lack of furnishings. He cleaned the bathroom and wiped the kitchen worktops, bought a Victoria sponge and a new one of those plug-in air fresheners Becky liked — Linen and Lilac.

Maureen arrived laden with carrier bags of newborn clothes. A grand gesture and total waste of money — she could at least have bought different sizes or, better still, bothered to ask whether there was anything in particular they needed. Once she'd cooed over Clover for a few moments, she got stuck in.

'What's your brother doing in a B & B when you've got all this space?'

'We were decorating the front bedroom for him, before.'

'That's right,' he agreed, determined to present a united front, though they still hadn't discussed it properly and Clover's arrival surely jeopardised the plan — he certainly hoped so.

'It's going to take us a while to finish things off, Mum. We had to buy baby things. There's no carpet upstairs and — '

'Of course, if you're worried you could always take Jim back to Portsmouth with you,' he said, and Becky's face fell; he'd promised not to cause trouble.

'Perhaps I should. When was the last time you saw him?'

'Last week,' he said. 'He came round for tea. I cooked. When was the last time *you* saw him?'

'This afternoon, before I came here. And he's not well. You'd know if you'd been looking out for him.'

'God, he picks his moments.'

'Don't, Darren.'

'There's no reason why one of you couldn't put the baby in her pram — '

'We haven't got one yet — '

' — and walk down there to check on him. It'd do you good, Becky. Get rid of some of that fat.'

'Cup of tea, Maureen?'

He didn't wait for an answer, he left the room as fast as he could, the expletives swimming in the pouch of his throat like fish.

As Maureen left, she took Becky to one side and, in a stage whisper, hissed, 'You'd better pull yourself together — brush your hair and get some make-up on. He won't hang around if you don't.'

He'd never felt more like punching her. He wasn't going *anywhere*. But later, in the evening, when he was washing the bottles, Clover started to cry and he discovered Becky sitting beside the Moses basket, staring into space, as if the baby was nothing to do with her. He decided he was doing quite a bit more than his fair share and called Colin.

'What're you up to?'

'I'm on the train, to Liverpool.'

There was a whoop and a few half-arsed cheers in the background and Darren experienced a stab of self-pity. He should be out having fun too; he hadn't asked for any of this.

'I'll wait for you at Moorfields if you like. How long do you think you'll be?'

'I'm not going on the pull with you.'

'Why not? I used to go with you.'

'We were pulling girls then,' he said, although what he really meant was *I need someone to talk to.*

'Oh, don't be such a baby. You'll love G-Bar, it's a right laugh, and it's mixed. *Come on!*'

308

'No, you're all right.'

He went out by himself. Walked down the road to the Blue Anchor and nursed a pint of cider while checking his watch. Clover should have had her ten o'clock feed. He hoped Becky was all right.

On his way home he went to Bargain Booze and bought a bottle of Malibu and two litres of Lilt. When he reached the end of The Grove the house was in darkness. He was glad: it meant Clover had gone down after her feed and Becky had followed suit; it made him feel better about leaving them. He watched crap on the telly and drank until he was nicely pissed. He went up to bed clumsily, stood on a pile of Becky's books, stubbed his toe on the corner of the bed and woke Clover.

'You have no idea how long it took me to get her to sleep.'

Her voice was weary and he realised that she hadn't been asleep at all but had, in fact, been lying there, wide awake.

'Sorry.'

'I'll get her, you're drunk.'

'Not drunk, just a bit pissed.'

'Pissed, then.'

'Sorry.'

Once she'd changed and calmed Clover, she climbed back into bed. He was half asleep, fuzzy, relaxed.

'I might do something,' she whispered, her voice so quiet that it felt like he was hearing her thoughts. 'Something stupid.'

He couldn't let it pass without comment.

'What do you mean by stupid?'

'I don't know.'

'You won't. You're not stupid.'

In the morning, when it was light, her words seemed imagined, nightmarish. And he didn't know how to ask her about them. His dad had talked a man off a bridge — where was *his* emergency reserve of words?

⋆　⋆　⋆

He noticed the missing clocks the moment he stepped into the house. The hall looked bare and unfamiliar.

'They were driving me mad.'

'Where did you put them?'

'Back in their boxes. In the dining room.'

'It looks shit now.'

'Get some pictures like a normal person.'

'There's no need to be — '

'You try staying here all day with five ticking clocks going off every thirty minutes, an alarm every three hours, and a screaming baby you weren't planning on having.'

'Okay,' he said. 'We'll put them back when you're feeling better.' And he pulled the nails out, just in case they snagged and hurt her as she passed.

⋆　⋆　⋆

Later that week he came home from work to find Clover in the basket in the lounge — face scrunched and purple, occupied almost exclusively by her

310

mouth, which had subsided into a wide, raging yowl. He attempted to calm her as he searched for Becky, heart pounding.

She was in the bathroom, sobbing quietly. She looked strange: there was something odd about her face. No, it was her hair. It was gone. *Gone* — fuck. It lay on the floor beside her, a bobble fastened around one end, the partially unbraided curls at the other fanning the floor. He cradled Clover in one arm and bent to retrieve the hair, stupidly holding it up to Becky's head for a moment, as if he might refasten it. Accepting the impossibility of his wish, he laid the hair to rest in the sink and went downstairs.

'Can you come?' he asked Kelly. 'With your hair things?'

'Is everything okay?'

'Not really,' he replied, experiencing the relief of making the admission to someone at last.

Becky sat on the side of the bath, her face mottled and swollen. She'd stopped firing blank, dry after-sobs; Clover, too. The crying over, he allowed himself to feel wronged. He loved her hair, she knew that. Yes, it was *hers*, but she could at least have told him, let him know what she planned. It was hard not to take it personally, to see it as a protest.

'Hiya, Becky,' Kelly called as she stepped into the bathroom. 'Darren says you fancy a — oh, you had a go yourself . . . ' She paused and studied Becky's lop-sided mop. 'Not to worry,' she said, smoothing her own hair, which was elfishly short and pillar-box red. 'I know the feeling! Sometimes I want a change and I can't wait.'

She lifted Becky's hair out of the sink, getting him to hold the bobbled end while she re-plaited the length. Standing like that, on the holding end of the job, opposite a chatting woman with busy hands and a concentrating face, reminded him of folding sheets with his mother when he was a boy, and he was struck by a bolt of missing her. Once she ran out of hair, Kelly dug in her bag for a bobble and fastened it around the plait so it was secured at both ends.

'You could do something with this, you know? Send it off to a charity, to be made into a wig.'

He didn't know what to say. The idea of someone walking around wearing Becky's beautiful hair made him feel queasy. Becky said nothing; she appeared, for the moment at least, to be past speaking.

'No? Well, you could just keep it, if you like. That'd be fine, too. I've got my nan's plaits. She had her hair cut when she was twelve. Wanted a grown-up style. If you ask me, she ended up looking like Paul McCartney — I've seen the photos — but she liked it, that's the main thing. She went to the hairdressers' after school and they started by chopping off her plaits. They let her take them home with her. Is there a chair you could carry up, Darren . . . no? Don't worry. Could you just swizzle round and face the tiles?'

Becky placed her feet in the empty bath and faced the wall, as if in disgrace.

'I'm going to comb through your hair, just to get rid of any tangles, okay? Anyway, I found them — my nan's plaits — in a drawer when I was about six. The hair was dark brown. Hard to

312

believe they were my nan's, because she was white-blonde by then. You know how some people go blonde to cover up the grey? I loved them. Used to play with them all the time.'

He was so glad to have her there, flattening his fright with her stream of ordinary words. She didn't know Becky terribly well, but she touched her like a friend, and although her words came fast, her hands were gentle as she smoothed the jagged hair at the base of Becky's neck in a stroking motion that seemed to say, 'There-there, there-there.'

'So, I'm thinking that we want to make your hair look uniform, but still hold a nice shape while you grow it out — if that's what you're planning?'

Becky didn't answer.

'Hair like yours is difficult — I mean, it's really lovely and you're very lucky, but it's tricky. And I haven't got much experience. You have to cut less than you want because curly hair shrinks. What I need to do is minimise bulk and maximise curl. Then you can wear it back from your face, like Andie MacDowell in *Four Weddings and a Funeral*. That'd be nice, wouldn't it?'

'Don't worry about all that, Kel. Just tidy it up.'

'All right,' she said, setting to with her scissors. 'So, have you got any holidays planned?'

Becky made a choking noise. 'Ask Darren,' she said.

Kelly glanced over her shoulder at him. He shook his head and she stopped talking and concentrated on Becky's hair.

'We should take Clover to Peacefields,' he said. 'Everyone will want to see her. And they'll be missing you.'

'I miss it.'

'Well, exactly. That's what I've been saying. *That's* why you need to get out, see people — '

'Going there will only make it worse.'

★ ★ ★

On his day off they took Clover to the clinic to be weighed.

'She cut her hair,' he told the health visitor as Becky undressed Clover.

'Looks lovely.'

'But she's always had long hair.'

'People often fancy a change after they've had a baby.'

'She did it herself. With the kitchen scissors.'

'That was brave! No harm done, it suits you, Becky.'

'She was very upset.' Becky was going to be furious with him, but his worry was finally bigger than his fear of hurting her. 'She was crying.'

The health visitor inclined her head. 'How are you feeling?'

'Tired,' Becky confessed.

'Emotional?'

'A bit.'

'Are you eating?'

'Yes.'

He couldn't understand what food had got to

314

do with it. 'Tell her what you told me in the night.'

Becky froze. 'What?'

'The other night.'

She looked from him to the health visitor, deciding. 'You mean when you were *pissed?*'

His mouth dropped open and the health visitor inclined her head again, this time addressing him.

'You shouldn't smoke — '

'I don't!'

' — or drink around the baby.'

'It was the first time I've left Becky alone with her at night, apart from at the hospital. I was a bit tipsy when I came to bed, that's all. Becky was looking after her.'

'What did she say that worried you?'

'I don't know what he *thinks* he heard, but he was pissed.' Becky placed Clover in the scales. 'Look at that!'

'Oh, that's great. I *thought* she'd put some weight on when I saw her. How many ounces is she having now?'

And, just like that, his concerns were cast off and replaced by a conversation about Clover's weight, sleep and bowel movements.

'I can't believe you did that to me,' he hissed as they returned to the car.

'The feeling's mutual,' she said.

★   ★   ★

The black skirt from Dorothy Perkins. It had been in the window, before, and she'd commented on it. 'That's pretty,' or something, she'd said. It wasn't in the window any more, but it was easy to find: red flowers, floaty, delicate.

'I bought this for you.'

There was a flicker of something in her expression, and he felt pleased with himself.

'Try it on. Go on.'

He waited in the lounge, but she returned still wearing her trackie bottoms and T-shirt.

'It's too small.' Her voice was small, hurt.

'But the waist is elastic.'

'I know.'

'And it was the biggest one they had,' he said, which made things worse.

*   *   *

Clover had been crying since he'd arrived home at six o'clock, longer if he counted the hour Becky claimed before his return. Fists clenched, knees flexed; two whole hours of screaming. His ears were ringing, his forehead and neck rigid with tension, his throat squeezed by a clenching anxiety.

There was a knock at the door and he answered, nursing Clover as she howled.

'COLIC!' Mrs Mackerel shouted. 'BICYCLE HER LEGS. Put some CAMOMILE TEA in her BOTTLE or get some GRIPE WATER.'

She turned to leave, changed her mind and stepped, uninvited, into the house. She took Clover from his arms and sat on the sofa with her. There was something in her confident, no-nonsense hands that stopped Clover's crying.

She moved Clover's legs up and down and spoke to her sternly.

'THAT'S ENOUGH. If you're going to keep SCREAMING I'll need some of that CAVITY WALL INSTALLATION.'

Clover paid attention.

'THERE'S ABOLUTELY NO NEED FOR THIS. Your mother looks AWFUL.'

Clover listened, eyebrows raised, forehead wrinkled.

'Get the GRIPE WATER *and* the CAMO-MILE TEA. Don't put all your CHICKS in one BASKET.'

'Eggs,' he said.

'NO, I DON'T think so. I wouldn't feed EGGS to a baby THIS SMALL.'

She passed Clover back to him and strode out of the house. But within moments, Clover was screaming again.

★   ★   ★

It's possible for a loving person not to love their own baby. He saw it, but didn't comprehend it; couldn't quite believe it. Becky had got off to a slow start, he decided. It was like the other kinds of love: sometimes it took a while to build. Once she had forgotten her chewed nipples and stopped leaking blood, once she had noticed what everyone else saw, that Clover was her in miniature, perhaps she would be able to forgive her for arriving.

★   ★   ★

317

There were sparks at the edges of his vision as he approached the end of The Grove on his way to the garage. It had been the worst in a series of worst nights. Clover was in the throes of her first cold. When she finally fell asleep the mucus bubbled in her nose and throat, keeping them awake. In the early hours she filled her nappy and the shit oozed past its waistband, right up to her shoulders. He changed and cleaned the Moses basket while Becky dealt with Clover. After her feed, Clover coughed, and the whole lot spouted into their bed. He changed the bedding and wiped the mattress while Becky changed Clover and prepared a second bottle. There were quiet moments during the rest of the night. He'd managed *some* sleep, dozing off each time Clover calmed down. But Becky hadn't slept at all. Every time he'd stirred during the previous few nights, she had been wide awake. She needed to sleep.

He turned back, hurried down the pavement and the driveway and tiptoed up the stairs. They were flat out. Clover, arms up, surrendered to sleep at last. Becky, completely under the covers, starfishing the bed in his absence. This memory is well worn; *lift the covers and kiss her goodbye,* he sometimes tells the self that stands in the bedroom on that particular morning. *Wake her and say you love her,* he instructs. *Better still, stay home, don't let her out of your sight.* But the self in the room scribbles a note, instead: *Clover next door for a couple of hours. Get some rest xx.* He lifts Clover out of her Moses basket, grabs a couple of nappies and the packet of wipes and tiptoes downstairs for the tin of formula and a pair of sterilised bottles.

Mrs Mackerel's bell played Brahms' 'Lullaby'. It was early, and her workmen were nowhere to be seen. The door whipped open and there she stood, feet planted, body braced, ready to be affronted.

'OH, it's YOU,' she said, apparently disappointed not to be accosted by an early morning, bell-ringing burglar. 'And *the baby*.' Her voice softened as he proffered Clover and the bag of baby things.

'Please,' he said.

* * *

He sits on the floor beside the shut door, head resting against the wall. How to tell Clover about what happened next? He can take the pieces of the story and arrange them this way, that way, but the fact is, he doesn't really know. He doesn't know whether he inadvertently cleared the way for Becky to do something stupid by leaving her on her own. He doesn't know whether he saved Clover by removing her after that worst of worst nights. He doesn't know whether it was an accident; a mistake caused by exhaustion. He doesn't know whether it was planned; an idea he could have cut off, uprooted, if he'd tried harder. And he'll never know. Right in the middle of him there's a not-knowing hole that he has filled with every kind of just-in-case and maybe-one-day thing he can find. And shame. A horrible, vacillating shame. Shame that she may have preferred death to a life with him. Shame at the comfort that comes from imagining her loss as an accident. It has been such a long time since he ploughed this ground. By the time Clover started school he was convinced that there weren't any new ways of getting at the pain, yet here he is, sitting in a room full of it — assailed by another instance of not-knowing.

There are tears on his cheeks. Idiot. He swipes them away with the back of his hand.

And then the bedroom door is opening and closing, and it isn't Clover but Dad entering the room, making a low whistle as he perches on the end of the bed.

Darren stares at Dad's high-topped feet and bare legs, at the tessellating veins and the slack skin that collects under his knees in a series of smiles.

'Well,' Dad says, and then he pauses to inhale.

Darren hears the steady, reeling sound of breath and awaits the cast.

'At least she didn't pour water over everything, eh?'

Darren laughs. It's a bark, involuntary, almost a half-cough — it certainly hurts like a cough, scuffs the back of his throat, bangs against the dread skinning his stomach.

'You kept all this, then?'

He nods and his neck burns.

'For Clover?'

He doesn't know.

'Is this what she's been doing all summer? Not a boyfriend after all?' Dad picks some papers off the bed. 'And you — you're all right with this ... *arrangement* she's made? You don't mind?' He pauses to allow Darren to respond.

He can't.

'But of course you mind,' he says. 'She's made a thing. A sort of guide to *this*.' He settles himself on the bed and examines the papers and a notebook.

'You remember Paul?' he asks, when he has finished reading.

'Mum's . . .'

'That's right, your mum's Paul.'

'Yeah, she had that picture.'

'She did. She kept some other things, too. Just a few. To remember. Her old ring, a necklace he'd bought her, a couple of cards from their wedding, the photograph. Different situation, hers, not like yours . . . This — this is . . . I'm not criticising, I'm just saying, son — this, what you've kept, *is a lot*.'

'It wasn't deliberate.'

'Well. That's time. Catches up with you.'

Dad gets up and opens the door. He comes back in almost immediately with a mug that Clover must have left for him. He makes a note in his B&B book before taking a sip.

The wall is hard against the back of Darren's head. His neck is knotted and when he swallows there are repercussions in his shoulders.

'I'm just going to wait here with you, son.' Dad takes another sip and Darren hears the water move down his throat. 'Warm water,' he says. 'It's good for you.'

The sun streams through the window:

summer's last hurrah. Soon it will be autumn again, another year drawing to a close.

'You and me, we were your mum's second chance. And she was happy. Wasn't she? People get them sometimes — second chances. Course, they have to be open to them. Receptive.'

Darren closes his eyes. He hears the sticky sound Dad's old mouth makes as it opens and he waits for the words, but they don't come. He hears the sound again and wonders what it is about these particular words that makes them hard to articulate.

'There are ways to love someone who no longer has a body.'

Darren opens his eyes.

'But you need to keep your best love for a person who breathes, someone who can love you back.'

'Just like you do?'

'I'm old enough to give advice that I've got no intentions of taking, it's a privilege of age, and if you've got any sense you'll listen instead of trying to smart-mouth me.'

Darren listens, wondering where all these words are coming from.

'Your mum used to visit Paul's mum every so often. Nice lady, kept his bedroom exactly as it was when he died. Dusted all his things, guarded them for years, as if she was expecting him back. It was a sort of pretending. People do strange things.'

'I'm not . . . it's not pretending. I just never got round to this.'

'You never got round to lots of things.'

'Yeah.'

'It's a shame.'

'You've not done much in recent times, either.'

'And?'

'I suppose you're going to say that's a privilege of age, too.'

' 'Sir, I am too old to learn' — that's *King Lear*, that is.'

'And you *learned* that when, last week?'

Dad chuckles. 'Touché,' he says, and raises his mug in a toast.

There is a relaxing of something between them, allowing Darren to ask, 'What shall I do with all this then?'

'It's up to you, son.'

He looks at the bin bags and the displays, the little pile of objects on the floor beside the bed, some of which aren't even his, and he feels lost.

'You've done really well. I wondered how you'd get on. No one to help you.'

'People helped.'

'No wife to help you.'

'No.'

Dad taps the side of the mug with his index finger. *Tap, tap, tap.* 'Would you like some help now?'

He shifts as he thinks about it, trying to find a more comfortable position for his aching neck. Today it's not so hard to believe that, once, his dad talked a man off a bridge.

Exhibit: 'Becky Brookfield — the Untold Story'

Catalogue

Object: Black T-shirt with 'I'm flying without wings' written across the chest in white letters. This was the name of a pop song from 1999 by the boyband Westlife.

Description: The very T-shirt Becky Brookfield (my mother) was wearing when Darren Quinn (my dad) photographed her in the hospital.

Item Number: 28.

Provenance: Becky Brookfield wore this T-shirt when she had to go to hospital after she'd had an unexpected baby (me, Clover Quinn) in the kitchen.

Display: Placed on a dressmaker's dummy.

Curator: Clover Quinn.

Keeper: Darren Quinn.

15

The next day Dad seems older, sadder. It's the combination of his stiff-necked stance and his *everything* face, the way he is wearing the hurts of the crash *and* the hurts of the past.

'I've asked Mrs Mackerel if you can go round to hers for the day.' His mug of tea settles on the worktop like a full stop.

'What? Why?'

'I know you were trying to do something nice. The display and the sorting, all the things you organised. I need to think about what to do with them.'

'I'll stay downstairs,' she says, not wanting to go anywhere while he messes with her exhibit; she hasn't even finished yet. And it's *hers*: the objects she has been looking after, the story she has been telling, the woman she has been building — all hers. He can't just mess it up. 'I won't come up. I'll keep quiet. You won't even know I'm here.'

'No, I don't think so.' His stiff neck is interfering with his facial expressions. His mouth isn't opening properly, which makes it difficult to decide if his stern face is intentional. 'Did you throw anything away?' It seems to have only just occurred to him. She wishes she could say no. 'Clover?'

'Yes. I did.'

'It wasn't yours. You can't throw away things

that don't belong to you.'

'Can I throw things away that are mine?'

'What things?'

'Things I don't want.'

'What don't you want?'

She thinks of all of the things in her room: the record player, the guitar, the books that are too young for her, the skateboard she has never so much as stood on, a bazillion soft toys she didn't want and doesn't like. Now's her chance to tell him. That would wipe the sad, poor-me expression off his face and make him consider how *she* feels, having spent all summer on her exhibit only for him to act like she's done something awful and mean. It's like he thinks her mother is just his. But he doesn't own her; she is hers, too.

'Nothing,' she says, in a way that lets him know there are lots of things, tons, in fact, but she won't stoop to name them right now.

'Let's not fall out,' he says, shoulders square, head immobile.

No, *let's*, she thinks. Let's fall out. Let's have a big fight like people on the telly. Let's say things we don't mean and get so carried away that you accidentally tell me all about my mother. Every. Last. Thing. She is angry. *So* angry with him. The anger swims around her insides, heating her cheeks, tugging at her face. If there was a mirror in the kitchen, her face would be a picture. Her anger must be *ad oculos* — obvious to anyone who sees it. And *wham!* Something else is *ad oculos*, too: Dad, who is calm, and kind, and frequently resigned, is *angry*. Really, really angry.

When he is upset, his *everything* face isn't made of everything at all, it's made up of what is missing: a great big helping of anger.

'I told Edna you'd be there any minute.'

'I *made* it. It's *my* exhibit.'

'Clover . . . '

'If the things were too important for me to touch, why didn't you look after them — '

'They aren't *important*, that's not why I — '

'Just because you're really angry — '

'I'm not *angry* with you, I'm just — '

'Just because,' she tries again.

'That's enough.'

'Just because you're really — '

'This isn't helpful, stop it.'

'Just because you're angry with — '

'I'm not *angry* with anyone, I'm just — '

'You can't keep her all to yourself. She's not *your* mother, she's *mine*.'

A burst of breath comes out of Dad's mouth. He tries to gather his words, but she finds some first. Full of her mother's story — the love, the surprise and the misadventure, the one, two, three of it — she says, 'Maybe you wish I was dead and not her.'

His feet stay put, but his top half sways, as if he has been hit.

What an awful thing to say. And it's not true. She knows it, right inside herself, in the exact spot where her feelings are made. It's completely untrue.

He picks his mug of tea off the worktop and holds it in both hands. 'Have you finished?' His face is set, determined, and she can see that the entire exchange has been a total waste of time. She has said some terrible things and she hasn't even changed his mind.

'Yes.'

'Off you go next door then.'

'All right,' she manages. 'I'll just get my stuff.'

★　★　★

The doorbell plays 'Amazing Grace'. She waits, holding a carrier bag containing the scarf she is knitting for Dad, and tries to rearrange her face into something neutral. The scarf hasn't got any longer since she was last here; Mrs Mackerel will tell her off.

The front door opens.

'ENTER at your OWN RISK!'

As she steps inside she is reminded of last summer when she was *much* younger, and she feels like a great big baby who can't be trusted to be left alone.

They have tea and digestive biscuits and watch people shouting at each other on *The Jeremy Kyle Show*: a man who won't look for a job argues with his mother, and a woman who has won some money on the lottery explains why she won't share it with her sister.

'SILLY GIRL. She should have stayed UNANIMOUS.'

Jeremy makes his concerned face and poses on the step of the stage as a fight breaks out behind him. Mrs Mackerel tuts and sighs.

'You're VERY QUIET today.'

'Hmm.'

'You're usually as HAPPY AS A BEE IN A DOG HOUSE. Are you WORRIED about your DAD?'

'No.'

'He's INJURED. You should be LOOKING AFTER HIM.'

'I know.'

'Well. Maybe it's YOUR AGE.'

Mrs Mackerel slides her feet out of her slippers. A little cloud of talc puffs and settles — the heels of her pop socks are dusty with it.

'I'm THROWING DOWN THE GOBLET. I'm going to BEAT YOU in a KNITTING RACE.'

She tucks her feet back into her slippers and leans over the arm of the chair, reaching for her knitting bag.

'Here, I'll do it.' Clover gets up and lifts the bag.

Mrs Mackerel digs in it until she finds a ball of thick mustard wool and a chunky pair of needles.

'Oh, not those needles. They're huge. You'll be way faster than me. It's not fair.'

'NOT FAIR? I'm OLDER and SLOWER.'

Mrs Mackerel waves her hands helplessly and feigns a tremulous, feeble smile. But as Clover puts the bag back on the floor beside her chair, she is already making a slip knot.

By lunchtime Clover is coming a poor second to the loose-knit mustard *thing*.

'What *is* it, anyway?'

'DOESN'T MATTER. You're being BEATEN by a PENSIONER. Better PULL your socks OFF.'

They share a plate of crab paste sandwiches and Clover has a packet of Frazzles and a carton of Ribena. When she goes to the toilet afterwards — 'Best have a WEE before *Murder She Wrote*' — there is blood in her knickers.

I am *hurt*, she thinks. I am *dying*.

Eyes closed, she searches for the pain. In the glittering dark she concentrates on the space behind her lids, where the part that is *her* lives, and then she thinks herself down, past her throat and into her stomach. And lower, feeling for the source of the leak. 'Are you all right?' she asks the meaty, inside parts of herself, the parts she has only seen on diagrams.

She sits on Mrs Mackerel's powder-blue toilet and waits. But there's no reply.

No pain.

Nothing.

She is fine.

Which means this is *it*. Her period. And although she knew it would happen one day, she is taken aback and experiences a strange feeling of separation from the body that has been making these arrangements behind her back. *Surprise*, it seems to be saying, *gotcha!* Surprises like this are part of being a woman, she thinks.

And she *is* a woman.

She is a *woman* — the thought is too big to think while sitting down, so she stands, shorts and knickers around her ankles, and stares at her reflection in Mrs Mackerel's mirror-fronted medicine cabinet: hair like her mother's; face all her own. For the moment at least, she looks exactly the same on the outside.

330

She wants to tell someone, but she can't think who. Kelly, perhaps. It might be nice to have someone make a fuss of her and tell her the things no one thinks to say — there's bound to be a big list, she's sure of it because there was when she got her bras: no one said the straps dig into your shoulders and sometimes slip down; no one said the label near the fastener would itch and it might be best to put the bra on back to front and then whizz it around before putting your arms in. She made these discoveries herself. Perhaps she will have to make the period discoveries on her own, too.

She wipes again. There is a little more blood. It's not like a nosebleed, it's less red and snottier, somehow. There's not much, but it might start to come faster — that's what happens, isn't it? What to do? She's been kicked out of home, *banished*, until at least four o'clock. If she was to return early for *this*, Dad would have to be nice to her. She entertains the idea for a moment and then discards it. She takes her stained knickers off, folds them in half and in half again, until they are small enough to squeeze into one of the front pockets of her shorts. And then . . . and then . . . she can do it . . . she reaches for the bag that sits on the floor beside the toilet.

The Tena pants are white with a picture of a purple dragonfly on one side. They feel exactly like a nappy, except the top part — the tummy and waist bit — which is thinner and softer than she is expecting. She steps into them. She doesn't remember wearing nappies, perhaps it felt like this. She pulls up her shorts and steps a circle around the bathroom to see if the pants make a noise when she walks. They don't, but she feels like a sumo wrestler.

★ ★ ★

She sits on Mrs Mackerel's sofa in her Tena Lady Pants (Discreet), knitting, watching *Murder She Wrote*, occasionally glancing up at the Virgin Mary on the wall, who is wearing an expression that is both surprised and pleased — the exact one Dad was supposed to adopt, in fact. She feels completely different on the inside and wonders whether it shows yet. She is half expecting Mrs Mackerel to notice and burst out with, 'I know it's NONE of my BUSINESS, but . . . ' just like the sharp-eyed Jessica Fletcher.

This is what life will be like when she is an old lady — knitting, afternoon telly and special knickers — but she isn't old yet and there's no way she is spending the whole afternoon on Mrs Mackerel's sofa.

'I think I need to go and water the allotment now.'

'Are you SURE? Your dad NEVER MENTIONED it. I don't want to get CAUGHT IN THE CROSSHAIRS.'

'It's fine.'

'When will you BE BACK?'

'I won't be long.'

Mrs Mackerel puts her ugly knitting on the covered arm of her chair and pushes herself up.

She looks slow and old and something tugs in Clover's chest.

'Just sit down,' she says. 'I'll show myself out. And I'll bring you a beetroot.'

'Oh, that'll be LOVELY.'

★   ★   ★

Clover sneaks around the back of the house and gets her bike out of the shed. Then she wheels it down the path and out, on to the pavement. The padding on her bottom acts like a cushion, it's a comfy ride up the hill and down, past the shops and the post office, *whoosh* — hair blowing behind her like streamers.

The gate hasn't been fixed: the smallest of nudges makes the catch slip and it yawns open. She slides off her bike and holds the warm metal. Gently, gently, she edges it, until *click*, it's shut again. She pushes her bike down the track, and as she approaches the allotment she notices that Dagmar is there, lying on the carpet beside her trolley, drawing.

'Hello,' she calls, rolling from her front to her side. 'I wait by the shop and you are not coming. So I think you are here. I just push the gate and it is opening. You don't mind?' She makes her dash of a smile, so fast you might easily miss it.

'No.' Clover sits on the carpet, too.

Summer is fading fast. There are gaps now, empty rows of disturbed soil where onions, potatoes and beetroots used to be; only a few sad stragglers remain, unharvested in the hope that they'll grow a bit more. The broccoli and pumpkins are coming into their own, but everything else is ending. Leaf tips are curling. Stalks are yellowing. The apple tree in the wild allotment next door is loaded with fruit. If no one picks it, it will all fall off and it will be wasp heaven, literally.

She looks at Dagmar's sketch pad. 'That's good. I like the way you've got the beans from the ground up, so they look like they're going really high. Like something from a fairy tale.'

'Thank you.' There's no fuss with Dagmar. No pretending modesty or fishing for compliments.

'Do you want to know something?' Clover asks.

'I don't know until after you have told me. And then it will be too late.'

'Something happened today.'

Dagmar waits, impassive, patient.

'I had a big fight with my dad,' she says, surprised by the words — she had intended to tell Dagmar about her period. 'And I said some horrible things.'

'You are being angry?'

'Yes.'

'*Hněv je špatný rádce.*'

'Hen-yev ye sh-patney rad-ste,' Clover tries.

'It means anger is a bad . . . helper. No, advice-giver? My mum is saying it. To my dad.'

'How is he?'

'It is a good week. He is sleeping every night.' She flicks her fringe away from her eye. 'And how is your dad, after you are being horrible?'

'I don't know.'

'You are sorry?'

She thinks about it. 'Mostly.'

'You will say it?'

'Yeah. I suppose.' She lies down too, back on the carpet, bum warmed by the Tena pants, and speaks the words she had originally planned to say. 'I started my period.'

'You are twelve. It is expected.'

'I *know*. But . . . '

'But?'

'I don't know! It's a big deal too, isn't it?'

'You are happy about it?'

She has no idea whether it is something to be happy about. She glances to the side, eyes shaded by one hand. 'I like talking to you. You say unexpected things.'

Dagmar looks flushed, pleased. 'I don't know what to say now.'

'That's okay.'

Although the sun is out and the carpet is warm there's something in the air, a smell perhaps, a slight spikiness that will sharpen the coming autumn mornings. The sun slips behind a flossy cloud and there's a bit of a whoosh as the wind brushes the tips of the big trees that border the allotments.

'Next week,' Dagmar begins, and Clover wants to shush her. Next week is not something she is allowing herself to think about. The autumn smell seems stronger now, and it is accompanied by an ending feeling: the nights will get darker, the allotment emptier and the mornings cooler. Dad will burn the rubbish. They will stand in wellies and jackets beside the licking flames, downwind from the billow of the smoke, and afterwards they will sprinkle the ashes on the soil, ready for the new things to be planted and grown next year. There will be Halloween, and Bonfire Night, and Christmas, and then it will be next year.

'Next week, we are going back to school and . . . you don't have to be knowing me.'

'But I *do* know you,' she replies, appalled that Dagmar is reconciled to the possibility of being ignored. Just thinking of it makes her feel sick. 'And anyway,' she says, realising, as she forms the words, that they are true and at least one good thing has happened this holiday, 'we are friends.'

'I am glad,' Dagmar replies, fiddling with her pencil for a moment. 'I am checking the name days and I find Cecílie on the twenty-second of November. It is the only girls' name with 'C'. So I am thinking it can be your name day.'

'Okay.'

'And I will bring you a present.'

'Epic!'

'Now I am drawing. And you are doing the gardening.'

★   ★   ★

Mrs Mackerel comes to the door with her knitting.

'YOU'VE BEEN GONE A LONG TIME.'

The mustard *thing* has grown. It's too wide to be a scarf and too long to transform into a section of jumper.

'I THOUGHT about COMING TO FIND

336

YOU. But it would have been like LOOKING in a HAYSTACK full of NEEDLES.'

'I'm sorry. Here's your beetroot, it's not very big, there's only little ones left now. I should go home and make the tea.'

'ALL RIGHT. I hope your dad GOT SOME REST for his NECK.'

'What are you knitting?'

'WAIT AND SEE.'

⋆　⋆　⋆

Once she has swapped the Tena pants for a sanitary towel and binned them in a pass-the-parcel bundle of knotted carrier bags along with the stained knickers, she makes the tea. She mixes runner beans with boiled cod and a packet of cheese sauce. When it's ready she knocks on the bedroom door.

'Down in a minute,' Dad calls.

She waits, planning her apology. As it gets later and later, and the plate cools on her lap, she begins to anticipate an apology from him, for spoiling the food. But when he finally appears he doesn't comment on the temperature of his tea.

'I've been thinking about this morning,' he says, between cheesy mouthfuls.

'Me too.' Her voice is small, mousy.

'I have *never* wished you dead. You know that, don't you?'

She nods. Of course she does. She tries to eat, too. The cheese sauce is horrible cold. It has grown a sort of skin. And the beans make a rubbery kind of squeak when pressed between her molars. 'I'm sorry for saying it.' She puts her fork down. 'I was angry.'

'I know.' The way he shovels the cold, squeaky slop into his mouth makes her wonder whether he has had any lunch. 'And what you said about me being angry?'

She nods again, her skin prickling with embarrassment.

'It made me feel angry — ha!'

She tries to smile at his joke, lips straining like a weightlifter's arms. She can't do it. None of this is funny.

'Do you trust me?'

'Yeah,' she says because it is the right answer.

'Look.' He pulls out his phone and shows her a series of pictures he has taken. Pictures of the dressmaker's dummy and the decorated walls; the magnet-spotted radiator and the made bed; the Becky Brookfield exhibit card and the MDF boards. 'So you can remember it,' he says, which makes her feel like crying, partly because it sounds like he has moved everything and partly because he is trying so hard to be kind. 'When I've sorted through it all, we'll go up together and talk about it, okay?'

'Okay.'

That's it. He doesn't ask about her day, so she won't tell him. He will realise about her period eventually, even if it's not until she writes 'sanitary towels' on the shopping list. In the meantime, she waits, withholding the news like a punishment. She won't say a word about it until he asks if she is all right.

She makes sure she has a pen and paper ready when *Bake Off* starts so she can write down any raspberry recipes, as promised. The bakers start with self-saucing puddings and two of them use raspberries. The recipes are complicated: one makes chocolate, lime and raspberry fondants; the other does strawberry, rhubarb, raspberry and orange puddings. The puddings are hard, but she makes some notes anyway.

Dad doesn't come downstairs, even though they always do this together. By the time the bakers get to the showstopper, she stops listening for him. The showstopper is baked Alaska, this amazing thing where you coat a cake with ice cream before smothering the whole thing in meringue and cooking it in the oven. Three of the bakers make their Alaskas with raspberries. There's mango, raspberry and coconut baked Alaska; pistachio, raspberry and chocolate baked Alaska; and raspberry ripple baked Alaska.

One of the Alaskas, not a raspberry one, melts because it is very hot in the tent where they do the baking. The ice cream just slides off the cake like butter. The baker gets really cross and chucks the whole thing in the bin. It's very exciting, and for a few moments she forgets that Dad is upstairs dismantling her displays. But when the programme ends and he doesn't appear with one of his daft treats — not a Cornetto or a meringue nest in sight — it's rubbish.

Still, she is a *woman* now. She is leaking actual

blood. She thinks she has heard Mrs Mackerel mention *the blood of life*, though it might have been bread . . . Anyway, *the blood of life* — it sounds good, doesn't it? She sits on the recliner, *the blood of life* seeping into the sanitary towel (with wings) that is fastened to her knickers. She feels ripe and responsible. Grown up. Until scenes from *One Born Every Minute* trickle into remembrance, and *blood of life* has other connotations — pain and screaming and umbilical cords, purple-knotted and pulsing. Actually, it's just *blood*, she thinks. Forget the *life*.

As an adult, she decides to take the high road and forgo her treat with good grace. She remembers something Mrs Mackerel says. She got it from Jesus, who was good at taking the high road: *forgive him, for he knows not what he does.*

Exhibit: 'Becky Brookfield — the Untold Story'

Catalogue

Object: Magnets & mugs.

Description: A small collection of fridge magnets and mugs (plus one egg cup and one tea towel) with sayings written on them:
'You can't scare me, I have children.'
'The first thirty years of parenthood are always the hardest.'
'I need a time out.'
'When I count my blessings I always count you twice.'
'Home is where the hugs are.'
'A family is a little word created by love.'
'To the world you may be one person, but to one person you may be the world.'
'God could not be everywhere and therefore he made mothers.'

Item Number: 30–37.

Provenance: Becky Brookfield (my mother) collected them. Perhaps she planned on having a kitchen like people on the telly. One with a fridge covered with pictures and plans of what every person in the family is doing. Clover Quinn (me) was born in the kitchen, so it is actually a special place and maybe that is why Becky Brookfield wanted to buy these things.

Display: Put the magnets on the radiator because it is magnetic. Display the other items on the floor beside the radiator.

Curator: Clover Quinn.

Keeper: Darren Quinn.

16

After the front door slammed he'd stood alone in the kitchen and finished his mug of tea, hands shaking, neck aching. 'Maybe you wish I was dead and not her' — how did such a thing get thought, let alone said? He'd never seen her like that before. Never imagined such a disagreement. It was fixable though, wasn't it? Almost-teenagers said all sorts, didn't they?

He rinsed the mug and went upstairs. Clover hadn't got around to his things. He was grateful, until he got stuck into them himself and realised that practically everything he had saved was rubbish. He uncovered school exercise books, swimming certificates and football cards. He opened another box and discovered a pair of aviator sunglasses, a Spiderman annual and his old school tie. In another he found cassette tapes, an insert template and some home-made single and album cover designs for his and Colin's band, Mad Scouse.

He fingered one of the inserts, a sketch of him and Colin — stick men with daft hair and boxing-glove hands — hanging out of the top window of a badly drawn tower block. Their first album was going to be called *Mad Scouse in the House*. He'd pestered for a guitar for his birthday and had been disappointed because the one Mum and Dad chose was second-hand and there were scratches on its body. At least they bought him a *How to Play* book, too. After he mastered the section titled 'Seven Basic Chords', Colin came round with his portable ghetto blaster and they recorded themselves, taping over the cassettes they'd previously used to record the Top 40 off the radio on Sunday afternoons. Darren's guitar playing was stilted, and Colin couldn't sing. They practised 'Sweet Caroline', 'Love Me Do' and 'Leaving on a Jet Plane', all sung and played with unscripted pauses as he worried the fingerboard between chords. They were crap, but imagined a day when they might be good. 'The next Oasis,' his mum said, encouragingly, and although they knew it wasn't likely, they basked in her optimism and scoffed the Curly Wurlys and cans of Tango she left on a tray outside the bedroom door. Mad Scouse: it was such a crap name for a band, an amalgam of northern pride — the whole Madchester thing — with reference to the nearest big city (Liverpool) and a light-hearted nod to BSE, which they found hilarious at the time.

In among the rubbish he found a packet of old photographs. Finally, something worth saving. There was only one roll of film and the pictures were pretty crap, truth be told. They were taken with a disposable camera. Maybe he could photograph them with his phone and filter and sharpen them, airbrush shiny foreheads and fix red eyes. They were of the house when he and Becky first bought it. There were far too many wasted shots of empty rooms. He wished he could go back in time and insist that either he or Becky be in each picture. But at least they were

344

in some of them. He flicked through the bundle: him, holding a paintbrush like a microphone; Becky, coating a strip of wallpaper with paste; him, rolled up in a length of old carpet, face creased with laughter; Becky, clasping a sheet of sandpaper, grinning into the camera. Sanding was such bloody hard work, but she *was* happy — there was the evidence. He studied her mouth and saw something of Clover in the sequence of her teeth and the creases on either side of her smile. By the time Clover was old enough to ask whether there were any pictures besides the one on the mantelpiece in the lounge and the one in her room, he could only remember the two of Clover and Becky together, which are awful. The pictures in the packet should be up somewhere, he decided. He'd give them to Clover so she could make a proper display, one they'd put up in the lounge — something real and genuine, so much better than her dead-end clues and half-baked assumptions.

★   ★   ★

It happened at the bottom of the bridge, just where The Grove meets the main road. If you stand on a chair and lean out of the front bedroom window, you can see the exact spot — another reason to cede the biggest room to Clover and retreat to the back of the house. The car hurtled over the hump of the hill and Becky stepped out in front of it. Those are the facts.

Here are some more: he was up to date with the shopping; there was milk in the fridge and tea in the caddy. She had her bag with her. The red one. It flew off and scuffed the tarmac. She had her purse and her keys and she was dressed for the weather, which was pleasant, warm. There had been only one phone call that morning. From the pay phone at Jim's B&B. Afterwards, the police assured him that there was no evidence she intended to leave him; it hadn't occurred to him until they said it.

On the day, the road was closed and the buses re-routed. He did a loop of the diversion before he knew; behind schedule, worrying about reaching his timing stops. They were waiting for him on Lord Street. Two police officers, a man and a woman, and Dave Newton, relief driver, ready to take over the shift. He climbed out of the cab, knees spongy, feet flat and clumsy. It was Dad, he thought: a heart attack, or a stroke. He braced himself for it as they escorted him to the car they'd parked on the double yellow lines behind the bus stop. There was time for a moment of embarrassment as he settled into the back seat alongside the female officer — did it look like he was being arrested? There was time to fasten his seatbelt, time to tense in anticipation of the blow. The woman started to speak, and time bent and stretched; he was newly aware of the intersecting muscles in his face and the effort it took to hold his mouth closed. He remembers the woman's shoes. As she spoke he counted the little holes that patterned the toes. There was something horribly wrong with her words. If he concentrated on the pattern, if he locked his jaw shut with cheeks and

346

teeth, he might contain the howl.

They drove until they reached the bridge. The police officer blocking it waved them through. They edged past a Land Rover sitting sideways across the road, fixed in the aftermath of a brake and swerve and crept to the end of The Grove. Mrs Mackerel came straight out, holding Clover. She followed Darren and the officers into the house.

'SIT DOWN,' she said, like she owned the place. 'I'll make him SOME TEA, *God love him.*'

'Would you like us to call someone?'

'No,' he said.

But they did. And over the course of the afternoon and evening they arrived. All of them: Dad, Jim, Colin and Maureen. Like the animals in *The Little Red Hen.* He'd asked for help and they'd refused, appearing only when there was nothing to be done. They were too late. He hated them.

★ ★ ★

In the days that followed one or other of them was constantly there.

'It's a good job Clover wasn't breastfed,' someone said as they scooped formula into a waiting bottle.

'You've got to stay strong for the baby.'

'You'll always have part of Becky with you.'

He was stunned by their stupidity, their need to fill the air with empty words. He could barely speak for fear of shouting. They talked as if

Clover's presence was a consolation, but she was not the part of Becky he wanted.

He wandered around the house, abstracted and surrounded by mysteries. He couldn't fathom how Becky's toothbrush existed when she did not. How the date on the tins in the cupboard extended past the end of her life. How letters addressed to her landed on the doormat. How her side of the bed could be empty. How the baby that woke him in the night was his responsibility for at least the next eighteen years — people spent less time in prison for murder.

They spoiled Clover. Held her all day. Showered her with all the love and sympathy they'd have given him if he'd let them. At night they left him on his own with her and she cried. When they returned in the mornings she seduced them with her newly acquired trick: the throwing of gummy smiles every which way — feed me, change me, play with me. He hated her, too.

★ ★ ★

Jim couldn't remember why he'd phoned. When asked, he said he thought he'd been calling to see how Becky was. Or to tell her about the new pet shop that had opened in town. Or to find out whether the number 60 on the washing machine was the wash cycle in minutes or something else. Or to say he'd lost the remote for the telly in his room and did she know where he might be able to get another one. Eventually, Darren stopped asking. What difference did it make, anyway?

The nights were the worst. His brain manufactured 'finding' dreams. He looked for Becky, searching in far-flung places: up mountains, across grassy planes, in crowded city streets, constantly seeking, always on the cusp of finding . . . and then Clover would cry. Sometimes he listened with disinterest as she howled so forcefully it seemed she might burst with rage. Sometimes he cried, too; matched her sob for sob in a peculiar anguish contest, and she would stop for a moment and listen, curious about the source of the other noise, the agony and anger pouring into the dark.

★   ★   ★

People tied flowers to the lamp post at the bottom of the bridge. What had the lamp post got to do with Becky? he wondered. Someone discovered that he lived right there, down The Grove, his house facing the bank of the bridge. Flowers appeared on the railings along the top of the bank, and then in front of the house. They were accompanied by cards addressed to 'The Baby's Dad' along with teddies and helium balloons for Clover. A pair of photographers stood in the driveway, cameras noosing their necks. 'Tragic Dad, Darren' — that's what they called him in the paper.

It rained, and the cards turned to papier mâché. Colin came with a pair of secateurs and a roll of bin bags. He started at the lamp post: cut everything off and stuffed it in a bag. Next, the railings. And finally the front wall and driveway. Pulped cards, soggy teddies, rotting flowers — he binned the lot.

It was better.

People stopped slowing down on the bridge to peep past the railings and trees to the house at the bottom of the bank. And the driveway no longer felt like a cemetery.

There were more flowers, after the inquest.

'Fucking idiots,' Colin said, bin bag and secateurs at the ready. 'Making a mess. Fly-tipping their crap everywhere. How'd they like it if I shat on their doorsteps?'

Darren felt he was pantomiming fury in an effort to sound him out, hoping to discover how he felt about the uncanny display of collective grief. He was angry, course he was. All those people who didn't even know Becky, co-opting his sadness. But the anger was dark and strong and he was already learning to spread it thinly like Marmite.

At twenty-four he was newly aware of the stretch of the years. He had no appetite for life, he was beholden to it — obligated, like a perennial, to keep on living because of Clover. And he was alone because of her, too — he allowed himself the thought, even though it was dangerous, a tightrope to be tested with the tip of one toe. Afterwards, he retreated to the edge of the precipice, where he waited, imperilled and unsteady.

★　★　★

350

He shopped late at night when the supermarkets were full of gruff blokes with pallet trucks, restocking the shelves. No one tried to talk to Clover, no one stopped to congratulate him for babysitting his own child.

He drove down to the allotment, lulling her to sleep with the drum of the engine, and placed her car seat on the old carpet while he planted rows of potatoes: red Desiree, Maris Piper and Charlotte; hard as pebbles, the life tucked inside them.

⋆　⋆　⋆

Clover's smiles were followed by sounds. Sometimes when she woke in the night she soothed herself with wordless babble and returned to sleep. She started to turn when he entered a room, extending her arms in anticipation of his embrace, sanding the worst roughness of his feelings.

He remembered that being loved keeps babies alive. And he loved her. Of course he did. She wasn't a consolation prize or an 'at least'. She was his daughter.

⋆　⋆　⋆

Edna took Clover while he worked. When he was on lates, Colin or Kelly would collect her from Edna's at six o'clock and entertain her at home until he got back. After Dad retired he sometimes helped, coming to the house with his B&B book, tying a hanky over his nose and

351

mouth if he had to change her, recording her input and output alongside his own.

He and Dad might have been a comfort to each other. But Darren noted the slope of Dad's shoulders and the drag of his feet and it wound him up, made him want to shout, 'I feel worse! I am the winner of this competition!' He made no concessions and allowed no comparisons between their griefs. By the time he realised how ridiculous he was being, the damage was done; the distance drawn, and delimited.

★　★　★

Every day he drove his bus over the bridge, past the house and the spot where the Land Rover hit Becky. It might help, he thought, to live out the middle of his life away from the places where his happiness began and ended.

He put the house up for sale.

It might help, the estate agent advised, months later, to have a bit of a sort out or, if he didn't mind her saying, to invest in some *storage solutions*.

He took the house off the market.

★　★　★

Clover was eighteen months old when the health visitor asked how many words she knew. He wasn't sure. Did he talk to her? she asked. Yes, he thought so. Was he saying things out loud or merely thinking them? she wondered. He didn't know, couldn't say. He should try a running commentary, like the football on the radio, she explained, in case he hadn't got it. Tell her what you're doing, as you do it; she'll like that. So he did: Daddy's making you some lunch; Daddy's putting the washing in the machine so your clothes will be clean; Daddy's taking you next door to play so he can go to work; Daddy's singing you to sleep so you're not afraid. The health visitor was right, she loved it. And the next time she came he had a list of words to tell her. But he felt guilty for his silence, if that's what it had been; he didn't know, he couldn't remember — *doesn't* know and *can't* remember those early years.

★ ★ ★

Colin appeared one day with a ukulele.

'Remember Mad Scouse? I did a house clearance and I found this baby guitar. Thought you could teach Clo. Maybe *she* could be in a band one day.'

'It's not a baby guitar.'

'Oh.'

'It's a ukulele.'

'Ah.'

'Nothing like a guitar.'

'Right.'

'Totally different things.'

'Okay.'

'And she's way too young to learn an instrument.'

'You can be a right twat sometimes,' Colin said as he went. But he left the ukulele on the table.

Clover played in the soil of the allotment with a bucket and spade while he planted and weeded. She watered the seeds and the resultant plants with her own little can. Time felt different there. More measured, less prone to speeding up and slowing down — the good moments felt longer, the bad, shorter.

It would be great if girls came in packets like seeds, he thought, watching her stomp through the dirt in her Peppa Pig wellies. If girls had instructions — *grow indoors with plenty of books*, or *likes sunlight and climbing frames* — he could buy the right equipment, create the correct conditions for optimum growth.

★ ★ ★

Around the time Clover started nursery, Colin came round and told him to pull himself together.

'It's time to think about getting back to normal,' he said. 'It was an accident. It wasn't your fault. If Becky hadn't been so self — '

Before Darren knew it, he was on his feet, shoulder-barging Colin from one end of the lounge to the other, as if they were on opposing teams in a penalty dispute. Colin raised his arms, indicating surrender. But the instant Darren gave up, Colin clocked him in the stomach. Hard.

'That's for Kelly, you shit.'

★ ★ ★

They were on the way to the corner shop to buy a tin of custard to go with some stewed apples, windfalls from the allotment next door. He had taught her how to cross the road in The Grove. It was safe there. *Stop, look, listen* — she knew exactly what to do. But she saw the shop from the other side of the road and dashed out. He grabbed her arm and hauled her back, lifting her off her feet. She swung like a monkey, light, elastic, and when she landed he smacked her, hard.

She sobbed all the way home. That evening, she wouldn't look at him. The flat of his hand stung, but it was nothing to the ache in his stomach when, at bedtime, he checked her leg and saw his fingerprints ranging across her thigh like tributaries.

For the next week he lived in fear of someone at nursery seeing what he had done. Clover forgot long before the bruise faded. But he remembered.

⋆　⋆　⋆

He studied her like a seismologist, on the lookout for waves, trying to map her interior in order to forecast the magnitude and timing of any future quakes. 'Is there anything you need?' he'd ask. And then he'd get her something anyway. Just in case. Often mistaking impulse for instinct. But it was better to be safe than sorry, he thought.

⋆　⋆　⋆

355

They marked her first day at school. Half past eight in the morning and the driveway was jammed with them: Edna, Dad, Colin, Jim and him. Clover stood on the doorstep, gripping a tiny PE bag and a Barbie lunch box; uniform stiff with newness, square knees peeping out from under her pleated skirt. They pointed their cameras at her, and Darren remembered other cameras focusing on the front of the house.

They were waiting for him outside Edna's when he got back from taking Clover. An intervention, that's what Colin called it. He hadn't been successful by himself, so he'd enlisted the rest of them. Dad appeared to have been press-ganged, while Jim looked like he'd won front-row tickets to a concert. Items on the agenda included the clutter in the house, the state of the garden, and his failure to *move on*. He gently told them to mind their own business.

★ ★ ★

Colin tried one more time, not long after he'd got together with Mark and Kelly had married Pete. Mark knew someone, a fellow nurse. She was pretty, dead nice. Just a date, he said. Just one measly frigging date.

Darren refused. One date would be pointless — an exercise in box-ticking.

Cock-sticking — it could be an exercise in that too, Colin joked, before clearing his throat and delivering a short speech about the importance of getting over things. The speech had a rushed, rehearsed quality. Darren listened. And then he saw him out.

People aren't speed bumps, you don't get over them. It wasn't that he was averse to another relationship. He could picture it, one day. It was the idea of beginning again that put him off. The prospect of getting it wrong. The possibility of not being enough. The knowledge that he had once started out with the intention of being the best thing to happen to someone and had ended up being the worst.

★   ★   ★

He opened Clover's notebook and read. Although she hadn't succeeded in conjuring Becky in the display, there were fragments of her on the pages, in the comments people had made and the stories they had told.

He thumbed the pages. Jim, Edna, Colin, Maureen, even Kelly — all there. Only his voice was missing. He had imagined he would find the words to talk about Becky often, that it would be natural and she would always be present, thanks to his inclusion of her in their daily lives. But why would he bring her up when it made him feel like shit? And what to say? He wasn't sure what to tell himself, never mind a kid. Once Clover was finally old enough for it to come up in conversation, there was nothing natural about it. He struggled for the right words and watched as her mouth clenched and her little face froze around it.

He likes to think that if Jim wasn't Jim and

357

was, instead, a reliable witness to his own life, they'd have been able to talk about his childhood, and together they might have formulated it into some sort of story that made sense: this happened, and then this happened, followed by this — an easy-to-understand, cause-and-effect sort of story, the kind you can share with children. Instead, it was all a jumble. And the confusion continued: Would Becky have coped better if she'd known she was pregnant? Was she already unhappy before she had Clover? Could he have done something, anything, different? Could he? *Could he?*

When someone dies you feel an urge to collect all the pieces of them and put them in one place, to hear every story from the people who knew them when you weren't there. By the time he felt the need to talk, he'd scared everyone off. But the urge to collect all the pieces of her and put them in one place remained. The wrong pieces, he realised, sitting in the bedroom. The wrong place. And he was struck by the impossibility of reconstructing someone via their possessions. Imagine if it was him: the motorbike helmets and tins of paint on the stairs, the ukulele parts and the boxed clocks, the saved newspapers and the boat engine — what would it all mean? It was the same here. All the *things* he had saved and stowed, all the stuff that sat suspended in the bedroom — it had no significance.

He unfastened the knotted tops of bin bags and was lifting out piles of Becky's clothes as Clover knocked on the door.

'Tea's ready,' she called.

'Down in a minute,' he said.

He started to hurry, but changed his mind, deciding instead to take his time. He straightened and folded; touched everything one last time. He's learned something during the past decade: grief never goes away. And that's no bad thing — it's only the other side of love, after all.

* * *

Thursday, and the lock of his neck and shoulders is somewhat looser. He can turn his head slightly from side to side and raise his arms without wincing. He eases himself out of bed and steps into the bathroom. There is condensation on the windowpane; he grabs a scrunch of toilet paper to wipe it off. When he goes to chuck the paper away, the bin seems unusually full and, on closer inspection, he notices the sanitary towels, rolled up in their bright, sweet-like wrappers. *Shit.*

He sits on the toilet, elbows resting on his knees, head supported by his hands. Beside the bath, opposite, the reduced-price Christmas tree rests on its side, still waiting to be lifted into the loft. If he looks hard enough, he can see the truth of things. Like the picture of the woman who is both old and young at once, the house is both a home and a mess.

He will have to speak to Clover. If it comes down to a choice between talking to him and talking to no one, she will prefer the former, won't she? He can't leave her like the chubby girl in the book about being a woman, bleeding and with no one to speak to. He won't send her anywhere today. She can lie on the sofa and watch telly or cycle down to the allotment or knit her secret scarf — whatever she wants.

Back in the room, he bags the remaining unneeded objects. He makes a small pile of things that should be kept, aware that they, along with her curly hair and sunny nature, are Clover's inheritance, and she should have some say in what happens to them. He removes the Blu-Tacked colouring pages from the wall, unsure about what they are meant to represent. Saints, that's what they are. Is it easier, he wonders, to turn a dead person into a saint than to remember them exactly as they were? When he is almost finished he sits on the floor, back propped against the closed door, and reopens Clover's notebook, wishing the past was the beautiful place other people seem to think it.

There is, he decides, a difference between what is true and what is necessary; between what is correct and what is kind. He picks up the pen he has brought with him.

'I met Becky on the 43 bus,' he begins.

★ ★ ★

Friday, and all the bin bags are piled on the far side of the bed, which has been stripped and is now a resting place for the stack of collapsed boxes. There is so much stuff here. It'll take him ages to get rid of it. He attempts to roll his shoulders up to his ears. A pain steers along his jaw and his collarbone and the knobbly bump of bone behind each ear, which must have a name but he doesn't know it.

If he isn't careful, the momentum of this moment will be lost, and he will close the door on a new, slightly tidier jumble. He can feel the impulse forming, the urge to put walls around everything. He stops himself and instead thinks about Colin, who has an annual permit for household waste and a temporary permit which allows twelve tip visits with bulky items. He also has a small trailer that he attaches to his car, which, along with a baseball cap and sunglasses, he uses to disguise himself as a domestic patron.

Darren pulls his phone out of his pocket.

'Hello,' he says. 'Is that the Handyman?'

'Yes.'

'I'd like to arrange a partial house clearance.' He paces along the space between the bed and the window, glancing out at the lawn. 'And some garden stuff, too,' he adds quickly, before he can talk himself out of it.

He is greeted by silence at the other end of the line which he waits out, until finally Colin replies. 'When would be convenient for you, sir?'

'How about this weekend?'

'I believe it can be arranged for Saturday. That would be tomorrow, in fact, sir.'

'Thank you very much.'

Another gap opens. Darren waits.

'But aren't you working at the weekend?'

'I'm off sick.'

'You okay?'

'Whiplash.'

'Crash?'

'Yeah.'

'Shit. Your fault?'

'No.'

'Phew.'

'Yeah.'

He can picture Colin, one hand holding his phone, the other rubbing the stubble on the back of his head, lips pursed, biting back a series of questions he wants to fire like arrows, but daren't in case they are startling, counterproductive.

'Saturday then, sir?'

'Yes.'

'Eleven o'clock?'

'Thank you.'

He sits on the end of the bed and thinks of all the things Becky has missed, things that would have made her love Clover. When Clover called the hail 'rattlestones' and her toes were 'foot-fingers'. The time she had 'a tummy ache in my head'. The way she praised him when he got something right: 'good girl, Daddy!' Their compulsory 'cuggles' at bedtime. The occasions when she 'misunderheard' him. The hamburgers from 'Old MacDonald's'. The 'Dalek bread'. Her requests for a 'pony head' when she first started school. The day she looped a buttered bagel around her finger and announced that she had decided to marry a giant.

There have been times when it felt like he was absolutely nailing parenthood. Once, he bought a bag of mini-eggs and laid them out along the top of the radiator, in a row. The heat melted their insides and when he and Clover put them in their mouths they burst, all warm and chocolatey. He still does it every so often. In the lead-up to Easter, when it's cold enough to have the heating on, he buys a bag or a tube and lines the chocolate eggs along a radiator before calling her. 'Oh, *Da-ad*,' she says, but he knows she likes it.

Once, she got nits. He bought the lotion, read the instructions and followed them *exactly*. What a relief to discover an aspect of parenthood with step-by-step instructions. He slid the comb past every one of the little bastards and wiped it clean with scrunch after scrunch of loo roll before flushing it away. Afterwards he watched a YouTube video and learned how to do a tight plait so that little wisps of hair couldn't escape. He checked for nits every Friday. He kicked arse when it came to nits.

And he remembers the shit moments. Collecting Clover from Edna's one day, catching the end of the children's history programme she was watching. Death appeared, scythe and all, and started singing a song: '*Stupid deaths, stupid deaths, hope next time it's not you.*' A Georgian barmaid poked a tiger, a king got blown up by his own cannon, and it was fucking hilarious. It's side-splitting when someone dies a really stupid, pointless death, isn't it?

He remembers picking her up from school. The way she'd lean over and turn off the radio. She never asked. Just assumed. That, or she'd talk over it. 'Someone trumped in carpet time, and Mrs Regan said she wouldn't read the story until the culprit owned up, but everyone was completely quiet, and we sat in silence for ten minutes . . . ' There were times when she bored him, her mouth motoring on about nothing, nothing at all, just spewing words. I'm not asking for much, he'd think. Just a bit of peace and quiet, a few moments to enjoy something. But later, when he checked on her last thing, before he went to bed, and saw her lying there, flushed, arms raised in the fling of sleep, eyelashes resting on her cheek-tops, he'd wonder how he could have been angry; he'd wonder what kind of a man would wish his own daughter away for a few moments' peace, and he'd tell himself it was good that she presumed, good that she positioned herself front and centre of everything, that she felt no restraint, that she was happy to talk, and talk, *and talk*. There was no hesitancy in her, she was certain of his affection and interest, and that had to be a good thing, didn't it?

This room, these things, the other day's outburst excepted — he's done all right, over all. Hasn't he?

Exhibit: 'Becky Brookfield — the Untold Story'

Catalogue

Object: Dust.

Description: Dust from between the slats of the old-fashioned wardrobe doors in the second bedroom.

Item Number: 38.

Provenance: This dust has been in the room for years. There are probably bits of human skin and hair cells in it.

Display: Display in a sandwich bag, so the dust is visible but contained.

Curator: Clover Quinn.

Keeper: Darren Quinn.

17

Uncle Jim sits on the end of the bed, a pile of collapsed boxes behind him. When he first sat down he pretended he was testing it for comfiness, but he only kept that up for a moment. The truth is, walking up the stairs has made him knackered, but he'd rather die than admit it. He only left hospital yesterday evening. She and Dad picked him up, stopping at South Garden on the way. They ate chips in Uncle Jim's bedsit, squeezed up on his sofa, greasy papers warming their laps. Then they had a bit of a tidy-up — Dad's on a roll! As they left, Dad asked Uncle Jim if he'd mind helping out with something. And Uncle Jim, pleased to be home and full of 'the best food he'd had for weeks', accidentally said yes straightaway, without pretending to think about it first. Which is why he's sitting here, today, in the second bedroom, still a bit wobbly, his skin bruised in the daylight, like an old apple core.

Dad has been busy. There are more bin bags. He has them organised into two separate piles, one pile for charity shops, the other for the tip. The dressmaker's dummy remains intact, but the walls are bare; the MDF boards and the various pieces of her artwork rest on the floor under the window, alongside a few other things that remain unpacked.

So, here they are: family, whether they like it

or not. She likes it; Dad and Uncle Jim don't look at all sure.

'Shall we get started?' Dad asks.

Uncle Jim presses his lips tight, which means he has thought of something rude and is trying not to say it.

'Right, there are probably some things here that you both want to keep.'

Uncle Jim looks like he might burst.

'So I thought we could go through — '

'Shit, Dazza — this is like finding out you've got bodies in the cellar or something.'

There. He's said it, and now it's Dad's turn to bite back words, which he does, before beginning again.

'Right, let's get started. We're here today to — '

Uncle Jim laughs. 'We are gathered here today,' he says in a posh voice, like a vicar in a film. 'We are gathered here today to witness the — '

'*Shut up.*'

He looks sorry. And then he bursts out with: 'I can't believe you kept her hair. It's creepy.'

'It's just hair.'

'I know what it is.'

'It's your sister's hair. Not creepy at all.'

'To you.'

'What should I have done with it? Buried it in the garden?'

'No.'

'Chucked it in the bin?'

'No.'

'Do you want it?'

'Do *you?*'

'No.'

'No.'

'Well.'

'Well.'

'I'll have it,' Clover says, and they look relieved, glad that *someone* is keeping it. 'But,' she adds, 'I'd like to know the story of it.'

'She cut it herself.' Dad's mouth makes the words carefully, deliberately. 'Are you sure you want to talk about this?'

'Yes,' she says, glad that their confinement and Uncle Jim's presence prevent the kind deflection he would usually employ.

'But you're pulling that face.'

'What face?'

'The face you do when I talk about her.'

'I don't do a face.'

Uncle Jim stares at her, too. Like she's got an extra head, literally.

'*What?*'

'Like this.' Dad closes his mouth tight and lowers his forehead until it hammocks his eyebrows.

Uncle Jim makes the face, too.

'I do *not* look like that.'

'You do, actually,' Uncle Jim says, unexpectedly agreeing with Dad. 'You look dead worried.'

'Well, I'm not. I'm just concentrating.'

'Are you sure?'

'You hardly ever say anything about her, and when you do, I have to remember it.'

Dad leans against the closed door. '*God,* Clover.'

'What?'

'Nothing.'

'You were talking about the hair,' she prompts, keeping her face as still as possible.

He lifts his chin and rolls his shoulders before stepping away from the door. 'Becky was upset. Really tired. I think she wished she hadn't cut it, later.'

'Was she upset with me?'

He looks uncomfortable. 'She was upset with everything, everyone.'

'So yes.'

'Here.' He reaches for her notebook, which is resting on the floor with the other things. 'I hope you don't mind.'

She takes it from him and flicks through it, starting at the back, searching for anything she might mind, worried that he might have crossed out details or removed pages. But he hasn't taken anything away. He has written on the blank page opposite her QUESTIONS heading; made a new column titled ANSWERS. She can see that some of the answers are brief — YES or NO — but they are there. She flicks further. He has made an addition to the THOUGHTS ABOUT BECKY BROOKFIELD section, which previously had pages headed UNCLE JIM, COLIN, KELLY, GRANDAD, NANNA MAUREEN. It now has a new section, headed DAD, followed by several pages of tiny writing. She squeezes the notebook closed, so his words can't escape.

'I think these might be yours.' Dad passes the envelope of teeth to Jim.

He opens it and laughs. 'I could do with

them!' He tongues the space at the back of his gums where the dentist removed two rotten molars. 'Becky always did the tooth fairy for me. I think she nicked the money from Mum's purse. I wasn't supposed to know it was her.'

'There's some notes, too,' Dad says. 'From you to Becky. I'm not sure whether you . . . they might make you feel . . . '

'Just hand them over, you arse-waffle.'

Dad does as he's told. Uncle Jim looks pleased, but makes no effort to examine them. He's probably saving them for later, too.

'What about this?' Dad asks, holding up the old school photograph.

'Bloody hell. I'd completely forgotten about that. Maybe Clover would like it?'

She would. But she can see that Uncle Jim also wants it, so she shakes her head.

'Would you like the school reports?' Dad asks her.

'Yes,' she says. 'What about the skirt?'

'Would you like to keep it?'

'Did *she* like it?'

'She never wore it.'

'Oh. Well, no then. Can I have the necklace?'

'If you like.'

'Did *she* wear it?'

'Sometimes. It's going green, though.'

'We can clean it.'

'I don't think so. The plating's coming off. It's not real gold.'

'Can I have it anyway?'

'If you like. Would you like the T-shirt?'

'Did *she* like it?'

'Yes.'

'Did she wear it?'

'Yes,' Jim and Dad answer together.

'I'll keep it then,' she says.

'Westlife were shite, though, weren't they? *What?* Oh, come on — they were! I bet you don't do any of their songs on your tiny guitar.'

'It's a ukulele,' Dad says, for the millionth time. He points to the few things left on the floor. 'What about these things? Do you want to keep them?'

She picks up the Little Golden Book. 'I want to keep this.' Dad opens his mouth, as if to disagree. In response she flips opens the cover and holds out the inscription: *Love from Mummy xxxx.* 'See?' she says. 'It's *mine.*'

'Yes,' he agrees eventually. 'It's yours.'

'And her magnets,' she says.

'They're junk, you don't want them.'

'I do.'

'They're not your mother's. They're mine.'

'Yours?'

'I used to . . . collect them.'

She looks at all the lovely words. 'And the mugs?'

'Yeah,' he says.

'And the tea towel and the egg cup?'

He nods.

'*When I count my blessings I always count you twice.*' Uncle Jim makes a puking noise.

'Let's put them in the kitchen!' she says, ignoring him.

'Ah . . . all right,' Dad says.

'Her art book.'

'It was mine.'

He has surprised her again. If the Rubens book isn't her mother's, she doesn't want it, but perhaps Dagmar would like it. 'I'll have it anyway,' she says. 'And I'd like the clown.'

'That's mine, too. It was a present, from her to me.'

'Oh. I thought it was mine.'

'No. She gave it to me the first time we went out. It used to hang from the mirror in my old car.'

'You two should talk about this properly some time.'

Dad's jaw tightens and not just because of his stiff neck. 'That's what we're doing, now.' He passes her the things which she made. 'You can decide about these. They're yours.'

Clover fingers the holiday board.

'Did she like holidays?'

'She liked sending off for holiday brochures and imagining where we could go.'

'Mum was always going on about it,' Uncle Jim says. '*Next year* we'll go on holiday. Next year, next year. I used to think we'd know when we'd stopped moving around and everything was settled, because *that's* when we'd go on holiday.'

Dad is listening as intently as she is. Perhaps he and Uncle Jim have never talked about these things, either.

'And because she'd stopped moving around and everything was settled with Dad, she wanted to go on holiday.'

'I suppose,' Uncle Jim says.

She fingers the pages from Mrs Mackerel's

colouring books. The heavenly messengers greeting the surprised women. 'This was a bad surprise, wasn't it?'

'Well . . . I *was* a bit shocked.'

'*I* was a bad surprise, wasn't I?'

Dad looks like his heart is in his socks. Uncle Jim glares at him and it is one of those moments when someone needs to say something but everyone is worried that it will be wrong. 'I thought you were a good surprise,' he offers.

That's it. No one says anything else. It is awkward and awful, and as it is her fault, she moves, picking up everything that is hers: the boards, the colouring pages, her notebook and the things Dad has said she can have. She places them on the bed, beside Uncle Jim, and arranges them into a stack. She'd like to be by herself for a bit, but she doesn't want it to seem like she's stomping off or flouncing out.

'*Ad perpetuam memoriam* of Becky Brookfield.'

'And what does that mean?' Dad asks, pretending patience.

'To the lasting memory. *Ad perpetuam memoriam.*'

'Absolutely,' Uncle Jim says, and he sings 'A-a-men' like a vicar and winks at her. 'I need a cup of tea.'

'You know where the kettle is.' Dad sounds cross, but he helps Uncle Jim off the bed, opens the bedroom door and calls 'Careful on the stairs!' as he makes his way down.

She steps to the doorway, holding her pile of stuff.

Dad places a black envelope on the very top of the pile. 'For you,' he says. They look at the room. It is already assuming the shape it will take when it is empty. 'Different, isn't it?'

She nods. 'The window's stuck shut,' she tells him.

He digs his fingers under the sash and pushes. She notices condensation on the inside of the glass. He tries an up-and-down manoeuvre. The glass rattles and finally the window opens and the last warmth of summer seeps in as her mother wisps out.

She steps on to the landing. 'Dad?'

'Yes.'

'There's some things I don't want. In my room.'

'Right.'

'When Colin comes, can he take them as well?'

He rolls his shoulders. 'If you're sure.'

Oh, it is horrible to hurt him. She turns to go to her room.

'Clover?'

She stops, waits.

'The most surprising thing,' he says, his words piling up and bumping into each other on their way out, 'was how much I loved you as soon as I saw you.'

*　★　*

As she stacks the things on the landing, she remembers all the times Dad has asked, 'Is there anything you need?' and all the times she has said, 'No.' Every time she has ducked his question and every time he has ignored her reply. All the occasions when she should have replied, 'I'd like to talk about my mother,' but didn't.

The bean bag shaped like lips, the record player, every babyish book she owns, ten different-shaped erasers, sixteen cuddly toys, a *Monsters, Inc.* pencil set — so many things. If she was to sort and arrange them into some sort of story, where would she be in it? The story would be Dad's, wouldn't it? It would be all about what he thought as he bought the things. And what *did* he think? she wonders.

She realises.

Clover — that's what he thought. Clover, Clover, Clover — *that's* why it's so hard to get rid of these things.

She leans over the banister and looks at the cluttered stairs, worried that Colin might fall and hurt himself as he carries everything down, and since Dad shouldn't be lifting things with his bad neck, she opens the front door and starts removing the stuff from the stairs and placing it in a little stack on the driveway: the pile of her old clothes Dad has never managed to give away, the books that were twenty pence each last year when the library closed, and the Dulux Black Satin paint — it probably won't come in handy. She puts the free newspapers and the motorbike helmets in the dining room. Maybe Dad will get a motorbike one day and they will ride it somewhere for a holiday — that would be epic!

⋆ ⋆ ⋆

375

'We'll start here,' Colin says, standing in the middle of the lawn, hands on hips, biceps like balloons. 'I'll point to an item and you've got five seconds to say whether you want it or not.'

'Is this what you usually do?' Clover asks.

'No,' he says. 'You're getting special treatment.'

Dad snorts.

The garden chairs and the table have been carried out of the shed and arranged on the grass. It might be the first time they've ever been used. Nicely played, Dad, she thinks — it's not as if Colin can take the seats from under people's bums.

Grandad has arrived, and Kelly has come too. Colin must have told her. Jim lights a cigarette and Kelly moves away from the smoke and takes her e-cig out of her purse.

'Anything that's too small for the current residents of the house will automatically be removed.'

'Hang on,' Dad says, but Clover agrees.

'That's a good idea. I don't need any of my old bikes for starters.'

'Maybe we'll just keep the first one you ever had,' Dad says. 'Remember practising? With the stabilisers, and then with me holding the back of your seat, running with you? Up and down The Grove, until you just took off all by yourself.'

Colin gets his phone out of his pocket and takes a picture of the stack of bikes. 'Anyone who wants to remember any of the bikes can look at the photo,' he says. 'Next: one paddling pool. Clo, when did you last use this?'

She can't remember.

'Any plans to come out here in the near future and stand in a couple of inches of water?'

She shakes her head.

'Maybe Kelly would like it, for the boys,' Dad suggests.

'They've got their own,' she says kindly.

'Bikes and pool — out to the trailer then.'

'Perhaps we could sell them.'

Next door, an upstairs window widens. 'OH NO YOU DON'T. You said you'd TIDY UP. You PROMISED.'

'I will. I *am*.'

'FINE WORDS BATTER NO PARSNIPS.'

'Don't worry,' Colin calls up to Mrs Mackerel. 'It'll all be done today. Why don't you come down and help?'

'*You git*,' Dad hisses.

'Aw, come on. Who doesn't want their parsnip battered?'

'I'LL BE DOWN IN A JIFFY.' She disappears for a moment before returning to momentarily dangle an enormous woolly mustard halo out of the window. 'I'VE KNITTED YOU A SNOOD, DARREN. For your NECK.'

The window clicks shut.

Jim laughs, and Kelly rolls her eyes at Clover, which feels nice, like they're on the women's team, against the boys.

★   ★   ★

Colin drives the first load of stuff to the tip and comes back for the charity-shop bags. Grandad goes with him because he thinks they should go to Cancer Research, but it's on Lord Street where it's difficult to park.

While they're gone Kelly starts cooking. She does sausages on one BBQ and chicken on the other. When Dad and Colin get back she smothers the chicken in Jack Daniel's sauce and tears it up before rolling it in wraps with salad. Mrs Mackerel isn't sure what to do with her wrap. She fetches plates and cutlery from the kitchen and puts them on the table.

'I MIGHT be going to AUSTRALIA,' she says as she attacks her wrap with a knife and fork.

Grandad sticks his hanky down the front of his shirt and holds it out with one hand to make a bib. 'I'll look it up for you on the internet,' he offers.

It feels like a party. A welcome-back Uncle Jim party, a tidy-up party, a goodbye-summer party. Dad makes tea and carries the mugs outside, two at a time, his neck and the top half of his chest hidden by the mustard snood.

Clover lifts her mug in a toast. '*Ad multos annos!*'

'Did she say *anus?*'

Kelly shushes Uncle Jim. 'What does it mean, Clover?'

'To many years,' she says.

'God, you're clever, you.'

'Or we could say *ad fundum*, which means bottoms up.'

'Cheers,' Kelly says, and everyone follows suit, preferring her toast to the special Latin ones — *ad interim.*

While Colin is driving back to the tip, this time with Uncle Jim, who has been persuaded to go along for the ride, and Mrs Mackerel is washing up in the kitchen, Clover slips away. She heads down the hall, past Grandad, who is trying to reattach the radiator, and up the stairs.

Emptied of the things she doesn't use or need, her room is different: bigger, airier. She opens the black envelope Dad gave her and arranges its contents on her bed. Dad says he will buy one of those special frames with lots of holes. She will be in charge of arranging the photos and then they'll put it on the wall in the lounge. The picture of her mother holding a piece of sandpaper is her favourite. But there are other good ones — her mother lying in the empty bath, fully dressed, grinning; her mother cutting a sheet of wallpaper, forehead creased in concentration; her mother standing in the back garden, arms spread, as if to say, 'This is mine, all of it.' *Here* is her mother. *Here* and *here* and *here.*

The notebook sits on her desk like a wrapped present. She opens it.

I met Becky on the 43 bus. It was April, snowing. Her face was pink and her hair sparkled. I thought she looked like an angel. Her bag was sitting in the cab behind me. Someone had handed it in when she forgot it, earlier that day.

This is not new. The bones of it are known to her, but Dad has attempted to cover them with tissue and skin: the snow, the sparkling hair, her mother like an angel. She closes the notebook. She will not read it all at once. She will ration it. Now the pieces are here, she will examine them one at a time.

She steps into the second bedroom. It is empty now, apart from the stripped bed. She stands at the window and, cloaked in one of the green curtains that have been here since before her parents moved in, peeps through the open sash into the garden.

And what she sees is this: Dad and Kelly, sitting on the grass beside the cooling BBQs, both leaning back, Kelly resting on her elbows, Dad propped on straight arms. Not a single part of them is touching, but their hands are a matter of inches away from each other, literally, and she can tell that they are both conscious of the inches and there is something electric there. Dad's legs are crossed and one of his feet twitches. He is *nervous*. She feels funny on the inside — slightly wobbly and a little bit disgusted, but interested, too.

Exhibit: 'Becky Brookfield — the Untold Story'

Catalogue

Object: Photographs.

Description: An envelope of photographs from before Clover Quinn (me) was born.

Item Number: 40.

Provenance: Darren Quinn (my dad) and Becky Brookfield (my mother) took these pictures when they first moved into the house where I was born.

Display: The exhibit 'Becky Brookfield — the Untold Story' has been dismantled, and the important pieces will be placed in the museum store. Keep the photographs in the envelope for the time being. Eventually, arrange in frame and display in a prominent place on the ground floor.

Curator: Clover Quinn.

Keeper: Darren Quinn.

18

He hadn't been expecting Kelly. She arrived in her work clothes, black leggings and a black vest top, a pair of disposable BBQs in one hand and a carrier bag of meat, buns and salad in the other.

'I'm all yours,' she said. 'Pete's got the boys for the weekend. About time, too — he's not seen them all summer.'

He almost missed the bit about Pete. He was too busy noticing that her hair was different, sitting on top of her head like a ring donut, exposing the bare back of a long, soft neck — *all yours*, she said. *God.*

It's just the two of them, for the moment. The garden looks empty, although he supposes it isn't really. The yellow thing Edna knitted rests on the grass beside them like a sleeping cat. The garden chairs and table are out. Clover's current bike leans up against the shed. Colin left a single milk crate: 'Here, keep one if it makes you feel better,' he said as he stacked the others before carrying them out to the trailer. He took the buckets and spades and the boat engine. He took the balls and water pistols. He took the slide and the lilos — 'Planning to go to Blackpool by sea, are you, Clo? No? Right, I'm having these then.'

After Colin and Jim went to the tip, Clover disappeared upstairs. Dad was busy in the hall re-hanging the radiator while Edna collected the plates.

'DARREN, I need YOUR HELP.'

He followed her through the back door and into the kitchen. 'Don't worry about the washing-up,' he said. 'I'll do it later.'

She ignored him. Put the plates in the sink and turned on the tap before pointing a wet finger in the direction of the window, at Kelly, stretched out on the grass, awaiting his return.

'A BIRD in your HAND is worth TWO in your BUSH.'

'Right. Thanks.'

God, what a day.

The ground is warm and dry. There's a bit of growing left in it yet. He can hear Kelly breathing, beside him. If he turns his head slightly, he can see the rise and fall of her stomach. He remembers when he imagined the world was divided into two groups — people who'd had sex and people who hadn't. He met Becky and the division shifted to those who'd been in love and those who hadn't. And then he was ungrouped, a remainder, no longer a part of anything.

'So,' she says.

'So,' he replies.

'This is good. Lots more space.'

'Yeah.'

'Well done, you.' She strokes the grass with the palm of her hand. 'You did the bedroom, too?'

He sometimes forgets she saw it. 'Yeah,' he says.

A train squeals as it crawls up to the station. They allow the interruption and listen to the wail of its brakes.

'And you're all right?'

'I'm fine.'

'I wouldn't presume to . . . I don't know what she'd want, and I wouldn't ever try to say . . . but she'd love Clover, wouldn't she?'

'Yeah.'

The train moves off again. They wait.

'Things might have been easier if you were alone.'

He isn't sure what she means. 'It's mad here today. Like Piccadilly Circus.'

'I don't mean today.'

'Oh. But . . . if I didn't have Clover, I don't know what I'd — '

She shakes her head. 'What I'm saying is, it's not as if you've really been on your own.'

'I don't get what you're . . . There hasn't been anyone.'

She looks straight at him, a firm, challenging stare. They've never talked about what happened all those years ago. He's not sorry for it. He *is* sorry for not knowing how to talk to her, afterwards. And sorry about the time she came round, many months later, with Colin, who said, 'Pete's asked Kelly to marry him.' They all, him included, awaited his response, which, when it came, consisted of an insipid 'That's nice'. He didn't know how to say he wanted her to be happy or how to explain that although a small part of him recognised it was a shame and believed something *might* happen between them one day, 'one day' had yet to feel any closer.

He opens his mouth but she waves a hand through his soon-to-be words. 'I was just a kid

384

and you weren't ready. It was all wrong.'

She's right. Yet, said like that, it sounds horribly final, and he finds himself wanting to disagree with her.

'You live,' she begins, and then she glances up at the window of the second bedroom, and at the almost empty garden, and pauses, before beginning again. 'You've *been living* in the . . . shadow of something unforgettable. *That's* not alone, is it? Not really.'

He is suddenly knackered. It feels as if his shoulders are fastened to the flap of his jaw. He stops leaning on his arms, draws his knees up and rests his elbows on them.

'Darren?'

'Yeah.'

'Do you think . . . '

She tails off. Although he has an idea of what she might be about to say, he holds fire in case he is wrong.

'Do you . . . Us — do you think we could . . . can we *see*?'

The words, though anticipated, scare him momentarily.

She pushes herself off her elbows and crosses her legs, so she is sitting right beside him. 'I used to think if I waited . . . And I did wait, for a while . . . '

He squelches the urge to apologise. He has no right. Despite what Colin says, she and Pete were happy for a while. And there are the boys.

'I just took it upon myself — the waiting. It was stupid.' She turns her head. Looks right at him. Waits.

'Yeah, I'd like us to . . . see.'

She smiles, containing it at first with pressed lips, before allowing it to burst open as she angles her head away. 'I'm busy at work,' she warns, still smiling — he can hear the shape of it in her words.

'I know.'

'The boys are a handful.'

'True.'

'Pete's a dick.'

'Yup.'

'I'm never getting married again.'

'Okay.'

'I don't want any more kids.'

'Right.'

'My new middle name is *takes-no-crap*.'

'Nice name.'

'Thanks.'

He hears the unspoken question in each jokey caveat: 'Are you sure? Please don't agree to us *seeing*, unless you're sure.' The more space she affords his retreat, the more comfortable he feels.

'Doesn't THIS look LOVELY?' Edna calls as she steps through the back door and into the garden. 'It's PROOF that a LEOPARD can CHANGE his STRIPES.'

Kelly's nose and forehead crease as she laughs. 'I think a tiger can change its spots, too.'

19

Mrs Mackerel and Grandad sit side by side, faces tilted up towards the hazy sunshine like flowers. Colin appears, holding Uncle Jim's elbow. He settles him into a garden chair and soon returns with a box of beer, which he places on the floor. He kneels to unfasten the cardboard and Clover watches as he passes beers to everyone, even Mrs Mackerel, who disappears into the kitchen and returns with a mug.

There have been times this afternoon when Dad looked caught, surrounded. But not now. Maybe he *wanted* to be caught, she thinks.

'You should get your tiny guitar out, Dazza.'

'It's not a tiny guitar,' Colin says.

Uncle Jim grins. He knows.

Grandad fetches the ukulele and asks for some proper music, which means The Beatles. Dad chooses 'I Wanna Hold Your Hand', an easy song because you can do it with a straight shuffle — down, up, down, up. They all join in and Clover presses a scrunch of curtain to her mouth because Colin *really* can't sing and Mrs Mackerel has one of those church choir voices that sound completely wrong when it comes to words like 'wanna'. Uncle Jim is torn between joining in and making fun. He glances around, hoping someone will take the piss, but they're enjoying themselves too much. Eventually, he joins in too.

This is happiness, Clover thinks, smoothing the drop of the old green curtain. The breeze in the bedroom. The singing in the garden. The periwinkle sky.

Colin waves up at her. 'Get down here, Clo. Your dad's going to do some Oasis next.'

Discovered, she leans out of the window to better hear them. Grandad mutters something about The Beatles, and Colin tells him that Oasis did a cover of 'Helter Skelter'. Dad says he doesn't know the chords and he can't imagine why anyone would do 'Helter Skelter' on the ukulele. Grandad wants 'With a Little Help from My Friends'. Uncle Jim groans — people are being far too nice to each other. Kelly leans across and whispers something to Dad, who plays the introduction to 'Do You Want to Know a Secret?' Uncle Jim carries on groaning and Colin, who was busy staring at Dad and Kelly, puts his beer down and wraps Uncle Jim in a gentle, jokey headlock.

'It's SIX OF ONE and a DOZEN of ANOTHER,' Mrs Mackerel says as she takes it upon herself to try to separate them.

Clover reaches up to close the window and then, fingers pressed against the warm wood of the frame, she changes her mind. Earlier, she let her mother out, but perhaps, given the opportunity, she will decide to come back. Her fingers fall to her sides. She likes it here. Her mother liked it too, once. Next time Dad says, 'Is there anything you need?' she'll ask if she can move into this room. Her mother's ghost is young, almost the same age as her. They can keep each other company. Perhaps Colin can strip the flowery wallpaper and redecorate. Maybe she will be allowed to help.

She is filling up with plans. When school starts next week, she will sit with Dagmar, and they will be themselves, together. In the evenings she will read Dad's notes. Little by little, a mouthful at a time, like spoons of Biscoff. Autumn will snatch the last of summer and brown and toast it, before dragging the sun down to the spot where it will ripen the apples and warm the bees through the last weeks of their work. The pumpkins will expand and the trees will undress. Conkers will pop from their shells and in the afternoons the air will turn hazy with wood-smoke. The harvest moon will glow orange in the sky and the soil will sleep.

Stepping away from the window and down the stairs, she is bursting, literally, with the feeling that there is so much happiness coming. It's just a matter of time. Of patience. Of waiting. And she is used to waiting. At the beginning of every year, she and Dad wait for the soil to soften and warm; for the planted seeds to show their heads; for flowers; for fruit. Each part of the wait has its own happiness. And sometimes it's the wait that's the best bit, isn't it? Knowing something's coming and enjoying the feeling of it being about to happen — like Christmas Eve, which is always better than Christmas Day.

Acknowledgements

I'd like to say some great big thank yous to some lovely people:

To Sarah Franklin for reading the novel at various stages of development. Thank you so much for your feedback and for our many conversations about Darren and Clover. I'm so glad we met — it's not often one finds a kindred spirit.

To Rodge Glass for reading the novel in draft. Thank you so much for your feedback and for our subsequent conversations over coffee.

To my bus driver friends Rob and Beverley for talking to me about your jobs. Thank you, Beverley, for reading through the bus bits, having me round for coffee and allowing me to pester you on Facebook.

To Eleanor Moffat, Curator of Maritime Collections at Merseyside Maritime Museum. Thank you so much for talking to me about your fascinating job.

To David and Lyn, my parents, for telling me about your three years in the Czech Republic and for sending me pictures and postcards. And to Iveta Kolková for chatting to me on Skype about learning to speak English.

To Rachael Sellers for pointing me in the direction of information about denied pregnancies.

To Deb and Bob at Retreats for You for

looking after me so well.

To my Facebook friends for being so entertaining as you answered questions about biscuits, beer, slang and a multitude of other things.

To my agent, lovely Veronique Baxter. Thank you for listening to me talk about Darren and Clover when everything was still fuzzy around the edges and for all your help and encouragement.

To everyone at Hutchinson for making me feel so welcome. To my splendid editor Jocasta Hamilton. Thank you for letting me get on with the writing when it was going well and for talking things through with me when I got stuck. Thank you for your quick responses to what, at times, probably seemed like an endless stream of emails. Thank you to Rose Waddilove. And thank you to Laura Deacon and Laurie Ip Fung Chun at Windmill Books. Also, thank you to Charlotte Bush for being such a lovely companion on some of the best adventures I've ever had. And to Millie Seaward and Jess Gulliver.

To various members of my family for providing linguistic mix-ups, including the following: 'He burned a jock-stick'; 'They've got an own-suite'; 'It was a racist Shloer'; 'I don't like rice pudding, I prefer salmonella.'

To Lizzy and Esther, my brilliant sisters, for our online chats and for listening to me worry.

Love and thanks to Sam, Daniel, Joseph and Alice for being utterly fabulous.

And to Neil. For everything.

We do hope that you have enjoyed reading this large print book.

Did you know that all of our titles are available for purchase?

We publish a wide range of high quality large print books including:
Romances, Mysteries, Classics
General Fiction
Non Fiction and Westerns

Special interest titles available in large print are:
The Little Oxford Dictionary
Music Book
Song Book
Hymn Book
Service Book

Also available from us courtesy of Oxford University Press:
Young Readers' Dictionary
(large print edition)
Young Readers' Thesaurus
(large print edition)

For further information or a free brochure, please contact us at:
Ulverscroft Large Print Books Ltd.,
The Green, Bradgate Road, Anstey,
Leicester, LE7 7FU, England.
Tel: (00 44) 0116 236 4325
Fax: (00 44) 0116 234 0205